BLACK WOLF

KATHLEEN KENT is a *New York Times* bestselling author and a two-time Edgar Award Nominee. She has also written the award-winning historical novels *The Heretic's Daughter*, *The Traitor's Wife*, and *The Outcasts*, and been published in the crime anthology Dallas Noir. In March 2020 she was inducted into the Texas Institute of Letters for her contribution to Texas literature.

ALSO BY KATHLEEN KENT

Betty Rhyzyk Novels

The Dime
The Burn
The Pledge

Historical Novels

The Heretic's Daughter
The Traitor's Wife
The Outcasts

BLACK WOLF

KATHLEEN KENT

An Aries Book

First published in the US in 2023 by Mulholland Books,
an imprint of Little, Brown and Company, a division of Hachette Book Group, Inc
First published in the UK in 2023 by Head of Zeus
This paperback edition first published in the UK in 2023 by Head of Zeus,
part of Bloomsbury Publishing Plc

9 7 5 3 1 2 4 6 8

A catalogue record for this book is available
from the British Library.

ISBN (PB): 9781804547908
ISBN (E): 9781804547861

Printed and bound in Great Britain by
CPI Group (UK) Ltd, Croydon CR0 4YY

Head of Zeus
5–8 Hardwick Street
London EC1R 4RG

WWW.HEADOFZEUS.COM

For Lowell A. Mint
Mentor and friend

Even Atlas would strive to withstand the glowing hot axis of the earth.

—Ovid

1

31 IYUL' 1990
TUESDAY, JULY 31, 1990
MINSK OBLAST, BYELORUSSIA

The man was so happy, he thought his heart would shatter. This surge of elation brought to mind the poem that every schoolchild grew up reciting:

There, the birch in silence
Slumbers all day long…

But at night. At night, with the warm summer breezes, the birch groves came alive, their topmost branches whipping carelessly in all directions. As did the tall, slender pines that stretched on formidably, lining both sides of the road like restless armies facing each other before a battle. The luminous shale road cut through the forest in an unbroken line—a white scar gouged into the land, shining pale and lustrous beneath a three-quarter moon.

The night air, as balmy, and as dense, as an evening spent on a Georgian holiday beach. The sky, for a few hours a shade blacker than black, punctured by a million pinpricks of light, bathed in the vaporous light of the Milky Way.

The man had rolled down all the windows of his car to let

in the breezes, but soon, overcome by his senses, he killed the engine and stepped out of the blue Lada. He stood in ecstasy, the poem inviting back so many memories of his childhood. The savory smell of shashlik roasting on an open fire, the clink of a metal spoon against glass as the small dollop of jam was stirred into his tea, the meaty slap of fish against the surface of the lake as they leapt to catch bottle flies. The lazy, hours-long hunt for mushrooms. Delighted, he shivered and hugged himself and laughed out loud.

He had another ten kilometers to go before he could rest, and so he climbed into the driver's seat, started the engine, and continued on his northeast journey. As he drove, he listened for any noise from his passenger in the backseat. It had been quiet for the past twenty minutes, but he glanced in his rearview mirror all the same, checking for movement. There was none.

He smiled and began to hum a song he'd heard on the radio. "You Will Come Back to Me" by the Russian star Tamara Miansarova. A bit saccharine, but far better than listening to the Red Army Choir butcher another Western rock melody. He sang along, loudly, extravagantly, appreciating his own warm baritone, which had charmed so many women. So many women…

He was tempted to turn off his headlights and let the reflective glow from the road guide him. It would feel like flying. But it would not do to veer off, to get stuck in a boggy rut or, worse, hit a fox or wolf or the occasional elk that ventured out at night.

Checking the backseat again, he once more admired the ingenuity of his handiwork. The simplicity, the subtlety, of his methods. He had been a student of Western history. In particular, American Colonial history, that all-too-familiar swamp of superstitious dread and cultlike devotion to the ruling magistrates. That culture of opportunistic accusations, as during the Salem witch trials, where the remnants of medieval British law held strong: guilty until proven innocent. But even with debtors' prisons and oppressive religious rulings, outright torture had been outlawed. However, like good apparatchiks, the black-coated judges and their willing constables found a cunning way around the ban. They devised the Bow.

Economically, it only involved two lengths of rope. A prisoner was laid prone on the ground, belly down. The first length of rope tied his hands behind his back. One end of the second bound his ankles, the knees then bent backward at a sharp angle; the other was formed into a slip noose and secured around his neck. The prisoner was forced to bow his back to keep the noose from tightening. Eventually, no matter how strong, the muscles in his back would give out. His head would drop, the noose would tighten, and, unless he revealed what the magistrates wanted to hear, he would strangle himself.

He would *strangle himself.*

Technically, by the letter of the law, the jurists would not be responsible. Their consciences could remain clear. Ingenious, really.

The woman lying contorted in the backseat had been a famous gymnast as a teenager. But since, she had become doughy and overweight, continuing to eat as though she were still lithe and active, in training for the Soviet Olympics. She had remained quite strong, though, and had held out longer than any who had come before. Almost four minutes. A record!

She'd also not cried or begged as the others had. Instead, she had spat and raged and sworn at him. A fighter till the very end. It had added immeasurably to the piquancy of their shared experience, accounting, perhaps, for his heightened exhilaration now.

He saw the turnoff to his dacha. For the briefest moment he thought to keep driving the dozen or so kilometers on to Khatyn. Now abandoned, it'd been the town where as a boy he'd dreamed about serving as a policeman. He'd imagined having a new uniform, and a warm woolen coat, with boots of good leather. But the war had started, and German soldiers were soon thick as flies across the countryside. In 1942, not yet twenty, he'd joined the Resistance instead.

There was something delicious about the thought of performing his planting at the official park at Khatyn. To return in the fall to watch scores of respectful visitors laying flowers on the war memorials, and then stooping to harvest the fruits of his labors. But there was no guarantee that he could return when the park was open in September. The fall would be a very busy time for him.

Momentous events were taking place. The Byelorussian Soviet Republic would soon declare its sovereignty, and full independence from the Soviet Union would follow within a year's time. Of that he was certain.

So he turned and drove around the dacha slowly, skirting the broad sweep of the lawn, thick with fibrous grasses and wildflowers, and pulling into the deeper shadows at the back of the house. He parked, his headlights illuminating a stand of birch trees. They'd been tall even when he was a boy. Opening one of the rear doors, he pulled a pocketknife from his coat and deftly cut the ropes binding the woman, gently pulling them from her stiffening limbs. He dragged her from the backseat and, with some effort, across the dirt, until he felt his shoes sink into the softened, spongy earth under the sheltering trees.

He retrieved a shovel from the trunk of his car and, removing his coat, began to dig. A trench a few feet deep would suit his purposes. He soon began to sweat, but the predawn breeze was pleasant, and he hummed quietly to pass the time. When he was satisfied, he stripped the woman until she was naked, her cool skin pearlescent in the headlights, and settled her in. Then he stroked her, running his callused fingers over her contours, kneading her mounds of flesh and marveling at their velvety texture.

"Moya ledyanaya printsessa," he whispered, laying his body over hers, sinking his teeth into her until he tasted the bright tang of blood. *My Ice Princess.*

But it wasn't until, in a building frenzy, he had packed her mouth and the tight recess between her legs with dirt that he could obtain an erection and gain release.

When he had finished, he rested for a bit, and then stood and shoveled the earth back over her form. She would rest beneath the surface, her body providing the necessary nutrients for the mushrooms to grow. He only ever planted the luscious ones. The others—the skinny, harping, bold-faced ones—he threw away like the trash that they were.

Later, he'd sprinkle on barn hay and horse manure for carbon and nitrogen. Then the spores would grow thick and fragrant. In a few weeks he'd return to harvest them, along with the many others growing in the grove behind the well-seasoned dacha—at least twenty-six patches of them. He'd cook them in soups and stews and his personal specialty, made in vast quantities: *draniki,* mushroom-stuffed potato pancakes. After all, what good was plucking the bounty of the earth if you couldn't share it with friends and colleagues?

Finally finishing, depleted, he entered his summer home, where he stripped and washed and fell heavily upon the bed that had once been shared by his parents and his grandparents before them.

He smiled in the dark, remembering the Tamara song. "You Will Come Back to Me."

Yes, you will, he thought. *Again. And again. And again.*

2

THURSDAY, AUGUST 2, 1990
MINSK

The small group of Americans arrived at Minsk-2 airport through a thick blanket of gray clouds and rain. The airport sat within a vast tract of silver birch forests about twenty miles east of the capital city. From a distance, the building had looked impressive, modern. Inside was a different story.

Melvina Donleavy stood at the baggage carousel a few feet apart from her three travel companions, taking in the crumbling masonry and cracked marble, the dangling and exposed wires, and long stretches of dark hallways. It had been pointed out by Dan Hatton, their team leader, that lightbulbs, among many other things, were in short supply.

The passage through immigration had gone relatively smoothly. The guard processing Mel's paperwork scrutinized her closely, matching her face—pale, with wide-spaced dark eyes and a slightly elfin chin—to her passport photo. She knew that in photographs she often looked startled, like a forest animal caught in the road. She was tall and slender but, despite her appearance of fragility, surprisingly strong, as her physical fitness test instructors, first at Quantico and then at the Farm, had discovered. Her mother, a college drama teacher, would often say that Mel had the outward demeanor of an Ophelia but the stealth, and secretiveness, of a Hamlet. At twenty-six years old, she was the youngest in her party.

The guard's gaze kept returning to a space above her head. It wasn't until her passport had been stamped and she had moved away from the window that Mel noticed that large, tilted mirrors had been placed over every cubicle, allowing the guards to scrutinize the backsides of travelers. Perhaps looking for some aging *babushka* smuggling in a black-market chicken.

A braying laugh from Dan snagged her attention. Dan was ostensibly her boss, but she knew that, of the four Americans, all sent by the Central Intelligence Agency, she had the highest security clearance. So high, in fact, that Dan was completely unaware that she'd been handpicked by the CIA's deputy director of clandestine operations on direct orders from a select Senate committee back in Washington. What the others *did* know was that this was her first mission, as she'd only just completed her Agency training. Mel couldn't—and for purposes of her cover story, wouldn't—hide it: she was, by turns, nervous and exhilarated. Nervous because there was as yet so much unknown, and exhilarated for the same reason. As was customary in Agency protocol, she'd spent a few weeks stateside prior to their trip getting to know her colleagues. And though they'd been friendly, and reasonably open, the other three already had years of experience as foreign field agents. She knew they'd be watching her, saving their final assessment of her reliability for after their mission was completed.

She'd been warned by her trainers that, at some point, the goals of her mission might conflict with those of the other three, and that she might cause friction within the team. But under no circumstances was she to reveal her true mission to anyone. She would share that only with her American intermediary, who she'd been told would contact her shortly.

It was this intermediary who would smuggle any intelligence she gathered out of Byelorussia and back to the States.

Her two other colleagues—Julie Reznik and Ben Franklin (born Benjamin Worthingham Franklin, according to his passport)—smiled indulgently at Dan's jokes. But she caught Ben throwing her a weary look and the slightest shrug.

He soon broke away and sauntered over, rolling his shoulders to ease the cramps in his back. It had been a long series of flights: DC to Frankfurt, Frankfurt to Moscow, Moscow to Minsk, with delays in between. It was now early morning, and there were few travelers at the airport. But the Byelorussians who had gathered to collect their baggage all gawked unabashedly at Ben. They'd probably only ever seen a Black person on TV, when the Communist state–run news propaganda ran images of impoverished, diseased Africans, or riotous African Americans hell-bent on destroying their own cities in the decadent West.

Mel had witnessed how Ben's immigration guard looked suspiciously from his passport to Ben and back again. But then he'd frowned and asked incredulously, "Like American president?"

Ben had barely suppressed a grin and answered, "Sure."

The baggage carousel lurched into action for a few seconds and then stopped again.

"More bad jokes?" Mel asked now, chucking her chin at Dan.

Ben adopted a rigid, military posture. "What is difference between Russian pessimist and Russian optimist? Russian pessimist says, 'Things can't get any worse.' And Russian optimist says, 'Oh, yes they can.'"

Mel snorted. "At least he's stopped with the Chernobyl jokes."

The carousel started up again, but as soon as the battered suitcases and boxes began moving, the overhead lights went out, plunging them into darkness. Ever resourceful, Ben dug a flashlight out of his backpack, and soon the four Americans were trudging toward customs, wheeling their bags behind them.

Dan directed the group to the shorter line for those with diplomatic status, which was also populated by a few German and Swiss businessmen with special visas. But it was still a full twenty minutes before two guards took up their post and started slowly and methodically inspecting every piece of luggage.

"God, it stinks in here," Julie muttered to Mel, who'd been studying the line ahead, impatiently shifting from one foot to the other.

Julie had sharp, Mediterranean features, a full figure—what some people would call Rubenesque—and a dry, stoic demeanor. But she could cut through corrugated iron with one caustic look. Grabbing a handful of her thick, curly black hair, she brought it to her nose, grimaced, and said, "Oh, God."

In Mel's experience, every foreign place had a unique smell. Bombay, cumin and stale sweat. Frankfurt, sausage and wet concrete. Rio, sunscreen and motor exhaust. "How do you say 'fermenting cabbage and disinfectant' in Russian?" she asked.

"Kvasheniye kapusty i dezinfitsiruyusheye sredstvo."

Mel shook her head. "I'm not even going to try that one."

Her three companions all spoke Russian, Julie being the most fluent. Ben and Dan were fairly conversant. Mel could only speak a few phrases. Just enough to find the toilet or hail a taxi. But, with the exception of Julie, they were all to feign ignorance of the language. People were more inclined to speak their minds if they thought they couldn't be understood.

Dan and Ben were processed through quickly. When Mel finally approached the inspection station, a long table behind which the two unsmiling guards stood, her suitcase had already been completely emptied—clothes, shoes, and underwear spread out for everyone to see. Her cosmetics bag had been opened and the older of the two guards was pawing through it. He upended the bag, noisily spilling out its contents.

Irritated, Mel took in a sharp breath, preparing to say something, but Julie closed her fingers gently around her arm. "Good opportunity to practice self-restraint," she whispered. Noting that Mel was young and used to speaking her mind, this had been one of Julie's favorite pieces of advice in their earlier talks. "To the Soviets," she had said, "nothing screams Western exceptionalism more than a blatant show of impatience."

Mel nodded, keeping her expression a careful blank.

The guard unwrapped a cardboard tube and looked through it as if it were a tiny telescope. Pulling on the blue string, he eased out the cotton cylinder and held it hanging in front of his face. He turned to his younger partner, who shrugged.

"What is this?" he asked Mel in Russian.

Mel turned to Julie in disbelief. "He's kidding, right?"

Julie responded quietly, but the guard still looked perplexed.

"Shto?" he asked loudly. What?

Julie grinned wickedly and, now matching his blaring tone, began a long-winded explanation of what the cotton cylinder was for, and where it was applied.

When the guard looked back at Mel, she nodded, gave him a practiced innocent look, and added a visual aid to clarify: a forefinger thrust forcibly upward.

The man dropped the tampon as though it had caught fire, shoved everything back into the suitcase, and motioned for Mel to move along.

"So much for the glorious Revolution liberating women," Julie said as Mel grabbed her bag. "Wait till they find out American condoms are ribbed."

In the main lobby, the group was met by an unsmiling, portly man wearing a terrible haircut and even worse shoes, holding a sign on which was printed in archaic-looking letters: hatton party + 3. Standing next to him was a harried-looking woman who rushed forward to shake everyone's hands, welcoming them in heavily accented English, letting them know that her name was Elena and she would be accompanying them to their hotel.

The cover story for the team was that they were on a fact-finding mission on behalf of the US State Department, which was considering offering American financial support to the newly sovereign—although still technically Soviet—republic of Byelorussia. Dan and Ben were posing as accountants, protective of the American dime, Julie as their official translator. Their true job was to report back to the Department about the realities of the fracturing Soviet Union. And what threats would be posed by this new republic, which would be the gateway to Western Europe.

There had been clandestine Agency forays into Byelorussia all throughout the Cold War, but this was the first time an official American delegation would circumvent the centralized politburo in Moscow. They had been invited by the newly declared Byelorussian Ministry of External Affairs, which would have been unthinkable only a year ago, before the warming effects of *glasnost* and the destruction of the Berlin Wall shattered Soviet control. But now Byelorussia needed money, and Uncle Sam was determined to help fill their coffers before other countries, like Iran, stepped in. The country that controlled the purse strings helped control the further proliferation of military weapons.

Mel's cover was that she was simply Dan's secretary. Therefore, the least prioritized and, more importantly, the least scrutinized member of the team. Internally, she'd been introduced to her three team members as an "independent observer." Meaning, as far as the other members of the group were concerned, she was to report on the reporters. This was not uncommon, but usually left to more experienced agents. The fact that she was so young and on her first mission did not immediately endear her to her team.

So it had taken Mel weeks of concentrated effort to win over her colleagues before their arrival. With Ben, his open, relaxed nature made it easy to strike up a conversation. She was a good listener, and a few well-placed questions revealed their common interests: reading, traveling, and psychology, especially as it related to true crime. They'd spent some deliciously dark hours after dinner discussing the possible motivations of the Zodiac Killer, John Wayne Gacy, and David Berkowitz, among others, hours that, for Mel, felt effortless. And, as he'd spent time stationed with the army in Germany, he was familiar with that country's own spectacular serial killers.

Mel also formed a quick attachment with Julie, after encouraging Julie's inclination to take on a protective role. This was a relief, as Mel's experience with police officers, through her father, a thirty-year veteran sheriff in Madison, Wisconsin, was that women in the force were often very competitive. When you were constantly being hit over the head by machismo, it was easier to punch down. But Julie seemed eager to play the role of big sister, and with half a dozen clandestine missions to Eastern Europe in her file, she was the most experienced of them all at maneuvering through Communist Bloc countries. Mel planned to stay close to her side, absorbing as much knowledge as possible as quickly as possible.

Dan was a harder read. He wasn't unfriendly, but he held himself slightly aloof, especially with her. Tall and slender, his hair worn longer than most men with the Agency, he dressed in expensive but rumpled suits and well-worn loafers. In his midthirties, he looked to Mel like the perennial Ivy League poly sci graduate from a wealthy family who'd joined the intelligence service out of boredom at the thought of doing real State Department work.

And even though he was constantly telling jokes, Mel quickly understood they were both a mask and a barrier to more intimate, unguarded conversation. Only through continual chatter during her training had she gathered that he'd been in some dangerous hot zones, and more than once, which would explain his cautious nature in relaxing his guard around an inexperienced, untried agent.

The success of her mission relied on the goodwill and cooperation of all three, and she intended to continue cultivating both, even as she was vigilant in hiding her true mission. When, at the end of a long day, she'd expressed worry about that balance to one of her Agency trainers, he'd sighed and snapped, "You took theater, right? Make it work!"

She was the only child of Walter Donleavy, taught to be fiercely independent and outspoken. But she tamped down her natural inclination to defend herself and absorbed the rebuke. "Understood, sir."

Elena, having at last gathered the group and all their luggage, was ushering them out of the airport and into a waiting van—the portly man abandoning his sign to climb ponderously into the driver's seat. From the passenger seat, she gave a running commentary on all the points of interest they'd see as they approached Minsk. Their driver's name, she explained, almost as an afterthought, was Anton. He would be their driver for the duration of their stay.

"Unfortunately, Anton does not speak very good English," Elena said, frowning, as though it reflected poorly on her. "But he is excellent driver."

Ben gave Mel a subtle nudge. It was impossible that anyone

would be assigned to foreign visitors without being fluent in several languages, including English. With his heavy brow, ham fists, and the bunched muscles Mel suspected hid under his stout build, Anton was most assuredly KGB.

As they entered Minsk from the northeast, Elena described in detail each notable building or park they passed.

"Here, as you can see," she said, pointing to a vivid redbrick building, "is the Red Church. Very famous."

A few minutes later: "Here is Victory Square...Here is Government House...Here is post office...Here is GUM, largest department store in Minsk, which you all must go and experience for yourself..."

To Mel, the dichotomy between the grandiose buildings and the somber, at times threadbare, pedestrians—the steep morning shadows engulfing the long lines of people waiting noiselessly to gain entrance into the state-run stores—was depressing. It worked to dampen her initial enthusiasm for being in an exotic, and until recently forbidden, country, despite Elena's rehearsed lauding of the city.

When Elena announced the KGB headquarters, a Western European–style four-story building in yellowish stone, Dan pointed and said, "That's the tallest building in Minsk."

When no one took the bait, he added, "'And why is that, Dan? Every building in this part of town is four stories.' Well, since you asked, it's because from the top floor you can see all the way to Siberia."

Elena stiffened visibly. But when Mel looked at Anton, he was smiling.

At last, Elena escorted them into the Planeta Hotel—a graying ten-story building, fronted along the roofline by a large blue sign—taking their passports and handing them personally to the manager. Their passports would be held until the group was driven back to the airport at the end of the trip. They were also all given rooms on different floors, in order to separate them, making it easier to monitor their movements. Mel had been briefed: their phones would be tapped, their rooms bugged, and the mirrors would be two-way.

As they waited for the elevator, Elena explained that the Planeta was of the highest order.

"It was built for party officials, high-ranking military, and only best athletes," she said emphatically.

As a child, Mel had been given a cardboard dollhouse, one that had to be assembled in pieces to reveal the idealized 1960s living room. It had come complete with shiny metallic side tables, sleek leather furniture in garish colors, and glistening wallpaper in improbable shades of burnt orange and silver. The lobby of the hotel reminded her of that beloved dollhouse, especially after the cardboard had begun to fray. She experienced an unexpected jab of nostalgia, combined with the lingering sense of emotional vertigo that such a space still existed, unchanged for three decades, in a "modern" city.

"Yikes," Julie muttered, taking in the spectacle. "People have been shot for less."

The five of them squeezed uncomfortably into the small elevator, along with the manager, who insisted on accompanying each of them to their rooms. He keyed the elevator to the top floor and, with a flourish, immobilized the doors so that they would all have to wait until he returned.

"Best rooms here," he said, nodding to Dan.

"Ah," Dan said. "Farthest to travel, and"—he lowered his voice, whispering into Mel's ear—"if necessary, farthest to fall."

He winked at her as he followed the manager out of the elevator. "Get a few hours' rest. Then we'll meet for lunch downstairs and get to work."

Mel was the last of the four to exit with the manager, leaving

Elena alone in the elevator. Her room was on the second floor, at the end of the hallway, past the *dejournaya,* the ever-present hall monitor. Every hotel in every city in the Soviet Union had them, and they performed many duties. Placing a call through the central switchboard to an outside number, if a guest needed it, or bringing tea, hopefully without too much grumbling, and safeguarding everyone's room key, which was returned to the desk whenever a guest left the floor.

But their most important duty was keeping an eye on the comings and goings of hotel guests and reporting them to the internal security apparatus. Mel's *dejournaya* was a middle-aged woman with narrow shoulders, ample hips, and an implacable mouth circled by deep smoker's lines. On her desk was a board labeled with the room numbers, each with a hook for the key.

The manager had taken the appropriate key and opened the door to Mel's room. Satisfied, he handed it to her but remained in the doorway for a few beats as she walked inside.

"I am Maksim," he said, leaning against the frame and looking pointedly at her chest. He was short and sturdy with protruding eyes that appeared never to blink.

Mel gave him a stony look, resisting the impulse to slam the door in his face. She heard Julie's voice in her head cautioning restraint. "I'll remember that."

Maksim snorted dismissively and then retreated. Mel closed the door and sat on the bed. The room was as she'd expected. Brown paneling, worn carpets, scratchy sheets, net curtains incapable of blocking out the sunlight that would stream through the windows starting at five a.m.

There was a large mirror over the shabby dresser. Rising again, Mel crossed the room and leaned in toward it, as though examining the dark circles under her eyes. Casually, she placed the tips of her fingers against the reflective surface, appearing to steady herself. In her peripheral vision she could see there was no gap between her fingers and their reflections. Definitely a two-way. She'd have to take care to always dress and undress in the bathroom. There was nothing she could do about the bugs in her room without arousing suspicion.

Resigned, she lay back on the narrow bed, fully clothed, deciding to unpack later. A few hours' sleep would be of more use. But it took a few minutes for her mind to still.

Dan had said that they'd begin work after lunch. But Mel had started working even before exiting the Aeroflot plane. It wasn't an active type of work per se. It wasn't even done consciously—at least, not completely. It was, instead, a skill that Mel had been born with, and one that she tried her best to hide. Revealing her unique ability to people was to invite, at best, probing questions she didn't have ready answers for. At worst, it triggered a profound discomfort in others, a reflexive pulling away.

In truth, she'd never intended for her ability to be discovered by her trainers either at the FBI or, subsequently, the CIA. She'd been found out during a training exercise at Quantico, and since then, her gift had been exploited by US national intelligence.

There was as yet no widely used category for Melvina Donleavy's ability, which was simply that she never forgot a face. Ever. Even if she'd not seen the person since childhood, she could, twenty years later, recognize a former third-grade friend, from thirty feet away, from behind. Just from the general shape of their head. Even if the person had changed their hair color, or had plastic surgery, or had been in a disfiguring accident. If their head was still attached to their body, she'd recognize them—the shape of their ears, their dimensions, the composition of their skull.

Every person she'd seen on the plane, every traveler at the airport and pedestrian on the street as they'd driven in, had been captured and committed to the short-term memory bank inside Mel's brain. And from that bank, she could recall anyone at a moment's notice. Whether she saw them in real time on the street, or in a still photograph or even grainy surveillance footage, she'd be able to pick out a preselected target almost immediately. At the Farm, they'd proven that her accuracy was close to one hundred percent.

Later, she would need to process the faces she'd seen today into the deeper recesses of her long-term memory. For that, she had developed a nightly ritual. One that she had practiced since she was very young. Without the ritual, after twenty-four hours, her head would ache and she'd start to see flashes of light at the periphery of her vision. After forty-eight hours, she'd begin feeling sharp pains jabbing at both of her temples. Beyond that, the pain would become excruciating, and debilitating. It was as though the images she collected over a day filled up her cerebral cortex, like water filling a balloon. And she harbored an irrational fear that without a release valve, her head, like a balloon, would burst.

It had been nearly twenty-four hours since she'd last been able to do her processing ritual and she already felt the pressure building behind her eyes. Like her gift itself, her ritual was another necessary secret.

She rubbed at her temples and tried refocusing on her current objective. Before leaving the US, she'd been shown photos of three preselected targets, all men, all from Tehran. And all committed to the acquisition of nuclear weaponry—or, barring that, weapons-grade uranium—from the fast-disintegrating and chaotic military infrastructure of the Soviet Union.

When Mel was growing up, she'd been all too aware, thanks to her father, of the violence perpetrated in society, usually by men. Shootings, stabbings, and assaults were, if not a daily occurrence in Dane County, not uncommon either. Particularly against women.

Later, at Quantico and the Farm, she came to understand that man's potential for violence could climb a monumental scale. A world-ending scale. The Middle East was on fire. Iraq had invaded Kuwait. And Mel had been sent to Minsk to confirm the rumors that Iran had initiated a clandestine pact with Russia. The project was named Persepolis. The Agency suspected that Russia was planning to provide nuclear experts, technical information, and fissionable material to Iran. In return, Iran would funnel vast amounts of currency back through untraceable Swiss bank accounts. It seemed the Soviet rats were beginning to leave the ship and needed resources for a comfortable lifeline.

What Mel had been tasked with—confirming that Iran was actively seeking nuclear weapons—seemed, on that first day, overwhelming, her narrow bed a life raft in a vast, gray sea, where she floated alone.

Mel closed her eyes and dreamed of burning cities.

3

THURSDAY, AUGUST 2, 1990

The dining room of the Planeta Hotel was two stories tall and had all the warmth of an airplane hangar. The walls were stark white, with long red curtains that only served to highlight windows that had probably last been cleaned when Chernenko was in power. A few scattered diners were seated at the two dozen tables; Mel immediately recognized a man from the swirl of travelers at the airport. He'd kept his face turned away, but she'd retained his image, reflected on the glass window fronting a money-changing kiosk.

The man looked at her briefly and then quickly lowered his head back to his newspaper. Assuming that Anton and Elena had been tasked with reporting from the road, here was Minder #3, presumably tasked with following them on foot.

Dan waved to her from the far side of the room, and she made her way past a tight knot of waiters, all of them arthritic and stooped, watching her with open hostility and grumbling impatiently in her wake. Ben and Julie were already seated, small bowls of what looked like coleslaw and pickles at the center of the table. Mel sat in the remaining empty seat directly across from Dan.

"Did you get some sleep?" Dan asked as she settled into

her chair. His sandy hair was still damp from the shower, an untamed lock falling boyishly over his forehead.

"I did, thanks," she answered, smiling, even though her head still throbbed. She lowered her voice. "Just so you know, we've got a Daniel Boone directly to my left."

Dan nodded, one eyebrow raised. "Impressive. Good catch."

Mel shrugged. "I remembered him from the airport." She'd have to be judicious about revealing who she recognized. But it was vital to the safety, and efficiency, of the group that they knew about their direct tails.

Dan motioned to the waiters, who promptly turned their backs and continued their conversation.

Julie speared a pickle with her fork. "They'll come when they're good and ready."

Ben drummed on the table good-naturedly with his fingers. "Welcome to my world. How's your room?" he asked Mel.

"Nice mirrors," she answered, and Julie gave a cynical laugh.

"You'll get used to the unpleasant waiters," Julie said to Mel. "It's almost a cliché that Soviet service people are the rudest on the planet. But they save their most potent vitriol for the hated Americans. It's like a badge of honor for them. At least now you don't have to look at their sour faces. The *dejournaya* on my floor actually hissed at me when I told her good morning."

Ben examined a spoonful of the coleslaw and decided against putting it in his mouth. "I thought the hall dragon was going to pass out when she got an eyeful of me. Five bucks says they're in our rooms right now rearranging our underwear."

This was not a surprise to Mel. She'd been advised that their rooms would be inspected, often and thoroughly.

"Huh," Julie snorted. "Five bucks says they're *stealing* my underwear."

A few minutes later, one of the waiters dragged his way to their table and stood begrudgingly, pen and paper in hand. Julie asked him in Russian what the freshest lunch selection was. The waiter mumbled, "*Kuritsa.*" Chicken.

"Which means fried cutlets," Julie added.

"What kind of vegetables do they have?" Ben asked, and Julie translated.

The answer: cabbage, potatoes, carrots. And mushrooms, lots of mushrooms.

Ben looked pointedly at the waiter. "But no meat in them, right? *Nyet myasa?*" he asked, in a purposely bad Russian accent.

Ben was a vegetarian. He'd been advised to bring a lot of dried fruits and nuts to stave off the real possibility of hunger in a country that served meat, in some form, at every meal. And very few, if any, green vegetables.

After taking their orders, the waiter shook his head, glowered at Dan, and sauntered away.

"Just be glad we weren't sent to Kazakhstan," Julie stage-whispered to Ben. "Or you'd be forced to choose between horse and camel."

"They're just mad because we changed tables. Twice!" Dan said, laughing quietly. "They tried to set us up in the middle of the room." He pointed discreetly to the decorative chandelier over the center table. "Directional mic."

"So, nothing under this table?" Mel asked, rapping her knuckles softly on the tablecloth.

Dan grinned. "Hopefully not. We'll have to play musical tables while we're here."

As if on cue, they all leaned in, and Dan gave them the meeting schedule for the day. "In an hour, we'll be taken to the Ministry of Finance building to meet the newly appointed minister of external affairs. We'll blah, blah, blah for a bit, scribble some notes, and then we'll be driven to the Byelorussian Heat and Mass Transfer Institute. Ben, you want to give Mel the official take there?"

"According to their reports to the US State Department," Ben said, "the institute researches energy-efficient transfer technologies in biological and nonbiological systems, and processes the properties of fluid mechanics and the internal structuring of strong influences."

Mel blinked a few times. "Meaning?"

"Exactly," Ben said, jabbing the table with his finger.

"Meaning," Dan said, "we don't really know what the hell they've been doing. It could all be for harmless thermoelectric devices. The development of computers, for example. But energy transfer has a more sinister reading as well."

"Igor's coming," Julie muttered, leaning back in her chair.

The waiter brought the plates on a large tray. On each plate was a small fried chicken cutlet, two boiled potatoes, and some colorless cabbage. At the center of the table he placed a platter of bright orange carrots and a large ramekin of baked mushrooms smothered under cheese and sour cream.

With a sigh, Ben offered his cutlet to Dan, who speared it onto his own plate. Julie carefully scraped the fried coating from the meat, which was thin and gray. She took a small bite.

"Well, it tastes like chicken," she said. "And the potatoes and carrots look fresh."

Mel was starving, as she hadn't eaten since early that morning—a stale roll and cold coffee on the plane. She'd never been a picky eater, thanks to the minimal cooking skills of her divorced father, and she followed his adage that the difference between a good meal and a great meal was about two hours. The food on her plate was not great, but it wasn't terrible either.

They ate for a few minutes in silence, waiting for the

hovering waiter to get bored and go back to his comrades. Finally, he retreated into the kitchen and they continued.

"I want everyone to wear their badge dosimeters from now on," Dan said. "In theory, we're far enough away from the Exclusion Zone to be safe, but we really have no idea what's been manufactured, or stored, in some of the labs we'll be inspecting. As soon as we return stateside, they'll be read, and we'll know for sure how much radiation we've been exposed to."

Mel stared at the carrots on her plate, wondering where they'd been grown. Seventy percent of the radioactive dust created by the Chernobyl explosion four years before had descended over Byelorussia, rendering a fifth of the country's best agricultural land dangerously toxic. That very swath of territory, to the south, bordering Ukraine, historically grew most of the best produce. And now it remained blanketed by soil that would stay radioactive for thousands of years.

As though reading her mind, Ben asked, "Everybody get a chance to look over that briefing on the growing cancer numbers here?"

"Scary," Julie said. "Especially for the kids."

Mel had studied the brief on the plane ride from Frankfurt to Moscow. Radiation exposure killed healthy cells, or mutated them. And because children were constantly growing, producing new cells at an accelerated rate, they were at a much higher risk. The orphanages and asylums in Soviet Byelorussia had been filled by an unknown number of abandoned babies and young children with developmental disabilities, some of them formed in utero. Thyroid cancer and leukemia too were prevalent.

Dan heaped more mushrooms onto his plate. "That's what one hundred and ninety tons of radioactive uranium and graphite will do to a country."

"You mean several countries," Julie added, nudging away her own plate still half full.

"Well, we're only here for a month," Dan said. "State is confident that we'll be okay as long as we're not strapping ourselves to a nuclear reactor."

Ben gave up trying to scrape the cheese off his mushrooms and set down his fork. "The real test will come ten or twenty years from now. When the family jewels swell to the size of cantaloupes and fall off."

Quietly finishing her own cutlet, Mel envied her colleagues their glib banter. She didn't think they'd be joking like this if they knew, as she did, how committed Iran was to building a fission bomb. And how likely it was that bomb wouldn't stay in the Middle East. There was a big black hole in American intelligence around Iran's timeline. The State Department, and by extension the American people, thought they were still years away. Intercepted Israeli intelligence declared with hair-raising surety it was only a matter of months. If Mel could confirm the presence of the three Iranian scientists, it would spark an immediate acceleration in the preparedness of US security forces.

As the waiter cleared the plates away, Ben asked for coffee.

"Eh," Julie said, shaking her head, the thick curls springing about her face, her pale skin and luxuriant black hair making her look like a Goya painting. "You're better off ordering tea. The coffee's going to taste like wastewater."

She ordered four teas, and after the glasses of dark amber liquid had been served, Dan continued his briefing.

"A year ago, the State Department really thought we'd have an embassy up and running in Moscow by now. But after spending a hundred and seventy million over the past twenty years, they've decided to demolish the current pile of bricks and start over. Fucking Soviets wouldn't let us examine the building materials before installation. And they kept putting bugs in the walls faster than we could find them."

He took a careful sip of his tea. "Goddamn, that's good."

Julie nodded smugly. "Told you."

Ben suppressed a grin and sipped at his tea. Mel lifted her glass but, feeling another throb at her temple, set it down again.

"And, of course, there's no embassy in Minsk yet," Dan continued. "So we don't have a dedicated SCIF."

Dan was stating the obvious, and Mel knew there'd be no SCIF. But he had directed it at her in case she'd somehow missed it in their briefings, a lapse that could put the team in jeopardy. A Sensitive Compartmented Information Facility was a room that was soundproofed and verified bug-free. Most other embassies, whether in an adversarial country or an allied one, had one. That was where intelligence and instructions could be given and received safely. No SCIF, no guaranteed secured place to exchange sensitive intelligence. Irritated at Dan's patronizing tone, she felt a buzz of nerves return and rubbed at her forehead.

"So, folks, let's stay sharp and remember that even the walls have ears. Literally." Dan signaled for the waiter. "Julie, let's settle the bill and take a walk before Anton picks us up."

There was a small park in front of the hotel and the group walked slowly around the perimeter, each casual step conveying *just four tourists going for a stroll on a temperate summer day*. Westerners, especially Americans, were still rarely seen on the streets of Minsk, and their presence was met with suspicious stares. Dan kept his head lowered, his lips barely moving as he continued his rundown in a quiet monotone.

"We'll meet our contact tonight, who will be the conduit for our reports. Everything will pass through him. Of course, we'll be keeping two sets of records. The first for Soviet eyes, which will be boring accounting tallies: keeping track of the widgets they show us. Those will be kept in our briefcases, which will most certainly be searched. The second set of reports will be written using the substitution cipher given to us by the Agency, with the stuff we don't want the Soviets to see. They'll be written up on Saturday afternoons, and then passed on to our contact later that night. He'll know how to get them to the right place."

"Who's the contact?" Mel asked, her gaze sweeping over the lush lawn and then lingering on a man and a woman pretending not to be watching the group.

"His name is Dr. William Cutler. An American chemical-nuclear engineer on loan from Oxford University, invited by the head of the Heat and Mass Transfer Institute for research purposes. He's lived in Byelorussia for the past year. He's not with the Agency, but he's been a fountain of information for us. He gives the Soviets just enough technical know-how to keep them interested—and to keep them from arresting him as a spy—but not enough to give them an edge. We'll be having dinner at his apartment. He'll let us know when and where we'll start handing over our findings."

Mel spotted the minder who'd been in the Planeta dining room. He'd wandered into the park, casually smoking a cigarette.

"Yeah, I see him," Dan said, looking at his watch. "Okay, Anton will be picking us up soon. Let's make his job easy and wait in front of the hotel."

Anton pulled up in his van exactly on the hour. Elena sat, alert and prim, in the front passenger seat holding a pocketbook the size of a duffel bag on her lap. She waited for the group to get settled, her eyes bright with enthusiasm.

"Did you have a good lunch?" she asked, putting an emphasis on the "a" to show she knew English well enough to add articles. Their lack was one of the most difficult peculiarities of the Russian language, at least for Mel. "Where is the toilet?" became *"Gdye toilyet?"* Where toilet? Admittedly, she'd taken two semesters of French in high school only to realize that her brain was not wired for foreign languages. Only for faces.

"Oh, lunch was great," Dan said, holding up both thumbs.

"Excellent," Elena responded. She caught sight of Dan pulling his dosimeter out of his pocket and clipping it to his lapel. "You don't need such here. We are far from Exclusion Zone."

"The US government provided them," Julie said. "They're insistent we wear them while in Minsk."

Elena blinked a few times and frowned. "Anyways, we go first to Ministry of Finance for brief meeting, maybe one hour, and then we will go to the Byelorussian Heat and Mass Transfer Institute. Where we will spend several hours touring the facility."

She cleared her throat and announced, "It's very important that you stay with the group at all times. There are sensitive places at the science institute which are clean rooms and cannot be contaminated."

"Of course, Elena," Dan said, giving her his best Boy Scout smile. "We wouldn't dream of contaminating anything."

The Ministry of Finance was a middling-tall building, blocky and gray, like most in the Soviet Union. Elena bustled her four passengers out of the van and into the front foyer, which was impressively large but murky from bad lighting. All of their bags were checked thoroughly. Dan's camera was removed from his briefcase and held aloft by a victorious-looking guard, as though he'd caught a prize fish.

"Kamery ne dopuskayutsya." No cameras are allowed.

Julie translated and Dan did his best to look sheepish. He could collect it again on the way out. The guard then turned his attention to Ben. Mel knew the camera in Dan's briefcase had only been a distraction. The important camera—a very small device camouflaged as a metal rivet—was in fact fitted into Ben's briefcase. As the guard picked up Ben's case, Mel upended her purse, its contents clattering loudly onto the floor, distracting everyone's attention. Acting profusely embarrassed, Mel apologized, allowing a guard to kneel and help her collect her things as the other guard shook his head and waved Ben along. Mel gave them both a dazzling smile when she passed through the security barrier.

Once everyone had been processed, Elena guided the group into another tiny elevator, pushing the top button.

Shifting his weight, Dan whispered in Mel's ear. "Thanks for that."

Mel allowed herself a small smile. In one of their early briefings, Dan had told them all that the sooner you gave the Soviets something to snag as *zapreshchennyy*, forbidden, the better. "It actually makes them cheerful," he'd said, grinning. "They think they've gotten one over on us, and that's when they'll let their guard down."

"Why are these elevators always so small?" Ben asked Elena, looking unusually anxious. "It's like being in a coffin."

Mel nodded and closed her eyes, willing the claustrophobic feeling to pass.

They exited onto the twelfth floor and Elena led the team down a long hallway and into a spacious receiving room. A young, attractive woman with porcelain skin and heavy eye makeup was seated behind a reception desk. She stood and opened an inner office door and, in her best Vanna White impression, gestured them into the minister's sanctum.

Minister Sergei Ivanov, a serious man wearing glasses with blocky, dark frames, rose from his chair to greet them. He wasn't tall or overly muscular, but there was a robustness to him that belied his pale complexion. Next to him stood a younger man who would act as his interpreter. It was not uncommon for each side to have their own interpreter, edging the negotiations toward a truthful, and accurate, exchange. The minister pointed to chairs set up in a semicircle in front of his desk, arranged as if they'd be listening to a concert. The group dutifully found their seats, pulling out their notebooks and pens and starting to take notes. Ivanov was the republic's first minister of external affairs: the man who would do the actual begging for US dollars. Without giving the impression of actually begging, Mel assumed.

The laborious process of call-and-response had commenced. Mel listened with half an ear to the back-and-forth, scratching out notes on her pad to fulfill her role as secretary. Through his interpreter, the minister began his long-winded prelude: "Byelorussia's commercial success depends on strong internal governance and on favorable external conditions, like funding from the United States." And then: "Our government will continue to enforce extensive long-term controls over economic activities...we must at all costs avoid shock reforms..."

Dan and Ben responding alternately: "Continued asset stripping will disrupt your commercial networks, and that will be very costly to the US, even in the near future..." And: "Your financial plans still constitute seventy percent of SOEs, state-owned enterprises..."

"Yes, but without government subsidies vulnerable start-ups will surely fail..."

Mel kept her pencil moving, even as she scanned, and retained, the faces of the guards, the receptionist, the minister, and the interpreter. Next, she memorized all of the faces in the numerous photographs on the minister's desk and nailed onto the walls. She couldn't name many, except for the obvious Soviet leaders such as Brezhnev and Gorbachev, and the current Byelorussian chairman, Kobets. But there was every possibility that she'd see some of them in the flesh, and soon.

When twenty minutes had passed, Mel leaned over to Elena and told her she had to go to the ladies' room. Elena looked momentarily flustered and then accompanied Mel out to the receiving area. The attractive receptionist leapt up, eager to assist. Elena instructed the young woman, Katya, to take Mel to the toilet.

Katya gestured for Mel to follow and they walked down a series of hallways to a door marked in Cyrillic.

"Please," Katya said in heavily accented English, indicating that Mel should enter, and then following her in.

The room was fairly large, but with only two stalls. The pungent, acrid smell reminded Mel of a poorly maintained port-a-potty. Inside the stall, instead of a porcelain toilet bowl, there was a hole in the tiled floor with two raised footrests on either side. She'd have to remove her slacks all the way to save the hems from being soiled on the filthy floor. Mel closed the door, removed her slacks as carefully as possible, hung them on a hook, and squatted down. When she was finished, she cursed herself for forgetting to bring American tissues in her pockets. Soviet toilet paper—dispensed in little squares—was as coarse as sandpaper and as absorbent as sheet metal.

When she was dressed again, Mel walked to the sinks to wash her hands, using the ubiquitous hard green-gray soap that never lathered and left a sticky alkaline residue. She took her time, hoping to engage Katya in conversation as the receptionist lingered by the door. From her training, Mel knew she should never underestimate a source of potential information. As soon as she'd seen Katya smile, Mel knew she had her opening. She'd been told that Russians did not often smile with strangers. Smiling here was not a sign of politeness, but rather a demonstration of insincerity and secretiveness. *Ulybka slugi.* A servant's smile, not to be trusted. But in Katya, she sensed genuine warmth. Or at the very least, youthful curiosity.

Katya continued watching her with frank interest, her head tilting from side to side as though inspecting a rare animal.

"American women do not wear dresses?" she asked finally. Katya was the only spot of vibrant color in the drab room, wearing a flowered blouse and emerald-green skirt.

"Yes, we wear dresses," Mel answered, realizing too late that there were no towels, paper or otherwise, to dry her dripping hands. "Pants are just more comfortable." She gave her hands a shake instead.

Katya sighed. "Not when going to Soviet toilet, yes?"

Mel nodded, not in the least embarrassed. Camping and hunting for years with her father had put an end to any squeamishness about answering nature's call. "I guess not. Your English is very good."

"I have no possibility to practice much."

Mel took a lipstick from her jacket pocket and Katya leaned in hungrily to watch as Mel touched up her lips, taking her time. She then retracted the lipstick, put the top back on, and held it out. Katya finally peeled herself from the door to approach. "Here, the color would look better on you."

"Really?" Katya brightened, smiling with delight. She took the lipstick and placed it in the waistband of her skirt. "Thank you. We cannot get here in Minsk. Not yet."

"Maybe soon," Mel answered. "Do you like working here?"

Katya shrugged. "Is okay. But very boring. You are secretary too. How much do you make in America?"

Mel sighed. "Not so much."

"But more than here."

"Yes, probably." Mel turned back to the mirror as though examining her hair. "But it's boring there too. What goes on in the city for fun? You know, for entertainment. Music or restaurants?"

Katya gave a dismissive snort. "Probably where you are staying now. Planeta Hotel, yes?"

"That's right. We're there for the next few weeks. You

should come one night. We can meet for a drink, and you can tell me more about Minsk. It'll be my treat."

Katya's gaze became more guarded. Her hip rested against the sink in a casual way, but she had crossed her arms in front of her chest. "Have you been at night? To the nightclub?"

"No, not yet. We only arrived this morning."

"You should be careful there. A very dangerous place. Don't go alone."

"Dangerous?"

"The women who go there? They are all prostitutes. And the men? They are all looking for prostitutes."

"Oh," Mel said, as though this news surprised her. She'd had enough Agency training to spot the obvious honey traps in hotel bars. "Most of the men I've seen at the hotel are Swiss and German. They don't look very scary."

Katya shook her head in a pitying way. She leaned in closer to Mel. "Women go missing from that place. And from other places too in Minsk."

"Missing?" Mel turned toward Katya, her eyes wide, maintaining the appearance of a naïve American. "You mean, kidnapped?"

Mel had been warned that there'd been a tremendous rise in sex trafficking over the past year in Minsk, as well as in other Eastern European countries. With the dissolution of the Soviet Union, factories and farms were closing down. People were not being paid. Vital supplies of food and medicine were drying up, leaving the black market room to thrive. People were turning to more desperate measures in order to survive. And for women, that desperation often came at a heavy cost.

"Not just kidnapped," Katya said. "Killed. At least six in past year."

This was news to Mel. They'd been briefed on the rise in crime and in retribution from the Russian Mafia—also known as the *Bratva,* the Brotherhood. But she hadn't heard of women being killed. "Prostitutes are being killed here in Minsk?"

"Not just prostitutes. Regular women"—Katya made a frustrated whooshing sound, her eyes wide—"some just disappearing—"

The door banged open, startling them. Elena walked in, a strained look on her face. She peered carefully first at Mel and then Katya.

"You've been gone for a long time," she said accusingly.

Mel finished drying her damp hands by wiping them on her slacks. "I wasn't feeling very well. Katya was kind enough to stay with me."

The receptionist turned away quickly, hiding her relief.

"Are you ill?" Elena asked. She looked worried, but Mel guessed it was more out of self-preservation than genuine concern for her charge's well-being.

Mel rubbed at her lower abdomen. "I think it was the mushrooms."

The three women walked back to the minister's office, where Mel slipped into her seat and resumed her note-taking. Within another twenty minutes the meeting concluded. Everyone shook hands, briefcases and purses were collected, and Elena ushered the group of four back through the receiving area. Mel looked briefly at Katya, who gave her the ghost of a smile, nodding her thanks. She had applied the lipstick Mel had given her. A dark slash of coral against her delicate skin.

Walking down the hallway, Dan quietly asked, "Anything?"

Mel waited for Elena to stride ahead, eager to press the elevator button. They were running late. "Six women in Minsk within the past year have been killed," she whispered. "And more have gone missing."

"The *Bratva*?"

"I don't know," Mel answered. "The receptionist looked scared, though."

"Well, fortunately our job description does not include avenging dead prostitutes."

His callousness caught her off guard. "Do you know what some American police note in their duty statements when they come across a dead prostitute? 'NHI.' No Human Involved. Does that sit right with you? You've got two women on your team."

"Oh, Christ," he huffed. "We're not here on a rescue mission." He caught Mel's expression and, to his credit, softened. "Look, see if you can get her to talk some more. We're here for a month. She might provide some useful information about the minister."

The Byelorussian Heat and Mass Transfer Institute was only a fifteen-minute drive from the finance ministry building. Elena continued her running commentary with the official history of the institute.

"There they are making progress for robotics, shock absorbers, and polishing aspherical optics for space program. And, of course, for making civilian life more—" She paused, searching for the right word.

"Comfortable?" Dan offered.

Elena brightened, having found her word. "Productive," she said.

"What about nuclear energy?" Ben asked, his face a mask of innocence.

"In the 1980s we had been building our own nuclear plant for heating and power about fifty kilometers south of Minsk," Elena said. "But, as you know, following the accident at Chernobyl, these plans were stopped." She paused her narrative to look suitably downcast.

Anton muttered something from the driver's seat.

"What was that?" Dan asked.

Elena made a dismissive gesture, giving Anton a cautioning look. But Julie translated into English. "He said, 'Now, with sovereignty, we can be a nuclear power again.'"

Ben chuffed air through his nose and looked out the window. "Yeah, good luck with that," he said under his breath.

Mel turned to her own window and thought, *Here we go.* Stepping inside the institute, potentially filled with visiting scientists, would be the true beginning of her private mission.

To no one's surprise, the institute was another gray, blocky building. The group was greeted just past the security checkpoint by the director, Oleg Shevchenko, a bulldog of a man. Despite having the face of a retired prizefighter, he'd earned a PhD in mathematics and now held the Communist Party title of academician, the highest honor in Soviet sciences. He gave a gruff hello in Russian before turning on his heel and marching away, not looking to see if the Americans followed. Elena beckoned and they rushed to keep up with him.

The director led them through a warren of offices and cramped workshops and labs, pausing only to give a brief explanation of each of the ongoing projects. Mel passed dozens of scientists and support staff, peering intently into each room, looking for any familiar faces. And though she quickly committed to memory each face, she didn't recognize any of them. Dan's camera had, again, been held by security, but Ben's briefcase would hopefully pick up anything Mel missed.

They were finally taken into the director's office, a large room with dark paneling, the walls covered in portraits of Soviet heroes. It contained an oversized desk and a conference table with a dozen chairs. The Americans were introduced to five scientists representing different branches of research at the institute—four men and one woman, all wearing white lab coats. Each went on to give a brief speech about their areas of expertise: thermophysics, chemistry, heat exchange, mathematical modeling, and plasma physics. Mel took particular note that the woman had a PhD in quantum physics. When they were all finished, the director turned to the woman and snapped something terse in Russian.

The scientist meekly left the office, returning ten minutes later with a large samovar and delicate china teacups. She served tea for everyone before returning to her seat. Mel caught the woman's eye and nodded her thanks. Things were not perfect in the States for women, but she thought of how humiliating it must be for a dignified, educated woman to be treated like a maid. And in front of her colleagues.

"And in which department do we find your nuclear experts?" Dan was looking down at his notes when he asked the question, as though it were of little consequence.

After Julie translated, the director gazed around the room with an exaggerated movement of his head. "I think you're in the wrong republic. The Ukraine is several hundred kilometers to the south."

Dan smiled. "Surely you still have scientists who are working on future nuclear-based projects?"

Shevchenko shrugged. "Byelorussia is too poor. Which is why I think you're here. To give us funding for our projects."

"But not for nuclear reactor development. Or for uranium refinement," Ben added quietly.

Shevchenko looked at Ben, his expression one of distaste. He murmured something under his breath, causing his translator to pause in uncomfortable silence. Elena and several of the scientists shifted in their seats and stared down at their hands. Julie's mouth tightened and she stole a look at Ben.

"Director Shevchenko assures everyone that there is no nuclear development within the institute," the translator said in English.

Ben nodded, giving Shevchenko a celebrity-style grin, with lots of teeth showing. But the good humor stopped short of his eyes.

"Good, that's good," Dan said, rushing in to quell the tension. "Then you won't mind giving us a broader tour over the next few weeks."

Shevchenko crossed his arms and leaned back. "I was led to believe you are accountants. The supply and order books I can give you. Take all the time you need to study them. But we have magnetorheological polishing laboratories for high-end optics, which must remain pristine." He held one fat thumb tightly against a stubby forefinger. "One speck of dust, one grain of sand, will destroy the lens surface." His face was flushed as though he could barely contain his outrage at the prospect of clumsy Westerners ruining months of work.

Dan held up his hands in a placating manner. "Okay, I get it. But American funding is dependent upon my bosses being certain that our money goes to civilian infrastructure and manufacturing. Not military." He pinched his lips together as though deep in thought. "Tell you what, Oleg, we'll take a look at your books. And you'll let us physically inspect what's safe and provide a building blueprint for the rest. We'll also need the names and countries of origin of all the visiting scientists and engineers. This is not negotiable."

Every scientist turned their gaze expectantly toward the director. Mel could sense their suppressed nervousness, like a heavy fog rolling across the conference table. She doubted they'd ever heard Shevchenko spoken to in such a demanding way, especially by a foreigner. Dan's facile manner had disappeared, leaving in its stead an unwavering forcefulness.

Shevchenko stared at Dan for a count of five. "This must be approved by the minister of external affairs, and the Byelorussian Academy of Sciences. It can take many weeks to get this approval."

Dan closed his notebook carefully and placed it in his briefcase. "Director Shevchenko, I'm sure that you'll find a way to help us out. We're here for a month. But if we cannot give assurances to our government that Byelorussia is free of nuclear research, we cannot recommend funding." He stood up, signaling to his group to follow his lead.

Dan held out his hand for Shevchenko to shake, which he did reluctantly. Ben followed suit, refusing to move until the director shook his hand as well. Mel and Julie were the last to leave the office.

"What did Shevchenko say to Ben?" Mel whispered to Julie. She could tell from Ben's rigid posture that he was still heated about the exchange.

"Technically, he called him a lackey, but it was much worse than that." Julie turned to Mel with a bitter smile. "The only thing some Russians hate more than Jews are Black people."

When they had all crowded into the elevator, Mel made sure she was standing next to Ben. The curious, suspicious stares of the local populace had taken an ugly turn.

"You okay?" she asked.

He looked at her for a moment, a complicated array of emotions washing over his face: disappointment, weariness, anger. "I'm getting there."

As Elena led the way to the van, Julie and Mel walked briskly on either side of Ben, while Dan followed close behind—the three of them forming a protective barrier around their colleague.

4

THURSDAY, AUGUST 2, 1990

When Mel entered her hotel room, it was five thirty and twilight was still four hours away. She stood in the entryway scanning for any changes. Nothing looked out of place, but when she examined the drawers in the dresser, there were subtle differences. She had purposely left a sales tag on a new sweater, price side down. It was now facing upward. Ben had been right about their rooms being searched. It would not be the last time.

She glanced briefly at the mirror. Being warned she'd be watched was different from the experiential creep factor of knowing that someone might, in that moment, be on the other side of the two-way glass. It wasn't so bad in the daytime, but the thought of being observed while she slept made the hair on her arms stand up.

She had half an hour to freshen up, so she took a change of clothes into the bathroom and carefully closed the door. By now, the headache had taken firm root behind her eyes. She began to run hot water into the tub, and not knowing how thorough the cleaning staff was, she placed a small washcloth at the bottom to sit on.

When the bath was full, she turned off the lights, plunging the room into darkness, and eased into the water. She leaned back and closed her eyes. It would be so easy to drift off to sleep, but she'd trained herself to stay awake until she had completed her ritual. Taking a few slow breaths, she started counting backward from one hundred. Soon a procession of the faces she had seen over the past twelve hours began to flow rapidly behind her eyelids; the features of each momentarily sharp and clear, like a carousel projector spinning photographs on overdrive.

It was always this way, especially after a day spent in an unfamiliar place, confronted with crowds of strangers. As she filed each face away, the headache began to ease, the muscles in her neck and shoulders relaxed.

She had started the ritual when she was young. Her childhood had been spent shuttling between her mother's house in Texas and her father's farm in Wisconsin. Perversely, the months spent in Houston fell during the summer, when the weather was at its most miserably hot and humid. The school year, including the biting, frigid winter months, was spent in Madison. Both extremes had driven her to spend long periods of time soaking in a bathtub—hot water for the winter months, cooler water for the summer. That was when she'd begun to realize its other valuable effects.

Her parents had been aware since Mel's childhood of her recognition abilities, which had alternately surprised and perplexed them. At first, it was little things, like recognizing adults she hadn't seen since she was a toddler. Or how once, when Mel was shopping with her mother in a large mall, she'd waved to a teenage girl who'd only frowned and quickly walked away.

"How did you remember that girl?" her mother asked. "Her family moved away from Houston the summer you turned four!" Mel had shrugged, but the question had lingered uneasily for months.

For all her easy acceptance of Mel's uncommon ability to

recognize specific individuals, her mother had had no idea that, from that day forward, Mel would be able to recognize not only that girl, whether she'd turned forty or eighty, but every other person Mel's gaze had fallen on in that crowded shopping mall too. As Mel herself came to understand this phenomenon, she kept the knowledge more and more to herself. Alice was a free spirit who believed in ghosts and the occult. If she'd known the extent of her daughter's abilities, Mel imagined she'd have spent many more hours of her childhood being dragged to visit mediums and psychics, looking for her mother's favorite thing, a supernatural explanation for the unexplainable. That and burning sage to keep the evil spirits away.

Her father, Walter Donleavy, on the other hand, seemed to understand intuitively that there was more to Mel's gift than she let on. Playing his usual role as an opposite to Alice, he encouraged Mel to keep her ability hidden. To use it when and where she could, but not to reveal it to anyone. He was a kind man, but a reserved, stoic one; he'd seen firsthand how the populace often reacted with hostility to the things they could not easily explain. And he knew all too well mankind's capacity for violence.

The year Mel turned twelve, she learned from one of Walter's deputies that, as a young cop, her father had been a part of the search for Ed Gein, the Butcher of Plainfield, one of the most sensational serial killers in the country, and certainly the most infamous in Wisconsin's history. Walter had been there on that cold day in 1957 when the police entered Ed's home and soon after arrested him. When Mel confronted Walter about the arrest, he refused to talk about it at first. Mel persisted, finally wearing him down, and, while he wouldn't give details about what he'd seen in that small farmhouse, he revealed that it had looked like the inside of a slaughterhouse. From that moment on, it had made him obsessive about teaching his daughter, his only child, how to defend herself. He would often turn ordinary household items into weapons—a wooden spoon applied with enough force to a vulnerable area, such as an eye, an ear, or the throat, was as deadly as the sharpest knife—and insisted that Mel practice eluding his capture.

It had started as a game, a kind of hide-and-seek through the forests, streams, and lakes surrounding their home, regardless of the season. But as Mel got older, they played farther and farther afield, with sometimes frightening seriousness. It was only after her father told her about the Plainfield Butcher that she understood what had driven him to prepare her this way for life in the outside world.

What Walter didn't know, at least not right away, was that contrary to protecting Mel from the harsh realities of the world, his revelation kindled an insatiable curiosity in her. Mel became obsessed with the men who came to be known as serial killers, and their methods. She kept newspaper clippings and true-crime novels hidden in her room the way her teenage friends hoarded magazines like *Penthouse* and *Playboy.* The stories both horrified and fascinated her, and she would often pester her father's deputies for details.

To Walter, his daughter's fascination was ghoulish, almost a betrayal of everything he'd tried to keep locked away inside his own troubled memories. But to Mel, her father had given her a sense of purpose. What if she wasn't just a freak, but someone who could help identify the killers? She'd studied photographs of the murderers, instantly committing them to memory as she did every face. But try as she might, she couldn't unlock the code, the telltale signs, the road map in their features that might reveal a brutal killer. In fact, other than an occasional deadness about their eyes, there were many, such as the good-looking Ted Bundy, who gave no clue that behind their smile lived a sadist. It was a source of frustration that Mel couldn't recognize the inner man as easily as the outer.

Mel learned over time how to hide not only her uncanny recognition skills, but also the internal conflict they often caused—was she gifted, as her mother stated, or was she a freak of nature? It wasn't until her first months at Quantico that she understood. Either way, she'd had her earliest training at being a spy: hiding her true self from the public.

Reluctantly, Mel opened her eyes and stepped out of the tub. The Planeta towels were thin and scratchy, but at least they smelled clean, and after she'd dressed in a fresh set of clothes, she felt relaxed, if bone-weary with jet lag. The last thing she wanted to do was go to a dinner hosted by a chemical-nuclear engineer. Even if he was an Agency contact.

She regarded herself in the bathroom mirror and sighed. In her simple slacks and button-down cotton shirt, she looked exactly like what she was pretending to be. A secretary. She'd inherited Alice's pale skin and brown eyes. But where Alice's hair was Gaelic red, Mel's was a dark brown. Black Irish, Walter had called her, teasingly.

Over the years, men had told Mel she was beautiful, but only because there was no better word for a grown woman who still looked like a garden fairy. Women sometimes found her otherworldly attractiveness disquieting—eyes a little too wide apart, a dreamy slackness to her mouth—what her mother had called fey. Mel's gentle demeanor belied a well-practiced self-reliance and often surprised, and dismayed, the men who'd mistaken her for helpless. She came to relish the surprise of this reveal—a quick takedown in a self-defense training, a sharp-tongued putdown to the women who bullied her, a well-timed thumb twist for the hand that sought to grope her on the train.

She sighed again. The lipstick she'd given Katya was her only departure from the restrictive Agency parameters: utilitarian apparel, monotone shoes, sparse jewelry, little makeup, and no perfume. Nothing that would call attention to Mel and prevent her from blending into the woodwork. As if such a thing were possible when her haircut alone would scream *American!* to anyone who wasn't blind. But the point was not to hide her Westernness, but rather to diminish her importance within that category.

Mel thought about brushing her shoulder-length hair back into a ponytail but was too tired to be bothered.

She picked up her purse and slipped into the hallway, leaving her key with the hall monitor, the same woman who'd been seated there earlier. There would be a different woman later tonight, as they sat in twelve-hour shifts. The monitor didn't smile, but she did nod, saying, "*Dobre vecher,*" as Mel waited for the elevator. Good evening.

Mel was the first of her group in the lobby. Hearing raucous male laughter, she wandered over to peer in the door to the place Katya had called dangerous. It was a spacious room with a curved bar at one end, a raised stage at the other, and clusters of café tables and club chairs in the middle.

Several groups of men were gathered, already well on their way to being drunk, all speaking German. A few young women sat among them. Mel watched one rise, darting away from a drinker's clumsy grab. The woman had been smiling at the older man's antics, but as soon as she turned away, the smile vanished, replaced by stone-cold indifference. As she neared, Mel was mesmerized; the woman was one of the most beautiful she'd ever seen, outside of a celebrity magazine. She had high Slavic cheekbones, full lips, and thick blond hair. Her dress was silky, the hem at midthigh, and she was fluidly graceful in the way that only a classically trained dancer could be.

The woman caught Mel looking at her and the indifference turned to defiance. On her way out of the bar, she purposely clipped Mel's shoulder with her own.

"Urodlivaya Amerikanskaya suka," she whispered. Ugly American bitch.

She turned to disappear into the women's toilet, leaving a scent of strong floral perfume.

A bit shaken, Mel withdrew to sit in the lobby. There was still no sign of her colleagues. She looked again at the sparkly sign over the bar's dark door. It read planeta mir. Planet Peace.

Within a few moments, Dan emerged from the elevator with Ben and Julie. They looked as tired as Mel felt and she was relieved when Dan said, "This is going to be a short evening, comrades. We all need some sleep."

Anton was alone in the van, hurriedly screwing the top back onto a large thermos filled with what smelled like chicken soup. When Dan asked him in English where Elena was, Anton waited for Julie to translate before growling in Russian, "At home. Having a real dinner."

William Cutler's apartment was a fifteen-minute drive away. Mel was alarmed to discover it sat across the street from the KGB building.

"Cuts down on transport time," Dan said, winking at Mel's dismay and climbing out of the van. He led the group into an extravagant lobby with marble floors and wrought iron balustrades. On Dan's insistence, a sleepy-looking desk clerk, sighing, locked the front door and accompanied them up to the third floor in an old-fashioned cage-style elevator.

"This is a damn sight better-looking than the usual Soviet buildings I've seen in Minsk," Ben said.

"The Germans destroyed most of the city during the Second World War," Dan said. "Afterward, the Russians used German prisoners of war to rebuild. That's why there was at least an attempt at beauty."

The desk clerk led them down a short hallway to a heavy oak door, where he knocked loudly a few times with the back of his knuckles. His sleeve was rolled up. Mel noticed the faint grayish numbers tattooed on one forearm just before he turned to face them. "Yes, the Germans were quite cultured." His English was perfect, if heavily accented. "You should have seen their gardens outside of Dachau. I saw them, through a barbed wire fence."

Dan had the decency to look embarrassed and Julie stared, visibly distressed, after the old man's retreat back to the elevator.

The door swung open and a rotund man with an abundant fuzz of white hair and a full white beard greeted them.

"Hello, hello," he said, motioning them inside. "I'm William Cutler. Welcome."

The apartment was spacious, with crafted oak paneling along the walls and intricate plaster moldings on the ceiling. Mel was relieved to see it was filled with worn, but comfortable, sofas and chairs in muted colors. A far cry from some of the stiff, garish furniture at the hotel. A Steinway piano glowed softly against a bay window.

William bustled to take jackets and sweaters, crushing them against his round belly as he ushered his guests deeper into the living room. On a trolley bar were bottles of whiskey and vodka, and on the coffee table were platters of meats, cheeses, and smoked fish. There was even a bowl of black caviar glistening wickedly on top of shaved ice.

However Mel had imagined their Agency contact, it certainly wasn't as a stand-in for Santa Claus.

"I think I may have insulted your desk clerk," Dan said, handing William his suit coat as well.

"Oh?" William asked, peering sharply over his glasses. "I

wouldn't worry. If the Nazis and the Stalinists couldn't kill him, I don't think a few thoughtless words from you will. Besides, he'll be living in Israel next year." He turned to Julie. "Isn't that what we always say at Passover? Next year in Jerusalem?"

A series of conflicting emotions washed over Julie's face, ending in a reluctant half smile, and she sank down onto the sofa with a small nod.

William took drink orders and, as soon as everyone had been served, joined them in the chair closest to the food. "Eat, eat, please."

Ben had remained staring with some dismay at the platters of animal products, and their host smacked his forehead with the palm of his hand. He leapt up, disappeared into the kitchen, and soon returned with a bowl of fresh lettuces, a selection of nuts, and strawberries.

"This is stellar, Dr. Cutler," Ben said, relieved. "Where did you get the fresh greens?"

Ben was directed to sit in a nearby chair. "Please, call me William. And all good Minskovites have gardens at their dachas."

"You clever old dog," Dan said, digging in. "How in the hell did you wrangle a dacha?"

William looked at Mel and smiled with mock shyness. "It's not really mine. It belongs to my girlfriend, Sveta."

Mel returned his smile. In the space of a few moments he had shown a masterful grasp of the group in his care. He had effectively deflated Dan's sense of self-importance while revealing his own Jewish roots to Julie, and had made a considerable effort to make Ben comfortable. She wondered what he was noticing about her.

William heaped his own plate full of food. "So, you met with the minister of external affairs today? He sent the caviar, by the way, so he must have been impressed."

"Or at least hopeful of our help," Dan added. "The problem is not going to be with the minister."

William immediately put his finger to his lips, set his plate aside, and walked to the piano, where he pointed to the strings, miming silence again. "I imagine Academician Shevchenko is not going to be keen on letting you see the entire institute. At least, not at first. But once you get to know him, he's quite an amiable fellow. Especially in a more relaxed setting."

He walked over to a lamp and pointed again. "Especially after a few vodkas. I'll be sure to throw a dinner so you can get to know him. But, for now, let's not talk business. You must be exhausted. How about I take you all on a walking tour of the city tomorrow morning? It should be a lovely day, and we could all do with the exercise. Especially me." He patted his stomach, retrieved his plate, and resumed eating.

Mel could feel the vodka tracing heavily through her body. The food was excellent, the fish oily and satisfying, the heavy dark rye bread pungent and filling. It was far better than the lunch they'd had earlier at the Planeta.

William had gotten to his feet again to refill everyone's glasses with vodka. After topping off Julie's, he said, "You have the keen appearance of a kibbutznik. It's in the eyes. There's steel there."

Julie gave him a skeptical look. "Yes, I spent a few summers at Ein Gev."

"Ah, right on the Sea of Galilee. Beautiful." He finished the vodka in his own glass. "There's a Greco-Roman city close by called Hippos. Have you seen it?"

Julie nodded.

William removed his glasses to clean the lenses on a napkin. "In Aramaic it's called Sussita, which is 'horse' in the feminine."

Dan said, "William speaks seven languages. Fluently."

William grinned roguishly. "Actually, it's eight. But who's

counting. In Arabic it's called Qal'at al-Hisn, which means 'Fortress of the Stallion.' It's interesting that fortresses and military might are usually referred to in the masculine. But I think it's the women who are the most adept at securing peace and security."

He turned his gaze to Julie. "During the Maccabean rebellion the fort hid the zealots. They were successful in creating an independent Jewish kingdom, in part because they had a vast network of spies." He touched the side of his nose playfully and then looked pointedly at Mel. "Many of them women."

"It didn't end very well for the Jews," Julie said.

"No," William said sadly. "It usually doesn't."

Julie finished draining her glass. "Cutler's not a Jewish name." There was a challenging edge to her tone.

He smiled indulgently. "But Wilhelm Kolwitz is. Born 1927 in Vilna, which was then Poland and is now Lithuania. You can't get more Jewish than that, which is why I changed it to Cutler after the war. It made things easier."

William gazed over at Ben, who was holding his vodka glass up to the lamplight, as though inspecting its purity. "Do you like the vodka?"

"Very much," Ben said, looking relaxed and happy. "I make it a point to try the native spirits as soon as possible."

"An old-fashioned in Georgia?" William suggested.

Ben looked briefly surprised before adding, "Schnapps in Germany."

"Jägermeister in Bavaria?"

"Oof," Ben said, grabbing his stomach. "I'll never drink Jägermeister again."

William nodded in sympathy. "I'm with you there, my friend. Have you tried bison-grass vodka yet?"

Ben shook his head.

"You should. It's a Byelorussian specialty, although

traditionally it's distilled in Poland. Every bottle has one blade of grass in it, which, as you are a vegetarian, should intrigue you."

Julie pulled a face. "Isn't *all* liquor vegetarian, strictly speaking?"

"Of course," William conceded. He turned back to Ben, one finger pressed against his nose again. "But it has a special, almost sacred, history with Byelorussia. In honor of your first night here, you should try it."

Dan laughed. "Uh-oh, don't encourage our young, energetic friend, William."

William directed a mischievous wink at Ben. "Just have one at the Planeta Mir and tell me tomorrow how you liked it. If you approve, I can get you several bottles to take home." He brushed the crumbs off his hands and stood. "Well, I think we can call it a night. You all look knackered."

They gathered their things, and their host escorted them to the door.

"Will nine o'clock be too early? For our tour?" he asked. "I'll meet you at the hotel."

Dan nodded. "I think that will be fine. Thank you, William."

The desk clerk watched the group solemnly as they exited. Dan waved good night, but he didn't return the gesture. They then spent several minutes searching for the van and discovered it parked on the street half a block away, Anton fast asleep in the driver's seat. Dan rapped on the window, rousing him, and they all climbed wearily into their seats.

As they drove away, Mel noticed that most of the office lights in the KGB building were still blazing. She knew from her training at the Agency that the KGB never slept. It was a tireless behemoth with countless arms and a multitude of teeth. Its motto was "Loyalty to the party. Loyalty to the motherland." She pulled her jacket tighter around her and murmured, "Looks like the night shift is in full swing."

"No rest for the weary," Ben said. "Can you imagine living across the street from them? I wonder how Dr. Cutler sleeps at night."

"Well, we know Cutler did his research," Julie said, yawning. "The kibbutznik comment was a little much."

"He mentioned Georgia," Ben said. "Sounds like he knew I did my basic training at Fort Benning."

"Sure," Dan said. "He probably did his homework on all of us, but it's almost impossible to put one past the old bastard. Don't ever play poker with him. He can read your hand by how much your pupils have dilated. I heard he plays chess every Friday night with the head of the Byelorussian KGB, Martin Gregorivich Kavalchuk. And usually wins. The guy may look like a Christmas elf, but he's got balls the size of boulders."

Anton said something in Russian, and Julie looked at him sharply but didn't translate.

When they arrived at the hotel, Dan told Anton that they would need neither a driver nor their guide, Elena, in the morning, but to come and pick them up after lunch. Mel was dizzy from exhaustion and the two glasses of vodka and almost staggered into the lobby behind her three colleagues. Ben had paused to look through the open doors into the nightclub. There was now a band playing rock music and the club was packed with men and women laughing and talking loudly.

"I think I'll take William's suggestion and try some of that vodka," Ben said. When Dan gave him a look, he said, "Just one. I promise. It'll help me sleep." He handed Dan his briefcase and disappeared into the bar.

"Watch your wallet," Dan called after him.

The other three got into the elevator, and when the doors closed, Mel asked Julie what the driver had said.

"He called Kavalchuk *Chernyy Volk,*" she answered quietly. "The Black Wolf. He said he's 'the wolf that eats men, women, and children.'"

They'd all been briefed on the head of the Byelorussian KGB. The man had risen through the ranks, first as an army colonel, then as a loyal and dedicated KGB officer proficient in the art of *mokroye dyelo,* or wet work: murder for the State. It was reported by escaped dissidents, or "criminals against the People," that even the Grim Reaper shat his pants when Martin Kavalchuk appeared. The team was to do everything possible to stay out of his crosshairs. Even hearing his name spoken in hushed tones, Mel felt the skin on the back of her neck tighten.

At the second floor, Mel was eager to retreat, waving good night to Dan and Julie and walking unsteadily toward her room. Although it wasn't late, her monitor had fallen asleep at her station, head on her arms. Passing by, Mel caught the fog of alcohol, most likely vodka, rising pungently from her half-open mouth with every exhalation. They'd been warned about the extremely high rate of alcoholism in the Soviet Union. Even when inflation skyrocketed, making many essentials, such as food and warm clothing, barely affordable, the price of vodka was always kept low.

The *dejournaya* never stirred, even when Mel took her own room key off the desk and proceeded down the hall to turn the lock and open her door. She paused for a moment, scanning the room for unexplained shadows and sniffing the air for any sign of another uninvited visitor. But everything was still, nothing out of place. She'd already started unbuttoning her blouse before remembering the two-way mirror.

"I hope you got your thrill for the night," she mumbled angrily.

She donned her pajamas in the bathroom, brushed her teeth, and at last collapsed into bed. Despite her fatigue, it was a while before she became drowsy. She knew that William Cutler would be their team liaison, smuggling their reports out to the States. But she didn't yet know who her special contact would be. She'd only been told that it would be a man and that he would reach out to her, identifying himself by repeating her special project name. A name no one else, save her handlers, would know. She'd just have to trust that he'd reveal himself when the time was right.

Her last waking act was to set her alarm for eight o'clock in the morning.

5

FRIDAY, AUGUST 3, 1990

Mel woke feeling remarkably well, with no sign of any ill effects from either the vodka or the jet lag. She dressed quickly and took the empty elevator down to the lobby, where she spotted Minder #3, settled into a large club chair, reading a newspaper. Mel walked toward the dining room, aware that the man had risen, folding his newspaper, and was following her. Julie was seated alone at a table to the far side of the room, and Mel slid into the chair next to her.

"How many times did you move tables this morning?" she asked, watching the minder taking one close by.

"We didn't," Julie answered. "Dan says we have to let them have their way once in a while. It gives them operational vertigo."

Mel stifled a grin and poured a cup of tea from a large samovar. "Where are the guys?"

Julie slathered what looked to be potted cheese over a piece of rye bread. "Dan was here with me, but he went to Ben's room to wake him. He thinks our vegetarian friend may have overdone it last night and missed his alarm."

There was an assortment of breads, meats, and cheeses on the table and Mel piled her plate with one slice of each. She was halfway finished with her breakfast when Dan joined them. He fell into his seat, visibly perturbed, his mouth set in a tight, thin line.

"What's up?" Julie asked.

Dan huffed in irritation. "He's not in his room."

Julie raised an eyebrow. "If we were in the States, I'd say he found some company last night. But in the Soviet Union? He wouldn't dare."

"I quizzed the hall dragon, and the woman just kept repeating that she hadn't seen him. I'm going to kill the little lettuce-eating shit. We've only been here twenty-four hours, for Christ's sake."

Dan stiffened, his nose pointed toward the main entry door like a bird dog. Mel turned and saw two uniformed *militsiya,* Byelorussian police. Even in the States, policemen showing up at the breakfast table was never a good sign. She thought of Ben disappearing into the dark chaos of the bar last night. Immediately, she got the feeling that something bad must have happened to him. Dan was on his feet before the *militsiya* got to the table.

The older of the two said in formal Russian, "Good morning, sir, ladies. I'm sorry to disturb your breakfast. I am Officer Boyko and this is Officer Yurov. I regret to tell you that there was an incident last night with one of your colleagues here at the hotel."

Dan took in a sharp breath. Remembering he wasn't supposed to understand much Russian, he gestured for Julie to translate, which she quickly did. "What incident? Which colleague?"

Julie, looking worried, released a torrent of her own questions in Russian. Boyko held up his hands and switched to English. "Your colleague by the name of"—he paused as he consulted an official-looking document, then enunciated carefully—"Benjamin Worthingham Franklin was arrested last night at the Planeta Mir."

Mel could see that Dan was struggling to keep his composure. "Arrested?" he said, his voice strained. "For what? You know he has diplomatic protection."

Boyko made a placating gesture. "Please, sir, we'd rather not say here. If you come with us, I'm certain that we can resolve the matter quickly."

Dan's expression was thunderous, his jaw clenched, chest expanded aggressively in what Mel would have labeled Full Outraged American Mode. The presumed poly sci major had been replaced by something much more formidable. "Go where, exactly?"

Again, the placating gesture. "Do not worry. He's not been taken to jail. He's at the procurator's office. It's very close. We can take you. You can sign some papers and he will be released."

Dan clenched and unclenched his hands a few times, working to control his anger. He turned to Mel and Julie. "Let's get this over with."

The three Americans followed Boyko to the lobby. Mel could only imagine how much more difficult this arrest was going to make Ben's time in Byelorussia. Yurov, the younger policeman, fell in step next to Mel.

"Don't be concerned," he said quietly in heavily accented English. "I can confirm that your colleague is okay."

Mel took in his features: the flat, slightly Asian facial structure of people from the Urals, but the gray eyes and thick blond hair of a Pole. Despite his Russian mannerisms—the stiff, formal way he addressed her—he smiled widely, and Mel felt the warmth of a blush across her neck and chest.

Flustered, she whispered, "Can you tell me what happened?"

He shook his head. "He will be back at the Planeta in time for lunch, I think."

"What exactly is a procurator?"

"It is like your American chief prosecutor, I think."

He smiled again and caught her hand, giving her a warm handshake. "I am Alexi Ilich, so that in the future you will know my patronymic." The handshake lingered, his thumb tracing over the top of her knuckles. "In the future" had an ominous ring, even though he maintained his friendly demeanor. She dropped her gaze, pulling her hand from his grip, and quickened her pace.

The five of them exited the hotel to find William just approaching the entrance.

"We're going to have to postpone our walk this morning," Dan said.

William took in their worried expressions and started grilling the two policemen in Russian.

"Oh, for heaven's sake," William said, disgusted, after getting the story. He turned to Dan. "Did they tell you what Ben was arrested for?"

"Not yet," Dan said, glancing angrily back at Boyko.

William lowered his chin, looking exasperated. "He was soliciting a prostitute."

Dan laughed incredulously. "*What?*"

Boyko adopted an apologetic air. "Prostitution is illegal in Byelorussia."

"You have got to be fucking kidding me. So, you're telling me you've arrested every German businessman at the nightclub?"

William placed a restraining hand on Dan's arm. "Look, this is all for show. Go with these officers, sign the papers at the procurator's office, and you'll have Ben back here within the hour, two at most. Take Julie as translator. Leave Mel here with me. While you're gone, I'll make some calls and grease the wheels." He leaned in closer to Dan. "They're just making a statement, my friend. It's a diplomatic pissing contest. Ben will get a warning and there won't even be a fine. In fact," he said, his lips twitching, "this may even be good for his reputation."

"I don't think the State Department will look at it that way." Dan turned to Mel. "You okay to stay here with William?"

William offered her his arm and Mel looped her hand into the crook of his elbow. "Of course," she replied, avoiding Alexi's gaze.

Dan and Julie followed the policemen to their car, and William said to Mel, "I think a walk would do us both good." He peered closer at her face. "Or maybe a drink?"

Mel shook her head. "Oh, no. That's the last thing I need."

She had a moment of indecision watching the police car pull away, thinking that she should have gone with Dan and Julie in support of Ben. She'd make it a point to talk to him later in private.

"Shall we?" William set off at a leisurely pace. He adjusted the silk scarf at his neck and took a few appreciative breaths of the pine-scented air. Mel fell in easily beside him.

He led her through the small park in front of the hotel, past the freshly painted gazebo, and back toward one of the main boulevards, Prospeckte Pobeditelei. The traffic was light, and they had no problem crossing. The weather was as good as it would ever get in Minsk. No clouds, and a pleasant, dry seventy-five degrees Fahrenheit. Across the road was another grassy park, sloping gently to the Svisloch River, which meandered gracefully through the heart of the city. With their easy, companionable pace, Mel thought they could be mistaken for any father and daughter out for a morning stroll. Not that her father was ever much for strolling. And he'd certainly never be seen wearing a silk scarf tied nattily around his neck.

"This river has been crucial as a major trade route since the tenth century," William said. "But it's also been a conduit to Minsk's destruction. By the Tatars, the Rus, the Mongols, Lithuanians, Poles, the Russians, the Germans—"

"And now the Americans," Mel said wryly.

William smiled and squeezed her hand where it still rested atop his arm. "You know, in Byelorussia there's a saying: 'If you live near the cemetery, you can't weep for everyone.' Centuries of bloody struggles have given the Byelorussian people a stoic, practical turn of mind. But they're like teenagers. They've demanded independence from Mother Russia, only to find themselves free, yes, but also naïve and without protection."

He led her to a bench, and at last they sat, facing the river.

"That's why you, and your colleagues, are here," he said, turning his face into the warmth of the sun. Mel noticed the deep lines scoring his forehead, lines that were not often found on the faces of academics and scientists who'd spent a lifetime sequestered in quiet libraries or research labs.

"You're here to take note of the bad actors," he said, finishing his thought.

She turned to survey the park. A small kayak was being paddled with the current, and a few couples with small children walked along the bank. No one looked familiar to Mel, and she didn't see Minder #3 anywhere close by.

"Dan says you're our Agency contact."

"That's right." William nodded, turning to face her, squinting one eye against the light.

"How will it be done?"

He smiled. "A very reliable courier service. Believe me, all your information will be in safe hands."

They watched a man and his son unfurl a kite, trying unsuccessfully to launch it into the breezeless sky.

"I hope Ben's all right," Mel said, feeling restless. She'd begun to wonder if she should have accompanied her colleagues. The park was pretty, but William could have given her this information at a later time.

"He'll be fine," William said, flicking away a small piece of lint on his corduroy pants. "He wasn't put in a jail cell. The most discomfort he experienced last night was probably a lumpy sofa in the procurator's office."

"Weren't you going to make some calls?"

William pursed his lips in a meditative way. He looked at her closely, as though coming to a decision. "I'm going to tell you something, but I want you to remain impassive. Can you do that for me?"

Mel nodded warily.

"I arranged for Ben's arrest."

Alarmed, she jerked her head back. Quickly she scanned the park and the river for any obvious signs of approaching danger, but everyone had moved farther away.

William placed a hand lightly on her shoulder and patted it. "Breathe, Melvina," he said.

She stared at him again, her muscles tensed and ready for flight.

"Just listen for a moment," he said calmly. "There was no way I could get you away from the others without raising suspicions. I'm the only one, outside of the Agency, who knows your security status. Not even Dan, am I right?"

Her status. She willed herself to relax. "What's my operational name?"

Without hesitation William said, "Medusa."

He had answered correctly. William was not only the team's liaison, but her own. That would simplify things, at least. She unclenched her hands and willed her shoulders to relax. "So you know my mission?"

William gazed dreamily up and down the riverbank. Only Mel clocked that he was checking for any listening ears. "Here's what I was told by my Agency contact stateside. You were trained at Quantico, but then were reassigned to the CIA shortly after graduation. Whatever your skills are, they must be impressive, but they were not revealed to me. All I was told was that I was to get you in front of as many scientists, support staff, and government officials as I can. And that directive takes precedence over any other."

William shifted on the bench so that he was facing her. "As for Ben, I promise, no real harm has been done."

"But how did you—?"

"How did I know Ben would be in the bar? I have a contact within the *militsiya*. After I made the suggestion that he go to the Planeta Mir, I called my contact to follow him. Ben did go into the bar, and he ordered the bison-grass vodka. My contact then arranged for the setup."

"I have a hard time believing that, even drunk, Ben would solicit a prostitute."

William gave her a pitying look. "Now who's being naïve?"

Mel felt a jolt of anger color her face. Ben'd had a rough enough time being possibly the only Black man in the whole of Byelorussia. The hostile looks, the insult from Shevchenko. "Dan said you're not with the Agency. Who are you?"

"Primarily a scientist. But I'm also someone who cares very deeply that the Americans get involved in the…shall we say refurbishment of this republic."

"You say 'Americans' as though you're not one yourself."

"Oh, I am. When I need to be." He stood up, smiling at her look of confusion, and motioned for her to follow. He began walking back toward the hotel.

"After today," he said when she caught up, "we'll probably only have fleeting moments alone together. So I want you to listen carefully to my instructions and follow them exactly. I don't need to tell you that you can never reveal my part in Ben's arrest to your friends. It would not be good for instilling trust." After a moment, still shaken by William's deception, Mel gave a reluctant nod.

He was silent as they crossed the boulevard again but

surprised her by stopping at the gazebo, where he entered and stood with his back to the hotel. The structure was on a slight rise, with an unobstructed view of the river and the rest of the park. There was no one within several hundred yards. William reached into his pocket and pulled out a rolled packet of Tums. He opened the foil, took one of the circular pieces, and handed the rest of the roll to Mel.

"Russian food can be heavy," he said, patting his belly. "So many Westerners find they need these. If your pockets are ever searched, no one will think twice." He palmed the piece and ran his hand across a section of the wooden railing about waist-high. "And wouldn't you know, it marks just like chalk."

When he removed his hand, there was a thin, barely visible white line on the painted wood. He popped the remainder into his mouth. "And unlike a piece of chalk, the evidence can be eaten comfortably after use."

He blotted his forehead with the edge of his silk scarf. "I'm too fat. It makes me sweat like a peasant, which is, in essence, what I am." He laughed and made a gesture that Melvina should join him.

"We can't be seen to be looking too serious," he resumed quietly. "The Russians get nervous when Americans stop showing their teeth." He reached out with his thumb and gently swiped away the white mark, as though chasing away a fly.

They stepped from the gazebo and again walked through the park.

"If you need to get in touch with me, make a mark where I've shown you. Do it around five o'clock in the evening. The KGB day shift is supposed to go until six o'clock, when the evening thugs take over. But in the Soviet Union you get paid whether you work or not, so they usually give up around four in the afternoon to drink some vodka before going home to the wife."

He slowed his pace as they approached the Planeta. "You might want to make it a habit to visit the gazebo daily, even if you're not trying to signal to me. Bring a book." His lips curled playfully under his mustache. "Something Russian. *Crime and Punishment,* perhaps. Turn your back to the windows of the hotel as though you're admiring the river. A boring thing done regularly becomes boring for the watcher as well."

"How will you know when to check for the mark?" Mel asked.

"It won't be me checking. But you've already met the messenger." He paused for a moment. "He's here patrolling the park five nights a week, Monday through Friday. He's my contact within the *militsiya.*"

Mel gave him a questioning look.

"Alexi Ilich Yurov."

"Yes," she said. "He introduced himself to me." She would certainly remember the young uniformed *militsiya* who had smiled at her, and had lingered over her hand, before escorting Dan and Julie to the procurator's office.

"If you've left the mark on a weekday night," he said, "I'll meet you here the next morning at six. We'll have to come up with something different for a weekend." He winked and kissed her cheeks, Russian-style, as though saying goodbye. He put both hands on her shoulders and leaned closer. "If we're lucky, the Russians will think we're having an affair."

Mel blinked a few times, not sure if he was being playfully serious or seriously playful. But, as instructed, she smiled as though in on the joke.

"One last thing," William said, handing her a business card. "If it's a true emergency, call me on this number. When I answer, say you're dying for some more caviar. I'll come by the hotel with a car to pick you up within one half hour."

He gave a friendly wave to the hotel doorman and said for the benefit of the man's ears, "Thanks for the pleasant walk, Melvina. I hope I haven't bored you too much. Your colleagues should be back anytime now."

She watched him turn and walk to the end of the hotel's driveway. Before long he'd disappeared onto a small side street.

6

FRIDAY, AUGUST 3, 1990

Mel got off the elevator on Ben's floor and hurried down the hallway toward his room. Dan and Julie had brought him back by eleven o'clock. She'd been waiting in the lobby for them, and, at first glance, Ben had looked tired, but certainly not as downtrodden as she imagined he'd be had he spent the night with the military police or the KGB. Dan had instructed him to get cleaned up, and they were to meet in an hour for lunch before going to the ministry and then back to the Heat and Mass Transfer Institute.

Mel had wanted to catch him before he rejoined the others. The growing guilt she felt over knowing the truth of his arrest made her want an unfiltered account of his night, and to offer any support she could. As she approached Ben's hall monitor, she noticed that the woman was making a note in her ledger, no doubt recording Mel's arrival. She was younger than Mel's *dejournaya,* but she had the same suspicious demeanor. Mel wondered if there was a special Soviet course that trained them in disapproving stares, or if the women, and they were always women, all started out that way.

She knocked and the door quickly opened. Ben had already dressed in fresh slacks but was still barefoot and in a white undershirt. The monitor, who had an unobstructed view, made a disapproving noise.

Ben waved to her in an exaggerated way. "*Spaciba,*" he called out, and then muttered under his breath, "you old cow."

Mel followed Ben into the bathroom, still steamy from his shower, and waited for him to turn on both the sink and the bath faucets before she perched on the side of the tub. Ben closed the door and sat on the lid of the toilet, rubbing a hand over his face in a tired gesture. He was deceptively slender, but with the muscled physique of a dedicated gym-goer. He was an attractive man, made all the more appealing by his self-effacing, easygoing manner. And, Mel thought, by the fact that he'd be the last one to recognize his own good looks. Unlike their colleague Dan.

"How are you doing?" she asked.

He looked up at her with a strained smile. "Actually, it wasn't too bad. I played poker with the procurator's deputy and some of his executive staff until two o'clock in the morning, drinking vodka and eating sardines. They got to practice their English and I got to fleece them out of a whole lot of rubles."

"Wow, that turned out better than my night," Mel teased with relief. "What happened at the bar?"

He gave a mirthless laugh. "I got set up, is what. I was minding my own business, getting pleasantly plastered. You know, on the vodka William was talking about."

Melvina nodded, hoping she wouldn't reveal her guilt at the mention of William's name.

"This woman kept coming over to me, trying to start a conversation. I'd have to be blind not to see she was a working girl. I didn't want to be rude, but I tried to ignore her. Finally, she sits next to me, puts her hand on my thigh, and slides it all the way up. Before I could move, there were two policemen behind me, breathing down my neck. They frog-marched me out while ignoring all the Germans practically getting lap dances from the other girls."

"I'm really sorry, Ben," Mel said. "That's so unfair."

"Dan told me it'll make a good story." He paused, his expression downcast, his usually cheerful demeanor subdued.

Mel wanted to reach out, to take his hand. But the intimacy of the gesture gave her pause. The times she'd been alone with Ben she'd felt comfortable, as with a good friend. But with forced close contact, loneliness, and stress—combined with his tight-fitting T-shirt and the steamy bathroom—for the first time she felt that their relationship could easily tip into dangerous territory. For one moment, she imagined another time, another place, where they might enjoy something more intimate. Ben was kind, he was intelligent. But he was also vulnerable in a way that the rest of them were not.

"He's right," she said instead, giving him a brief pat on the arm. "This'll blow over. I'm sure Dan will downplay the incident in his reports. And besides, Byelorussia wants our money too much."

"You know," Ben said, raising his head to look at her, "I've never been arrested before. If I'd been arrested in the States for soliciting a prostitute, a *white* prostitute, it'd be because I'm Black. But here, I got the feeling that was irrelevant. My Blackness was a novelty, but not a crime. I just happened to be the one they made an example of."

Mel blinked. "Why would they want to make an example of you?"

"The guys last night made a lot of CIA jokes. They suspect we're all Agency. I think it was a warning. To let us know they know."

Mel shook her head. "Christ, we can't turn around here without being watched."

"Ah," he said, "there's being watched. And being *watched*.

You know, the deputy actually asked me why I'd want to work for a government that had instituted slavery. When I told him Uncle Sam had paid for my college education, he said that was because I'd given four years of my life to the military. The guy knew I'd served. That was not on the bio the State Department sent to the Byelorussian government."

A bead of sweat glistened along his hairline, and he grabbed a towel and blotted his face. Mel had been warned that the Soviets had access to information on the Agency's employees. Still, having it confirmed sent chills up her spine, despite the room's heat.

"I'll let you finish dressing," she said, getting up to go.

He followed her back to the door. "You want to hear the best joke of the night? From the procurator himself. You know why the CIA and the KGB are alike? Because a CIA agent can stand in front of the White House and yell, 'I hate President Bush.' And a Russian agent can stand in front of the Kremlin yelling, 'I hate President Bush too.'"

Mel smiled, squeezed his arm, and walked out into the hallway. She got into the elevator and, before the doors closed, watched the hall monitor busily make another note.

On her own floor again, Mel was retrieving her key when she heard a door opening down the hall. She looked up in time to see Maksim slipping out of a room a few doors from her own. He was tugging at the zipper of his pants and then smoothing his hair. Catching her eye, he grinned obscenely. Before she could get her own room open, he walked past her, near enough for her to smell the aftershave and rancid sweat from his body.

He said, in English, "I make you smile—"

She faced him so abruptly that it threw him off-balance. "Come close to me again and I'll break your nose."

She was already angry on Ben's behalf, and Maksim's reflexive recoiling gave her a fierce satisfaction. He scowled and shook his finger at her as he would at a naughty schoolgirl. He walked down the hall and into the elevator, where he turned to stare at her, unblinking, until the doors closed.

Lunch was uneventful but quiet without Dan's usual banter. Ben's arrest had put him on edge, and he kept giving their minder—sitting alone, as usual, at a table nearby—dark looks. When the group had finished, Dan picked up the newspaper he'd been reading, a *Washington Post* that was a week old. As they exited he dropped it on the minder's table, saying, "Here, something to practice your English on, Comrade."

Anton and Elena were waiting outside in the van. Elena asked stiffly, and without turning around in her seat, if they'd had a comfortable evening. There was no doubt that she'd heard about Ben's arrest.

Dan barked a cynical laugh. Ben gave an exasperated sigh, and they finished the drive to the Ministry of Finance in silence.

Minister Ivanov greeted them solemnly, as he'd done the day before. Again, the group was escorted into his office by Katya, still wearing her emerald-green skirt, but today she'd paired it with a tight-fitting cotton sweater in a brilliant shade of coral. It perfectly matched the lipstick Mel had given her. Mel tried a smile, but Katya frowned and avoided eye contact, quickly returning to her desk.

In the minister's office they continued their back-and-forth over the terms offered by the US team, with Ivanov giving the same tired excuse that the central Soviet government still demanded "oversight" for any joint venture. Mel dutifully took notes, the pauses for translation helping her to keep up.

"You must understand," Ivanov said at last, "that we are still tied to Moscow. Three-quarters of our people still identify as *Soviet citizens,* not Byelorussians, even though we have officially announced our sovereignty—"

"And Gorbachev is still your president, I know, I know," Dan said, Julie translating. "But it may not always be so."

Ivanov stirred uneasily, pulling himself straighter in his chair.

Dan smiled sympathetically and continued. "Right now, Gorbachev is being squeezed between the hard-line politburo and the emerging independent republics. You may be having your own elections within a year or two."

Ivanov shook his head. "This is pointless conjecture," he said forcefully. "I have been tasked with facilitating your fact-finding mission. But nothing can be finalized without approval from Moscow."

Dan held up his hands and then gestured for Ben to continue, drilling down into the details of how, when, and where the American funds could be applied.

While Ben was talking, Dan motioned discreetly at Mel.

"Mel," he said, barely looking at her. "Would you go find us some tea? I think we're going to be here for a while."

Mel blinked, looking around at the impassive faces of Ivanov's team, and then nodded reluctantly. She rose and slipped out of the room, feeling Elena's eyes boring into the back of her head. But even for Elena, an errand for tea was too menial. She didn't bother to follow Mel back to reception.

Closing the door behind her, Mel allowed herself a fleeting smile. The ruse had worked. Earlier at lunch, Dan had encouraged her to try engaging Katya again. Who knew what details, no matter how seemingly innocuous, about ministry operations, or the minister himself, she might have overheard. There might not be time to cultivate her as an official asset, but a few encouraging words, along with a bottle of hard-to-obtain scotch, or chocolate bars, might provide useful information.

Mel crossed to the oversized desk and waited for Katya to look up. The receptionist took her time finishing a note. Mel noticed that her smoky eye makeup looked uneven, as though it had been blurred with sweat, or tears, and hastily reapplied, and she felt a pang of concern.

Mel put on a hopeful expression. "Katya, would it be possible to get some tea?"

Katya shrugged, keeping her gaze lowered. "It may not be possible."

Mel leaned forward. "Could we find out?"

Katya gave a long sigh but picked up the receiver of the heavy Bakelite phone and barked a few quick words. "Someone will bring a cart." She set the receiver down sharply.

"So, how are you?" Mel asked after a pause. When Katya didn't respond, she said, "That lipstick looks really good with your sweater."

Katya's eyes flicked nervously to the minister's closed door, and then she turned her gaze to Mel. "I'm sorry, but I am very busy just now."

Someone must have spoken to her yesterday, after their bathroom chat. There were dark circles under Katya's eyes, making the flesh look bruised and tender. This was the double-edged sword of recruiting assets and allies within the everyday Soviet populace: they would take the brunt of the reprisals.

"Oh, I totally understand. Well, anyway—" Mel pulled a chocolate bar out of her jacket pocket and placed it on the desk. She'd sampled enough Soviet chocolates to know they were overly sweet and chalky. And curiously, sold almost exclusively alongside vodka and beer. Russia's three staples. "I thought you might like one of these. I've got more than I can eat." She pulled playfully at the waistband of her slacks. "My pants are getting too tight."

Katya stared at the glossy foil wrapper, her frown finally giving way to a slight curling of the lips. "*Spaciba,*" she said finally, slipping the bar into a drawer. She glanced briefly at the minister's door again and whispered coyly, "I heard about your colleague. At the Planeta Mir."

Mel laughed quietly and made a face. "Wow, news travels fast. It was an unfortunate misunderstanding."

"Hmm," Katya hummed with mock seriousness. "It happens often with men. This kind of misunderstanding."

They grinned at each other for a few beats.

"You know," Mel said, leaning closer, "I've been thinking a lot about what you told me yesterday. About the missing women. What do you think is going on?"

Katya frowned and looked away. "We should not talk about this here."

The handle of the minister's door rattled and Elena peered out, her expression suspicious.

Mel nodded politely and said, "We're just waiting for the tea cart."

Elena made a dismissive noise and spoke a few hurried words to Katya in Russian. Mel understood enough to know that it was a warning: *Mind your own business.*

After the door had closed again, Mel stage-whispered to Katya, "She's like the barber Ivan Yakovlevich's nagging wife."

Katya's eyes widened. "You've read Gogol?"

"In English, of course. 'The Nose' is one of my favorites."

"Most Westerners only know Tolstoy. Too much tragedy. I like Ray Bradbury best."

Now Mel was the one surprised. "You like science fiction?"

Katya smiled cynically. "Censors allow us to read it because they believe it is too impossible to be real. Therefore, too crazy to be dangerous."

The outer door opened and an older woman rolled a cart into the room. On top was an elaborate silver tea service that wouldn't have looked out of place in a Tsarist palace. The woman exchanged a few words with Katya, who pointed her toward the minister's office.

"Well, I better get back," Mel said. She began walking away and then quickly turned. "Are you sure you won't have lunch with me? Or tea? I'd love to see more of Minsk, and," she said, lowering her voice, "get away from my boss for a bit."

The older woman had opened the minister's door, revealing Ivanov. He glowered out at Mel from behind his desk, until his gaze fell on Katya. It stayed there until the cart had passed into the office.

As soon as the door had closed, Katya looked at Mel and whispered fiercely, "Yes, I would like to meet with you. I will leave word at Planeta."

The security scrutiny at the Heat and Mass Transfer Institute an hour later was even more thorough than the day prior. Multiple guards searched every bag, and every pocket, ignoring Elena's scolding. Finally the group was released and escorted to Shevchenko's office. This time, the director didn't rise from his chair. Dan was given a stack of purchase documents for the materials used in the various labs, but also told that the actual budget was known only by the Academy of Sciences in Moscow.

"So you don't make budgetary requests?" Dan asked, Julie translating.

Shevchenko crossed his arms. "The academy gives us our directives."

Ben had explained to Mel that modern accounting practices in the Soviet Union were much like those in the US: debits and credits, revenues, expenses, assets, and liabilities. But instead of going to shareholders, profits were relinquished to the State for equitable distribution to the workers. In theory.

Ben wafted a thin folder. "And what if you need more funding than you're given for a particular project?"

Shevchenko's head swiveled. Mel could almost hear the muscles in his neck creaking.

"We are a fully accredited member of the Soviet Academy of Sciences. We do important work for the State. If we need it, I ask for it, and it is usually given."

"Could we at least have the total amount of the budget, year to date?" Dan asked.

Shevchenko gestured to the folder in Ben's hand. "If you add up all the materials listed, you will have our budget."

Dan sighed, chuckled humorlessly, and shook his head. "This is bullshit. Don't bother translating that, Julie, I'm sure Director Shevchenko knows the word." He stood up. "I've been to this rodeo before. We'll ask for something and you'll give us ten percent of what we need, telling us to come back tomorrow. And tomorrow, and tomorrow. Here's what I want. I want a list of all the institute's employees and their job functions. I want real budget figures, and copies of your balance sheets. And then I want access to all of the labs. Including the rheological polishing labs. We'll put on hazmat suits if necessary."

He cupped a hand around one ear. "Do you hear that, Director Shevchenko? That's the sound of the old Soviet Union falling apart. Nine months ago the wall came down, and Gorbachev is holding on by his fingernails. Do you think that a year from now Russia is going to give a damn about a satellite republic whose best agricultural land has been rendered useless? Or one that, unlike Kazakhstan, has no uranium deposits? Or oil?"

Mel could almost see the desk vibrating beneath the director's anger.

Dan gestured for his group to stand. "We'll be back on Monday. I suggest you talk seriously with the ministry. The US government is willing to render aid, but we're not going to start writing any checks until we know how the money will be spent."

They could still hear the angry bellowing from the director's office even after the elevator doors had closed.

Dan looked at Mel, his lips curled into a smug grin. "God, I love holding the purse strings."

Julie looked unsettled, and her eyes cut to Dan. She said, "You made that abundantly clear."

"Let's hope that show of strength didn't derail our talks," Ben muttered.

"Are you kidding me?" Dan asked, striding out of the elevator and into the lobby. "He wouldn't have respected anything else."

As soon as the Americans walked into the hotel, Dan announced that he would buy everyone a drink in the Planeta Mir. When Ben balked, the older man put his arm forcefully around his shoulders. "Oh, no, we're not going to let them dictate what we can and cannot do. You gotta climb right back into the saddle."

They sat at a table in the middle of the room. Dan took their drink orders and went to the bar, singing "American Woman" loudly enough to make the German businessmen turn and scowl. There were three young women at the bar, including the beautiful blonde Mel had seen the day before. Dressed in bright colors, they appeared like tropical birds trapped in a dark cave. They looked painfully bored in between bouts of animated gossiping, but were especially enthusiastic after spotting Ben.

Mel glanced down at her own lusterless slacks, a dull contrast to Julie's more fashionable attire, which, despite her full figure, always looked custom-tailored. Never one to be overly concerned about clothes, Mel promised herself that when she got back to the States, she'd buy something frivolous and colorful.

"You know," Julie said, studying Dan's back for a moment, "I've decided that he can be quite the asshole."

"Yeah, he can be irritating," Ben said, turning to Mel. "But the guy's more than a talking head. Julie knows this, but I don't think you were fully briefed on Dan's history. He spent several years in and out of Peshawar arming the *mujahideen* in Afghanistan. When he wasn't eating dust and battling dysentery, he was ducking bullets as he escorted armed conveys through the Khyber Pass."

So the gossip about the "hot zones" he'd experienced was true. It explained Dan's excessive, at times annoying, confidence. Sauntering into a meeting with an uncooperative academician was nothing compared to walking blind into a desert canyon populated by armed insurgents. Dan soon returned to the table with bottles of beer for everyone. "Too early for vodka," he said cheerfully. He had a manic glint in his eye that made Mel think these weren't the last fireworks they'd see during their negotiations with the Heat and Mass Transfer Institute.

He raised his bottle to toast. "Here's to *glasnost*."

"To openness and transparency," Ben clarified, clinking his bottle against Dan's.

Julie took a sip of her beer and made a face. "There's a Serbian word that would better describe what happened today."

"What's that?" Mel asked.

"*Skolski,*" Julie answered, making a wavy motion with one hand. "Literally, it means 'school,' as in a school of fish. But it describes the side-to-side motions fish make when they swim. Or Soviet functionaries who can't move in a straight line."

Dan drained half his beer in a few swallows. "Mark my words, we'll spend the next month storming the beach by inches. The minute we get up to go to the airport they'll make concessions. Trust me, what the Agency should do is wait half a year as Moscow slowly starves Minsk of heating oil and come back in February. Then they'll be lining up to sell us the damn missiles, pennies on the ruble." He finished off his beer and loosened his tie.

Mel had started peeling the label off her bottle. The beer was heavy and bitter and had increased her thirst instead of slaking it. The four German men sitting at the nearest table were the same ones as yesterday. They talked and acted as though they were drunk, even though it was only late afternoon. But in studying them more closely, in observing the way they stopped their conversation whenever her group commenced theirs, she realized that they weren't as inebriated as they pretended to be.

"We're not the only country with money," she said quietly.

"Believe me," Dan said, catching and holding her gaze, "I know how important this trip is. Do you know how many operational strategic nuclear warheads Russia has—?"

Ben made an impatient move, as though to redirect the topic.

"Relax, Ben. I'm not going to say anything that any other country's intelligence services don't already know." He patted Ben on the shoulder loudly enough to draw more looks in their direction. He turned back to Mel. "Russia has over seven *thousand* nuclear warheads. Ukraine, over fifteen hundred. Kazakhstan, more than a thousand. And little old Byelorussia? Eighty. Only eighty. But they're a hell of a lot closer to Paris and London than the ones in Moscow. And a lot more vulnerable to outside players. You know, Iranians, Pakistanis, former Stasi members…oh, excuse me…" He made air quotes with his fingers. "Now it's the Office for National Security. *Amt für Nationale Sicherheit.*" He said the last using a cartoonishly guttural German accent.

Dan was also acting as though he'd had more to drink than he actually had, unless he was one of those individuals whose brain darkened at the first hint of alcohol. But then his eyes met Mel's and she realized that he was not drunk, not even close. Just jazzed. Hypervigilant. And enjoying taunting the Germans.

In that moment the table of Germans erupted in raucous laughter, as though an off-color joke had been told. Dan grinned wolfishly.

"You know why East Germany has such lousy football teams?" he asked loudly over his shoulder. The Germans stopped laughing. "Because they always clump together in groups of three: one who can read, one who can write, and one to keep an eye on the other two intellectuals."

Mel watched as the Germans swiveled around to glare at Dan. "I don't get it," she said to Ben.

"The East Germans consistently have the worst teams in the world, which they're *very* sensitive about," he answered, grinning, "*and* the Stasi are mostly illiterate thugs." He shrugged. "It's an old Cold War joke."

Smiling broadly, Dan leaned into the table. "Just letting them know that we know who they are. Now, who's ready for more beer?"

Mel watched Dan walking to the bar, for the first time admiring his swagger instead of being annoyed by it. The guy in the expensive suits and loafers was not going to be easily intimidated. She murmured to Julie, "Maybe not such an asshole after all."

By five o'clock Mel was seated on the railing of the gazebo, book in hand, just as William Cutler had suggested. She'd packed *Bonfire of the Vanities,* hoping that the novel would lessen the tedium of the long flights over. But as engaging as the story was, both the location—the tough streets of Manhattan—and the people felt unfamiliar. The hard glitter of relentless competition, even among the minor characters, was intended to be satirical. But the mean-spiritedness of the story felt less darkly comedic than deeply cynical, and very far from how she thought of home.

That society of constant hustle was something Mel had never experienced before joining the intelligence services. After graduating high school, she'd moved as far away from Texas and Wisconsin as she could get, enrolling at St. John's College in the green and leafy hills of Maryland. The peace there had been a balm; her childhood had been fractured not only by the bitter winters of the north and the blistering summers of the south, but by the straining polarity of her parents' personalities.

Her father, Walter, was hardworking, and uncommunicative to the point of being taciturn. Alice, on the other hand, was as shiny as a firefly trapped in a jar. Ever an optimist, she considered herself an eternal hippie, and her favorite encouragement for Mel was a reference to the Jefferson Airplane song "Go Ask Alice." "It's just the drugs, Alice," she'd say, meaning that, just like a bad acid trip, the disruptions to a happy and balanced frame of mind were merely chemical and, more importantly, transitory in nature.

But moving from one household to the other year after year was disorienting, like being shuttled from Mercury to Pluto. Her parents had divorced when she was a baby, her mother fleeing the harsh Wisconsin weather as well as her husband's growing paranoia. Mel's escape had been to read anything and everything, and the thought of a college where undergrads could immerse themselves in the classics sounded like heaven. The summers in Annapolis were mild, the winters were relatively kind, and life on campus was safe and serene and unchanging in its commitment to cultivated studiousness.

Feeling drowsy, she lowered herself to the floor of the gazebo, leaned her head back against a wooden trellis, and closed her eyes. The day had been warm, but a cool breeze wafted over the park, bringing with it the damp smell of the river. She would leave no chalky mark for William today, as there was nothing yet to report. Instead, the book rested in her lap and she turned her face to the sun.

A shadow fell over her and, for a brief moment, she felt a jolt of irritation. Squinting, she opened her eyes, expecting to see another park visitor. But it was Alexi Yurov in his full uniform—tight-fitting dark gray jacket with red and gold epaulets, and tall black boots with the trouser legs tucked in.

"Hello," he said. "Are you enjoying this day?" He spoke precisely, but haltingly, as though searching for the correct words in English.

She started to get up and he gave her his hand to assist. He pulled her in close, their faces a few inches apart, her shoulder briefly bumping into his chest, but immediately let her go. He then clasped his fingers behind his back and turned away slightly to face the river. It could have been just an awkward maneuver, and yet their contact seemed intentional. His breath had felt warm on her cheek. She averted her face to keep him from seeing her blush.

"Yes," she said. "It's a nice place to rest."

He gestured to the book in her hand. "And to read, I think." He bent his head and slowly sounded out the title. "Is it good? This book?"

"I haven't decided yet." She studied his rigid, formal posture, his assessing stare: a local policeman, politely, but firmly, inquiring into a foreign visitor's activities.

"What is this book about?" he asked.

"People behaving badly," she teased.

He nodded with exaggerated seriousness, as though considering this universal theme. "Will you come to this place again?"

"Yes," she said. "I may come here every day, when I can. It's beautiful."

He threw her a cautious smile and then returned his gaze to the river. Although quite slender, he had the body of an athlete, hardened by more than just a few hours on a weight machine. His palms were callused by work, like the dairy farmers she'd known in Wisconsin, and he exuded the good health of a man who'd spent most of his time outdoors. He smelled of cut grass and clean sweat. It was sensual, and arousing, in a way that a man's heavy cologne could never be. She shifted her gaze away so he wouldn't catch her wide-eyed staring.

"You have talked with your friend Dr. Cutler?" he asked quietly.

"Yes." Her gaze swept the park, and she spotted Minder #3 sitting on a bench, pretending to read his newspaper. A woman with a little girl in pigtails passed in front of him on their leisurely way toward the gazebo. Mel recognized the woman immediately. It was the same one who had been on the riverbank yesterday too.

"I think Dr. Cutler's your friend as well?" she added hurriedly.

"Yes, a good friend. I will see you again soon. Goodbye, then." Yuri nodded curtly, tugged on the visor of his cap, and walked briskly away.

In the half hour since she'd come to sit at the gazebo the wind had gotten much cooler. She tucked the book under her arm and hurried back toward the hotel. When she walked by the woman, chatting in rapid-fire Russian to the little girl, the woman pretended to ignore her. And Mel, as she'd been instructed to do, ignored the woman as well.

After dinner, Mel begged off going back to the Planeta Mir, wanting to retire early for bed. It was Friday night, and though it wasn't yet eight o'clock, she could hear the raucous sounds of musicians warming up onstage. Listening to a Russian band singing American rock songs in Russian was not something she thought she could manage without vodka. And lots of it. Further, she was still jet-lagged and Dan had told her that William was hosting a party for them tomorrow night. It'd be a chance to mingle more informally with ministry appointees and various academicians and scientists. The vodka, he'd assured the group, would be flowing until late into the evening.

Ben had been quiet all through the meal and had offered to see Mel to her room when she begged off. He was exhausted as well, having slept very little on the procurator's lumpy couch. He looked strained while he waited for Mel to retrieve her key from the hall monitor.

"You okay?" she asked, unlocking her door.

"Just tired." He paused, as though contemplating what to say. "I'm pretty sure Dan's having an affair with Julie. I think it started a few weeks ago, stateside."

Mel looked at him doubtfully. Julie had earlier called Dan an asshole. In fact, temperamentally, they seemed to be polar opposites. "How do you figure?"

He tapped his nose. "She smells of his aftershave."

"If so, they've done a good job hiding it."

"Mel," he said, leaning in and whispering, "we're spies. We're supposed to be good at hiding." He smiled at her and shrugged. "It happens. Stress makes strange bedfellows."

For an instant Mel wondered if this was Ben's veiled attempt to flirt with her too. Testing the waters. "Why are you telling me this?"

"Dan's got a bit of a reputation with women," he said, shifting uncomfortably. "I just wanted to...This is your first mission and I'm just looking out for you."

Mel studied his face—his expression earnest, his gaze sympathetic—and she realized that he was not being paternalistic or patronizing. He was being protective of her, looking after her as though she were simply a vulnerable, inexperienced young woman as yet untried with the Agency and not yet capable of defending herself. She thought of her training with her father and wondered what Ben would have said if he'd known that she could probably kill him with a cheese grater. She had an impulse in that moment to hug him.

There was an impatient rustling from the hall dragon behind them.

Ben threw the woman a poisonous look. "Want to come for a walk with me tomorrow? I need to get out from under Big Brother for a bit."

They agreed to meet in the lobby at eight o'clock and Ben wished her a good night. Before he turned to go, he winked at the *dejournaya* and laughed when she huffed in outrage. His steps seemed lighter as he retreated to the elevator.

After she'd completed her usual processing ritual in the tub, Mel changed into pajamas in the bathroom and then settled into the one comfortable chair, next to the window. It would be light for only a short while more and then she'd have to turn on the floor lamp to continue reading her book. The chair faced the mirror, and, after a few uncomfortable minutes, she got up and scooted the chair so her face pointed toward the view instead. Unfortunately, it was of the rear of the hotel, overlooking a parking lot and an industrial building of the same sad, gray concrete as almost every other building in Minsk.

She had a hard time concentrating on her book, instead revisiting all the exchanges she'd witnessed between Dan and Julie, going back to their first Agency briefings. They'd certainly been discreet, which protected the integrity of the mission. And their affair didn't affect her agenda. She smiled, remembering Ben's protectiveness—she was young, but she wasn't naïve. She felt confident that she could handle any overtures from Dan. Or anyone else.

This wasn't wholly unexpected. Her innocent appearance often lulled people into thinking she was inexperienced. Again, she thought of her parents. Her mother had always been overly concerned for Mel's safety, and particularly once Mel had been accepted into the academy at Quantico. But her father had been excited, in his way, and encouraged his daughter to join the FBI. He saw it as a respectable profession in law enforcement and, in his opinion, safer than police work and with real job security.

"You'll be a good analyst," her father had assured her. "You're smart, you're dedicated, you're happiest working alone, and you're hard as nails."

This expression of praise was about as loquacious as Walter ever got. But it meant the world to Mel that he was proud of her.

Her mother had been absolutely horrified by Walter's support. When she found out that Mel had been inducted into the Central Intelligence Agency too, she'd lost it.

"Like a lamb to the slaughter," her mother had intoned. Her response had not been surprising. Mel had inner resources of strength that her mother had never personally witnessed. She'd spent almost an hour on the phone with Alice reassuring her that all would be well. Just boring class work and a few well-supervised weapons training sessions.

But Mel hadn't told either of her parents about her trip to Byelorussia. It was Agency policy to tell no one, except a spouse, of a placement inside the Soviet Union. Which was, admittedly, a relief, especially where her mother was concerned. Her parents believed she'd been assigned to Frankfurt for a month of training. She pictured them each, going about their days—her father spending most of his time chasing down petty thieves, her mother in rehearsals for the next college play—unaware of the existential threat she'd been sent to thwart.

It was, of course, also against Agency rules to have sexual liaisons with colleagues while on assignment. Unless the agent had specific orders to engage a target in a sexual tryst, a mission Mel hoped she'd never encounter. But humans had needs, which was why the Agency used so many married couples on foreign operations.

It was also why they'd all been advised of Soviet State School 4, which trained male and female honey traps, called ravens or swallows, to seduce and then bribe and blackmail important officials. Her mind turned to Katya's revelation of women missing and murdered, some of them prostitutes, some of them not. Sex workers, male and female, were always more vulnerable to violence. But women who were not in the sex trade? The Soviet Union had long held that murder was a Western vice; in Comrade Stalin's utopia it had been decreed that murder was a capitalist disease, which to Mel was a ridiculous notion. It was like saying that Soviet men were inured to the violent impulses that plagued the rest of the world. As if Stalin, and his minions, hadn't murdered two million of his own people. She decided, if she got the opportunity, to question Katya more about the killings.

Inevitably, the thought of honey traps turned her mind to Alexi Yurov. William Cutler had told her that the young *militsiya* would be a go-between. Alexi was handsome and unnervingly friendly. Her mind wandered to Alexi's strong body and his winning smile. His breath on her face had felt as intimate as a kiss. Had he been flirting with her, or just establishing a friendly rapport? She'd had lovers in college, but not, by anyone's standards, passionate affairs. More like the inevitable tumble after spending long hours in the close, friendly confines of paired study groups.

Mel forced her concentration back onto her book. Within twenty minutes the words began to swim, and she closed her eyes.

★★★

Something had changed. Some indefinable sound or shifting of the air pressure caused Mel to open her eyes. She still sat in the chair, noticing that the bright light outside the window had vanished. The glass was now a rectangle of black, the room completely dark. Unnerved, she stood, fumbled for the floor lamp, and turned the knob next to the bulb. It clicked several times, but the light didn't come on. Fighting panic, she purposely steadied her breath. When she looked out the window again, she realized that the building across the parking lot was entirely dark too. There must have been a citywide blackout.

She heard a sliding metallic noise coming from the door. A key being fitted into the keyhole. With a jolt, Mel realized she hadn't engaged the internal lock earlier. Before her fear could root her in place, she bolted forward, careening blindly off the edge of the bed, and threw herself against the door. The rattling stopped, but she sensed someone was standing just on the other side.

Heart pounding, she jerked it open. A second of nothingness and then a blinding light shone directly in her face. She instinctively covered her eyes with one arm and backed away.

A disembodied voice with a heavy accent said, "I just check to see if you're okay."

It was Maksim, the manager. His voice was breathy and tense, as though from some heavy exertion. The beam of the flashlight raked the front of her pajamas. For a moment, Mel stood frozen, but then the lights in the hallway and the floor lamp inside the room came on all at once. Blinking against the glare, Mel saw that Maksim was holding a key in his hand and the hall monitor was gone. His eyes were heavy-lidded and red-veined, and he still had the flashlight beam pointed at the thin cotton material over her crotch. She could smell the alcohol rolling off his body in acrid waves.

The adrenaline she had felt only a few moments ago was now funneled into a growing anger. "What were you doing at my door?"

He shrugged, looking more entertained than concerned. "Like I say. Lights go out. I check on you. You are alone. You maybe need help."

For an instant she thought of driving her fist into the soft middle of his belly.

"I don't need any help." Pushing him away, she slammed the door and double-locked it. Mel could feel Maksim's indignant rage seeping through, along with his incoherent mumbling.

Finally, one word, spoken in English. *"Whore!"*

A few minutes later she heard a heated exchange between a man and a woman. The hall monitor had returned. Soon afterward, the elevator dinged once and then everything was quiet again. She checked the time; it was not yet ten thirty.

A man with a master key to every room, rooms where single women were staying.

She would need to say something to Dan in the morning. She'd been warned that being caught alone while traveling abroad could be treacherous. The previous year a female intelligence agent in Greece had been raped and beaten in her room by a hotel employee. She'd been assigned to the US Embassy in Athens, but even with her official status, the Greek police had taken no action, saying she must have invited it as she'd been seen drinking in the hotel bar earlier that evening. She'd been hospitalized for her cuts and bruises and, Mel knew, later furloughed from the Agency following a breakdown.

After her heart had stopped pounding, Mel splashed cold water on her face. Crawling into bed, she left all the lights on and, mindful of the mirror, pulled the covers over her head. After more than an hour, she fell into a troubled sleep.

7

FRIDAY, AUGUST 3, 1990

The blue Lada crept eastward on Prytyckaha Street, a main east-west avenue that intersected with the First Ring, a beltway that encircled the center of Minsk, and its most important cultural, judicial, and administrative buildings. The circle was pierced north and south by the Svisloch River, which snaked its way past Gorky Park, the Bolshoi Opera House, and the Planeta Hotel at its northern edge.

Sitting like a bull's-eye in the middle of the beltway, cradled on all sides by the river, was the Island of Tears. The man driving the car held in his mind's eye the memorial: the gargantuan statues dedicated to the legions of mourning women—mothers, sisters, and wives of the Soviet soldiers who'd died so bravely in the long Afghanistan conflict, their faces masks of tragedy and suffering. A far cry from the stoic women who daily trudged their way into the heart of the city to work in its office buildings, its courthouses, its hotels. Some to do the upstanding labor of the daylight hours. And some to do indecent work under the cover of night.

His own mother had been a Hero of the State, part of the Resistance who hid in the labyrinth of the forests, gunning down Germans who crashed through the undergrowth like lost and wandering water buffalo. He'd been sixteen when the invasion came, his mother only thirty-two, and he was left behind to defend, as best he could, their small homestead and his younger sister and brother. That first winter of 1941, both his siblings had died slowly of the cold, and of hunger. He'd managed to survive by eating grass and moss, scraped from beneath the ground frost with broken and bleeding fingernails. He didn't see his mother again until the following spring, when she'd brought him some bread and salt and, after a few days, left again with her comrades. Her parting words were that he was free to join the Resistance now that he was seventeen and unencumbered.

As he drove, the man inspected the few pedestrians moving briskly along the sidewalk, looking for the right woman who would catch his eye. It was growing dark and anyone not walking with a sense of purpose could be stopped and questioned by the *militsiya*. He saw a flash of color coming out of the Pushkinskaja underground train station and instinctively slowed to get a better look. It was a young woman with dark hair, wearing a green skirt and colorful sweater that reminded him of an Easter egg. He drove past her, but did a U-turn after a few hundred meters, circling back around. She seemed to sense that she was being scrutinized and held her purse tightly to her chest. She quickened her pace.

When he passed her the second time, he got a better look at her face. He realized he knew who she was.

He pulled his car over to the curb and waited, his heart pounding with anticipation. He leaned over the passenger seat and, rolling down the window, called to her, asking if she needed a lift.

Instead of responding, she raised her chin and moved determinedly ahead. The cheeky little bitch.

Pulling forward until he was abreast of her again, he called out loudly for her to "Halt!" And, as he knew she would, she instinctively obeyed the iron in his voice.

She finally looked in his direction and he saw recognition flare in her eyes.

He flung open the passenger door and told her he'd drive her to wherever it was she was going. Still, she wavered. He reminded her it wasn't safe to walk alone on the street. That she was vulnerable in the dark. But it wasn't until he tried molding his lips into a persuasive smile that he saw alarm flare in her eyes.

"You'll come with me. Now," he ordered abruptly.

After a last, fruitless search for someone she might join instead, she eased into the passenger seat and sat rigidly upright, her knees pressed tightly together.

"Spaciba," she whispered, her voice timid and breathy. She then told the man she was going to the Planeta Hotel, but only to leave a message for a friend.

The man grunted, giving her a skeptical look, and began to lecture her on the dangers that awaited women at the Planeta. She sat, silent and still, as he continued talking. When he drove past the turnoff to the hotel, she made only a few weak sounds of protest. He continued on to the Svisloch River, stopping at a cul-de-sac just south of Victory Park.

He extracted from his pocket a small Makarov pistol and told her she had to come with him. That it would only take a few minutes, and if she was cooperative, and didn't fight him or call out, he would take her on to the hotel. But only afterward. He'd even wait for her to deliver her message and then return her to the train station, if she'd like.

When he pulled her from the passenger side, she was unresisting, resigned. He could tell she'd been through this before. A brief, uncomfortable fumble. She even pulled a handkerchief from her purse in preparation for the inevitable cleanup. Though she was distressed, she thought she had no reason to fear anything worse than a few sharp thrusts between her legs, and another secret kept.

It disgusted him, her acquiescence. Had she stayed at home, had she not volunteered to visit a place where women enticed men into weakening themselves, this would not be happening. The thought of the Planeta angered him more. The women there! Their very boldness robbed men of their virility, leaving them soft and helpless as infants. And then they'd dare to laugh when they couldn't perform like circus animals.

He'd known women and girls like this all through his youth. Females who'd made fun of the dirt on his clothes and under his nails. Who'd held their noses at the stench and ungainliness of his body, as if his poverty were his choice. It was only after he'd served as a policeman, clothed in his immaculate service uniform and fatted through the largesse of the State, that women eyed him with appreciation and respect.

By the time he had prodded the woman into a stand of trees, he was more than angry. He was enraged at this slut, this whore who didn't even try to escape. At least the gymnast had put up a valiant fight. He lashed out, hitting her in the back of the head with the butt of his pistol. She fell heavily to the ground and he quickly pulled the two slender ropes from his belt, going to work. As a final touch, he stuffed the handkerchief into her mouth.

She only came to as the weight of her legs tightened the noose around her neck. He watched with savage delight her growing horror as she realized he was enjoying her struggles. Soon, she gave a few brief shudders, and then she was still. She'd made very little noise, but he was still alert for any curious *militsiya* patrolling the riverbank.

He sat for a few moments, quieting his breath, feeling the anger evaporate from his body like the sweat from his exertions. It was disappointing, this ending. It was rushed and couldn't be savored. He wasn't even aroused. It had been an opportunity, pure and simple, to vent his rage.

Suddenly, the distant streetlights cut out. There descended

a massive, all-encompassing darkness, as though the city were being swallowed entirely by an inky cloud. Minsk was experiencing another blackout. He smiled at the timing. The darkness would further ensure that he wouldn't be discovered. But it would make it difficult to maneuver back to the car, so he sat with the patience of a monk, breathing in the soft summer air, the rankness of the river smelling, to him, like the secret, wicked parts of a woman.

In little more than an hour the electricity came back on, light rippling through the surrounding buildings like the start of intermission at the Bolshoi Theater.

Sighing, he stood and hoisted the body up by the rope. He dragged it into the water, throwing her purse in afterward. He watched as the woman sank into the dark water, and he checked his watch. It was not yet half past ten.

If he hurried, he'd be home before his wife went to bed. She would heat up his dinner for him without too much grumbling. He'd been having stomach pains for weeks and hoped that she'd skimmed off any extra fat from the soup as he'd asked. Just in case, however, he took a roll of antacids out of his pocket—the chalky little tablets that his American friend had given him—and chewed one thoroughly, thinking. There were four more Americans in Minsk now. As a people they could be immensely entertaining, if arrogant and shortsighted. And of course, they brought a new future for Minsk. He looked forward to getting to know them better. In particular, the females.

He turned to walk back to his car, thinking that, all in all, it had been a very good evening.

8

SATURDAY, AUGUST 4, 1990

When Ben stepped out of the elevator into the lobby, he looked rested and energized, last night's gloom erased. But when Mel stood to greet him, he furrowed his brow.

"Uh-oh. Somebody didn't sleep well last night."

She had dark circles under her eyes, her eyelids puffy, so, of course, it would be obvious. Mel sighed and told him about the power outage, which was news to Ben.

"I completely missed it. Slept right through it."

Then she told him about Maksim. "He scared the bejesus out of me. I think if I'd stayed asleep—"

Ben stilled; every bit of exuberance drained from his expression. He stared unblinking at her for a few seconds.

"Son of a bitch," he whispered. His head rotated slowly toward the lobby desk, and Mel realized that her usually good-natured colleague was truly angry. His protective instincts had kicked in and it looked like he was ready to do something rash.

She reached out and grabbed his arm. "I need to tell Dan first. Before we say or do anything."

His gaze stayed fixed on the male receptionist until she tugged on his shirtsleeve.

"Ben," she said. "Let's take our walk. We could both do with the fresh air."

Reluctantly, he shook himself and followed her out. They walked through the small park, not speaking, making their way toward Victory Park.

Mel could already tell that the day was going to be exceptionally warm, the sky intensely blue with only a few diaphanous clouds. But by the river the morning air was still cool and damp, the abundant trees lush and unmoving. They passed only a few other walkers, mostly men and women dressed in monochrome colors, hurrying to work. Ben got a second look from every passerby, but he didn't seem bothered by their scrutiny. Or if he was, he was practiced at ignoring it. He remained loose-limbed, fingers unclenched, his face a mask of polite neutrality, seemingly over his anger at Maksim. They chatted about inconsequential things to keep the mood light, what they both missed about being stateside: MTV, pizza, ice in their drinks. For Ben it was American sports, and all things Michael Jordan. For Mel it was spending afternoons wandering through bookstores. Then their conversation turned to Saddam Hussein's bloody crimes. He was not a "serial killer" per se, not in the way the two of them would define one, but a vicious tyrant nonetheless, responsible for the deaths of millions.

They slowed their pace to a stroll, finally stopping at a Great Patriotic War memorial: a cluster of charging men, bayonets fixed on their rifles, cast in bronze. Ben pulled a bag of dried fruit out of his pocket and offered some to Mel, who took a handful gratefully.

"Notice how every war monument in this city looks like it's melting under its own weight?" he asked.

Mel studied Ben's somber face. She'd seen the old men standing patiently at bus stops, crowded rows of Soviet military ribbons and medals proudly covering the fronts of their threadbare jackets.

Mel held out her hand for another dried apricot. "You said you were in the army?"

Ben nodded. "I spent four years in Germany at the Dagger Complex in Augsburg. I worked INSCOM, army intelligence, supporting the NSA. It was a no-brainer joining the Agency after that."

"Where'd you learn accounting?"

"College. University of Illinois. My dad was an accountant in Chicago. After the army I thought I'd be following in his footsteps." He turned to Mel, smiling. "I discovered pretty quickly it wasn't for me."

Mel returned his smile. She could well imagine how hard it would be for such a vital, athletic man to be trapped behind a desk five days a week.

They turned away from the monument and continued walking.

"You went to St. John's in Annapolis, right?" he asked. "How come you joined the FBI first? The Agency does a lot of recruiting out of St. John's."

A group of three moved past them, talking in hushed tones, their eyes first flicking to Mel and then lingering on Ben. She scanned their faces, committing them to her faultless memory.

"My dad is a county sheriff," she said once they were out of earshot. "He was always suspicious of the CIA. Called all agents ghosts. He told me if I wasn't going into local law enforcement, the best thing would be to join the FBI. So that's what I did."

"Why the switch to the Agency?"

Mel picked up her pace, hoping to distract Ben from any more probing questions. "I was asked to join."

But Ben had paused to admire a large metal fountain in the

river. Shaped like a giant lily, it had a pulsing spray of water that flashed rainbow colors in the sun.

"It's kind of unusual," he continued. "Being transferred from the FBI to the CIA." His brow furrowed, both hands jammed into his pants pockets. "Mel, what exactly is your role here? I mean..." His voice trailed away, and he smiled apologetically. "You spying on us ghosts?"

Her Agency trainer's voice sounded loud in her head. *"You took theater, right?"* She adopted the outwardly innocent guise of Ophelia. "What makes you think that?"

He faced her, his expression serious. "You just answered my question with another question."

He wasn't going to let this go. "Ben...I'm not spying on you. On any of you."

There was a nearby bench, and he abruptly sat. Mel joined him, perching at the far end. About a hundred yards away, a young couple played tag in a group of trees. The woman shrieked joyfully a few times as the man reached out to grab her.

Ben opened and closed his mouth as though reluctant to speak. "When I was with INSCOM, Defense Intelligence had a program called Project Center Lane. It'd been going on for years, under several different names. It's kind of a poorly kept secret within the intelligence community." He turned to face her. "Ever hear of remote viewing?"

Mel looked at him warily. She *had* heard of remote viewing—it was something the CIA publicly discounted but had secretly tested for decades. Once the Agency caught wind of her recognition abilities, her division chief had fought like hell, to her immense relief, to keep her from the Stargate Program, which studied remote viewing methodologies. The last thing she wanted was to be stuck interminably in some lab, used like a rat.

She turned toward the river, as though enjoying the view, and asked casually, "You mean as in parapsychology, precognition, that sort of thing?"

"Right," he said. "The Soviets have been experimenting with it for decades. The army started their own program in the seventies." He stared down at his hands clasped together between his knees. "I got to watch footage of the experiments as part of my training. The test subjects would all enter a kind of altered state, almost like they were hypnotized." He waved his hand in front of his face. "There was something about the eyes. They were definitely in a different place."

The young couple had gone quiet, their shapes barely discernible in the shadows of the trees. Mel sat rigid and unmoving, sensing that Ben was leading up to questioning her about a forbidden subject.

"Mel," he said quietly, "I watch you looking at everyone we pass. You get that same look. It's like you've gone somewhere else."

There'd been very few people, outside of her trainers at Quantico or the Agency, who'd documented the change in her demeanor or situational awareness when she scanned people. Ben was a sensitive, empathetic person. But even so, it shocked her that he had grasped something so fleeting and subtle.

She was hyperaware of the Soviets' single-minded and decades-long commitment to their psyops program. And though her ability had nothing to do with the supernatural, she'd been warned by her operations officer that if any hint of her abilities were to become known to the Soviet military, they'd certainly take an interest. She'd disappear into a black hole in some unmapped city, to reappear only when she was secretly buried in a Siberian pine box.

From now on, she'd have to carefully monitor herself in his presence.

A shrill scream rang out. Then another. The young woman ran panicked from the trees, followed closely by the man.

Ben and Mel were both on their feet instantly. The woman was sobbing loudly and pointing in the direction of the riverbank, where the branches tangled in the water. Ben began to run, Mel following close behind, joining a tide of alarmed parkgoers.

Three men talking excitedly in Russian rushed to the water's edge, only to recoil as one and go silent.

Ben jostled his way through the growing number of onlookers to join them, staring at the gentle lapping of the river until Mel moved to his side.

In the water was a woman, facedown. Wrists and ankles tied somehow to her neck, her dark hair floating gracefully in the tide. Her emerald-green skirt billowed aloft, like seaweed skimming the surface, seeking light, or air, or a final escape.

9

SATURDAY, AUGUST 4, 1990

Mel knew, even before the figure was dragged ashore, who the woman was. Katya had been dead for a while, because rigor mortis had already set in. And when the ropes were finally cut, it was only with great difficulty that her limbs were stretched out enough for her to be laid on her back. Despite the bloating of her waterlogged skin, her contorted expression spoke of a painful death, most likely by strangulation. There was a deep indentation circling her throat, the flesh still scarlet and angry-looking. Her eyes were open, as was her mouth, her lips still coated in a bright slash of coral lipstick.

Mel had seen death before—the bedside visitation of an aged, deceased grandparent whose body had been neatly arranged for viewing—but, apart from in photographs, she'd never been a personal witness to such a violent end. Especially the apparent murder of someone who'd recently been so vibrantly, fulsomely alive. Her eyes filled with tears, and she turned away from the crowd—not to hide her sadness, but to conceal her anger. Katya should not have fallen victim to such brutality.

The Byelorussian *militsiya* arrived quickly, detaining and questioning both Mel and Ben—the only foreigners among the growing crowd of curious onlookers—for close to an hour before letting them return to the hotel. Instinctively, Mel knew to pretend she didn't recognize Katya; anything else would only complicate an already tenuous relationship with the Ministry of External Affairs.

Finally, they were escorted back to the Planeta by a tight-lipped policeman. They found Dan and Julie having breakfast in the dining room.

Mel was aware of the abrupt silence in the dining room as she and Ben entered. As much as she had tried for calm, she could only imagine that her body language mirrored Ben's: taut and wary, poised for action.

"We need to talk. Outside," Mel said quietly to them both, and the four quickly exited. They made their way to the park and stood close together, their backs to the hotel.

"A body was just pulled from the river at Victory Park," Ben said grimly. He looked at Mel to continue.

"It's Katya, the receptionist from the ministry." A renewed surge of helpless anger made her voice quaver and she paused to collect herself. "She'd been strangled and dumped in the water."

Julie drew in a sharp breath, her hand flying over her mouth.

"Jesus Christ," Dan said. He rubbed at his brow, and then realization seemed to hit him. "Wasn't she the one who told you women are being killed in Minsk?"

Ben blinked. "Women are being killed in Minsk?"

"Do you think her death is related somehow?" Julie asked. "To these other killings, I mean."

"I'm not sure," Mel said. "But it seems an awful coincidence."

Dan did a quick check to make sure no one had wandered closer to them. "Did anyone overhear your conversation with her?"

Mel thought for a moment. "We were alone in the bathroom. But this is the Soviet Union."

Dan pinched his lower lip and frowned at the river. "Look, I think the best thing to do is to talk to William tonight. He will have gotten the news from his contacts with the KGB and local law enforcement. We all have reports to write in our rooms."

He glanced at his watch. "Let's meet again in the dining room at one o'clock for lunch, okay? And then Anton will pick us up at five o'clock. Stay alert, and if you get strong-armed by the *militsiya,* raise bloody hell until I'm notified."

Everyone nodded and trailed back into the lobby. Dan reached for Mel's arm and motioned for Ben and Julie to continue on in the elevator without them.

"Will you be all right?" he asked after the elevator doors had closed.

The remembrance of Katya's stiffened, contorted body made her shudder. But she needed to reassure Dan that this incident wouldn't derail her focus on her job. "I'll be fine."

Dan's hand lingered on her arm. "Would you rather not be alone right now?"

She looked up at him sharply. His expression seemingly one of simple concern, the lock of hair flopping carelessly over his forehead, his eyes clear and earnest. Ben had told her that Dan had a history of seducing women. Mel's instincts told her that Dan was testing the water to see how vulnerable she really was. But whether it was an operational probe—a team leader assessing a colleague's weaknesses—or a genuine seduction attempt, she didn't yet know. Either way, her response would be the same.

She pulled her arm out of his grasp and shook her head. "Thanks, but the quiet of my room will do me good," she said, all business. "You go ahead. I'm going to get some tea."

Turning on her heel, she walked into the dining room. When she returned a few minutes later with a cup of tea and a sweet roll, the lobby was empty.

Upstairs, Mel retrieved the key from the hall monitor and entered her room, leaning against the closed door and shutting her eyes. She couldn't seem to banish the image of how the rope had been pulled from Katya's neck, like kitchen string being peeled away from an oven-baked pheasant. She walked to the window and stood looking out over the dreary scenery while drinking her tea and eating her roll.

Despite her efforts to calm down, the tension from her body seemed to vibrate in the very air around her. From Ben's suspicions to the discovery of Katya's body, she felt deeply shaken.

And then there was the matter of Maksim. She'd planned to speak to Dan about it, but her unease over his solicitous offer had driven the incident right out of her mind.

She looked at the tea growing colder by the minute in her hand and set the cup down on the bedside table. Her reflection in the mirror caught her attention. She looked pale and drawn, clearly upset over something, and she quickly turned away, not wanting the ghosts behind the mirror to chronicle anything notable about her appearance. She gathered her notebooks and report sheets and sat at the desk, willing herself to concentrate on her work. Soon she was immersed in the comforting routine of identifying facts: dates, times, names, and places. She would write nothing that couldn't be seen by both the Americans and the Russians. In fact, that was the point. She'd leave the reports in her briefcase, unlocked. They would be examined, photographed, and shared with the Soviet Academy of Sciences, as well as the politburo. Her secretarial reports would reassure their Soviet minders that all was as it appeared to be. Anything clandestine would be shared with William face-to-face, or for her, with her CIA officers stateside later.

After reflection, Mel decided not to mention Katya in the reports. She strongly suspected that no one else in her group, including Dan, would mention her either. If anyone had thought of Katya as a productive asset, an attractive lead for cultivating information at the ministry, that possibility was now terminated.

But despite her best efforts, Mel kept remembering Katya's whispered agreement to meet up. And it led her to recall the dark, threatening look the minister had thrown at them while the tea service was being delivered. The thought that her attention to Katya had put the woman in danger refused to go away. She wasn't merely a prospective asset to Mel. Under different circumstances, she could have been counted as a friend.

Mel finally broke for lunch just before one o'clock and sat in the dining room next to a somber Ben. Julie appeared nervous too, wired up and hardly touching her food.

The only one who seemed normal was Dan, who began lunch by teasing Ben about the frustrations of reconciling Soviet accounting practices in his report to the State Department.

Ben sighed, trying to play along. "There's no accurate accounting for substandard or malfunctioning material returned to the institute. It's just modified or repaired and then added back into the quota for the next batch."

Dan turned to Julie. "There's no actual term for 'quality control' in Soviet production, isn't that right?"

She nodded. "Literally translated, quality control is *kontrol' kachestva*. But there's no real process in the Western commercial sense. At least, not yet."

Mel knew about the State quality mark of the USSR, but she'd been informed that the goods receiving the stamp of approval were often substandard by international comparisons. Everything from automobiles to television sets, from shoes to watches—if it was manufactured in the USSR—would be stamped with the official certification before delivery. But meeting a factory quota was more important than keeping the bar high for excellence, as any Soviet citizen on the street could tell them. If they felt free enough to talk.

Dan tossed his napkin on the table. The corners of his mouth twitched. “I knew a State Department accountant who visited Moscow a few years back. He’d been warned that things were dire, but he’d been tasked with reporting back on the true state of affairs for the average Russian.”

Mel groaned inwardly and caught Ben’s eye. Another joke.

“If the living conditions were found to be adequate, he’d write his report in black ink. If, however, the conditions were less than favorable, he’d use red ink. After a few weeks, the accountant sent his first report. It was written all in black ink and read as follows: ‘Dear State Department, things in the Soviet Union couldn’t be better. I’m free to go wherever and whenever I want, the standard of living is high, and there is no shortage of anything. Well, there is one thing in short supply. There’s no red ink.’”

He looked around the table and pulled a face at their lack of response.

“Fine, since apparently no one’s eating, playtime’s over,” he said. “Back to the salt mines. I’ll see everyone in the lobby at five.”

As they left the dining room, Dan once again dropped his newspaper on Minder #3’s table. “Nice little verbal spanking by Gorbachev to Saddam Hussein on page three,” he said. “In case you missed it in today’s *Pravda*.”

The man remained expressionless, but he calmly pulled the newspaper toward him and began thumbing through. The four trudged to the elevator, and Mel was relieved to get off on the second floor. But the hall monitor was not at her desk, and the key to Mel’s room was missing. She walked to her door and turned the knob. It opened easily.

Inside, the hall monitor stood frozen in front of the short dresser, the top drawer open like a gaping, surprised mouth.

Mel's new sweater, the one with the price tag still attached, lay rumpled atop a pile of other clothes.

Mel and the woman stared at each other, unblinking, for a few seconds. Then the monitor gave a backhanded push to the drawer, closing it completely, and mumbled something in Russian. She straightened herself to her full height and walked out the open door, closing it gently behind her.

"What the hell—" Mel murmured.

She'd known their rooms had been searched. But she'd been assured that the hotel *dejournayas,* although tasked with reporting on their comings and goings, were relatively honest.

Angry at first, she replayed in her mind the way the woman had gathered herself with shabby dignity and walked from the room like vanquished royalty. She began to suspect that the woman was merely curious, not a thief. The woman had worn the same clothes for the past few days running, the only change in her appearance a different cheap plastic barrette in her hair. Maybe she'd just wanted to see what the young American woman had brought with her from the West?

Another thing occurred to Mel. If the woman was just snooping, there was no way she would have entered, knowing that, behind the two-way mirror, some fervent apparatchik was documenting her every move. Mel had never seen or heard anyone entering or leaving the door next to hers, behind which the recording equipment would be kept. It would be useful to know when she was being observed and when she wasn't. The *dejournaya* would certainly keep tabs.

Mel worked for another few hours until the pressure in her head demanded attention. She drew a bath and soaked in the hot water, committing to her daily processing. She got dressed slowly and at four o'clock left the room, her purse in one hand, and the new, as-yet unworn sweater in the other.

As she passed the hall monitor, she placed the sweater on

the desk. It was an oversized pullover, in a loose weave, a lovely shade of lilac.

"Etot sviter luchshe dlya tebya," Mel said in her awkward Russian. This sweater will look better on you.

The woman looked up at her, surprised, but Mel walked on without pausing to the elevator. As the doors closed, she caught the woman stroking the sweater with her fingertips as she would have a shy cat. Alone in the elevator, Mel gave a satisfied exhalation, remembering one of the Moscow Rules, the unwritten strategies for avoiding detection in the Soviet Union, which was: *Lull them into complacency*. Mel had memorized the rules as soon as she knew she would be assigned to Byelorussia.

Mel went straight from the lobby into the Planeta Mir. Dan had told the team to be on alert, but he hadn't told them not to have a drink in the bar. The same half dozen Germans were sitting at the café tables, and she wondered if they ever even pretended to have a job outside the hotel. They stopped conversing and looked her over with interest. It was not unusual for a local, enterprising woman to appear alone. It was highly unusual for a Western woman, obviously there on official business, to enter without male accompaniment.

She made the snap decision to sit at the bar, placing her handbag firmly in her lap, her back to the Germans. The bartender was a stout, thick-waisted man with a badly set nose. He was dressed in an ill-fitting suit coat, so tight across the shoulders that one good flex would probably rip out the seams. His tie was badly knotted and was as broad as her palm. He finished wiping a glass and placed it with exaggerated care on the shelf behind him. He rested both palms on the bar in front of her and cocked his head, stretching his full lips into an amused grin.

"You old enough to drink, little girl?" he asked in broken English.

"Well," she answered, folding her hands primly on top of the bar, "I am certainly younger than your tie."

He clapped a hand to his chest as though wounded, and asked, *"Pivo?"*

"Nyet," she answered. *"Vodka."*

He nodded, impressed, and poured a healthy shot into a glass.

Mel downed it in one go. *"Snova, pozhaluysta."*

Again, please.

He threw back his head and laughed, and Mel realized it was the first unfettered expression of amusement she'd seen since arriving in Minsk. The bartender poured a few more ounces of vodka into her glass and moved away, still chuckling.

The alcohol coursed through her system like hot water through frozen pipes, and for the first time since early that morning she began to fully relax.

She heard conversation to her right and recognized two of the women who'd been at the bar the previous afternoon, one dark-haired, the other the remarkable blonde. They were throwing guarded looks in her direction and whispering.

Mel decided to ignore them and stared into her glass. She found she was looking forward to tonight's gathering at William's apartment. After the events of the past few days, she was hoping to steal a few brief moments alone to talk to him. She realized she missed her father's calm, steady guidance, and in William she felt some of that same protection.

For as far back as her memory could take her, she had often felt set apart, isolated, even in a room full of people. Maybe especially then. It was more than social awkwardness. Over the years she'd overheard the comments from her teachers, coaches, and friends describing her as odd and, once, disturbing. And that was even before they got a sense of her recognition abilities.

At one of the few high school parties she'd attended, she'd finally been introduced to Sam, someone she'd nurtured a silent crush on for the entire year, but to whom she'd never spoken. She would have bet her father's badge that he'd never noticed her before.

But that night, his smile had seemed genuine. He'd said hello, and even offered her a sip of beer out of his red party cup. It was the first time she'd overindulged in liquor and she was well on her way to being drunk.

She took a big swallow, desperately trying to come up with something to say; anything that would keep his interest. "You're wearing the same school jersey you wore last October at the Badgers' football game," she'd said, slurring her words. "You were in section E, fourth seat from the aisle. My dad and I were in section S. That was a great game..."

A curtain of silence settled around them. Mel swayed unsteadily against someone standing behind her.

"Dude," someone had said. "That stadium holds, like, seventy thousand people—"

She'd never forget the look on Sam's face. It was not a look of surprise, or even of confusion. He'd been afraid.

Mel had learned at a young age to keep herself to herself. Even while in training at the Farm, she'd felt as though she lived in some kind of bubble, where she could see and be seen but never touched. Despite her growing ease with Ben and Julie, the secretiveness of her mission, by necessity, kept her at arm's length from any true friendship.

"*Izvinite, pozhaluysta.*" The voice was so close to her ear that Mel jumped.

The dark-haired woman was standing next to her. She was dressed in a short, flowered dress, and she looked nervous.

"I don't really speak Russian," Mel said, disoriented and hoping to discourage any further conversation.

"Excuse me, please," the woman repeated in English. "There was woman, in park this morning—" She broke off and eyed her blond friend, still seated at the far end of the bar. "You saw this woman? She was dead, yes?"

Mel took a breath. "Yes, a body was found in the river this morning."

The woman slid into the seat next to Mel. "But not drowned." She lowered her voice to a whisper. "Killed, yes?"

Out of the corner of her eye, Mel could see the blonde approaching them. She sat on the far side of her dark-haired companion, her challenging gaze firmly fixed on Mel.

No way out of this, then. "Yes, it looks like she may have been murdered."

The blond woman nodded and pulled a cigarette out of her purse. The bartender appeared and lit it. She took a deep drag and then dismissively waved him away. She turned back to Mel. "You're with the Americans. What's your name?"

The events of the day, and the blond woman's demanding, prickly veneer, had all worked to buff out the need for social niceties. Mel held up her vodka in a parody of a toast. "Ugly American Bitch. What's your name?"

The woman reared back and looked at Mel as though seeing her for the first time. A slow smile crept onto her face. "My name is Nadia Ivanovna," she said, giving her patronymic. "We have no last names here."

Mel held out her hand. "My name is Melvina. Mel to my friends."

Nadia's fingers were slender and warm, her grip firm. She ordered three vodkas from the bartender, and the dark-haired woman introduced herself as Larysa.

As soon as the drinks were placed on the bar, Nadia tamped out her cigarette and changed seats so that she was seated to Mel's left. And as the two women questioned her, Mel was forced to swivel her head back and forth between them. They asked her where she was from and how long she was staying in Minsk. Larysa's English was poor, and she used Nadia as translator.

Nadia offered Mel a cigarette, which she declined. The cigarettes were German-made, instead of the common Russian brand. Nadia placed one between her lips and lit it with a small, expensive-looking gold lighter.

"Did you know who is this woman, the one pulled from the river?" Nadia asked, blowing smoke above their heads.

Mel looked down at her drink, but she could still sense both pairs of eyes boring into her. "I think…I think it was someone who worked at the Ministry of External Affairs?"

Larysa fired off a few rapid questions in Russian and placed her hand on Mel's arm as if to give greater weight to the words.

"Larysa wants to know was this woman tied with rope?"

Mel nodded, surprised at how quickly the details of the killing had circulated.

"*Svisloch Dushitel!*" Larysa murmured, her eyes wide.

While the two women leaned in, trading urgent, emotionally charged whispers, Mel gestured to the bartender and ordered three more drinks. She knew that if she wasn't careful, she'd be sliding toward inebriation, but already the sensation was like a warm blanket, tempering the upheaval of the past few days.

"*Svisloch* is the Minsk river," Mel said, breaking into their exchange. "What does *Dushitel* mean?"

Nadia set her cigarette in an ashtray. "It means—" She put an imaginary noose around her neck and yanked it tight with one hand. "This man has killed many women."

A serial killer. Here in Minsk. How had she not thought of it that way?

The fresh vodkas were set in front of them, and they drank in silence. Mel gratefully embraced her sense of relief. Perhaps she'd had nothing to do with Katya's death. Maybe it was just a terrible coincidence; Katya had simply been at the wrong place at the wrong time.

Larysa said something mournful in Russian.

"She's worried about her son, Vassily," Nadia explained. "If something happens to her, there is no one to take care of him. She's from Ukraine. Husband dead from Chernobyl. Parents dead too. The son was born with heart outside of body. She comes to Minsk for surgery for him. He's only four, but will not live much longer, I think."

At Vassily's name Larysa pawed through her purse and brought out a laminated photo of a small boy with huge eyes and a head too big for his frail body. She handed it to Mel as she might a religious icon.

The photo was heartbreaking. The boy looked as though he were made of parchment. "He's beautiful." Mel wasn't sure what else she could offer and handed the photo back to Larysa. "Do you have any children?" she asked Nadia.

In that moment, a hulking form draped itself noisily over Nadia's shoulder. It was one of the Germans, very drunk and sweating profusely. He whispered something in her ear and Nadia pushed him away so forcefully that he almost lost his footing. He staggered backward, his entreaties becoming more insistent, and belligerent. But before the bartender could move out from behind the bar, Nadia released a torrent of Russian insults so acidic they needed no translator.

The German only laughed and staggered back to his tablemates.

Nadia turned to face Mel, her outrage already cloaked behind well-practiced contempt. "Do I have any children?"

She laughed bitterly. "Yes, that *mudak* sitting there is one. They are all like children." She lit another cigarette, exhaling loudly.

"What does *Idi no hoi* mean?" Mel asked.

After a pause, the bartender barked out a laugh, and Nadia and Larysa both grinned.

"Idi na hui," Nadia corrected her. "It means 'go to the dick.'"

Mel hoisted the last of her vodka in a kind of salute. "Okay, then. *Idi na hui.*"

Larysa, still sitting to Mel's right, nodded in the direction of the entrance. "Your boss?"

Mel turned and saw Dan standing in the doorway, a strange smile on his face. "My boss for now," she answered. "Have another drink on me."

Mel took a handful of rubles out of her purse and laid them on the bar. But when she passed Dan, she realized his focus was not on her, but on the dimly lit interior of the Planeta Mir. Nadia had swiveled her chair to face him, her long legs crossed provocatively, her skirt pulled tight across her upper thighs. Her generous lips were stretched in a seductive smile, a burning cigarette held in one graceful hand.

Dan caught up with Mel as she walked out of the hotel, looking expectantly for Anton's van. She spotted it parked at the far end of the driveway, Ben and Julie already seated inside.

"You're making friends all over the place," Dan said, stepping in front of her. "Hold up. How many drinks have you had?"

He was smiling but the question felt invasive. Especially after remembering her drunken high school incident. Defensively, Mel started to brush past him. "More than one, less than ten."

"Find out anything interesting?"

"*Svisloch Dushitel,*" she answered. "The Svisloch Strangler. He kills with a rope. I think the authorities here have a bigger problem than crimes of passion, or Mafia vengeance. Minsk may have a serial killer."

Dan made a dismissive sound. "You don't know that for certain. Besides, official Soviet policy is that there are no serial killers."

Mel opened the door to the van and turned to look at him incredulously. "That's nonsense and you know it. You really think Soviet men are fundamentally different? If it looks like a duck, and quacks like a duck—"

Dan leaned in, blocking her from entering the van. "Mel," he said quietly, "be very careful who you say the words 'serial killer' to while we're here. Even *talking* about certain crimes is a criminal offense with the KGB. Promise me you'll only discuss it with our team, and only when you can't be overheard, okay?"

She met his gaze and nodded. He moved out of the way, and she climbed into the van, sliding into the back row next to Ben. Elena gave her a brisk nod over her shoulder.

"Wow," Ben said to Mel as she settled herself awkwardly into her seat. "Somebody's already gotten a jump start on the weekend." He waved the air in front of his face and pulled out a roll of breath mints, offering her one.

She looked at him, feigning indignation. "I was improving international relations in the bar."

Julie snorted, and in that moment, Mel caught Anton's face in the rearview mirror. He met her eyes for a moment and grinned.

Ben said, "Okay, but you're looking a little pale."

Mel did, in that moment, feel a bit dizzy. The comfortable fog of alcohol was retreating, and when she closed her eyes, she had the sensation of being locked in an overcrowded, airless closet.

Mel leaned her head back against the seat and stared up at the stained, upholstered roof, taking deep breaths. She thought of the fear in Larysa's and Nadia's eyes as they talked about the Svisloch Strangler.

She was unprepared for the van's abrupt stop and yelped when she was pitched forward. Through the windshield she could see that the car in front of them, a small green Volga, had been stopped by a group of men standing in the street. They had turned onto a small side avenue where there were no other cars and no pedestrians. It was after five o'clock, but still fully light, and Mel had no trouble making out the faces of the men, all of whom had turned to face their van. They looked young, and very fit, dressed in expensive-looking leather jackets and jeans. Elena sat forward, her back rigid, grasping the dashboard until her fingers turned white.

"What's going on?" Dan asked.

Anton didn't answer, but Mel could see the muscles in his neck and shoulders bunching tensely. He leaned forward, retrieving something from under the driver's seat.

Dan stirred restlessly. "Hey, Anton—"

Anton turned his head slightly and snapped, *"Spokoyen!"* Quiet!

Two of the men broke off from the group and approached the van in a leisurely fashion. Anton rolled down the driver's-side window and propped something metallic against the bottom of the frame. When the older of the two was a few feet from the driver's side, his companion circled the van, peering into the interior, taking note of all the occupants. When Mel scanned his face, she immediately pegged him as one of the kitchen workers from the Planeta. A waiter, carrying an empty tray, had opened the swinging doors to the kitchen, and she had caught a glimpse of the young man in his service whites, smoking a cigarette. Now, he pointed at her and grinned unpleasantly as though he recognized her as well.

Anton rested one beefy arm on the window frame, raising what was in his other hand slowly. It was a revolver, the size of a small cannon. He rested the barrel steadily in the crook of his elbow. The man saw it and took a few steps back.

Excited voices erupted from the Volga, and the driver was pulled from the driver's seat and thrown roughly across the hood, his pockets searched. He was then manhandled into the backseat, where glimpses through the rear window revealed what looked like a brutal beating.

"What's happening?" Dan asked again, his voice tight.

Anton still ignored him, keeping firm eye contact with the lead man. There was a brief exchange between them in Russian—the words spoken too rapidly for Mel to understand—and the two men returned to the Volga at last. The older man sat in the driver's seat, his younger companion in the front passenger side, and they drove away, the original driver still in the backseat with his attackers. The rest of the group scattered and disappeared into the alleyways.

Replacing the gun under his seat, Anton put the van in gear and continued their drive toward William's apartment.

Dan turned to Julie, clearly angry. "Will you please ask Anton what in the holy fuck just happened?"

Julie asked, in Russian, if they had just witnessed an undercover police action.

Anton let out a cynical laugh. *"Nyet. Bratva."*

That one, Mel did understand. The Brotherhood.

10

SATURDAY, AUGUST 4, 1990

Mel and her group arrived at William's apartment building, still shaken, and were greeted by the same doleful desk clerk as before. The ghostly sounds of someone playing a piano echoed down from an upper floor. The melodious chords partnered with the deepening evening shadows to transport the ornate lobby into an earlier time, before the Great Revolution, and before the end of Romanov finery.

Without a word the clerk led them to the elevator and pressed the button for the third floor. As the cage rose, the music grew louder, until it became clear that the playing was coming from William's apartment.

"What's that?" Dan asked Julie. "Debussy?"

Julie shrugged. "Chopin, maybe?"

Mel searched her memory for the composer. She knew the melody. It was one that her mother often played when she was in the doldrums.

The clerk rapped his knuckles on William's door, and the playing abruptly stopped. He exhaled as though irritated by the exchange of opinions and gave Dan a scornful look. "It's Satie." As he returned to the elevator, he threw over his shoulder, *"Je te veux."*

William's expression was somber when he opened the door.

He ushered them inside, saying, "Terrible about the woman found this morning. Evidently, she worked for the minister of external affairs. I'm just sorry that Melvina and Ben had to witness it."

William gestured for them all to sit in the living room. "The body is with the medical examiner now," he explained. "This is not the first time this type of killing has happened in Minsk."

He grew even more subdued as Dan explained what had occurred when their van was stopped. "The Minsk Mafia is growing bolder by the day," William said when he'd finished.

"I know there's increased chaos because of Soviet dissipation, but where are the police?" Dan asked. "The abduction, or whatever it was, was done in broad daylight, on a main street. Nowhere in our briefings were there warnings about the Mafia in Byelorussia."

William sighed. "It's becoming a war that the Soviet officials are ambivalent about pursuing. Most of the *Bratva* in Minsk are young men who fought in Afghanistan. They're hungry, and they're angry. And, because of the black market, they're now better armed than the local Byelorussian *militsiya*. Some of whom, I might add, are being paid better by the Brotherhood than the State. *Inter Arma Enim Silent Leges*."

He turned to Julie. "And our resident language expert translates it as—?"

"In times of war," Julie said without hesitation, "the law falls silent."

William nodded with approval. "What did your driver do?"

"He pulled a gun from under the front seat," Dan said.

"Good, that's good. It means you won't have to worry about him letting the Mafia kidnap you for a hefty ransom."

Dan started to laugh, but the seriousness of William's expression stifled it.

"I'll be sure and let the appropriate officials know what transpired," William said.

"'The appropriate officials' such as your friend Martin Kavalchuk?" Julie asked. Her tone was sharp, but William smiled.

"Indeed. He'll be here tonight, by the way." William took note of the Americans exchanging concerned glances. Dan frowned with displeasure and shook his head. Mel was torn. Her impulse, and training, told her to stay well away from the head of the Byelorussian KBG. But, at the same time, a perverse curiosity to observe the man named the Black Wolf gave her a jolt of nervous energy. The same kind of excited energy she got from reading about serial killers. Only this time there'd be no prison bars or courtroom bailiffs separating her from the monster.

William stood and wandered over to an antique chess set positioned on a small table. The set where, Mel assumed, their host played chess with the Black Wolf every Friday night.

"You know," William said, carefully moving one of the pieces, "there's a Russian saying, 'The wolf and the dog can always agree about the goat.'" He looked briefly at Mel, as though sensing her nervousness. "Right now, in Byelorussia, the Americans and the Russians share a common cause. We want to do business, and they want to do business."

"But that won't be possible with a strengthening Mafia," Ben said.

William nodded his assent. "If anyone can put a leash on the Brotherhood, it will be Martin."

Dan poured more vodka into his glass. "I've heard that the Afghanistan veterans are popular with the people."

"But," William said, holding up a finger, "the more crimes they commit, the faster that sympathy will wane. Trust me, Martin is waiting for his moment."

Julie turned to Mel and muttered, "Gosh, if I'd known

Martin Kavalchuk was going to be here, I would have dressed more suitably for the gulag."

William clapped his hands together, signaling a change of subject. "So, the rest of the guests will arrive about six thirty. There will be some from the ministry, some from the institute, and some from internal security, along with their wives and ornamental incidentals. Security will be listening in anyway, so I might as well make it easier on them. Besides, the more vodka they drink, the shorter their memories.

"Dan, why don't you assist me in the kitchen for a few minutes. The rest of you can help yourselves to refreshments."

Dan, carrying a file of notes, all converted to code, followed William into the kitchen, and Mel trailed after Julie and Ben into the formal dining room. The large table was covered with platters of food, and a sideboard held bottles of vodka, whiskey, and Russian champagne.

Mel could hear the water in the kitchen sink running, a teakettle bubbling forcefully on the small stove, and pans being rattled noisily, all to mask the men's voices. Their first information dump to their liaison had begun.

They piled food on their plates and returned to the living room to eat. Both Julie and Ben had helped themselves to vodka, from bottles nestled in a large bucket of ice. But Mel poured herself a glass of tea from the samovar, hoping it would clear her head before she had to mingle and, more importantly, remember all the other guests. She was beginning to regret her overindulgence at the Planeta.

The three sat quietly for a while, Julie only nibbling at her food and Ben restlessly rattling something in a prescription pill bottle. It took a moment for Mel to realize that it wasn't a lone pill making noise, but the tiny roll of film that had been extracted from the Minox camera in his briefcase. Ben would pass that along to William too.

Out of the corner of her eye, Mel could see him studying her.

"Before, in the van," he said finally, "I got the feeling you recognized the younger Mafia guy."

Mel kept her expression relaxed. "I remembered him from the hotel. He's one of the kitchen workers."

"I've got a pretty good memory for faces, but I don't recall ever seeing him."

Under different circumstances his close attention could have been flattering. Few had ever tried so hard to know her. And fewer still had taken note of her abilities. But here, with so much at stake, his scrutiny made her increasingly uncomfortable. Regrettably, she'd have to be more cautious around him now too.

At that moment, Dan stuck his head out of the kitchen, crooking his finger at Ben to join him.

Julie made a sour face as the door closed again. "Left out of the boys' club once more, and last on the totem pole. They do know we won the right to vote, right?" She swallowed the last of her vodka. "William's idea, no doubt."

The vehemence of her words surprised Mel. Julie could be prickly in her assessment of people, but Mel had assumed her colleague had the same perception of William that she did: that he was a brilliant, resourceful man with the full confidence of the Central Intelligence Agency. "What's your problem with William?"

"My problem? I don't trust him."

"Why?" Mel asked. Uncomfortably, the memory of Ben's arrest resurfaced.

Instead of answering, though, Julie got up and wandered over to the piano, her brow furrowed in thought. The cover was still up, and she pressed a finger firmly onto one of the black keys, letting the tone ring out. She was wearing a formfitting dress with a tight bodice instead of one of her usual practical pantsuits—like the one Mel was wearing now—her plentiful black hair back-combed for more fullness. The diffused light from the table lamps softened her angular features, and Mel, in that instant, wished she had taken more care with her own appearance. She felt drab by comparison.

Ben was right about Julie and Dan, she thought. *Julie's dressing like a woman who's concerned about keeping someone's attention.*

Julie struck the key several more times in rapid succession and grinned. "That ought to blow the eardrums out of the Crazy Ivan listening in."

She came back to the couch and sat close to Mel. "I don't trust William because he's too glib," she said in a whisper. "He talks a lot without revealing much. It's all folktales and clever sayings. I also don't understand how an American can work, and socialize, so closely with Soviet functionaries, and the KGB, and not be considered a spy. Unless—"

"Unless?"

"He's playing both sides."

Mel sat back in her chair. She'd never seriously considered this possibility. Julie was a seasoned agent and had spent years in and out of Soviet Bloc countries. She was experienced in assessing people's true intent, discovering their hidden agendas and their deceptions. Mel wondered, and not for the first time, what she was missing through her inexperience. She had placed her trust in William, but this new thought gave her pause.

Mel was the last one to join William in the kitchen. Her three colleagues had ultimately been seen all together, their reports handed over, but she was called into William's presence alone. He had turned off the faucet but had switched on a small radio, tuned to a classical music station, the volume turned up high.

"You know, this is not going to endear me to my coworkers," Mel said. "Being debriefed without the others."

"Is that so important to you?" he asked. He had just pulled a porcelain baking dish out of his oven and placed it on top of the stove.

"It's important that my colleagues trust me. How are you going to explain that you're seeing me alone?"

"I've told your three colleagues that you, tasked with being 'the secretary,' don't need to be included in their debriefings. It will serve to cement your omega status." He grinned. "Thus, hiding you in plain sight."

William dipped a large spoon into the mixture in the dish and offered it to Mel to taste. It was a stew, dark and rich, and pungent with mushrooms.

"The mushrooms aren't fresh, unfortunately," he said. "They're dried, left over from last year's harvest. You'll still be here when the gathering season starts in two weeks, though. I think you'd enjoy it. I'll take you, if you like."

She gave a nod, not certain she'd actually enjoy stooping for hours over the forest floor. She handed the spoon back to William.

Mel moved closer to him, keeping her voice low. "Ben asked me this morning if I was spying on the group."

"And what did you tell him?"

"I told him I wasn't."

"And did he believe you?"

"I don't know. He also..." She paused, considering how much to reveal. "Ben is uncomfortable with my methods of observation."

William took his time, carefully nestling a decorative cover over the dish to keep the stew warm. "There's an Arabic saying that, loosely translated, means 'Get together like brothers, but work together like strangers,'" he said. "A little seed of doubt is never a bad thing, especially for someone in the intelligence field. It makes you depend more on yourself, and less on those around you."

The core of Mel's conversation with William had centered around trust—her colleagues' trust in her, and, in return, her trust in them—to ensure success in their mission. But Julie's lack of total trust in their host had planted a dark seed in Mel's mind. A "little seed of doubt" that William seemingly encouraged.

"Especially if that distrust between coworkers is encouraged by an outside party with an agenda," she offered, watching closely for his reaction.

He peered at her over his glasses and gave her a friendly, grandfatherly smile. "Now you're thinking like a spy. Melvina, my only agenda, besides passing along your reports, is to foster your access to foreign scientific visitors. That begins tonight, and the less your compatriots know about it, the better, don't you agree?"

She studied him for a moment longer: an older, roundish man dressed in a worn but bespoke suit, improbably wearing a woman's full apron to keep his shirt and tie pristine. To any outside observer, he might appear to be an aging professor, or an antiquarian bookseller. He certainly didn't look like a man smuggling clandestine state documents out of the Soviet Union. And that was probably the point.

"How do you get the reports, and Ben's film, out of Byelorussia?" she asked suddenly. "It can't be easy. I mean, you live right across the street from the KGB."

"Again, hiding in plain sight," he answered cheerfully. "If nothing else, I've learned to be conspicuously invisible. Something, I have a feeling, you've learned to perfect as well."

So, it wasn't just Ben who saw below the surface of things. After the cold, impersonal evaluation of her trainers, it was comforting to be assessed, and appreciated, beyond the parameters of her mission. William was smart, but he was also warm and approachable. Another one of the Moscow Rules: *Trust your gut*. Mel was about to ask him if he'd heard about the Strangler when there was a loud rapping at the front door. "Ah," William said, glancing at the wall clock and taking his apron off with a flourish. "That must be Sveta."

Disappointed at being interrupted, Mel followed William out of the kitchen and rejoined everyone in the living room. Ben made room for her on the couch, and Julie handed her another glass of tea. It took her a few minutes to realize that William had avoided answering her question about how their reports would be smuggled out of Byelorussia.

William opened the door to a small, attractive woman who greeted him with a volley of rapid-fire Russian and the Slavic triple kiss on both cheeks. She looked middle-aged in a well-constructed woolen dress, twenty years out of fashion, and a single strand of pearls, and sported a rigid helmet of hair, lacquered into immobility.

"William's girlfriend," Dan muttered, suppressing a smile.

"Everyone, this is Comrade Sveta Ulanova," William said, his arm wrapped snugly around her shoulders. "She doesn't speak any English but I'm leaving her in your good hands for now." He nodded and smiled encouragingly at Sveta while guiding her to a chair next to Julie.

He whispered into Julie's ear, "Careful, she's probably wired for sound."

Julie grinned impishly and whispered back, "So you suggest we speak loudly into her bosom? Don't worry, I think I can handle Comrade Ulanova."

William laughed, wagged his finger, and said something Mel didn't understand.

"What was that?" Mel asked.

"It's Hebrew," Julie answered, looking pleased with herself. "Dr. Cutler is charming, I'll give him that. He said, '*Tafasta merubeh lo tafasta.'* It means, don't bite off more than you can chew."

Soon after, the next guest arrived, a young captain of the KBG's elite Alpha group, all jutting chin and restless eyes, sent in advance to ensure the safety of the invited guests. William busied himself carrying several bags of kitchen garbage out into the hallway while the captain searched every room and every cupboard, and Mel realized that this was a commonplace occurrence.

Things moved quickly after that. Within half an hour there were at least forty invitees filling the apartment, most of them talking animatedly in Russian, some in halting English, helping themselves to food and drink as though they'd been rescued from a desert island. There were more men than women, and those who were not wearing tired-looking suits were dressed in full military uniform, heavily freighted with ribbons and medals. The women sparkled among them, wearing brightly colored cocktail dresses in shiny acrylic fabrics that Mel was certain would flare like acetylene torches if touched with a lighted match.

William walked them around, introducing the Americans to his Byelorussian guests in their official capacities as accountants, translator, and secretary in that order. Ben and Dan were greeted enthusiastically while Julie and Mel were welcomed in a more formal way. At least by the men. The women looked them over like prize hens at a 4-H exhibit, scrutinizing every article of clothing and piece of jewelry brought from the West. Julie, in particular, trailed hungry gazes as she moved around the room. Mel, in her plain blouse and slacks, was immediately dismissed, which suited her purpose perfectly.

Sipping her tea, she scanned the room and recognized at least a dozen men. Some she had seen in person, and others she recollected from the many photographs in Minister Ivanov's office. But others were wholly unfamiliar. Their faces were absorbed into her memory for future reference.

She noticed Ivanov talking discreetly to two men in military uniforms, the lenses in his dark-framed glasses fogged from the heat of his body. As though sensing her gaze, he turned toward her, his face unreadable, and she wondered how he felt knowing his receptionist had been found dead that morning. Again, she remembered the glowering look he had thrown at Katya. And how Katya's makeup had looked tearstained the last time Mel spoke to her.

A loud voice distracted Mel, and she turned to see Academician Oleg Shevchenko holding court with some of the male scientists she had met at the Heat and Mass Transfer Institute. He'd probably been a good-looking man at one point, but now he had the dense network of broken capillaries across his nose and the paunch of a lifelong drinker. He snuck frequent appraising glances at the female guests, who by now had all gravitated toward one another at the far side of the room. They pretended to ignore him while they sipped at the caustic Russian champagne. He caught Mel's eye several times and raised his glass in a friendly salute. His attention at first startled her. Next to the other women, she thought herself to be nearly invisible. But Mel collected herself and smiled back. Maybe William was right. Given more time, Oleg might put on a more amiable front.

William had earlier fitted a music cassette of Western pop songs into a large Sony Boombox and now the music buzzed softly from the dusty speakers. Mel hadn't been listening closely to the songs, but in that moment, she recognized the plaintive voice of a popular British rock star singing "Russians." She smiled at the irony. Or perhaps William had purposely included the song for his own amusement.

A curious sensation, like a fingernail dragging along the base of her skull, made her suddenly turn to see a man standing next to her, just behind her left shoulder. She hadn't heard him approach, and she hadn't noticed him mixing with the crowd. It was as though he'd appeared out of thin air.

He was not tall—perhaps an inch or two taller than she was—and he gave the impression of being both slight of frame and yet, at the same time, solid with dense, compacted muscle. He appeared to be in his late sixties. His skin was pale but not sickly, his gray hair cut close to the scalp and bristled like a fine wire brush. He was dressed all in black, and Mel instinctively looked to where his shirt was buttoned at the neck, expecting to see the white band of a clerical collar. There was none.

But his eyes were extraordinary. They were a dark hazel, liquid and expressive. Intelligent, inquisitive, those of a man attuned to the ways of the world and of the vagaries of history. It was seldom that Mel locked eyes with a stranger so deeply. His gaze was probing, relentless, and utterly pitiless, but she couldn't look away. And from this she knew who he was.

As a child visiting the zoo, she had thrilled at standing close to the jaguars. She'd loved the excitement of taunting them just by her presence on the other side of the glass. Feeling the delicious swell of fear as they stared hungrily at her, putting her faith completely in the frail barrier that kept them back.

In the background, the orchestral interlude of "Russians" had begun. One by one, every hair on Mel's arm stood up. She blinked and looked at the other guests, searching for one of her team members.

"Prokofiev, yes?" Martin Kavalchuk asked in English. His voice was mellifluous, as gentle as a priest asking if she had anything to confess.

Mel took a breath. "Yes."

"For the film *Lieutenant Kije,* I believe."

"That's right."

"And, just now," Kavalchuk interjected, seeming genuinely curious. "What is he singing?"

Mel forced herself to turn fully toward him and meet his gaze again. "Just now he's saying, 'I hope the Russians love their children too.'"

Kavalchuk nodded thoughtfully as though this was a given. "Who is the artist?"

"His name is Sting."

Surprisingly, Kavalchuk gave a restrained smile. He made a slight jabbing gesture with his forefinger. "Like a wasp."

Mel was aware that the general volume in the apartment had dipped, and that many pairs of eyes were now watching the two of them. She could see Dan in her periphery, edging closer. She managed to work the muscles around her mouth into a smile as well. "That's right."

"The point of art, to be sharp on the senses, yes?" He peered at her, unblinking, his head cocked to one side as though intensely interested in her answer. Mel realized her blouse had dampened from sweat and was sticking to the small of her back.

"That's right," she said, resisting the impulse to look away. "When it's allowed."

Kavalchuk ducked his chin as though considering her last comment. "Melvina is an unusual name for a woman."

Not surprising that he knew who she was, but chilling too. "I inherited it from my aunt."

"Yes," he said, as though answering a question only he could hear. "It's a strong name. And are you as strong as your namesake?"

He put an emphasis on the word *strong,* and Mel wondered how many men, and women, had given up their deepest secrets to him through broken teeth.

He continued to stare at her, waiting for her to fill the

silence, a silence that rose around her like a tidal wave. Finally, she blurted, "My aunt was a farmer's wife in Wisconsin."

"Where the cold lasts as long as a Siberian winter—"

The Alpha officer appeared at Kavalchuk's side and whispered something into his ear.

All traces of polite civility vanished from his expression. "I must leave," he told her. He turned on his heel and left the room, the crowd parting carefully around him.

Dan appeared, pressing a glass of vodka into Mel's hand and guiding her to a chair. William had seated himself at the piano and began playing a Russian tune, with several of the female guests singing boozily along.

"You okay?" he asked before returning to the crowd. She nodded and downed the vodka, surprised to see that her hand was steady, her grip on the glass firm.

When she looked around the room, the guests had all resumed their partying. Even straitlaced Sveta had cozied up to William as he played, her head thrown back, crooning along with abandon. Julie sat close to Dan in quiet conversation while their eyes constantly surveyed the room. Oleg Shevchenko stood behind the women gathered at the piano, one large hand surreptitiously massaging the buttocks of a different woman than the one he'd arrived with. Ben was in a lively discussion with an attractive young woman she recognized from the external affairs ministry.

Everyone seemed to have made a connection. The only other person, besides herself, who sat apart from the enthusiastic partygoers was Minister Ivanov. He had placed himself in a far corner, his face a blank behind his black-rimmed glasses. He was completely motionless, and she realized he was staring in her direction.

She averted her eyes, scanning the group again for late arrivals, finding no new faces. And, frustratingly, no matches to any Iranian scientists. But there were plenty of eyes pointed in her direction. Her attempt to remain invisible had been defeated by the Black Wolf, and no matter where she moved, she felt the inquisitive, and sometimes hostile, stares of the party guests.

The air in the apartment was close and too warm, weighted with the scent of floral perfume and civet-heavy cologne. A light touch on her arm made her jump. It was Ben, offering her another vodka. The liquid in the glass looked viscous and cloudy, with a powerful odor of fermented potatoes. She stood abruptly, the feeling of claustrophobia overwhelming.

"I'll be right back," she said, and walked quickly for the front door.

The hallway had been dark and cool. And would be much quieter. She opened the door and stepped out at the exact moment the desk clerk was stooping to pick up a couple of grease-stained paper bags. He startled and almost dropped them.

Mel apologized and he stared at her nervously for a few seconds.

"I'm collecting the garbage." He said it defensively, as though she'd challenged his presence.

Still holding the bags, he wheeled around and walked rapidly toward the elevator. Without a backward glance, he stepped inside the cage, keyed the floor, and descended until he was lost from sight.

She removed her jacket and leaned back against the wall, purposely slowing her breathing and locking her knees so that her legs would stop shaking. She had fully expected to be scrutinized and surveilled by Byelorussian intelligence. But she had had no expectation of speaking one-on-one with the head of the KGB. And though she had been briefed by the Agency on the Russian Mafia, her American contacts were not yet aware of how brazen, and dangerous, the organization was quickly becoming.

She'd also not been prepared to witness the discovery of a murdered woman—a woman she had just befriended. She thought of Nadia yanking tight the imaginary rope around her neck, and Katya's green skirt floating in the river. She made a promise to herself that before they left Minsk she'd corner William, if necessary, to get his take on the killer.

From inside the apartment, she could hear someone, in heavily accented English, saying, "William, you are the chairman of all good times!"

And William responding, "I'm not a *chair,* I'm a *love seat.*"

There was a wild outbreak of laughter and William transitioned from playing Russian pop music on his piano to an American rock song Mel vaguely remembered hearing on the radio as a young girl. Something about Red Riding Hood looking good. She couldn't recall the name of the group, but she did remember the singer at times howling like a wolf. William sang the lyrics in English and at the appropriate moment the group of revelers howled along with him. It must be in his regular party repertoire.

During any other occasion, she would have considered his performance silly, humorous. But she had a dark, disquieting sense that the timing of the song was intentional. Meant as an exclamation point to the end of the sentence: *The Black Wolf of the KGB has left his mark here!*

11

SATURDAY, AUGUST 4, 1990

The first of the partygoers began to leave around eleven, and by midnight the rest of the guests had staggered out the door in groups, or two by two. But it was another half hour before the four Americans appeared. The man in the blue Lada had left the party earlier, but he'd returned to sit in his darkened car, the engine off, waiting for another glimpse of the black-haired woman whose figure made his mouth water with longing.

The older American woman was full in the breast and her skirt hugged tightly to her backside in a way that suggested it would be firm to the touch. The tone of her voice was not pleasing, nor was the way her mouth twisted in frequent derision. But he knew how to silence that voice, to still that mouth.

The younger woman was interesting, to be sure. But she had a slightly neotenous face that did not inspire immediate passion. And yet…the more he sat with her image in his mind, waiting in the night, the more desirable she became.

He imagined how luminous her naked skin might look in the dark. How her wide-set eyes would grow enormous with fear. How he could twine her hair around his hand like silk thread around a spindle as he pulled her head back and slipped the noose around her neck. She'd had a clean smell, like freshly laundered bedsheets.

The Reznik woman smelled of expensive perfume, heavy and briny, like the odors following sex. Yes, he could well imagine the older woman naked. Her body still and pliable beneath his fingers. He knew she would be fertile. As her body gave up its nutrients to the earth, surely the mushrooms would grow thickly around her like a little army of conquering soldiers.

The fact that she was American heightened his anticipation. She would be clean-shaven, with strong, straight teeth and painted toenails. She'd have no dirt under her nails, no calluses on her feet, no venereal diseases, even though he could tell that she and the American *kozyol* were sleeping together.

The man dressed like a disgusting *degheneraat,* with his Western shoes only serviceable as slippers, his expensive suits and hair as long as a woman's. But it was common knowledge the man was a spy, and beyond his self-satisfied smirk, he had the exacting gaze of a long-distance sniper. He'd been a soldier at one time, of that the man in the blue Lada was certain. So, the difficulty would be getting the black-haired woman away from the rest of the group. Away from her lover.

He watched as the Americans climbed into their van, one by one, and as they were driven away, back to the safety of their hotel.

The man in the blue Lada sat for a few more minutes, windows down, breathing in the smells of Minsk. Every city had a unique scent, and during the hot nights of August, his smelled of pine and river and the softening bones of a million comrades lying beneath the blood-soaked earth of his beloved Byelorussia.

12

SUNDAY, AUGUST 5, 1990

The loud jangling of the boxy telephone next to Mel's bed brought her roughly to consciousness. Her dreams had been dark and chaotic. It seemed that, for the entire night, she had wandered through a nightmarishly constructed house, a labyrinth with a seemingly endless series of rooms. Wandering through the darkened spaces, she could hear a woman crying, but try as she might, she couldn't find her. When she opened her eyes, Mel thought first of Katya.

She squinted against the sunlight streaming through the gauzy curtains. The phone was still ringing. After a few clumsy tries, she pulled the heavy receiver to her ear.

"Melvina, good morning." William's voice sounded alert, and much too loud. "Did I wake you?"

She rubbed at her eyes and sat up. "That's okay. What time is it?"

"It's eight o'clock," he said cheerfully. "Look, I've already phoned Dan and he's given the okay for you to take a little excursion."

"An excursion?" She looked at the bedside clock to confirm the hour and groaned.

She and her three colleagues had stayed at William's to review the evening long after all the other party guests had departed. Who'd said what and to whom. Disappointingly, there was no important information to share, other than who was cheating on their spouse.

Curiously, it seemed no one had brought up Katya's murder.

"It's as though she was just erased," Julie had said, her eyes sad. "Shouldn't a murder be a juicy item of gossip at a party?"

"Ah, but don't you know there's no murder in paradise?" William said, smiling cynically.

As William walked them all to the door to say good night, he'd turned to Mel and said, "I'd be happy to bring you that caviar you asked me about. Tomorrow, if you'd like."

As she hadn't recognized any of the guests as her targets, Mel had declined the offer.

Shaken by the many events of the day, she hadn't fallen asleep until two o'clock in the morning.

Now, too early, William was talking about an excursion. Her head throbbed and her shoulders ached. She wanted nothing more than to pull the covers back over her head.

"I've arranged for a guide to pick you up in one hour. You'll take a little tour of the Byelorussian countryside," he said. When she didn't answer he added, "It will do you good. I think last night put a bit of strain on you. Be out front in one hour."

She made an impatient sound. "William, I just don't—"

"Melvina," he interrupted her. "You need to trust me. A few hours out of Minsk this morning is the best thing."

He hung up before she could protest or ask any more questions. The tone of his voice brooked no dissent. Thinking of how he had orchestrated Ben's mishap, Mel realized that William's message was clear: she would be spending the day outside Minsk.

She showered and dressed, leaving just enough time to have

some tea and a sweet roll in the dining room. None of her collcagues were around, and she wondered, enviously, if Dan had fallen back to sleep after speaking to William.

At nine o'clock she walked out of the hotel and into a brilliantly lit summer day. There was a strong fragrance of pine trees and damp, rich soil in the air, and despite her reservations about the unexpected change of plans, she was glad William had gotten her out of bed. The emotional hangover from her disturbing dreams had begun to fade. Left to her own devices, she probably would have spent most of that Sunday in her room reading. She hoped that whoever the guide was that William had chosen, he, or she, wasn't too talkative. She'd like nothing better than to sit back and enjoy a peaceful, restorative drive into the country, away from the ever-present Soviet scrutiny.

A long black car was parked a few yards from the front entrance, and a man stepped out of the driver's seat. He wore a summer-weight linen shirt and pressed slacks, so it took Mel a few moments to recognize him.

Alexi grinned and said, "I think you don't know me at first."

She almost laughed with relief, afraid to acknowledge the thrill she felt that she'd be spending the day with him.

Alexi walked to the passenger side and opened the door for her. She met his gaze for a moment—eyes clear and strikingly gray—and his grin widened. She slid into the seat, marveling at the beautiful interior, the polished chrome and wooden paneling. The seats felt like rolled cashmere edged with leather. When he closed her door, the thunk of metal sounded like the closing of a cavernous bank vault.

He took his place at the wheel and started the engine before turning to her, his arm resting casually along the back of the seat. A few more inches and he'd touch her shoulder. His movements were relaxed, almost languid, putting her at ease and banishing her nervousness over seeing him again.

She couldn't remember the last time she'd felt this weightless around a man.

"William has instructed me to give you a day without any worries. Or I will have to answer to him."

Alexi's tone was serious, the words delivered in a formal, exacting manner. But he gave her his quicksilver smile and placed both hands lightly on the steering wheel. He put the car in gear and eased out onto the Prospeckte Pobeditelei.

"Where are we going?" Mel asked.

"To the real Byelorussia," he said.

When they crossed over the river, Alexi pointed out the Bolshoi Opera House, which had been built on a hill. He told Mel that nothing in Minsk could be built higher than the Bolshoi because it could then be seen from Poland, a country that, for the first time in forty years, had a non-Communist leader.

"We Byelorussians are like children playing hide-and-seek," he said. "We think that if we can't see the other players, they won't be able to see us."

After that they drove a long way in silence. He seemed to sense that she needed quiet. All the windows were rolled down, and he drove at a sedate speed until they were beyond the last of the blocky apartment buildings and warehouses at the outer fringe of the city.

From time to time, she watched him surreptitiously as he drove. The kaleidoscope of ash and silver in his hair, the tendons at the base of his neck, the way the muscles in his forearms flexed. She liked the alertness of him, his economy of motion, the way he seemed completely at ease in his own skin.

"This is a beautiful car," she said at last, wanting to hear the sound of his voice again.

"Yes," he said. "Unfortunately, it's not mine. It's our friend William's car. I believe the suspension in my car would break your spine. Byelorussian country roads are sometimes not so good."

He arched one eyebrow as he talked, giving her a playful smile.

"Where did you grow up?" she asked.

"Close to where we are going today." A truck had pulled up behind them, and he waved for it to pass. The driver tapped his horn in exuberant appreciation as it pulled ahead. "I was raised in a village called Dubrova. Very small. Very old-fashioned. Farming and fishing and fighting and not much else."

"Does your family still live there?"

"I was raised by my grandparents. My mother died when I was very young."

"And your father?"

There was a slight tensing of his jaw. "My father was…my father was out of my picture." He turned to her. "Is that how you say it?"

The earnestness of his question made her smile. "Out of *the* picture."

He nodded and quietly repeated the correction. "But I have an uncle who looks after me, so I am not without family. And you," he asked, "where in America did you grow up?"

"Summers with my mother in Texas, the rest of the year with my father in Wisconsin."

He gave her a sympathetic look. "It sounds…complicated."

They were just then passing open fields thick with ripening summer grain and dense groves of pine trees. The shining plots smelled of rich earth, malt, and molasses. Mel was instantly flooded with memories of the fall harvests around her father's farm. She filled her lungs with air and smiled. "We made it work. I was happy to spend most of my time with my father."

"He is also quiet, like you?" Alexi teased.

It had been months since she'd spoken to her father, and she missed his calm and reserved manner. "Very much so."

Soon, groupings of small houses—summer dachas and year-round dwellings built some distance away from the road—began to appear less frequently. Every five miles or so brightly painted bus stops sheltered lone travelers, most elderly.

They had been driving for almost an hour when he turned off onto a wide dirt path. A few minutes later, he parked in front of a small wooden house painted bright yellow with green trim. A small table and two chairs stood under a rustic awning out front. Alexi quickly got out and opened the door for her. He pointed for Mel to be seated in one of the chairs as an ancient woman came out of the house, her arms outstretched toward Alexi. She couldn't have been more than five feet tall, wearing a worn housedress, a colorful head scarf, and woolen slippers.

She screeched happily at him in Russian, her lips rubbery over her prominent, toothless gums, and pulled him down so she could kiss him three times noisily on both cheeks. They spoke for a few minutes and she disappeared back inside the house.

Alexi took a seat in the other chair, rubbing his cheeks.

"Is that your grandmother?" Mel asked, charmed by the rustic setting. Alexi was right; this felt like the true Byelorussia.

"She is *everyone's babushka,*" he answered. "Dubrova is close by. But my own grandparents are now gone."

They sat in the shade, quietly watching bees hover over a small garden patch of flowers, and the graceful, halting movements of downy white hens pecking in the dirt of the yard. Soon the woman returned, carrying two glass canning jars filled with a foamy brown liquid. She set the jars on the table and hovered nearby, smiling and murmuring softly in Russian.

To Mel, the beverage looked like a dark ale. But when she

tasted it, it was bitter with a musky aftertaste. "Is it beer?" she asked.

"It's kvass," he said. "Made from rye. It's a Byelorussian specialty. Everyone drinks it in the summertime. Even the children."

The woman stroked Mel's cheek with one arthritic hand and said something to Alexi that made him color slightly and shake his head. She soon shuffled back inside, waving and throwing them kisses.

Mel took a few more courtesy sips of her drink while mapping her surroundings. The house had no indoor plumbing, as evidenced by the decorative outhouse and a stone well where water would be drawn up by a bucket. It wouldn't have looked out of place in a watercolor scene painted a hundred years ago. Or even two hundred. She could hear the old woman singing a folk song inside the house, her voice thin and reedy.

She began to feel drowsy from the summer heat and the cooing of pigeons in the eaves. A small, cautionary voice suggested that perhaps the setting was a bit too pastoral. That maybe the house and the old lady were part of a set, designed to put her off her guard. Mel realized that her expectation had been a park, or a national monument, more of a tourist destination. Her training had insisted that she not take anything, or anyone, in the Soviet Union at face value. William seemed to trust Alexi, but Mel wasn't sure she completely trusted William yet.

She took another drink, observing Alexi under her lashes, curious about his role for the State. "How long have you been a policeman?" she asked.

"Six years," Alexi answered.

"And how do you know William?"

He smiled. "Everyone in Minsk knows Dr. Cutler. He knows my uncle and through him I met William."

She didn't want to press too hard, too soon. A flash of bright colors caught her eye, a green-and-red scarf hanging on a clothesline. The vibrant green made her think of Katya again.

"What do the police think of the murdered and missing women in Minsk?" she asked.

His smile faded and he looked away. "I have, of course, heard of this. But it's not in my..." He struggled for a moment to find the right word.

"Jurisdiction," she suggested.

"Yes, jurisdiction." He leaned forward, clasping his hands together over the table. "I have lost sleep over these women. For several years now."

He held her gaze as though willing her to see how important these crimes were to him. She was relieved to know that the murdered women hadn't gone unnoticed after all.

"Do you know how many Russian jokes begin with 'I was beating my wife the other day...'?" Alexi continued, growing angry. "A husband, according to Soviet law, cannot rape his wife. Any abuse that does not include broken bones falls under the legal category of 'light injury.' Mother Russia is not a gentle place for women."

He sounded both bitter and exasperated, and she was surprised, and moved, by the passion in his voice. Aware of the gravity in his expression, he sat back and ran a hand across his forehead. Alexi was treading on dangerous territory for a Soviet *militsiya*. Officially, there was no violent crime in the Workers' Paradise. But it was as though he needed to unburden himself of these rebellious thoughts.

"A woman told me about the Svisloch Strangler," she prompted.

He looked at her steadily, his expression serious. "For many women, it's less frightening to think that only one man is responsible. Not as frightening as the truth: that there are many men in Minsk capable of such violence."

He was quiet for a moment, staring out at the garden, his face in profile. His shirt was open at the neck, and she watched the pulse at the base of his throat beating strongly. When he turned to her again, he was smiling. Mel felt the breath catch in her throat, thrilled at the effect his direct gaze triggered in her. But he'd also seemingly turned off his anger like an electric switch. "I should not sour the day by such talk. Time to leave."

Alexi stood and called out a goodbye. He walked with Mel back to the car, humming the folk song under his breath.

He drove back to the main road and headed east again, farther away from Minsk. And for the next fifteen minutes they sat without speaking, Mel still pondering Alexi's unpredictable emotions.

She noticed that the pine trees had begun to grow more closely together and were very tall. At an unmarked dirt road, Alexi turned and drove north for a few miles until the road ended at a large, flat meadow. Surrounding the meadow, like a dense curtain, was forest. Alexi killed the engine. There had not been another house, or human being, for several miles. Mel sat with her heart beginning to race, wondering why he had driven her to such a remote location.

Alexi got out and opened the trunk. After lifting something out of the back, he closed it and began walking to her side of the car. A bright spasm of panic gripped Mel's chest.

But when he opened her door, he merely smiled and held out his hand. In his other he held a loosely woven picnic basket.

"Our friend William has provided lunch," he said.

She looked at him, confused. First the rustic Russian peasant house, and now a picnic? "William did all this? Why?"

"Because William's greatest pleasure is feeding people."

Mel barked a laugh. "That certainly seems to be true."

He helped her out of the car, and she followed him the short distance to the grassy field carpeted with tiny white flowers that looked, to Mel, like baby's breath. It was a setting that would have delighted her, if not for her nagging doubts about why William had sent her out of Minsk. Alexi led her to the middle of the clearing and pulled from the basket a thin blanket, which he spread on the ground. He motioned for her to sit and began to unpack the basket, taking out a loaf of dark bread, sausage wrapped in wax paper, and a brick of cheese. China plates, glasses, and utensils were unwrapped from linen napkins. And finally, he withdrew a bottle of French champagne.

"I think the champagne is not much cold now," he apologized, pouring her a glass and saluting her once he'd filled his own.

Luckily, the champagne was still cool and felt like frothy gold on her tongue. Much better than whatever had been served last night. She'd have to be careful not to drink too much again. Nothing like alcohol to blunt the senses and inhibit healthy caution. After preparing plates for the two of them, Alexi sat back on the opposite corner of the quilt and stared off into the forest.

"I used to go fishing not far from here. Just beyond those trees," he said, pointing to a narrow path.

Mel could imagine him as a serious-minded boy, precisely threading a worm on a hook. "I went fishing with my dad a lot," she said. "When I was little."

Alexi began removing his shoes and socks and rolling up his pant legs. "Tell me more about your family."

So, between bites, she told him about her split life. "I have no siblings," she said, "and so all of my parents' best, and worst, efforts were expended on me."

"I have no brothers or sisters either," he said, plucking a few long blades of grass and weaving them together. "I think maybe you were a lonely child?" He expressed it as a question and then added, "Like me."

His insight surprised her. She had been a shy child and socially awkward. But she'd always tried to paint a picture of a reasonably happy, safe, and predictable childhood. She set the champagne aside, deciding she should stick with water.

"Perhaps I am too personal," he said apologetically.

Normally she would have agreed with him, distancing herself from conversation that revealed too much. But it had been a while since she'd felt so at ease.

He stood and beckoned her to come with him. "I want to show you something."

"Shouldn't we be heading back?" she asked.

"It will only take a few minutes."

She let him help her to her feet, and he led her down the narrow path, a few hundred yards between the pine trees, to a narrow, shallow stream. Following behind him, she watched his bare feet rising and falling, pale like flags of surrender, the bones and tendons flexing strongly beneath his skin.

"Take off your shoes," he said when they came to the bank of the stream. Mel thought about resisting, but the water looked cool and inviting. It had been years since she'd gone wading in a river, carefree like a child. Alexi held her hand for balance as she removed her flats and rolled up her own pant legs. He continued to hold her hand as he led her down a gentle slope.

The water was clear and, when they waded into it, bone-achingly cold. Mel gasped and laughed with the shock of it.

"In the springtime it is much bigger," he said. "And full of small river fish. Pike, I think you call them. I spent many hours here when my grandparents were working."

"What did your grandparents do?"

"They were collective farmworkers. Maybe half of all Byelorussians work in this way."

"And the other half?"

He grinned. "Mostly for the military complex, or the politburo, which is sometimes the same thing."

She thought of how formal and stiff he had looked in his uniform, and how relaxed he now appeared in civilian dress. "Does that include policemen?"

"Yes." He composed his face as though commencing a stern lecture. "The half that oils the workings of the State must be fueled by the other half. The sickle cuts the grain, which feeds the hammer."

She gave him a playful scowl. "Sounds like propaganda."

"This is first-year academy knowledge, Comrade," he said, shaking his finger at her.

"Your English is very good."

"In school there were three choices of compulsory languages—English, Spanish, and German."

"Spanish?"

He leaned in and whispered conspiratorially. "Cuba."

"Oh, of course." The Soviet spy base within ninety miles of the Florida Keys. A missile base at one time as well. "But you chose English."

"More like English chose me. In primary school our abilities were assessed, and we were...encouraged. I excelled in mathematics. So my teachers decided that, as English is the most difficult—" He made a gesture as if to say, *And here I am.*

They stepped out of the stream when their feet went numb, and climbed onto the bank to rub feeling back into their toes. He held her hand again while she put her shoes back on. When she stood upright, he moved in close, close enough for her to feel his breath against her skin, and gently plucked a few leaves from her hair.

"Otherwise," he said, with a sly grin, "people will wonder what kind of picnic is this."

Mel, in that moment, was wondering the same thing. She

had an unwise impulse to lean in closer, to give in to the moment and pretend it was just a lovely day spent with a handsome man. Moscow Rule number three: *Everyone is potentially under opposition control.* Instead, she quickly turned away before he could sense the storm of emotions insider her.

Returning to the blanket, Mel purposely sat on the opposite corner, a safe distance from Alexi. She allowed herself one more sip of the champagne, as well as a few furtive glances at Alexi. She'd never been on such an elaborate picnic with a man before. A very attractive, engaging man. The closest she'd ever come to it was in Wisconsin in high school—sitting in the open bed of a pickup truck with a boy her age, sharing a soda and a few pieces of elk jerky. The elk shot and smoked by the boy's dad.

She'd never have imagined that the first time she'd have such a romantic interlude would be in the Soviet Union with a military policeman. She allowed herself the briefest fantasy: sitting with Alexi anywhere else, drinking the entire bottle of champagne, letting her guard down.

Except for the calls of a few birds, the silence was almost absolute. Mel hadn't experienced such quiet since she last visited her father's farm outside of Madison over a year and a half ago. No traffic, no airplanes, no human voices. She closed her eyes and tilted her head back for the sun, now at its zenith, to shine fully on her face. When she opened her eyes again, Alexi was studying her with an almost unsettling intensity.

Flustered, she ducked and said the first thing that came to mind. "Did the old woman in the village ask if I was your girlfriend?"

She had asked it teasingly, but he stared into his glass for a moment, and just when she thought she'd made a mistake, that he'd somehow taken offense, he raised his eyes and looked at her. The moment stretched on, but he didn't look away. Of this she was certain: she'd never experienced such a signaling of desire. There was no nervousness from him, no apparent fear of rejection, or uncertainty of purpose. If he had stripped her naked in that moment, she wouldn't have felt more exposed.

Her breath came faster, and she began to feel light-headed. If he tried to kiss her, she wasn't certain she'd be able to stop him. The truth was she wanted him to touch her.

Instead, he stood abruptly and said, "We should go."

The sudden change in mood startled her. Had he rallied to save her further discomfort—or was it something more manipulative?

They gathered up the picnic items—carefully moving around each other as in an awkward dance—and returned to the car. There was no more conversation as Alexi returned to the highway and headed back toward Minsk.

Mel stared out the passenger window, feeling shaken by the depth of her emotions. Perhaps her powerful response to him was only the result of being unexpectedly freed from the constraints of the Soviet machinery. Big Brother was always watching.

And maybe that could also explain her elevated senses. The longer she probed her feelings, though, the more she realized it was more than just a release from the constant scrutiny. It was as though the air immediately surrounding Alexi Yurov were richer in oxygen. She imagined burying her face in his chest and inhaling deeply, like a patient on life support.

But the one remaining troubling thought was that this had all been orchestrated by William Cutler.

Within an hour the forest gave way again to fields, and the fields gave way to the boxy, gray warehouses and apartments of Minsk. The denser the mammoth buildings grew—vestiges of a still-formidable Soviet Union—the greater Mel's doubts about William's motivations. And Alexi's as well. The bucolic glow of the Byelorussian countryside was dimming, the memory sliding away like a sidewalk chalk painting in the rain.

What was William's hidden agenda? And why use Alexi, a handsome Soviet *militsiya,* as a tour guide?

A thought, like the flash of a camera bulb, startled her. As far as she could tell, no one from Minsk had been following them while on the road. It appeared there had been no surveillance at all. If they had been followed or observed, their watcher would have had to be almost invisible.

"Alexi," she said quietly, "what is William Cutler to you?"

Alexi took a few breaths and said, "He is…my friend."

"Is that all?"

He looked at her, his face guileless. "Is that not enough?"

She kept her expression neutral but answered his question silently. *Not in Soviet Russia, it's not.*

Alexi dropped her off in front of the Planeta with a friendly, but formal, goodbye. She thanked him for the picnic and the drive into the countryside, and when he pulled away, she stood a moment at the entrance of the hotel, trying to reorient her feelings.

The first was a sharp spike of annoyance. She'd allowed herself to be momentarily immobilized by a strong sexual attraction for a man she hardly knew—a man who most likely was a Soviet intelligence gatherer. She wasn't a high school student anymore, paralyzed by shyness and crippling self-doubt.

The second was a lingering frustration; if Alexi, a member of the police, knew women were mistreated and murdered in Minsk, why was no one in a position of power talking about it?

And the third was a seductive warmth she couldn't shake, an appreciation for a day away from the city, out in rolling fields so much like her home; the past few hours forming a powerful blend of nostalgia and novelty.

Walking into the lobby, she was surprised to see Dan sitting in a chair and looking worried. When he saw her, he stood and approached her as he might someone who'd just walked away from a car accident. Or a hostage situation.

He took her elbow and guided her back out and into the park. Mel reluctantly took her place on a bench, and he surreptitiously looked around, making sure they were out of listening range.

"Are you all right?" he asked quietly.

"Yes, I'm fine." His elevated concern was raising her own anxieties. "Didn't William call you this morning? He told me he'd called you about arranging some kind of excursion for me out of the city."

"Yes, he did. But he didn't tell me you'd be spending the day with a Soviet policeman." He leaned in closer. "But that's not the main reason I was concerned."

"Why? What's happened?"

He angled his body away from the windows of the hotel. "About a half hour after you left, two KGB officers showed up looking for you."

"For me? Why?" Diplomatic status or no, Melvina Donleavy was a lowly secretary. No one but William should know different. And despite her high clearance within the Agency, there might be very little the State Department could do if she was arrested for espionage.

A nicely dressed man had walked out of the hotel, casually lighting a cigarette and strolling in their direction.

"That guy," Mel said, lifting her chin in the man's direction, "is a hotel guest. He's been keeping an eye on us."

Dan quickly looked at him and then back at Mel. "Never seen him before. You sure?"

"Very sure."

He grasped her elbow and they walked on to the gazebo. She could feel the tension rolling off his body in waves. They both faced the river as though taking in the view.

"They found something when they pulled Katya from the river," he said, his lips barely moving.

For a moment Mel stopped breathing. "What kind of something?"

"They wouldn't tell me. They would only say that it's something that ties Katya to you." He flashed a warning look at Mel. "Did you give her anything compromising? A note, or a telephone number?"

"I gave her a used tube of lipstick and a candy bar, that's all." But of course, they'd planned more. "The last time I saw her at the ministry, she did say she might meet with me for a drink, or a meal."

Dan exhaled sharply and gripped the railing. "I'm to bring you to KGB headquarters for questioning tomorrow morning."

It was one thing to learn about the Committee for State Security, the *Komitet Gosudarstvennoy Bezopasnosti,* in the safety of an Agency briefing. But it was another thing entirely to be summoned by them. Mel sat very still, considering the possible implications. Her name, in the mouths of a universally feared military machine.

"Okay..." Dan took a few steadying breaths. "I called William as soon as they'd left and he's going to meet us tomorrow morning, early, for a prep talk. He said he'd try and get as much information as he could tonight. So maybe we'll know what it is they've got."

The hotel guest was slowly making his way to the gazebo.

He was contemplating his shoes as though deep in thought. Dan and Mel left the cover of the structure and continued their walk through the park.

"Look," Dan said, "I don't want you to worry about this. You've done nothing wrong. This is probably what William calls a fishing expedition. Just stick to your backstory, no embellishments, no ad-libbing, and you'll be fine. Remember your Agency training and don't try to fill in the silence." He stopped and faced her. "You believe me, right? I won't let anything happen to you."

In that moment, Mel realized that Dan was more nervous for her than she was for herself. She was an untried asset, whose skills had not been clearly defined by their Agency contacts. He was uncertain of her ability to withstand questioning and maintain her cover. He needed reassurance that she could carry her weight.

"Dan," she said, forcing her voice to remain steady, "you don't have to worry about me. I wouldn't have been sent on this mission if the Agency felt I wasn't ready. I can handle a question-and-answer session. Trust me, I won't let you down."

As they walked back to the hotel, Dan advised her to spend the rest of the day in her room. Mel nodded, relieved to be going to the solitude, and relative safety, of her room. She would crawl into bed and sleep.

When she got out of the elevator on the second floor, Dan held the door and said, "Anyone knocks, you pick up the phone and ring my room, or Ben's. Don't let anyone in until one of us is with you, okay?"

She nodded and walked down the hallway toward the *dejournaya*. It was not the same woman to whom she'd given the sweater. This one, presumably the weekend monitor, was older and hard-eyed, and when Mel asked for her key, she passed it to Mel grudgingly, and in silence.

13

SUNDAY, AUGUST 5, 1990

Mel did her memory processing in the bathtub at five o'clock. The faces were few—the old *babushka* from Dubrova, the lone people waiting at the bus stops, the few truck drivers passing on the highway—but she immediately felt the usual physical and mental relief. At six thirty, Dan appeared with her dinner. He lingered in the open doorway, as though wishing to be invited in. Not wanting to give him any encouragement that could be misconstrued, she assured him she was all right, no one else had come knocking, and she'd be going to bed early. They agreed to meet in the lobby at eight o'clock the next morning for their briefing with William.

Mel closed the door and sagged against it. It was exhausting trying to decipher people's true intentions. She exhaled forcefully—but that was exactly her job now. To assess, to report, to act appropriately on the intelligence gathered. But where was the truth when you were always acting a part, along with everyone else? A remembered quote came to her: James Jesus Angleton, the godfather of the CIA for twenty years who ended his life stark raving mad from the paranoia of trying to ferret out the truth from a cesspool of lies. His dying words were "The better you lied and the more you betrayed, the more likely you would be promoted."

The plate of food Dan had given her consisted of cabbage, some kind of stringy meat, and carrots, which had all gone cold. Mel only picked at it before setting it aside. She sat in the chair, its back turned toward the two-way mirror, and stared out the window.

In the quiet, she thought about her father and their last face-to-face conversation. That had been before she'd left for her CIA training, at the beginning of 1989. It was after Christmas, which she'd spent at her father's farm just outside Madison after completing her twenty weeks at Quantico.

Her academy graduation day had been December 21, 1988. The day that Pan Am Flight 103 crashed violently into the southern Scottish town of Lockerbie, after a suitcase filled with plastic explosives had detonated, ripping the plane apart and killing 259 passengers and crew, 190 of them Americans.

The explosive device had been concealed inside a cassette recorder, which was then packed inside a suitcase and stored in the plane's cargo area. Suspicion fell on Libya and its leader, Mu'ammar Gaddhafi, but even without proof, the attack rattled the intelligence community. Already, the FBI seemed to have a new goal: to counter the expanding threat of terrorism.

Standing at graduation, Mel had already been aware that something new and deadly had begun taking shape on the international stage. Extremist groups were being formed by disgruntled fundamentalists in the Middle East; wealthy facilitators, like the rising Osama bin Laden, who had been emboldened by the surprising victory of jihadists over Soviet forces in Afghanistan. Had Melvina stayed with the FBI, she would have asked to join this new counterterrorism task force.

But at her ceremony, she'd been pulled aside by the director of special projects—a short, compact ex-Marine nicknamed the Bullet for his bald head—and presented to a mild-mannered man in a gray suit. He'd introduced himself as Special Agent Thomas Hunter from Washington, DC, and handed her a card upon which was printed his name, title, and central intelligence agency. No address, only a phone number.

They'd entered an empty classroom, where the Bullet left the two of them alone.

Agent Hunter had perched on a desk, brushing invisible wrinkles from his trousers, and gestured for her to take a chair. "May I call you Melvina?"

She nodded and sat down, wary.

He looked at her for a few beats and then asked, "Melvina, what do you know about fissionable material?"

She'd flown into Madison the evening of December twenty-third. Her father had picked her up in his battered work cruiser, driving the twenty-five miles home through a softly falling snow. The farm had been in Walter's family for three generations and encompassed a modest two-story house and a barn that had, at one time, held fifty milk cows. Now it only housed two. With no spouse or other children to help him run things, and with the long hours demanded of him as a sheriff, there'd been no time left for Walter to tend livestock or grow crops.

During the drive they'd chatted sporadically about the lousy, but unsurprising, season the Green Bay Packers had had, and the surprising statewide win by Dukakis over Bush. Her father groused about the $90 million spent on the new Bradley sports center, and Mel remarked that the ice crusting the shoreline of Lake Mendota looked like beautiful lace.

Walter had ducked his chin into his collarbone but smiled. "You sound like your mother just now. It's good to be reminded you got some of her poetry and not all my rough edges."

She studied her father's face, wondering how in the world

two such different people could have set up house and had a child together. She accepted, maybe for the first time, that she was not just Sheriff Walter Donleavy's daughter—strong, capable, and self-sufficient—but Alice's daughter as well. At times prone to imaginative flights of fancy and romantic imagery. This realization gave her a surge of confidence. She was an Ophelia who could swim.

As they passed horses in a snow-drifted field, thick-coated as woolly mammoths, he reminded Mel of the time she rode a green broke mare, contrary to his warnings not to.

Mel smiled. "We rode over a bevy of quail, and she bucked me off. Broke my ankle. Took me forty-five minutes to catch her again."

His grin widened with pride. "And yet you walked home, close to two miles, leading that mare. Swearing all the way. Had to cut the boot off your foot."

Once they'd gotten home, she'd dropped her bags in her childhood bedroom and followed her father out to feed the cows. It had stopped snowing, and a brisk wind had chased the clouds northward, leaving the night sky a brilliant, clear turquoise. The snow reflected ambient light so that it was bright enough to navigate between the house and barn without a flashlight.

The smell of the barn, yeasty and warm, flooded her with old memories: the delicious expectation of being caught while playing hide-and-seek behind mountainous bales of hay; hours of solitary reading in the loft, watching shafts of sunlight march across the stalls; burying her face in the yielding and bristly haunches of the sad-eyed Guernseys. The farm had always been a place of refuge and comfort for Mel, timeless, changeless. And she wondered now how long it would be before she'd be able to return to it.

After he poured grain into the feeding bins, Walter turned to her and asked, "You gonna tell me now what's bothering you?"

She should have known he'd sense her apprehension. He always could read her, especially her silences. So she told him about the mild-mannered man from the CIA and his offer.

Her father's knuckles whitened on the handle of the bucket. "And what did you tell him?"

She reached out, stroking the nose of the nearest cow. Stalling would not make it any easier; she owed him the truth. "I said yes."

He started shaking his head. "Guatemala, Laos, the Bay of Pigs—"

"I know how you feel about the CIA, Dad."

"Then why, Mel? You just spent twenty weeks completing your FBI training. You could be applying for a post with the Feds right now."

She took his hand and they walked back to the house. They sat at the kitchen table, the table that had been built by her grandfather, and Walter poured a generous measure of whiskey into two small jelly jars, one for each of them. She'd drunk her breakfast juice out of those glasses for most of her childhood.

Mel had folded her hands on the table and stared at the patterns in the wood. "Something happened at Quantico. They know about me."

Understanding flared in her father's eyes. "Danny Delvecchio."

She nodded.

In the fall of 1980 when she was sixteen, Mel had gone with her father into the nearby town of Sauk City to get feed supplies. She sat in his truck, radio on, windows down, and stared dreamily at the colors of the turning leaves. At the end of the street was a bank with a van parked in front, the engine idling. She thought it strange that the driver had left the vehicle running.

Then the door to the bank was flung open and a man wearing a ski mask ran out. He yanked open the passenger-side door of the van. In the driver's seat another head popped up, putting the van in drive and roaring down the street toward her. As the vehicle raced by, the passenger pulled his mask off, giving Mel a brief, but indelible, look at him. The driver was wearing a cowboy hat with the brim pulled low. But a split-second view of his mouth and jawline was enough. She recognized both of them from their photos in the local paper. They were both high school football stars, and the getaway driver was Danny Delvecchio, the mayor's son.

Walter had run to the bank to offer assistance, so it was a few hours before Mel could talk to him alone about what she'd seen. With her father's encouragement, she gave an official statement through the sheriff's office, certain that she had correctly identified the robbers.

The reaction from the mayor's office was swift, and brutal. The mayor gave an interview to the local paper, intimating that the Donleavy girl had some hidden, vengeful agenda against his son.

When the DA asked Mel about her motivations, she looked at him with a steady gaze and said, "Because it's the truth."

The DA ultimately wouldn't believe that Mel had been able to identify two boys she'd never met, and Walter Donleavy's position as sheriff was threatened unless his daughter dropped her ridiculous claims. The mayor's son had never gotten so much as a traffic ticket. It was the first time Mel had brought her abilities out from the shadows in such a public way, and for many years to come, it'd be the last.

Soon after she reluctantly recanted, Mel began to receive anonymous, threatening phone calls. They lasted for months.

Her sophomore year was a misery, and she spent more and more time at the farm.

One winter evening when Walter was working late, Mel was alone with only her father's aging sheepdog. She'd let the dog out just before bed and soon afterward heard a high-pitched squeal. The roar of a powerful engine brought her to the door in time to see a red truck tearing away from the house, throwing dirt and rocks in its wake. When she rushed into the yard, she found their dog howling in pain, shot with an arrow in its haunch. The dog survived the injury and, as importantly to Mel, she'd recognized the truck. It was the prized possession of the mayor's son.

A few days later, she'd said good night to her father and climbed the stairs to her bed. After a few hours, fueled by a simmering anger, she'd eased out of the second-story window and walked the six miles through the snow to the Delvecchio home, carrying a bottle of bleach. She'd emptied the entire bottle into the red truck's gas tank. After returning home, winded from walking twelve miles in drifts up to her knees, she lay down next to the injured dog, burying her face in his fur. It had snowed again later that night, covering any tracks she had left.

Later, when questioned about the ruined vehicle, her father swore to high heaven that Melvina Donleavy had been in bed asleep the entire night.

Following that event, bad luck seemed to stalk Delvecchio junior for months. Cow pats were left in his school locker, a hard-core porn magazine turned up amid his school reports, and several large carpet tacks were strategically placed inside his football shoes. One of the puncture wounds became infected, benching him the entire spring. However much the injured jock suspected Mel, she always seemed to be elsewhere—across campus, in the library, erecting sets for the school play. He alone was left believing that the angelic-faced

Melvina Donleavy was responsible for exacting revenge for her injured dog and making his life miserable.

The following year Danny Delvecchio was arrested trying to buy a muscle car with the marked bills he had stolen from the Sauk City bank. On the day of the arrest Walter sat with Mel at the kitchen table.

"You're as honest as the day is long," he had said, "which is why I never asked you directly about Danny's misfortunes. I want you to know that I never doubted that you recognized him that day. And I respected your wanting to do the right thing with the DA. But Mel, now you know why I warned you to keep it under wraps. Your mother and I have different views on this, but..." He paused, as if uncertain how to go on. "Sometimes you're more than a little spooky with this recognition stuff, and some people are going to misunderstand it. Or they'll try to use it to their own advantage. Do you recognize *everyone* you've seen before?"

She nodded.

"For how long?"

"Forever."

Walter finished his whiskey and poured a little more into his glass. "What happened at Quantico?"

"Do you remember the Tompkins Square riot last summer in New York?" He nodded. "The mayor reached out to Quantico to help identify some of the police officers engaged in excessive violence. Seems he didn't fully trust his police commissioner. In our cadet training, we were shown five photos of uniformed police officers who'd been sanctioned for violence. I was the only cadet who picked out all five from TV news footage, from a crowd of about five hundred people. Two of the officers were filmed from behind. They were never filmed face-on."

"So your instructors took notice," Walter said.

"Yes. They began testing me. My hit rate was close to a hundred percent. They've finally coined a name for people like me, Dad. They call us super recognizers."

"How rare is it?" Walter asked.

"There may only be a few hundred of us." Mel watched her father closely.

"In the country?"

"In the world."

The full impact of Mel's abilities, their rarity and vast implications, stunned him into silence. He stared at her as he would have a stranger. "And that's when the CIA became interested in you."

Mel reached out and covered his hand with both of hers, fearing that this revelation would widen the gulf between them. She needed him to understand that, without a purpose, she worried her abilities would keep her at the fringes of society forever, merely a mistake of nature.

"Islamic extremism is on the rise. The Soviets are being crushed right now by the cost of years of war and the fallout from Chernobyl. Their old guard is being destabilized by Gorbachev's *perestroika*. The Soviets have thousands of nuclear weapons and fissionable material that will go to the highest bidder if money is needed.

"Do you remember showing me pictures of the aftermath of Hiroshima? An entire city and thousands of people incinerated. I was shown photos of the aftermath of Chernobyl. Dad, it was terrifying. People will be dying of radiation poisoning for generations."

She squeezed his hand, willing him to understand. "Iran is talking to the Russians about developing a nuclear program. Not as a power source. But for making bombs. Intelligence thinks I can be of help. To identify those bad actors."

She paused, gathering up the words she hoped would make

him see what she saw so clearly. "My whole life I've felt set apart. Different. But something happened to me when Agent Hunter was talking about the possible threat of nuclear war. Every moment of my life crystallized into one purpose. You've always told me to 'do no harm when you can and do good when you must.' I've spent most of my waking hours trying to hide this…gift, if you can call it that. It's been something that I've been almost ashamed of at times. Other times it's actually scared me. Now I can use it. Direct it. And all I have to do is keep my eyes open."

He studied her face for a long time, worry wearing grooves in his face. "What now?"

"More training. The full Agency program, eighteen months."

"And then, what? Working as a covert officer? You'll be sent into the belly of the beast."

"I'll go wherever they send me. Wherever they need me." The next bit of information would be the most difficult to impart. She'd always shared almost everything with her father—her hopes for the future, her fears—and now that would have to change. "But you know I won't be able to tell you about any of it. You know that, right?"

He stood up from the table, his expression pinched and sorrowful, and gave her a brief hug before climbing the stairs to bed.

It snowed through most of that Christmas week, as she'd tried to retain each moment spent at the farm. Her dad making mountains of pancakes every morning, even though it was just the two of them. Hiking on snowshoes into the pines at the edge of their property to cut down a tree and drag it back into the house. Exchanging presents on Christmas Day: a new pair of slippers for him and a soft cashmere scarf for her. The two of them reading contentedly together next to the Franklin stove.

They never again talked about her joining the Central Intelligence Agency.

Mel made several calls to her mother, wishing her a happy Christmas. Alice congratulated her daughter on completing her FBI training, although Mel was vague in answering her questions about where she would be assigned stateside, steering the conversation back to her mother's theatrical plans for the upcoming school year.

Three weeks later Walter drove Mel to the airport for her trip to Langley. "I'll contact your mom soon and tell her you'll be very busy and out of touch for a little while." He chewed the inside of his cheek, his jaw tightening. "I want you to listen to me. I know you'll be going through a lot of training, and that some of it will include resisting interrogation. You'll be put in stressful situations. Little or no sleep. No food for days. Heat or excessive cold. Sensory deprivation. Solitary confinement—"

"Dad, I'm strong—"

He waved his hand to silence her. "I know you're strong. I've taught you to be that way. You'd go naked in a snowstorm to get the job done and please your instructors. But that's one of your two biggest weaknesses, Mel. Your desire to please. The one thing they won't teach you is that the most dangerous interrogator will present himself as your friend. I'm telling you, don't get killed with kindness."

"What's my second weakness?" she asked.

"Your dogged persistence, especially where a wrong has been done. You put yourself out on a limb for that old mangy mutt. Imagine what you'd do if a human being you cared about was harmed. Hell, I've had stockyard bulls that gave up a fight before you did."

She was, in that moment, overwhelmed with love.

They drove for a while without speaking.

"I found your newspaper clippings after you left for college," he finally said. "I'd tried to shield you from all that."

Mel studied his profile, heavy with the weight of knowing that no matter how high he had tried to build his protective fence, human carnage had managed a way in.

"You've dealt with it your whole life," she said.

He looked at her. "But at what cost?"

The muscles at his temple worked nervously for a moment. "Maybe it's better that you've always known. Now that you'll be in the thick of it."

She held his hand in silence the rest of the way.

Mel insisted on being dropped off at the airport curb. She hugged Walter for a long time, promising him she would be careful. She waved at him until his truck disappeared from view.

14

MONDAY, AUGUST 6, 1990

Dan met Mel in the lobby at eight o'clock and they walked out a side door to William's waiting car, the same one that Alexi had driven the day before. William drove them to the greenbelt fronting the river, where he parked and led the three of them to a bench on a slight rise, giving them an unobstructed view of their surroundings.

"How are you, Melvina?" William asked formally once they were situated. "Did you get a good night's sleep?"

Mel had not, in fact, slept well. She'd been anxious and restless, filled with questions about what might have been found on Katya's body. She woke at four and watched the windows brighten until she was forced to get up and take a shower. She'd observed her own dark circles and worry lines in the bathroom mirror and thought, *This is the face of a guilty person.*

"Have you eaten anything?" William asked when she stayed silent.

She shook off his question impatiently and asked, "Why am I being called in for questioning?"

William sighed. "From one of my contacts I found out that Martin Kavalchuk left my party early because the coroner had found something in Katya's pocketbook. Apparently that was retrieved at the same time as her body."

"What was it?" Mel asked.

William looked at her apologetically. "That, unfortunately, was something I couldn't find out. But I was informed in the wee hours of Sunday morning that you would probably be getting a summons from the KGB. It's why I called Alexi and directed him to take you out of Minsk for a few hours. I needed time to get as much information as I could, and also give you time to prepare for the interview. It will most likely just be conducted by a minor functionary."

"Thank you for the heads-up," Mel said. "I'll be fine."

William studied her for a moment. "Of course, it's possible that they found absolutely nothing but needed an excuse to bring you in. You're the youngest and, seemingly, most vulnerable of your group. They may just be trying to get more information out of you."

"Just stick to your backstory about why you're here and you'll be fine," Dan said. "William and I will be with you, if not in the interro—"—Dan caught himself and bit off the word—"interview room, then right outside. I've already put in a call to the State Department in DC using an open-channel phone line, so the Soviets know that our government has been given a heads-up."

Mel's backstory, her "legend," was virtually the same as her real personal history. As a simple secretary, she'd been raised in Wisconsin by a father who was in law enforcement and had attended St. John's College. Of course, her time in FBI and CIA training was filled instead with her working as an admin for Dan, who'd been given a fake work history for a large accounting firm in DC, his years as a CIA plant in Afghanistan scrubbed from public records.

All of Mel's training at the Farm had been a dress rehearsal for the real thing. She quieted her mind, willing her body to relax. She was not alone, and had the full weight of American intelligence behind her. "Thanks, Dan. I know my story. It's going to be fine."

They returned to the car—Dan sitting in the front passenger seat and Mel sitting in the back—and William drove them the short distance to the KGB headquarters, the sprawling yellow stone building that covered an entire block facing Ulitsa Nezalezhnastsi. The complex sat along a narrow park decorated with a bust of Felix Dzerzhinsky, the founder of the much-feared Cheka, the predecessor of the KGB.

While William stopped at a traffic sign, Mel stared at the bronze bust, which stared soullessly back across the wide avenue. Her palms were damp, and she rubbed them discreetly against her pant legs.

"So Alexi took me out of Minsk knowing that the KGB might come looking for me?" she asked William.

"Yes."

"Wouldn't that get him into trouble?"

The car behind them honked impatiently, making Mel jump, and William eased forward. "Not if you and I don't tell anyone." He glanced at her meaningfully in the rearview mirror. "It was a picnic, Melvina, pure and simple. Alexi was your guide as a favor to me."

He turned left on Ulitsa Komsomol'skaya, passing his own home, and pulled into an underground parking space below the headquarters.

"We won't go through the front entrance. That's for visiting dignitaries and high-profile political prisoners. It's a shame, really, because it's quite grand, really impressive."

"I think we can do without the tour," Dan muttered, frowning.

William opened the car door for Mel and took her arm to lead her to an elevator. He exchanged a few brief words with a guard, and the three of them entered. The guard keyed the panel for the first floor and the doors closed. The elevator shuddered and began its slow and noisy ascent.

Mel worked to contain her nervousness, but the tiny space seemed to be closing in on her. "Why do they make these elevators so small?" she asked.

William squeezed her arm. "So only a few people can gather. Makes it difficult to foment dissent. Or rally a coup." He winked at her and smiled. "It's easier to shoot four people coming out of an elevator than ten."

The elevator shuddered again and jerked to a stop between floors. Mel's nervousness swelled.

As though sensing her anxiety, William said cheerfully, "Don't worry. The KGB has the best building engineers in the city. The longest we'll have to spend in this box is twenty minutes. Moscow has more elevators than New York City. And more elevators mean more engineers, most of them trained by the Soviet military. You know, Martin Kavalchuk actually showed me the 'brains' of the building's elevator system. The bank of electronics was initially designed to raise and lower rockets stored underground."

The elevator groaned to life again and soon the doors opened to another guard waiting to receive them. They followed him through a long series of narrow, silent hallways, passing closed and numbered doors. Everything was painted an industrial blue-green and there were no ornaments—no obvious exit signs, no warning posters, no wanted posters, no information boards.

It was anonymous, labyrinthine, and disorienting in the extreme, which, of course, was the point.

The guard left them in a small waiting area with exactly three hard-backed chairs, telling them, in Russian, "Sit. The interview will begin soon." The guard looked at Mel for a moment, as though memorizing her face in return, and then left.

Mel closed her eyes, slowed her breathing, and emptied

her mind as she'd been taught to do before an interrogation. She'd learned many skills at Camp Peary, some of which she'd already mastered at Quantico, such as firearms handling and marksmanship. Admittedly, she'd been comfortable with guns, as she'd grown up hunting with her father.

But of the specific "spy" skills—everything from code work and lock-picking to opening packages, following targets without detection, and evading hostile pursuers—withstanding capture was something no one could truly prepare for. Still, the Agency did their best to simulate the discomfort, and at times terror, of enhanced interrogation. After a few days of no sleep, little food, extreme cold, and stress, the human animal inevitably begins to unravel, physically and mentally. For Mel, in particular, if she could not process her facial scans after forty-eight hours, the consequences were incapacitating.

Her trainers had known this and decided to push the envelope anyway. The night she'd been taken, along with two male trainees at the Farm, hooded, bound, and driven in a van for several hours to some unknown location, she'd understood that it was necessary. None of the trainees had known when their time would come, and the "capture" was always executed in the middle of the night.

Mel would later learn she'd spent close to sixty hours in a room that was, alternately, pitch-black, then suddenly filled with blinding light from directional spotlights mounted in the ceiling. She was left untied but provided with only a thin mattress and a bucket for a toilet. A tape of someone screaming played erratically at ear-popping decibels so she could never really sleep.

Without warning, men wearing formfitting ski masks would come into the room and demand information. Some of the information was banal, some of it deeply personal, like when she'd lost her virginity. The men screamed at her in Russian, and then in English, that she'd been kidnapped by double agents and that this was not a simulation. They asked her about her CIA training, details of which she was not allowed to divulge to anyone but her trainers.

For Mel, the unraveling began with the insistent drone of her headache, a dull, unpleasant tugging sensation inside her skull, like a powerful vacuum cleaner threatening to suck her eyeballs out of their sockets. She tried to ignore the noise and the stabbing lights, breathing deeply, trying desperately to find a place of meditative isolation in which she could settle the unprocessed images into her subconscious.

During her training in advance of her interrogation, a veteran field agent—a man who'd been captured while fighting in Vietnam by the Vietcong—had suggested picking one phrase, the more absurd the better, and repeating it over and over again while being questioned.

"It works like a meditation mantra to focus your thoughts," he'd said. "And it confuses the hell out of your interrogators."

In a panic, she'd settled on her mother's often-used saying—"It's just the drugs, Alice"—which she repeated over and over again, until the words became meaningless.

After what seemed an age, the dull ache in her head became sharp, stabbing pains at her temples, as though the connective ligaments of her jaw were being wrenched free. She held her chin firmly in both hands to keep her face from disintegrating.

At some point, her interrogators got tired of hearing the same hysterically uttered phrase. They poured buckets of ice water over her head, three of them hovering over her, screaming their demands, poking her with their fingers.

Mel would have no memory of what happened at the fifty-eight-hour mark, although the camera recording for training purposes would capture every second. When she was finally pulled from the room, one of her interrogators had been bitten savagely in the neck, requiring stitches, a second had been head-butted in the crotch, and the third was scratched so deeply that a piece of Mel's fingernail was embedded in his flesh.

At her evaluation, her assessment team stared warily at her as though she were a specimen. But their expressions of doubt became expressions of surprise when she correctly identified one of her reviewers as one of her interrogators. Even though he'd been hooded and masked, she recognized the shape of his head, jawline, and eyes. Despite her exhaustion, the pain of her bruises, and her torn fingernail, Mel had proven herself a force to be reckoned with. She looked at her astonished evaluators and smiled defiantly.

"Donleavy," the reviewer had said, "you look like a Disney character, but you're fucking scary. That's going to come in handy when someone underestimates you."

Mel's only regret was that she had no memory of her attack. They never showed her the video.

It was officially against Soviet ideology to torture a prisoner. But, conveniently, the Soviets did not consider enhanced interrogation torture. Mel knew they'd become modern and forward-thinking in their methods. Experimenting with psychotropic drugs was reportedly a new favorite.

Her controlled breathing had slowed her heartbeat, and she could feel the force of it beating against her spine. She was strong, and prepared, and with a sanctioned American delegation. She had nothing to worry about. Melvina Donleavy was simply a secretary who would probably be questioned by a minor Soviet functionary.

The guard came back into the room and gestured for Mel to follow him. Dan started to stand, but the guard said, "*Nyet. Tol'ko eta zhenshchina.*" No. Just the woman.

Dan's face reddened. "You can't take her in by herself. I won't allow it."

William also stood and began a heated exchange in Russian with the guard. A second, wearing a pistol in a holster, entered the room.

"I'll be fine," she said to Dan. Her voice sounded overly loud in the crowded space, but firm. "Really."

She turned to the guard, and he led her through a different door and down another long hallway, William's shouts echoing until the door firmly closed. The guard opened a final door and gestured her into a large, windowless room with concrete walls and a floor that slanted slightly toward the middle. At the center was a drain covered by a mesh plate, which had been bolted to the concrete. The room smelled strongly of disinfectant. There was a desk with an accompanying chair, set to face a single chair situated close to the drain. Mel sat in the lone chair as the guard left.

After a few minutes a door at the opposite end opened and a young Alpha officer—the same man who had searched William's apartment the night of the party—came in and sat at the desk. Mel straightened her posture, remembering to keep her breathing deep and regular. She composed her face into a pleasant expression: a young American woman, eager to please. The officer shuffled some papers in a file but didn't address her, or even look at her.

It's just the drugs, Alice, she thought, reminding herself that if she could get through enhanced interrogation stateside, she'd be able to answer the young officer's questions without breaking a sweat.

The door at the far end opened once more. Martin Kavalchuk stepped into the room, dressed, as usual, all in black. Mel felt an immediate acceleration of her heartbeat as the adrenaline surged through her body. He made little sound as he walked toward the desk, as though pulled along on greased ball bearings.

He has the moves of an assassin, she thought, admonishing

herself again that there was no reason to panic. Dan's voice played in her head: *This is probably what William calls a fishing expedition...*

Kavalchuk stood behind the Alpha officer and placed one hand lightly on the man's shoulder. The officer immediately stood, turned stiffly on his heel, and exited, his footfalls echoing on the hard floor.

But why would the head of the KGB want to question her? Maybe he had uncovered her true mission...*You're making things up,* she scolded herself. *Stay calm, stay focused, stay alert.*

Kavalchuk sat at the emptied desk, closed the folder, and interlaced his fingers over it. Finally, he looked at her and said, "*Dobrye utro.*"

She remembered his mellifluous tone, his mildly curious gaze. For an uncomfortable moment, she wondered if he was personally interested in her, but that was nonsense. This was no social setting.

"Good morning," she responded in English.

He smiled benignly and cocked his head. "*Ya dumayu ty nemnogo govorish' po russki. Vernyy?*" I think you speak a little Russian. Correct?

She gave him a shy smile in return, as Melvina the young, inexperienced secretary would. "*Nemnogo. Ochen' malo.*" A little. Very badly.

"Then we will speak only in English," he said. He opened the folder and ran his fingers down the first page. "Did you have a pleasant visit to the countryside yesterday?" He asked the question without looking at her.

"Yes," she said. Despite her measured breathing, her heart rate continued to increase. It seemed she and Alexi had been followed after all. "It was lovely."

There was a moment of silence, and Martin looked up expectantly as though waiting to hear more. When she didn't try to fill the quiet, he looked back at the file, slowly and methodically turning the onionskin pages of the report.

He began to read the history of her life. "Melvina Donleavy, born in Wisconsin, 1964. Father, Walter, mother, Alice. No siblings. Four years university at St. John's in Maryland. Did you enjoy St. John's?"

It took her a few beats to realize that he'd asked her another question. She'd been momentarily caught off guard by the mention of her parents. That had not been supplied in her official bio. She had expected that simply keeping Walter and Alice Donleavy in the dark would keep them safe. Now she wasn't so sure.

"I enjoyed St. John's very much," she answered.

"Maryland, I hear, is quite beautiful. And then you went to work for Mr. Hatton as his secretary."

"That's right."

He closed the file again. "It all seems very straightforward."

Again he paused, his probing eyes studying her face. She resisted looking down at her feet, and the covered drain. She smiled, but it felt strained, false. *Remember to stick as close to the truth as possible*. The less she fabricated, the fewer details she'd have to commit to a falsified memory.

"Do you know why you're here?" he asked.

"Dr. Cutler said it had something to do with the woman found in the river."

"Yes. Katerina Mikhailovna Shushkevich. Katya. You recognized her."

"Yes."

"How well did you know her?"

"I met her at the Ministry of External Affairs. We only spoke a few times."

"What did you speak about?"

"I knew she enjoyed reading science fiction. We talked about Russian literature. Not much else."

"Did you give her anything?"

"I gave her my lipstick and a candy bar. She was a nice girl. I liked her."

"Did you give her anything else?"

"No."

Another moment of silence followed, in which he looked at her, his brows raised as though surprised. "Were you going to meet her outside of work?"

She pretended to think about it for a few seconds. "Well, I did ask if she could show me around Minsk. Share a meal. Nothing definite was planned."

He slipped a piece of paper out of his pocket. It was crumpled and darkened, as though it had been soaked and then dried. "We found this in Katya's pocketbook. It's a note addressed to you. Do you know what it says?"

A fine line of sweat beaded against her hairline and she resisted brushing it away with her fingers. "No."

He put the note back in his pocket. "You were in the presence of Alexi Yurov yesterday. What did you talk about?"

He asked the question lightly—as though it were merely small talk—but Mel intuited that he was zigzagging the interview, trying to put her off-balance. Like a dance instructor trying out a new pupil.

"We talked about our families, our schooling," she said, her voice steady. "He talked about fishing. I tried kvass for the first time. We had a picnic, provided by Dr. Cutler. Then we returned to Minsk."

A ghost of a smile appeared on his face when she mentioned the kvass, but she couldn't tell if it was out of nostalgia or pity. "William seems to like you. You are, after all, an attractive woman." The last was expressed bloodlessly, as a statement of fact.

Mel managed to blush. "Dr. Cutler was only being kind. He said he wanted me to experience the Byelorussian countryside."

"Yes," he said thoughtfully, studying her through a seemingly passive gaze. He stood, picking up a writing pad and a pencil from the desk. He positioned himself in front of Mel, handing her the pad and pencil.

"I would like to dictate a letter to you. Will you be so kind as to write down what I say?"

"I don't understand. I'm not giving a written statement—"

"No. Nothing like that." He made a conciliatory gesture with one hand. "But, as you are a secretary, and no doubt have learned shorthand, you'll have no problem writing down what I dictate to you."

She took the pad and pencil and waited, her pulse thundering in her ears. She could type decently, but she'd never learned any kind of shorthand. She'd have to rely on her memory to fill in the gaps in her handwriting. He moved to stand behind her, and the skin at her neck tightened and goose-bumped as though an ice bag had been laid across her shoulders.

He began speaking rapidly and she struggled to write. "The holy features of your face. Detained in darkness, isolation, my days began to drag in strife. Without faith and inspiration, without tears, and love and life—"

She pressed so hard trying to scratch out the words that the lead broke. He stopped speaking and stood motionless behind her. Mel held up the broken pencil, and after a moment, he collected it, along with the writing pad, and returned to the desk.

"You're not a very good secretary, are you?" He said it without rancor.

"Mr. Hatton is satisfied," she said defensively. If she couldn't pass as a competent office assistant, maybe he'd accept the cliché of the "ideal American secretary." If not qualified, then beautiful. If not talented, then accommodating.

"Perhaps," he said doubtfully. "Did you recognize the poem?"

"I think…maybe, it's Pushkin?"

He exhaled and nodded. "We'll speak again soon, Melvina. Very soon."

She looked at him, alarmed. There would be more sessions.

"You have something more to say?" he asked.

Again he adopted the pose of the waiting father. Patient, expectant, receptive.

"Do you have any idea who murdered Katya?" She asked it plaintively, as any young woman in a strange city might.

"It's being investigated."

"I've heard mention of the Svisloch Strangler—"

His expression darkened. She'd pushed the "naïve American" too far. He turned and exited the way he had come in. Soon the Alpha officer escorted her back to the small waiting room where Dan and William sat worrying.

The two men flanked Mel as they left the building, exiting into the parking lot. No one spoke until William had steered his car back onto the main avenue, headed toward the hotel.

By the time Dan turned to her, Mel had unclenched her jaw and returned her breathing to normal.

"What happened?" he asked.

"Martin Kavalchuk questioned me."

She caught William's sharp gaze in the rearview mirror.

"He asked how well I knew Katya and showed me a note they'd found in her pocketbook."

"What did it say?" William asked.

"I don't know. He didn't let me read it. He then asked me about Alexi. I told him we had a picnic and talked about fishing." She took a breath. "He knew my parents' names."

Dan's eyes cut to William. "That tells us his intelligence has poked a hole in our cover stories. Did he say anything else?"

Mel glanced again at the menacing bronze bust of Felix Dzerzhinsky as they drove past. "Yes. He found out that I was a lousy secretary. And said he'd see me again soon."

Dan twisted in his seat to stare at William. "Why would the head of the KGB want to interrogate her again?"

"I don't know." For once, William looked at a loss. "But if he knows more about Mel's background, we need to be prepared."

The three fell silent. Mel didn't mention that she'd questioned Kavalchuk about the Strangler. It had been spontaneous and lay outside the boundaries of her mission. But the memory of Katya's distorted face haunted her, demanding answers.

15

MONDAY, AUGUST 6, 1990

Martin Gregorivich Kavalchuk sat inhaling his one cigarette of the day. It wasn't that he wouldn't have preferred to indulge himself with the entire pack. It was a matter of personal will that he only allowed himself one. He'd finished his usual lunch. Soup, always soup, and two slices of rye bread. Good, rustic, country-style bread with enough grit in the dough to keep the pipes clean.

He stubbed out the last of the cigarette and signaled for his tray to be removed. In its place a single file was presented by his personal aide—whom he'd handpicked from the elite Alpha antiterrorist group, organized only a few months before by the State Security Committee of Byelorussia.

Kavalchuk waited for the officer to leave before he opened the file. It was stamped in red ink sekretno, or Confidential, for his eyes only. Inside were three densely typed pages detailing matters important to state security. If an issue was urgent, it was stamped sovershenno sekretno.

The first page was a status report on the Iraq-Kuwait conflict and a detailed analysis of when, and if, the United States would get involved. A lifelong soldier who'd studied Western intelligence agencies for forty years, he had no doubt that there would be American boots on the ground within a few months, as well as an international coalition of military forces. What was more interesting was a report from a Russian source inside Israel. It stated that Israeli intelligence had completely missed what Russia already knew, which was how close Saddam Hussein was to successfully developing missiles that could deliver nuclear payloads to Tel Aviv. If not for the invasion of Kuwait, Hussein would have had a viable nuclear program in six months.

The second page dealt with the covert assassination of Gerald Bull, a Canadian engineer who was secretly working with the Iraqis on their nuclear program. He hadn't been a spy and wasn't motivated by ideology. He'd strictly wanted money, more than he would have made working in Canada for decades. He was killed entering his apartment door, fumbling with his keys. It wasn't as if the Mossad hadn't given him plenty of warning. The report included the weapon used: a Makarov pistol with a silencer. A good choice, Kavalchuk thought. He preferred the Makarov for wet work himself. Reliable, compact, powerful.

The last page was the most problematic, but not so surprising, considering recent data from the Byelorussian health committee. It was the as-yet-uncensored report sponsored by the International Atomic Energy Agency. These findings by the International Chernobyl Project had been completed in May, but Moscow had sat on them for months before sending them on to Minsk. They'd decided the total contaminated area was estimated to be 25,000 kilometers, 15,000 of which were found in Belarus: a larger amount of irradiated material than had fallen on Russia and the Ukraine. The ground concentrations of cesium-137, even outside the Exclusion Zone, had likely already caused thousands of cases of thyroid cancer and birth defects. And those numbers would continue to grow for many years to come. Infant mortality rate was 300 times greater there than in the rest of Europe. It was estimated that only twenty percent of newborns were born healthy. Heart defects were so common that doctors had named the condition Chernobyl Heart.

The numbers would have to be massaged to prevent further panic, of course. Smoking and excessive alcohol consumption would be the usual designated causes for children born with defects.

The scientists with the investigative Chernobyl program had complained loud and long about incomplete or missing health records and the protracted delays in being given permission for on-site testing. He exhaled a short bitter breath.

"*Pozhaluysta.*" You're welcome.

Of course, Byelorussians were tough, and stubborn. People had moved back into the Exclusion Zone, back to their farms to try to grow their fatal crops, to pick the mushrooms that would light up a Geiger counter like a New Year's sparkler.

Behind the last page of the report was a recent photograph of a stillborn piglet from Gomel, about a hundred kilometers north of Chernobyl. He'd seen the photographs of the stunted and deformed children abandoned to orphanages, but this was something out of a nightmare. Four front legs, one of the rear legs splayed into tentacles. Teeth growing out of the top of its skull. Eye sockets, but no eyes.

He slipped the photo back into the folder and closed it. Only too well he knew what was *not* written in the report. That the next Chernobyl...would be Chernobyl. Inside the shielded coffin of Unit Four, which still housed a molten slurry of uranium fuel rods, graphite control rods, and melted sand, it was suspected that the neutron levels were rising. Another nuclear disaster in the making.

And yet, there were some arrogant fools in the politburo and the Academy of Sciences who preferred to once more play ring around the reactor, helping foreign entities in exchange for money, not caring that the weapons could just as easily be fired at Minsk as at Jerusalem. The ground close to Chernobyl would stay radioactive for *twenty thousand years* and would as easily kill a good communist as it would a corrupt capitalist. He was not a sentimental man, but he was a patriot and the unnecessary waste of life angered him almost as much as the rampant stupidity.

He dropped the file into a drawer, which he then locked. The world was filled with troubling events over which he had no influence. But he did have power within the interrogation rooms of the *Komitet* headquarters. There were few men better at extracting information than the Black Wolf. Hardened soldiers had wept like newborns as they poured out their most closely held secrets after long and uncomfortable confinements, aided by a judicial application of physical pain.

Melvina Donleavy had secrets, he was sure of this. She was no secretary, of this he was also certain. Her colleagues were obviously CIA, and experienced agents at that. Melvina was young, but something about her disquieted him. Despite his long experience in accurately assessing his targets, he couldn't immediately identify her purpose in Minsk.

For a brief moment he allowed himself to acknowledge that he found his interactions with her pleasant. She was self-contained, keenly observant, intelligent, and poised. She met his gaze straight on, without flinching. Most females cowered in his presence, whether they knew of his reputation or not. Yuri Andropov once told him that he, Martin Gregorivich, wore menace the way other men wear expensive cologne.

"You can smell it coming a mile away," Andropov had said, grinning like a death's-head mask.

An urge for another cigarette washed over him. He sat with the cravings until he'd mastered them, returning his body and mind to a sense of homeostasis.

The wolf eats only what it needs to survive. He stays alert for any trap, lean for the hunt, and hungry for the next kill.

16

MONDAY, AUGUST 6, 1990

When Mel returned to the Planeta, Ben and Julie were waiting in the lobby. William had dropped them off in front, saying he'd meet them at the Heat and Mass Transfer Institute later. It took Mel some time to reorient herself to the idea of following schedules and business meetings, because, of course, their meetings would have to continue. While Dan spoke quietly to Ben and Julie, bringing them up to date on what had transpired that morning with Martin Kavalchuk, Mel stood, frowning at the metallic wallpaper with the orange flowers, wondering how it was possible to reconcile the Soviet obsession with soulless function over aesthetic form. Like blocky, soundproofed interrogation rooms with drains in the floor in close proximity to walls plastered with garish colors now seen only in retro dollhouses.

The four of them had an early lunch and Mel did her best to follow the course of the conversation. But she was keenly aware of their concerned looks and, far from reassuring her, it made her feel like the younger sibling who'd fallen off her bike, instead of a capable member of the team. Ben had even asked if she needed some time to recover before they went to the ministry.

Mel finally set down her fork. "I'm fine." She gave Ben a pointedly grateful nod. "The best thing for me now is to get back to work."

She excused herself for the restroom and left the dining room. Julie caught up with her in the lobby, linking her arm through Mel's. She waited outside the bathroom stall, and then at the mirrors, handing Mel some crackling beige squares that passed as paper towels to dry her hands on. She leaned against the sink, much as Katya had done a few days earlier. Mel closed her eyes against the memory.

"You really okay?" Julie asked.

"Honestly?" Mel asked. "It was pretty nerve-racking. I didn't expect to be interviewed by the Black Wolf himself."

Julie studied her through narrowed eyes, head tilted, as though assessing Mel's anxiety level. "I was in Poland two years ago. Lots of workers striking, trying to force labor solidarity against the Soviets. US intelligence was there to stir the pot. I got picked up and hauled in front of the Ministry of Public Security. My interrogator was a woman who made Cruella de Vil look like Mother Teresa. She was low in the pecking order, but even so, I was terrified. Forty-eight hours in a cell with no outside contact. And this at the exact time they were executing *priests*. But the State Department made a stink and got me released."

"I have a hard time imagining that anything could frighten you," Mel said, smiling.

Julie nodded. "It would seem that way. I work hard enough to cultivate it. But this kibbutznik with steel in her eyes, as William would say, is mostly bark and no bite." She took hold of Mel's arms and shook her playfully in mock seriousness. "Trust your training. You wouldn't have been sent here if the Agency didn't think you were ready. And remember, you've got your team."

⋆⋆⋆

Twenty minutes later they were being driven in Anton's van to the Ministry of Finance building, to meet with the minister of external affairs, Ivanov. Elena, as usual, sat stiffly in the front seat.

Dan turned several times to study Mel, his brow still creased with worry. Finally, he leaned over the seat and asked, "You okay?"

It was the exact question that Julie had just asked, but to Mel his concern seemed overwrought and patronizing, as though he was playing the role of the responsible team leader.

"Yep, I'm good." She held up her hands. "Look, no thumbscrews, and no rack. Just questions. I'm confident that's all it's going to be."

Dan raised an eyebrow and faced the front again. But when she caught Anton's gaze in the rearview mirror, he slowly winked at her.

It was a shock to Mel, walking into Minister Ivanov's office, to see a different woman sitting in Katya's place. She was young and attractive, like Katya, but she didn't smile at the Americans and was formally efficient as she led them into the minister's office. They stayed only long enough for Dan to explain that they wouldn't be returning until they'd been given access to the entirety of the Heat and Mass Transit Institute.

"There's no point in our discussing any financial terms," he reiterated, "when we can't be certain where the money will be going."

As they left, the minister stared pointedly at Mel, and his lack of expression was more unnerving than if he'd scowled openly. In passing the reception desk, she noticed that the new woman was finishing the chocolate bar she'd given Katya.

Mel felt Elena crowding her from behind, shepherding her out, close enough that she could smell the garlic from the woman's lunch. She had the strong urge to offer Elena one of Ben's breath mints.

William was already at the institute when the group arrived at Shevchenko's office. The two were snickering, as if William had just told a slightly off-color joke. The academician greeted the group more cordially and Mel imagined that William had been greasing the wheels with his affable charm. That, and the half-empty bottle of vodka on the desk.

Shevchenko announced that he would start the tour of the institute at the Department of Mathematical Modeling, which, it was explained, was a think tank exploring a wide spectrum of problems: thermal processes, hydrodynamics, chemical kinetics, among other dynamic systems. They were led through room after cramped room of researchers—dry, emotionless men, staring at equations written in chalk on blackboards.

In one such room Shevchenko launched into an interminable lecture about the utmost importance of proving mathematical equations in support of the physical sciences. Julie looked pained as she tried to keep up her translation. Mel had stationed herself at the very back of the room, willing herself invisible while she memorized every researcher.

As Shevchenko went on, William joined her and leaned close, whispering, "Oleg has a background in the army, and has risen to be head of the institute, but he's purely a theoretical mathematician. He's not an engineer and has no real practical experience studying physics. Do you know who Richard Feynman was?"

Mel nodded. Fascinated, she'd followed the American physicist's testimony to NASA after the *Challenger* disaster—the space shuttle that had exploded four years before, killing all on board. It was Feynman who'd pinpointed the failure of the rubber O-rings, made rigid by the freezing temperatures at launch.

"I met him when he was lecturing at Caltech," William continued. "Brilliant man, part of the Manhattan Project. He once said 'Physics is to mathematics what sex is to masturbation.'"

Mel covered her mouth, hiding a smile. As if sensing joy, Elena craned her neck around, frowning. As she stood to join their conversation, William motioned to Mel and they slipped out of the room into the hallway.

Elena urgently whispered to them to come back, but William ignored her. He took Mel's arm. "Come with me."

He led her down a series of halls, walking with surprising alacrity given his size. Mel was relieved when Elena didn't try following them.

"One of the advantages of being a man in the Soviet Union," he said. "We don't have to answer to a woman. I hope you don't mind, but I've been dropping hints that we are indeed cultivating a *skandal*. An *affaire de coeur*."

She looked at him, bemused. "And that's not frowned upon?"

He gave her a sideways glance. "My dear, in Russia a man without a wife is considered a field without a fence. But without a mistress, he'd be a field of stones. It's absolutely expected!"

"Where are we going?"

"Toward the Department of Thermophysics. We won't get in, but they know my face, so hopefully we won't end up in a gulag. If we're stopped along the way, I'll just say you're my assistant."

"What exactly is it that you do here?" Mel asked.

He'd spoken glibly before about giving the Soviets just enough information to keep them interested. *Glasnost* aside, she once again wondered how the institute tolerated a Western scientist in their midst, even one who was under surveillance 24/7.

"Right now, I'm doing a series of lectures on nanotechnology in computer chips." He leaned in, grinning. "I'm happy to say the Soviets are behind the US in this technology."

Their progress came to an end in front of a set of wide double doors, a guard standing to one side. He was tall and wiry with a joyless look. He held up a hand in warning and demanded of William, in Russian, what he was doing in that part of the institute. William pointed to a large glass case filled with grainy black-and-white photos, medals, and banners, and answered him in Russian. He steered Mel to stand in front of the exhibit.

"What did you tell him?" Mel whispered.

"I told him I'm trying to impress my American girlfriend. Just nod and follow along," he said quietly, and started pointing to the photos. "This is dedicated to Comrade A. V. Luikov, founder of the institute and recipient of the Red Banner of Labor." He squeezed her arm as a prompt. "Look impressed, Melvina."

She made a suitable sound and William continued. "I don't think the guard can speak English, but I'm going to speak softly nonetheless. A little birdie told me that there is a new delegation of scientists coming to the institute imminently. I couldn't find out any more than that."

"Did you help coordinate our tour today?"

"I suggested to Shevchenko that he start his tour at the Department of Mathematics. Arrogant as he is, I knew he'd jump at it so he could use it as a stall tactic. But it's also close to a space that has, for six months, been closed off to most of the institute, me in particular. And which has been bringing in a lot of mysterious equipment."

"What do you think is going on?"

"I'm not sure. But if we can see who's visiting, that will tell us a lot."

The guard made some impatient noises and gestured for them to move along.

"Odin moment, pozhaluysta," William said, smiling apologetically. One moment, please.

He pointed Mel's attention to a photo of a former scientist—a worn, desiccated-looking man wearing a white lab coat. The guard, now bored, looked away.

"Take a peek at this," William muttered, pulling a pen dosimeter out of the breast pocket of his coat.

Mel turned her back to the guard and briefly held the pen up to the overhead lights to read the graph. "It's at forty millisieverts."

"About what you'd be exposed to getting an X-ray."

"But higher than normal. So whatever it is they're bringing in is bleeding radiation."

William gave her a sober look. "That's right."

Exposure to one hundred millisieverts a year was the beginning of risk for cancer.

Elena appeared, gesturing impatiently. "Please, everyone is going back to Comrade Shevchenko's office. You must return. Now, please."

They followed her back to the academician's office, her rigid, unforgiving posture punctuated by hostile glares and a lecture, in English for Mel's benefit, about the necessity of staying with the group. Within ten minutes, the Americans, minus William, were led back to the van.

As Anton pulled away, another car approached the institute: a sturdy black Volga, with two men seated in the back. One wore the uniform of a high-ranking KGB official. The other, his sharply defined profile crowned with a mop of luxuriant black hair, Mel immediately recognized. He was an Iranian scientist named Farhad Ahmadi, and he was, as far as American intelligence could tell, one of the driving forces behind Persepolis. The CIA had been tracking him for several years, but he'd fallen off the radar twelve months ago. Was this the reason Shevchenko was so eager to have the Americans leave?

Mel knew Ahmadi was Oxford-educated and had labored for several years as a researcher in the uranium enrichment facility Eurodif in France. Most recently, he had worked closely with Argentina's National Atomic Energy Commission in order to supply Iran with low-enriched uranium.

His code name was Lion, and the Lion was now in Minsk.

Having identified one of her targets, Mel felt electrified. Yet, despite her inner elation, she sat quietly in the van, calmly listening with half an ear to the conversation of her colleagues, aware of the occasional critical glance from Elena. She could almost hear the woman's censuring thoughts: *Shameful, throwing yourself at a gentleman old enough to be your grandfather.*

She would need to signal William that she'd seen one of her targets. She'd leave a mark at the gazebo at the agreed-upon time. If everything went as planned, Alexi would report the mark to William, and he'd meet her tomorrow morning at six, hopefully before the rest of her team was awake.

She knew that in the coming weeks, other Iranian scientists might appear at the institute. The thought gave her another frisson of excitement. She looked at Dan, chatting away, telling jokes, feeling in full control of the mission, and she thought there was a good chance that he might never know the purpose behind the purpose of their assignment. Such was the inequality of Agency security protocols. She turned to face the window next to her and smiled at her reflection, deciding she liked the feeling of having knowledge that Dan Hatton didn't have.

As soon as the group was returned to the hotel, Dan stated that he had work to do, and Julie complained of a headache.

They disappeared into the elevator together and Ben arched one eyebrow. "Uh-huh, *some* kind of work."

Mel, still on a high from recognizing one of her targets, and too restless to return to her room, lingered with Ben in the lobby. They stood together, looking out the large plate glass window as though admiring the park, their backs to the reception desk. Reflected in the glass, she could see Minder #3 rising from his usual chair and sauntering up behind them.

"Come on," Ben urged, also seeing the reflection. "It's been a long day. I think we both need a drink."

Grateful for his arm entwined in hers, Mel walked with Ben into the Planeta Mir, which was unusually quiet for a late afternoon. The broken-nosed barman had not yet lowered the window shades, leaving the usually gloomy space uncharacteristically bright. Only a few Germans were present, and Nadia was at her usual place at the end of the bar sorting cocktail napkins. The stocky man whom Nadia had previously called a *mudak,* an asshole, was trying to engage her in conversation, making kissing sounds and blowing in her face. There was something menacing behind his teasing and Mel wondered why the barman didn't intervene. Nadia met Mel's gaze briefly and gave her a weary smile, but then ducked her head. Her usually hard exterior had wilted, as though the constant harassment had worn her down.

Ben ordered two vodkas, and the barman poured generous measures into iced shot glasses.

Ben held up his glass. "The red, white, and blue."

"The red, white, and blue," Mel echoed, draining her glass in one go.

"Jesus, if I have to listen to any more of Shevchenko's palaver, I'm going to slip into a coma." He sipped at his drink. "You disappeared with William. Where'd you go?"

Mel studied her glass. "He showed me a commemorative exhibit for the founder of the institute."

Ben looked at her for a few beats. "Really?"

"Really." To a degree, she was telling Ben the truth. Here it was again, that peculiar push-pull. This was what it must be like to cheat on a spouse, she thought: every encounter compartmentalized so that nothing incriminating was revealed. The cheater smiles, reassures, misdirects.

Mel smiled at Ben. "The Soviets do love their scientists."

"It sure put Elena into a tizzy," Ben said, signaling for two more vodkas.

"Everything puts Elena into a tizzy."

"So..." There was a slight pause. He turned to her, concerned. "There's no hanky-panky coming from William?"

Mel looked at him, surprised but also moved. He was being protective again. "Not at all. He's just become a sort of mentor." She placed a hand on his arm. "Really, that's all it is."

"Okay," he said, pausing as the bartender put the drinks down and walked away. "It's just that I get the feeling that... you two have a secret. And if it's not romantic, strange bedfellows and all..."

Ben was already aware that something was off about Mel. And now she'd boxed herself into a corner by refuting the very rumor William was cultivating to give them cover. Mel reached for her vodka, but then paused. She needed to play this carefully. And keep her emotions out of it, even though a small part of her was disappointed that Ben would even entertain the notion.

"Mel," he continued. "I'm not going to ask you what you're actually doing here, because even if I did, you wouldn't be able to tell me. But you're not just keeping an eye on us. Am I right?"

She met his gaze, unblinking. "Ben, I can't talk about this."

"Is it going to put you in increased danger?" he asked.

"It shouldn't."

"Is it going to put the rest of us in increased danger?"

"Absolutely not."

He gave her a broad smile and finished his drink. "Oh, boy. That sounds like the answer you get from your recruiting officer. 'Sir, am I going to regret joining the army?' 'Absolutely not, son.'"

Mel allowed herself a laugh, which broke the tension, and after a last searching look, Ben began settling the tab. A yelp from the end of the bar drew Mel's attention. Nadia had slapped the German—Mel could see the red mark across one fleshy cheek—and he'd grabbed her wrist, hard. His face was contorted in rage, his eyes unfocused and wild. For the first time, Mel saw real fear in Nadia. Before Ben could vault from his stool, the stocky barman rushed over, his ire directed solely at Nadia. As he yelled in Russian, Mel was relieved to see Nadia rally and give as good as she got.

"Come on," Ben said, helping Mel from her barstool. "I think it's time to retreat."

As Mel walked reluctantly from the bar, her last sight was of Nadia, looking fragile and harried, sandwiched between the two larger men.

Moving through the lobby, Mel and Ben gave a friendly wave to Minder #3 and then got into the elevator. Mel exited on her floor, saying she'd see Ben at dinner.

As she approached the *dejournaya,* she saw that the original woman had returned and was wearing the lilac sweater. She'd also found a plastic barrette in the same color for her hair.

"Ochen' krasivyy," Mel said, pleased. Very beautiful.

The woman gave her the ghost of a smile as she handed over the room key. *"Spacibo."*

As she was unlocking the door, the *dejournaya* made a noise, as though she was clearing her throat. When Mel glanced at her, the woman pointed at the room next to hers—the room that backed the two-way mirror—and whispered, *"Pustoy."*

Empty. Mel nodded her thanks.

Cautiously, she approached the observation room and stood for a moment, listening. There was no sound coming from inside. If she could get a glimpse of the equipment, she'd know how serious Soviet intelligence was about recording her movements. Was it just audio, or visual as well?

Mel turned to the hall monitor. "*Mozhno mne chayu?*" May I have some tea?

The woman looked at her, momentarily alarmed, her eyes drifting back to the door. She set her mouth into a hard line but stood and headed to the opposite end of the hall where the tea service was set up. Mel twisted the doorknob. It was locked. Sneaking a quick peek at the hall monitor, who was taking her time, Mel moved swiftly to the desk and removed a key from the hook. She would only have a few moments. Slipping the key into the lock, she opened the door.

Inside the observation room was a desk upon which sat two phones, a journal, and an overflowing ashtray. A narrow cot was pushed against the far wall. An audio recording deck with headphones was next to the desk, and, placed against the two-way mirror, a video camera on a tripod. The hairs on her arms bristled.

The signal bell on the elevator pinged. Someone had arrived on her floor. Mel reversed and locked the door, throwing the key onto the desk, and hurried into her room. She caught sight of the monitor rushing back to her station. The whisper of footsteps approached and then the door next to hers was opened and then quietly shut. Whoever was watching her had returned.

A sharp knock startled her. Cautiously, she opened her door to find the hall monitor, a glass of tea in hand, glaring angrily. Mel took the tea, whispering her apologies, and closed the door again.

Resting her forehead against the doorframe, she waited

for her heart to stop hammering. At Camp Peary she'd seen a reconstructed observation room based on intel from an Estonian Soviet hotel, where an entire floor was devoted to spying on guests. They'd been assured the Estonian equipment was at least a decade old. The equipment here at the Planeta was a vast improvement. She'd have to tell Dan. Whatever goodwill she'd fostered with the *dejournaya* had been used up. Luckily, she didn't fear the *dejournaya* telling the authorities about the breach, as she would have to admit how Mel had obtained the key.

Purposely ignoring the mirror, Mel spent only a few more minutes freshening up, although she wanted nothing more than to lie down and sleep. It was only five o'clock, but the day had seemed to last for an entire week. She would stick to her schedule and go to the park, spending a short time at the gazebo, reading. Time enough to leave her chalk mark for William. But she wouldn't wait for Alexi to appear. It would simplify things, for her, if she could avoid him. No use dwelling on an impossible situation.

She gave her key back to the hall monitor—the woman refusing to meet her gaze—and left for the park. The afternoon was still, with no breeze from the river to soften the heat. She entered the shade of the gazebo and leaned against the railing, gazing out toward the banks of the Svisloch, doing her best, and failing, to not think of Katya. She eased the roll of antacids out of her pocket and put one in her mouth. Palming another, she swiped it carefully against the railing where William had indicated.

Then she sat back and opened her book and began to read. She was about halfway through *Bonfire of the Vanities,* deep into the trial of Sherman McCoy, but she found herself rereading passages several times before she could absorb the plot. The slanting rays of the sun were making her drowsy and, though she'd only been there for a quarter of an hour, she decided to return to the hotel for a quick nap before dinner.

A noise startled her, and, for an instant, she hoped that, despite all her earlier resolution, it might be Alexi. She craned her head around to see a young man in service whites on the path behind the gazebo. He flicked away a lit cigarette and effortlessly vaulted over the railing, grinning. She recognized him. The kitchen worker who had aggressively circled Anton's van the evening of William's party. A member of the *Bratva*.

He sauntered up to her and stood close, casting a shadow over her book.

"Kak dela, milaya devushka?" How are you, pretty girl?

He was very skinny, with bad teeth, and when she stood up, she was just as tall as he was. She noticed he was wearing an expensive gold-toned watch, which she was sure he could not have afforded on his hotel salary.

She set her face to stony indifference and walked down the steps of the gazebo and onto the path back to the hotel. He bounded down the stairs and stood in front of her, blocking her way.

He had pulled out another cigarette. "You have a light, lady?" he asked in English.

She shook her head, but as she passed him, he grabbed on to her wrist. He was still grinning, but his grip was tight. "Come for a drink with me," he whispered hoarsely.

As she'd been trained, Mel put her other hand firmly over his, swinging his arm up and around so that he was forced to face away or suffer a broken elbow. Torquing his arm further brought him to his knees. He squirmed and yelped in pain. He looked back over his shoulder at her, his expression as shocked as if he'd roughhoused with a puppy and it had bitten off his hand.

A blur of motion in her periphery made her flinch, and for an instant she thought another member of the *Bratva* was coming to his aid.

But it was Anton, something metallic glinting on one hand. He smashed his clenched fist down on the back of the younger man's head. There was a dull crack and he fell heavily onto the path.

Anton let loose a string of insults as he pocketed his brass knuckles. He kicked the prone man once and then said politely to Mel, *"Pozhaluysta."*

"Spacibo," she said quietly.

Without looking at her, he said, in English, "They teach such to all American secretaries?"

His face was expressionless, but he'd said it in a wry, almost playful way.

"It's dangerous to be a woman alone," she said, straightening her blouse. "In America as well as Russia."

"Pravda," he conceded.

He began to accompany her back to the hotel, leaving the kitchen worker still writhing on the ground.

"We didn't order the van," she said. "But you were here, watching."

Amused, he looked at her as if she were a lost tourist. "We always watch." He handed Mel her book, which she was startled to realize she'd almost left behind. His expression turned serious. "For our mutual protection, yes? Yours *and* mine."

They walked into the hotel lobby together, and as she stepped into the elevator, he gave her a subtle salute.

On impulse, Mel took the elevator to Julie's floor, hoping she would be in her room without company. She listened at the door, her heart still racing, ignoring the hall monitor making disapproving sounds at the apparent eavesdropping. Hearing no sounds from inside, she knocked tentatively. Julie opened the door, and Mel was relieved to see that she was alone, and fully dressed. And she could detect no lingering scent of Dan's cologne.

"Anton speaks perfect English," Mel said quietly.

Julie, noting the alarm in Mel's face, opened the door wider and invited her in. She had the same dresser and mirror that Mel had in her room, so they both went into the bathroom and turned on the shower. Mel told Julie about the *Bratva* bully in the park, and of Anton's subsequent rescue. Julie motioned for her to sit on the lip of the tub and offered her a drink.

Mel shook her head. "No, thanks, I had several with Ben in the bar."

"Have you told Dan yet?" Julie asked, perching next to Mel.

"Not yet. I guess I just needed—"

Julie held up a hand and gave her a sympathetic look. "You just needed another woman to talk to. I get it. If we were stateside, I'd make you some chicken soup, get you really drunk, and commiserate with you about what bastards most men are. You're lucky there are two of us on this assignment. I'd done several missions before being paired with another woman."

Julie stood up, filled a glass of water from the sink, and handed it to Mel. "Look, it's one thing to hear the disparaging comments and all the sexual innuendo, but it's another thing to have someone put their hands on you with violent intent."

Something darkened in Julie's expression. Her usual sarcastic demeanor was gone.

"It's happened to you," Mel said.

Julie ducked her chin and crossed her arms. "Several times." She shrugged, pushing her curls out of her face. "It can be part of the job. But, hey." She suddenly grinned. "At least you fought back. I'd love to have seen you put that jerk on the ground."

Mel blew out a breath. "I'm just glad Anton was there."

Julie gripped one of Mel's hands with both of her own. "I wish I could say it'll never happen again. But it will. And you'll handle it. You'll also get better at sorting out who the good guys are."

"Like Ben," Mel said. *And perhaps Alexi,* she thought.

Julie nodded. "Like Ben."

She walked with Mel out into the hallway and watched until the elevator doors opened. "Remember, don't look back," Julie called.

It was the fourth Moscow Rule: *Do not look back, you are never completely alone.*

After returning to her room, Mel lay on her bed, the events of the day swirling around in her head like startled birds. Beginning with the KGB, and ending with the Byelorussian Mafia, the day'd had an irregular cadence of fear and staggering boredom, thanks to listening to Minister Ivanov and Academician Shevchenko. She'd been warned that the *Bratva* had gotten bolder in Moscow, but the State Department still considered Minsk safe for Westerners. Things were unraveling quickly. She barked out a laugh. Ironic to think she'd been aided by a likely KGB agent.

But even more worrisome was Kavalchuk. He'd promised to interview her again soon. She probed the thought like she would have touched an aching tooth, gently and cautiously. The interview had not been overtly menacing. And the Pushkin poem that he had chosen for her to transcribe was an odd choice. It was romantic, titled "I still recall the wondrous moment (When you appeared before my sight)." It had been part of her literature studies in college. She would have thought Kavalchuk would have her scribble out something by Marx or Lenin, not a lament for lost love.

She would meet William at six tomorrow morning. The rest of the operation would be determined, and executed, by more experienced agents. She, at least, was doing her part. She tried to recapture the elation she'd felt after recognizing the Lion.

Mel had thought to nap before she took her bath. But sleep

wouldn't come. The image of Nadia arguing with the two overbearing men made her restless. And enraged.

Fueling the fire was the memory of the kitchen worker's hands.

Frustrated, she threw off the blanket and went into the bathroom, filled the tub with hot water, and began her processing ritual. No sooner had she committed all the new faces to her long-term memory than Nadia's face appeared again in stark relief, frozen into an expression of fear. Her image faded, and in its place appeared the German's face: pockmarked, puffy from drink, his mustache stiffened by too much grooming wax. He'd looked at Nadia as though he wanted to kill her.

The Svisloch Strangler. Could he be real? In Washington the Green River Killer was still at large. He'd spent years murdering young female runaways and sex workers, knowing their disappearances would go unnoticed. He too had murdered his victims by hand as well as using ligatures. Maybe Alexi had it wrong; a single man could do so much more harm than Soviet society was ready to accept. The Green River Killer remained so elusive that the detectives were consulting with Ted Bundy, collecting his insight into the mind of a serial killer.

In the US, victims were often alone, vulnerable, and disposable. Just like Nadia. Anger propelled Mel from the bath, and she dressed quickly, adrenaline evaporating her exhaustion, and headed for the Planeta Mir.

When Mel walked back into the bar, Nadia was still sitting at the far end, smoking and staring dejectedly into space. The large German had returned to his usual spot, where he sat with two companions, shot glasses and bottles of beer crowding the table. They were loud and very drunk.

She sat down next to Nadia. She'd set her face to stone, but Mel noticed that her eyes were veined and red.

"You okay?" she asked.

Nadia turned to her, exhaling smoke through her nose as her mouth twisted into a parody of a grin. "As you see."

Nadia's wrist was already beginning to bruise.

The barman approached, asking Mel if she wanted something to drink. She ordered two vodkas and, as soon as he walked away, said angrily, "Why didn't he defend you?"

Nadia tapped her cigarette against the ashtray. "You don't know how things are here in this place."

"Then explain it to me."

Licking her lips, Nadia leaned closer to Mel, her expression fierce. "We pay *him,*" she said, jabbing her finger at the barman, "to let us sit here. *They,*" pointing her finger at the Germans, "pay him too, to let us service them. They pay better, so they are treated better."

Mel looked at the men. "Do you think the big German is capable of violence?"

Nadia held up her injured wrist.

"No," Mel said. "I mean, do you think him capable of killing a woman. Strangling her?"

Craning her neck, Nadia studied the men for a moment. "Maybe. But it's not the *Sviloch Dushitel.* He's only been in Minsk a few months."

"Do you want to go somewhere else?" Mel asked. She thought of dinner, and all she had to tell Dan, but realized she didn't care anymore today. "Somewhere safer, maybe get something to eat?"

Nadia said something in Russian, her eyes filling with tears. The barman set the vodkas on the bar and walked away, shaking his head. They both downed their drinks in one go.

"Come on," Mel urged. "There's got to be somewhere safe

where we can spend a few hours talking. I want to understand." Mel squeezed Nadia's hand. "I want to help."

"You want to help." Nadia exhaled a bitter laugh. She collected her cigarettes and gold lighter and dropped them into her purse. "There's only one place in Minsk that is safe for women tonight. The *banya.* You want to go, we go. But I pay for everything, okay? First-time visits to *banya* are always paid by host."

"Okay," Mel said. "The thing is, I didn't bring a swimming suit—"

Nadia snorted. "You have your skin, yes? That's all you need."

She slipped off the stool, smoothing her hair and tugging down the hem of her short skirt. "First, I have phone call to make. Meet me out front in ten minutes."

Mel watched the men watching Nadia walk out, catcalling obscenely. One of the Germans pulled a pack of cigarettes out of his coat, which was made from heavy black leather and draped across the back of his chair. All three had the same one. The much-valued, expensive coat worn by the East German Stasi when they weren't in official uniform. And even though the Stasi had been dissolved earlier that year, the ex-members still wore the coats proudly as a badge of distinction. It was a coat that would cost half a year's salary for the officers wearing them.

Mel noticed that Nadia had left a cigarette still smoking in the ashtray. Signaling the barman, she ordered a whole bottle of vodka, paying for it with rubles. When he wasn't looking, she broke off the filter, which had been marked by Nadia's lipstick, leaving it in the ashtray. She then palmed the burning end in her left hand. Grabbing the bottle of vodka with her right hand, she walked up to the table, standing closest to the big German. She leaned over the table and slammed the bottle into the middle with a big smile. At first startled, the Germans laughed and cheered when they realized the crazy American woman had bought them an entire bottle.

While they were distracted, she pried open the big German's coat pocket with two fingers and dropped in the still-burning cigarette. She gestured for them to enjoy themselves, turned, and began walking out of the bar. Her last view of the boisterous table was of the men drinking, smoke curling from the German's coat.

17

MONDAY, AUGUST 6, 1990

Nadia picked Mel up in a little burnt-orange sedan fitted with mismatched tires and a cracked rear window. She rolled down the driver's-side window and waved.

Mel had left her purse at the front desk with a note for Dan that she wouldn't be joining the group for dinner, and not to worry, that she was going to the *banya* with a girlfriend. This, after all, was still within her directive. She'd placed her Maryland driver's license and some rubles in the pocket of her coat.

When she got into the car, Nadia arched one eyebrow, an unlit cigarette planted between her lips. She'd wiped off all traces of makeup and had changed into jeans and a T-shirt. "Mondays. *Idi na hui,* yes?"

"Absolutely," Mel answered.

The car immediately stalled. "Fucking Škoda," Nadia swore as she pumped the gas pedal. After a few moments, the engine caught, and the sedan leapt forward. As she drove, she jammed in the cigarette lighter and, when it glowed red, ignited her cigarette with a flourish.

"It's a piece-of-shit Czech car, but it belongs to my cousin Vladimir, and I get to borrow it whenever I want."

She turned up the volume on the radio and sang along to a pop song in Russian.

Nadia sighed. "Hopefully, I won't have to work at the Planeta much longer. I think I will soon have a patron. This guy, he's old and fat, but he's Swiss. And he's loaded."

"What does that mean exactly, a patron?"

"It means," Nadia said, flicking ash from her open window, "that I won't have to suffer under those *svoloch'* Germans no more. I'll have a new car maybe and a better apartment."

Within ten minutes they had reached the *banya,* a square concrete building only one story tall, with a sturdy metal door at the front. Nadia parked and pulled a small gym bag from the backseat.

"The country *banyas* are better, but this is one is clean," she said. "They will provide everything that you need."

Whatever Mel had envisioned, this squat, ugly building was not it.

They entered a small receiving room. An older woman in a wrinkled housedress sat behind a desk, reading a body-building magazine. The captions were all in Cyrillic, but the glistening, tanned male bodies spoke a universal language.

The woman handed over two large white bath towels, two pairs of rubber slippers, and two oversized felt hats without speaking a word. Nadia provided a few rubles, and the woman pressed a button, opening the internal door to the spa.

Nadia led Mel past a sitting area furnished sparsely with a few worn couches and chairs and into a pristine tiled shower room. All the shower stalls were open, with no curtains or doors for privacy.

"There are no locks on any of the lockers," Mel said.

Nadia made a face as she set down her bag and started removing her T-shirt and jeans. "There's nothing worth stealing." When Mel looked doubtful, she added, "Don't worry, your things will be safe here. Theft only happens in the decadent West, right?"

When she was completely naked, Nadia coiled her long blond hair on top of her head with a few deft moves, securing the bun with large hairpins pulled from her bag. She motioned for Mel to turn around and secured her hair too. There was something almost sisterly in the gentle way she smoothed Mel's hair away from her face.

Mel had gotten used to being one of the only females in the room during her training. And among the other female trainees there was often a stiff formality—because the competition to get plum assignments was keen, and because it was hard emotionally to make friends with women you might never see again. Mel was comfortable in the company of men, but she realized in that moment that, apart from Julie, she hadn't had a female friend in a long time.

Nadia seemed so different in this place, away from the Planeta Hotel. Her hard, cynical veneer had been replaced with a more playful vulnerability. She was beautiful, almost flawless as far as Mel could see. But there was no explicit eroticism in her nakedness. She was more like an ivory statue, to be contemplated by a museum-goer.

Nadia then moved into one of the shower stalls and turned on the water. She seemed completely at ease with her nudity, and Mel followed suit, stripping down and showering in the neighboring stall. Nadia wrapped herself in a bath towel, slipped her feet into the rubber slippers, and, taking both felt hats, motioned for Mel to follow her into the sauna.

The blast of heat was like being physically assaulted. Mel felt momentarily breathless when the door closed behind them. There were three rows of wooden benches and they sat on the lowest.

"The temperature here is about eighty degrees Celsius,"

Nadia said as she fitted one felt hat over her head and the second one on Mel.

Mel did a quick calculation and realized that in Fahrenheit, the temperature was about 170 degrees. Hot enough to slow-roast a chicken.

"The felt hat is to keep the brain from frying," Nadia said, smiling cheerfully at Mel's alarmed expression. "Don't worry. We will only be here less than ten minutes."

"We seem to be the only ones here," Mel said.

"Mondays and Wednesdays are only for the women," Nadia explained. "But Mondays, usually everyone is still recovering from the weekend. That's why this is the safest place in Minsk."

Nadia moved up another row, laying her towel down on the bench and stretching out on her back, like a cat relaxing in a beam of sunlight.

Mel lay back as well, thinking that if she passed out, at least she wouldn't hit her head. She had hoped their chatter would reveal more information about the Strangler, but she'd have to wait until the environment wasn't surface-of-the-sun hot. Just when she thought she couldn't take anymore, Nadia sat up and led her out into another tiled room with a large, water-filled pool.

They climbed a few steps to its lip.

"Don't think, just jump," Nadia said, pushing Mel in.

The water was ice-cold and Mel shrieked with the shock of it. Nadia had plunged in after her and came up for air, gasping and laughing.

They bobbed and shrieked some more, and Mel found herself giggling uncontrollably.

"Oh my God," she said, shaking with laughter. "You almost gave me a heart attack."

"No," Nadia said, splashing water into Mel's face. "It's good for the heart. Makes it strong and"—she paused, searching for the word in English—"*elastichnyy.* Like rubber band."

"Elastic," Mel translated, and instantly the word, the entire concept of a rubber heart, made her laugh even more. She felt light-headed and, for the moment, happy, and the two of them bounced in the frigid water until their teeth chattered and their fingers and toes started to prune and go numb.

"Come on, back into the sauna," Nadia said, rising like a dimpled Venus from the ice pool.

This time the heat felt exquisite to Mel, and she sat next to Nadia on the middle row of benches.

"We do this three times," Nadia said. "Hot and cold. *Then* comes the special Russian massage."

By the third plunge into the ice pool, Mel felt alert and energized in a way she hadn't in weeks. Her body felt toned and supple, and she could sense the blood thrumming through her arteries like water through a spring river.

Finally, Mel followed Nadia into another small room, with two benches perpendicular to each other. They lay on their towels, facedown, and soon two *banshchiks*—large, half-naked women the size of sumo wrestlers—came in, both carrying what looked to be tree branches laden with fragrant, dried leaves. They began to thrash the branches over Mel's and Nadia's backs with such vigor that the flesh on both the masseuses quivered and shook.

The sensation wasn't exactly unpleasant, but it was not the kind of massage Mel had been expecting. She'd been hoping for a long, relaxing Swedish-style rubdown that would put her to sleep.

Nadia once lifted her head and smiled mischievously. "Birch leaves to drive out all the poisons, yes?"

"Oh, definitely," Mel said, burying her head in her arms, hoping the birch branches would leave no permanent scars on her tender Irish flesh.

After what seemed like forever, the woman working on Mel stripped some of the leaves from the branches and began to rub them briskly over her skin, from her neck to the soles of her feet. She ground her knuckles into Mel's arches, karate-chopped Mel's calves, and finally kneaded the flesh of her back as though readying dough for the oven.

Cool water was then sluiced over her, washing away the birch leaves, and Mel was patted dry like a baby with a coarse towel. Then, as silently as they had arrived, the two bath attendants left. Mel got up from the table feeling hollowed out, both physically and mentally, every muscle relaxed into a jelly-like state. And she was ravenously hungry.

She followed her companion into the showers again and, after they were dressed, Nadia led her to a small café tucked into the back of the spa, where a cheerful-looking grandmother served them a multitude of small dishes of salty, pickled vegetables, slices of black bread, and two bowls of fragrant borscht, each topped off with a mountain of sour cream. She also placed on the table two glasses of tea. When Nadia asked for vodka, the old woman shook her finger, but soon reappeared with a small bottle and two shot glasses.

Nadia giggled. "It's usually the men who drink the vodka. The women are discouraged after the spa. Old wives' tales say it will make a woman infertile." She held up a glass filled with vodka in a toast. "Which is all the more reason to drink it, I think."

They toasted and began to eat. The soup was earthy, thick with bits of beet and onions, the bread dense and chewy. Mel groaned with pleasure.

Nadia smiled. "No matter what else turns to shit here in Minsk, you can always get good borscht."

Mel laughed and nodded. And noticed she now had the trifecta for mining information from a source: food, liquor, and a safe place to talk. But as they ate in silence, she realized that what she wanted to know was more about Nadia's personal life. "Where is your father now?"

"Lying under a Russian cross in a cemetery in a small village outside of Vitebsk."

"And your mother?"

"She's here, in Minsk. She lives with me. Or, I should say, I live with her." Nadia poured another round of vodkas. "When I get a new apartment, she'll move with me."

"You're close to your mother, then?"

Nadia's expression turned serious. "My mother sacrificed everything for me. For years she worked two jobs to make money to send me to study ballet. I auditioned for the Belarussian Bolshoi. I was accepted into the company." She downed her glass. "Two days before I was to start, I was hit by a car. I broke both my legs and spent many months in hospital. The driver of the car was so drunk he couldn't stand up."

Mel thought of the graceful way that Nadia moved, every limb in harmony. "I'm so sorry."

Nadia shrugged and poured more vodka into Mel's glass. "It could have been worse. At least I can walk without looking like a cripple."

Mel took a sip of her vodka and went to set the glass down on the table.

"No, no," Nadia said, putting her hand under it. "It's bad luck not to finish. We say 'to the bottom' and must drink it all."

Mel finished and then placed her hand over the glass. "No more," she said, gasping and laughing.

"You have boyfriend?" Nadia asked between bites of bread.

Mel shook her head. Nadia had asked the question casually but reflexively, turning attention away from herself. "Not for a long time."

"That's too bad." Nadia reached across the table and smoothed back a lock of hair that had fallen across Mel's forehead. "You could be really beautiful. Maybe with some makeup. Maybe different haircut."

Nadia had worn lots of makeup while working at the Planeta. But even now, sitting comfortably in an old T-shirt and jeans, her hair damp and tangled, her face scrubbed of all artifice, she could still stop traffic.

"No, you're the beautiful one," Mel said fervently. "You could be a model in Europe or America."

Nadia frowned into her glass. Her features had begun to harden again. She looked at Mel. "No. I'm too old now. Besides, it's all prostitution anyway. At least what I do is an honest exchange. No games. No bartering."

Mel thought of how vulnerable Nadia had looked sandwiched between the barman and the big German. Katya too had been a vital, lively woman. And yet she had been overpowered. "Aren't you ever afraid? Doing the work you do, I mean. It leaves you exposed to such men as the Strangler."

Nadia poured the last of the vodka into her glass. "The Strangler does not only target women like me. He made to disappear office workers, young students also. To be a woman in the world is to be born a victim, I think."

She slipped a folding knife out of her gym bag and showed it to Mel. "*Berezhonogo bog berezhot.* God keeps those safe who keep themselves safe."

"Are there rumors about who the Strangler could be?" Mel asked innocently, taking Nadia's knife and admiring its workmanship.

Nadia spread her hands out expressively. "Yes, of course. Every woman in Minsk has a husband or a boyfriend or a boss who it could be." It was close to what Alexi had said, but it was clear Nadia thought one man was the killer.

She frowned thoughtfully into her glass, and Mel asked, "What?"

Nadia looked to make sure the old woman was not within

earshot. "There are some rumors that this man is very high up. But no one knows for sure."

She said it dismissively, but Mel got the feeling that Nadia had an opinion about the matter. "But you have an idea of who it might be?"

"Perhaps. But my mother says to talk about the Devil is to invite him into your house."

Mel reached out and placed her hand over Nadia's. "Look, I'm not here very long, but if you learn anything concrete, you can come to me, and I'll do everything I can to help you."

"You know why I like you?" Nadia asked. "Because you don't make judgment on me. Do you know what Larysa did in Ukraine before she came here? She was electrical engineer. I have girlfriend who works at the Planeta Mir who was a doctor! But there is no possibility of finding such work now in Minsk. Everything is falling apart. If you don't work *pod stolom*, under the table, you can't get much money."

She studied Mel for a moment and shuddered involuntarily, as though throwing off thoughts of the Strangler. "What I want to do more than anything is travel. You are free to go anywhere. You've been to foreign places?"

Mel nodded, feeling loose-limbed and, more dangerously, loose-tongued. She would have to be careful. She had taken a gap year between college and beginning her training with the FBI. If asked, she'd have to remember to say that she'd begun working for Dan immediately after returning to the States.

"Following college," she said. "I took a year and traveled. I went to Rio de Janeiro with my mother. After that I went to India. I started in Bombay and backpacked north for months, almost to Kashmir."

Nadia's eyes widened. "And you did this alone?"

"I had no traveling companions, if that's what you mean. But I assure you, you're never alone in India."

Nadia leaned in, resting her chin on one palm. "Tell me one true thing about India."

Mel thought about her months wandering, often on foot, through villages, temples, and marketplaces, pressed in on all sides, and at all hours, by countless numbers of aimlessly moving people. She had always heard the expression a "sea of humanity," but it was the first time she had experienced such immense, seemingly limitless, crowds of men, women, and children—thousands, millions of them flowing together like a vast, impenetrable ocean. But she had absorbed each person she'd seen. She'd wondered if she would one day come to the end of her capabilities, like a water tower filled to overflowing. Or if, like the ever-expanding universe, her neuronal pathways would continue to retain an infinite number of faces.

Mel smiled, flooded with memories. "I think that some Westerners, in their arrogance, imagine that so vast a population will end up looking all the same. But I realized that everyone is unique. No two humans are alike. Their eyes, their noses, their ears, all different. Even identical twins have differences, if you know where to look."

"Okay, like snowflakes," Nadia said teasingly. "I get it. But were you never frightened, to be without any friends, I mean?"

Mel took her time scraping the last spoonful of borscht out of her bowl, unsure how to answer Nadia's question honestly. "You know, being a foreigner, I felt watched all the time. And sometimes crowds of kids would follow me. But it was merely for curiosity's sake. I never felt threatened by it."

One eyebrow rose, and Nadia's mouth twisted unpleasantly. "In Soviet Union we're watched all the time and it *definitely* feels like a threat. Even Stalin said, 'I don't trust anyone, not even myself.' Okay, so what was the most beautiful thing you saw in India?"

Mel turned over in her mind all the astounding places she could mention: the Taj Mahal, the tiger enclaves around

Jaipur, the immense Kailasa Temple cut from a rock cliff face. After a moment of reflection Mel said, "Prashar Lake in the north. It has a natural floating island that constantly changes its position, and a guardian temple built in the thirteenth century. No one has ever reached the bottom of the lake, and at night, if the clouds have cleared, the sky is white with stars. I took a small raft out onto the water and lay on my back and watched the stars for hours."

Nadia stared at Mel, her lips slightly parted in rapt attention. "I can only dream of visiting such places. I've never been farther away than Moscow to study ballet. It takes money to travel." For just an instant the edges of her mouth turned downward, her eyes glistening with sadness. But then she rallied, giving Mel a playful grin. "But my new prospect has money. Maybe he'll take me to Switzerland."

She held her glass aloft in another toast. "Here's to the true capitalists in Byelorussia."

Nadia downed her drink, threw some rubles on the table, and gestured for Mel to follow her out into the street again. The evening breeze felt cool compared to the swampy air of the spa. Nadia dropped her bag onto the sidewalk and, extending both arms in a sweeping arc in front of her body, executed a few effortless pirouettes, ending with a heart-stopping arabesque. She winced in pain and collapsed back to standing.

She bent down and slowly picked up her gym bag. "I could beg for a job at the Bolshoi as assistant to wardrobe mistress for a few miserable rubles a month, but then I would live and grow old in Minsk, which, believe me, is worse than dying in this city. Just ask my mother. She has no youth, no beauty left, which, other than money, is the most important currency in Minsk."

If Nadia had had the chance to travel, she would have discovered what Mel already knew. That it was the same all over the world. Youth and beauty could be used as a tool, or a weapon. But it could also make you a target.

They climbed into the Škoda, and, after a few stalls, the engine ran true and Nadia drove back to the Planeta, the windows down, the radio turned up high. This time, though, there was no singing. Nadia smoked her cigarette in thoughtful silence, her earlier cheerful mood muted. Mel knew she was partly to blame. Her probing questions about the Strangler had brought the specter of "the Devil" into the *banya*. She couldn't give Nadia her friendship, not fully. But perhaps there was something tangible she could give her to thank her for the evening. Among her things in the room she had a turquoise silk scarf that would go well with Nadia's blond hair and blue eyes. It wouldn't be life-changing, but it might bring Nadia a little joy.

Mel got out in front of the hotel and watched as the Škoda pulled away. One languid arm emerged from the driver's-side window and gave a royal wave goodbye.

Mel took a few deep breaths of the cooling air, relishing the lingering pleasant haze in her head. For a moment she thought about walking to the gazebo, forestalling the return to the stale, claustrophobic atmosphere of her room. The night sky was still pale and silvery above the pine trees, only blending to a deep indigo at the very top of the infinite dome over her head. She looked for stars, but there was still too much ambient light. Her mind touched for an instant on Alexi Yurov meeting her in the dark. She immediately brushed the thought of him away and turned to go into the hotel. If he'd come by the gazebo to check for her mark, he would have done so hours ago. It was too dangerous to stay outside in the shadows. And it was pointless to engage in wishful fantasies of a Byelorussian policeman.

18

MONDAY, AUGUST 6, 1990

The man watched the young American entering the hotel. He was close enough to follow, through the large plate glass window, her progress across the lobby and into the elevator. He'd been close enough to see that her skin was still flushed from the *banya,* and that tendrils of dampened hair floated temptingly loose around her neck. She hadn't noticed him standing motionless in the dark, so preoccupied was she by her own thoughts. He could have, after taking a mere twenty steps, placed a chloroform-soaked rag across her mouth and nose and stared into her frightened eyes until both lids closed and she sagged senseless into his arms. Imagining her vulnerability in such a moment aroused him in a way that he hadn't experienced in many months.

Since the night of William Cutler's party, when he'd initially been attracted to the black-haired *shlyukha,* he hadn't been able to get Melvina Donleavy out of his head. The way she moved through a crowded room, erect and stately, as though she were the only person inhabiting that space. The way her enormous dark eyes seemed to take in everything without giving away the thoughts behind them. The manner in which she spoke—cautiously, and yet concisely. As though each word out of her mouth were a fragile egg dropped carefully into boiling water. She was steel wrapped in velvet. The thoughts of her prolonged struggles against the rope, naked and helpless, were so overwhelming, so titillating, that he had to steady himself against his car. Next to Melvina, the other American woman was utterly forgettable.

When he had recovered, he got behind the wheel of his blue Lada and drove away. After a few miles he spotted the battered Škoda parked, or stalled, in front of what was once a school, now boarded up and abandoned. There were no street lamps and the burnt-orange car looked like so much industrial rust within the curtain of blackness. He parked behind the Škoda, killed the lights, and got out. Releasing the ropes from his belt in one practiced movement, he quietly approached the woman sitting in the driver's seat. Her car windows were open, and he could see the glow of a lit cigarette, its smoke curling into the night air.

She had called him earlier that evening from the Planeta Mir, telling him she would be going to the *banya* with Melvina, and arranged to meet him after in this place. So she would not be surprised to see him approaching. He had only to move in swiftly behind the driver's seat, slip the noose over her head, and pull until she passed out. It would be so easy. But he hadn't come for that. At least, not yet. He had something else in mind. He climbed into the front passenger seat, hooking the slender ropes back into his belt and out of sight.

"You're late," she said, flicking the stub of her cigarette out of the window.

She was irritated, but he could tell she was also nervous because she immediately lit another.

He sat quietly for a moment, relishing her discomfort. "Well?"

"Where's my money?" she asked without looking at him.

"In good time. Tell me everything."

So she told him about the evening at the spa. What Melvina had told her, about not having a boyfriend, traveling for a year, her initial shyness.

"She's like a virgin nun," Nadia said. "Shy about her own nakedness."

"That's because she's not a whore," he said. "She trusts you?"

"Oh, sure." Nadia's mouth twisted into a cynical smile. "I'm like a big sister to her now."

She handed him the driver's license that she had lifted from Melvina's coat pocket.

He tucked it into his own pocket. "Good, Nadia Ivanovna. That's good."

She finally turned her head toward him and held out her hand. "I did what you asked me to do. To keep an eye on the American. Now you can pay me."

He pulled a wad of rubles out of his wallet and placed it in her hand. As soon as her fist closed over the money, his other hand shot out and closed hard around her injured wrist. She winced in pain, but his grip only hardened. "There's a month's worth of fucks in that pile. I expect you to remain on good terms with the girl."

Nadia pulled her hand painfully from his grasp and shoved the bills into her gym bag. "What about the Swiss businessman you told me you'd introduce me to?"

"Soon," he answered. "Soon."

"What now?"

"I'll let you know." He opened the door, preparing to step out.

Nadia tossed the second cigarette out of the car. "What do you want with her? She's not going to fuck you."

He turned to her and smiled, and for the second time in her life—the first time being when, for a split second, she saw the car that would crush her to the pavement—Nadia caught a glimpse of approaching disaster and found herself unable to move out of its path.

"I don't need to fuck her," he said softly. "That's what you're for."

He got back into his Lada and drove away. He could hear the old Škoda starting and stalling and Nadia's frantic swearing, and, despite the now-constant burning discomfort in his gut, he breathed an immense sigh of contentment.

19

TUESDAY, AUGUST 7, 1990

Gorky once observed that the Russians were especially good at cruelty," William mused. "It's a 'peculiar, cold-blooded cruelty,'" he quoted, "'which tests the limits of human endurance for suffering.' And he would know, as he was exiled from Russia, not once but twice, for proclaiming that Lenin and Trotsky had both been 'poisoned with the filthy venom of power.' Fortunately for him, he died before he experienced the sum total of Stalin's insanity."

He and Mel were sitting on their usual bench in Victory Park, as yet the only visitors except for a few park attendants sweeping the walkways. It was still early morning, and William had brought a thermos full of strong tea and several large *vatrushki,* pastries filled with sweetened cream cheese and fruit.

As planned, William had picked her up in front of the hotel at six and had driven them to this secluded place, where they could see anyone approaching from some distance away.

William turned to her. "So, you're sure you saw one of your targets?"

"Yes," Mel said.

"His code name?"

"The Lion."

"Where did you spot him?"

"He was in the backseat of a car approaching the institute as we were leaving."

William's brow wrinkled in concern. "So you only caught a glimpse of him."

She saw the doubt in his eyes. A lot of Agency wheels would be set in motion on her say-so. It was natural to feel some doubt, after only the briefest glimpse. But for Mel, it was enough.

William finally nodded and looked toward the river. "Remarkable that the same country that gave us some of the most sublime music and poetry in the world will also kill their own people *in the millions* just to stay ahead of the West. The fact that they'd willingly try to develop a nuclear program so soon after Chernobyl is astonishing, but not surprising."

"'A single death is a tragedy, a million deaths is a statistic,'" Mel quoted.

William gave a bitter laugh. "Good old Stalin. The question is what to do now that you've seen your target."

"How soon will you be able to get the information stateside?"

"Tonight. Tomorrow if tonight's not safe."

"Do you trust the messenger?"

"With my life."

"Can you tell me who it is?" If Mel had been forced to guess, she would have named Alexi Yurov as the most likely candidate.

"For your own safety, and for theirs, I can't." William offered her another pastry, which Mel declined. "And speaking of your safety—"

His voice trailed away, and he looked at her, concern wrinkling his brow. "There are some troubling developments with our friend Martin Kavalchuk. His secretary called to tell me we'll have to suspend our Friday-night chess games, indefinitely."

"What does that mean?"

"It means he's distancing himself from those whom he suspects of being *vrag naroda,* enemies of the state. Or in close communication with those who are suspected. He's wrapping himself more tightly in his official role as chair of the State Security Committee."

The memory of the interview room and its single drain reared its ugly head. "Is this to do with me?"

William dropped his chin and regarded her over his glasses. "Perhaps. The problem is that this may dampen my flow of information. If Kavalchuk is pulling away, it means he'll be scrutinizing everyone much more vigilantly. I would suggest that from now on you stay close to the group whenever you're out of your room."

Mel thought of the time spent at the spa with Nadia, and the few hours of relative freedom she'd experienced. Last night she'd slept better than she had since arriving in Minsk. A deep, satisfying sleep with no dreams. She genuinely liked Nadia and thought that if she could spend more time with her, she could glean more clues about the Strangler. But she saw the wisdom in forgoing any more unofficial excursions.

"Kavalchuk said he'd be interviewing me again. Should I be worried?"

William glanced around casually, as though appreciating the scenic beauty of the park. "Melvina, does anyone in your team know the true nature of your mission?"

"Ben intuits something, and he's asked without actually probing, but I've revealed nothing to him. That goes for Dan and Julie as well. So if there are any leaks, it's not coming from the American side." She took a cautious look around too. "I got a peek inside the room next to my own. They're videoing me. With a Zenit."

William nodded, impressed. "Anything worrisome they could have captured?"

"Besides the *dejournaya* rifling through my things? No."

Standing up and brushing pastry crumbs from his pants, William held out a hand to Mel. "Let's make sure we keep it that way. No late-night confessions, no more excursions. It's too dangerous now. The best way to keep the wolves at bay is to stay well within the flock. I'll let Dan know about the cameras."

He helped her up and they walked together back to his car. When they were seated inside, he said, "As long as we have something the Byelorussians need, in this case American dollars, we have leverage. If you're called in again for another interview, stay calm, stay focused, and, most of all, stay boring. Remember, you're just a secretary."

He dropped her off at the hotel, promising to let her know when his message reached the State Department.

It was only seven when she entered the lobby of the Planeta, and she was surprised to see Dan seated in one of the oversized chairs. He stood immediately and, taking her arm, led her back outside. He looked angry, his face flushed, his eyes narrowed to two slits.

Once they were across the street in the small park, he turned on her. "I want you to tell me what's going on."

She took a step back. "What do you mean?"

"What I mean is I want you to tell me why you left the hotel last night, by yourself, with a known prostitute, and then disappeared this morning with William without clearing it with me first."

Keeping her expression neutral, she asked, "Are you more upset that I'm developing a source without getting your permission, or because that potential source is a sex worker?"

"Both."

What she wanted to tell Dan was that her discussions with

William had nothing to do with him, that she didn't answer to him even though he was ostensibly the team's leader. And that his holier-than-thou attitude was offensive, and hypocritical. It would feel so satisfying to finally put him in his place, but antagonizing him would not make her job any easier. And, as William had warned, her safety depended on remaining solidly within the group.

"It won't happen again," she said, hoping to end the conversation. "I'll check with you first next time."

"The rumor with our Byelorussian friends is that you're having an affair with William, which I know is crap. What's really going on?"

"You're right, it is crap. William knows I'll be interrogated again by Kavalchuk, and he's preparing me."

He studied her for a moment. As good as she was at maintaining a mask of innocence, he was more experienced at reading people. "Bullshit. There's more to it."

She took a steadying breath. She could see he wasn't going to let this go. "Dan, you need to talk to clandestine operations stateside. Contact the deputy director. He can answer these questions for you."

He looked at her, incredulous. "The hell I do." He started walking away, but then stopped, turned around, and walked back.

"I sure as shit know who *I* am," he whispered forcefully. "Ben consistently has one of the highest scores on a shooting range, which makes him invaluable in a hot zone. Julie speaks several languages and is a black belt in jiujitsu. Both of them are field-tested agents. But who the fuck are you? I mean really, who are you? Why are you here? I don't get it. You don't serve any purpose, or have any special talents, that I can see, other than scribbling notes. And yet you've already been called in for an interview by the head of the KGB."

Mel looked at him for a long moment. Dan was a veteran

of some of the most dangerous missions, and she could easily see how he intimidated people. He was older and more experienced than she was, taller and physically stronger. And yet, despite his aggressive stance, he looked unnerved, as though the questions about her "otherness" had been eating at him for some time. Her entire life, Mel had seen the same disquieted look on people's faces. The same guarded expression, as if they were gazing at an expanding glow on the horizon and wondering if it was an approaching forest fire.

"What's your security clearance?" he demanded. He'd turned defensively, his body in profile as he would have done if someone had been pointing a gun at him.

She took a deep breath and met his gaze steadily. Her refusal to be cowed seemed to be aggravating him further, and for a moment it gave her a perverse satisfaction. "You'll need to ask the deputy director about that."

Brushing calmly past him, she walked back into the hotel. If he'd been a thermal-triggered IED, he would have detonated.

Once she was in her room, Mel sat in the reading chair, her back to the mirror, trying to order her thoughts. Growing questions could be expected. But the depth of Dan's ire and distrust did not bode well. She expected that the station chief would inform Dan that Melvina Donleavy's role, and the subsequent intelligence that she gathered while in Byelorussia, were on a strictly need-to-know basis. Two things had been revealed to Mel too about Dan's character: he had a temper and a sizeable ego. Whatever the Agency decided to reveal to, or withhold from, Dan, she wasn't certain that the knowledge would assuage either.

Her earlier sense of well-being had evaporated, and she felt a pang of sadness at suddenly having to distance herself from Nadia. She'd offered the woman help, and now it would be difficult, if not impossible, to deliver it. This was a part of the job, though. Making people believe you were their friend.

A literary quote flitted across her consciousness. Something about how a person living a solitary life, outside of normal social constructs, would have to be one of three things: a god, a monster, or a philosopher. Hard as she tried, she couldn't remember where she'd read it.

Perhaps she was a fourth thing—a yet-unnamed thing.

At eight thirty Julie rang the room, telling Mel that she'd missed her at breakfast and that the team was meeting in the lobby to go to the institute.

Everyone, including Anton and Elena, was quiet on the drive. Dan's silence had an edge of hostility, and a few times he stared hard at Mel, as though trying to decipher a code. William, as he'd been the day before, was already in Oleg Shevchenko's office. Dan's greeting to both men was curt, and barely civil.

The academician, on the other hand, seemed to have warmed to his visitors and had sweet rolls and tea brought in. He presented to both Mel and Julie small but expertly painted *matryoshki,* or nesting dolls.

"Is tradition to give for ladies visiting Minsk," he explained in his barely intelligible English.

Dan seemed almost disappointed when Shevchenko agreed without hesitation to a tour of the high-end optics polishing labs, as though Dan had been looking for a fight. Some of the lab's lenses had reportedly been used for top secret laser guidance systems for the Soviet military, and Dan was eager to see what was still in development. Ben held his briefcase strategically to take photos of the labs.

The Americans stood behind several large, hermetically sealed windows, watching as technicians wearing full suits, masks, and booties ran equipment and made notes. Several times Mel caught Dan looking from her to William and back again.

As they viewed the lab, Shevchenko began another long-winded lecture. Julie translated, putting an exaggerated emphasis on every word he stressed, so that she sounded, at times, like an announcer for a political ad. Once, she caught Mel's eye and grimaced.

"What you are seeing in this lab is history-making. Our Byelorussian scientists have been the *first* to successfully develop magnetorheological finishing techniques for precision optics. The surfaces will eventually be polished by a *computer-controlled* finishing slurry. Unlike conventional rigid materials, the MR fluid's shape and stiffness then can be *magnetically manipulated...*"

The day unspooled in a blindingly tedious way, with only a brief respite for lunch.

As they walked into a private room, Julie turned to Mel and muttered, "Do you love me?"

"Of course," Mel answered, giving her a puzzled look.

"Good," Julie rasped, making a comic face. "Then kill me now before the next lecture. I thought Oleg was actually going to kiss our hands when he gave us the dolls. Honestly, I think I prefer the old, grumpy version."

Julie sat next to Shevchenko to translate during the meal, and William guided Mel to the far end of the table so they could speak quietly.

A dull, persistent headache from exhaustion and stress had started behind Mel's forehead and she rifled through her purse looking for the small bottle of aspirin she traveled with. Moving aside her wallet, she noticed that her driver's license, usually nestled in a clear pocket, was missing. She remembered that she'd placed it in the pocket of her jacket, the same one she was wearing now. But the license was not there. Maybe it had fallen out at the *banya*? She'd have to ask Nadia.

"What's the matter?" William asked.

"I think my driver's license is missing."

William pursed his lips. "We'll ask around. I wouldn't worry too much about it. It's not like a missing passport." He took a few sips of his tea, gazing at the group over the rim of the cup. "Dan seems a little tense," he observed. "More so than usual."

Mel told him about their confrontation earlier. "I think he's going to be contacting clandestine operations in the States. That will be going through you, of course. He doesn't like that you and I are, without his knowledge, meeting apart from the team."

William patted her on the arm. *"La parfaite valeur—"* he began, and then broke off. "Do you understand French?"

Mel shook her head. "I had one year of it in high school."

"I'll translate La Rochefoucauld's phrase into English then. 'True valor is to do in secrecy what you could just have easily done in front of others.' Hang in there, Melvina." He looked at Dan thoughtfully. "And don't worry about him. I'll handle it."

By the end of the week, the group had been paraded before all the optical, chemical, and microtechnology labs. Ben had been buried under mounds of accounting reports, all in Russian, which had to first be painstakingly translated by Julie. Often, they worked late into the night.

Every evening before dinner, the four colleagues went into the Planeta Mir for a drink, waving performatively at their German counterparts. By Friday, the team was bone-weary and short on patience. They sat at the bar staring into their glasses. Dan's cold-shoulder treatment had continued with Mel all week, but he seemed too weary to summon outright hostility by now. Especially as Mel refused to rise to the bait.

She'd swallowed her retorts, gritted her teeth, and maintained a smooth, placid front each day.

What was really bothering Mel was that Nadia hadn't been in the Planeta Mir for several days. Mel's thoughts turned to the Strangler, and to a million other mishaps that could befall a beautiful woman in a high-risk profession. Larysa was also conspicuously absent.

As a child, Mel had once gone to the Gulf of Mexico with her mother for vacation. The beach was painfully rocky, the temperature blistering, and the water murky, with treacherous riptides. It had been the middle of August, the height of jellyfish season. Her mother had slathered her with sunscreen and then told her to go and have a good time. Mel had stood at the edge of the tide, sharp pebbles boring into the soles of her feet, the sun baking her like a tender sponge cake. She'd wanted desperately to cool off in the water, but she could see the colonies of jellyfish floating on the waves.

Thinking she'd be safe if she just stayed away from their gelatinous bodies, she waded in. She didn't realize that their tentacles could reach six feet in length. She spent the next two days with a fever, covered in painful welts. All she'd wanted was a cool dip in the water, and it seemed unfair that there were so many treacherous barriers. Now the memory was an apt metaphor for being a woman in Minsk. There were dangers you could see, but many more that were hidden until they wrapped their tentacles around you.

Grimacing, Ben tapped Mel's arm and begged for a few aspirin for his own headache. She gave him the tablets and then stood up, rubbing his shoulders until he groaned with exaggerated pleasure.

"Jesus, Ben," Julie said. "You are *such* a cheap date."

"Yeah, well," he said, "you take joy in Minsk where you can find it."

Mel gently slapped his shoulder and said, "Just don't get used to it."

The band had begun setting up for the evening, the drummer testing out his kit with careless abandon. Fishing a few rubles out of her purse, Julie hopped off her stool and walked to the stage. After a short conversation with the band members, she walked back to the group, her expression a studied blank.

Counting down from four in English, the musicians—drummer, guitar player, bass, electric keyboard, and accordion—crashed into a song that sounded vaguely familiar.

Dan frowned. "What is that?"

The lead vocalist began singing in mangled English.

"You've not lived," Julie said loudly over the electric instruments, "until you've heard a Tina Turner song butchered in Russian."

Ben laughed, almost falling off his stool. He sang along with the band, "*Rollin', rollin' on the river...*"

Dan made a face and rose, saying, "This is where I draw the line. I'd rather be in the desert being shot at."

As he walked out of the bar, Mel caught sight of the big German standing next to the entrance, his right coat pocket prominently scorched. He was looking at the band, but his gaze shifted and settled on her face. It was a look she remembered from the mug shots of killers, slack-jawed, humorless, eyes brimming with malice and full of suspicion. Another jellyfish with tentacles reaching who knew how far.

Ten minutes later, the German was joined by several of his comrades, and they took a table at the far side of the room. Mel excused herself and slipped out to retrieve her book from her room. Within five minutes she'd left the hotel and made her way through the small park.

Since spotting Ahmadi at the institute, Mel had not seen any of the other targeted Iranian scientists. William had pointed out that all the institute tours for the Americans had been as far away from the locked and guarded Department of Thermophysics as possible. But she knew to keep up the afternoon routine, even if she only stayed for twenty minutes or so.

She was almost finished with *Vanities*. Tomorrow William would be having his usual Saturday-night gathering at his apartment, and she would have to remember to ask to borrow another book. She hoped she could find one in English that was not a scientific journal, or a philosophical tome by a long-dead aristocrat like La Rochefoucauld.

The late afternoons had begun to turn cooler. Even though it was still August, the chill of autumn would be in full bloom in another month. As she approached the gazebo, she was disappointed to see that someone was already sitting under the domed canopy. It was a woman, with long blond hair, her head lowered to her chest in contemplation, or in sleep.

Mel stood on the bottom step and asked, "Nadia?"

The woman raised her eyes, which were bloodshot and unfocused, her hair wild as if it hadn't been combed in a while.

"Melvina! I've been waiting for you."

Nadia's voice was slurred and, as Mel approached, she could smell the alcohol rolling off her body. "You haven't been at the Planeta. I was worried about you."

Nadia held out both hands and pulled Mel down next to her. "My mother has been sick."

"How did you know where to find me?"

"Ask *anyone* in the hotel. They know where you are always." She dug in her purse and held up two pieces of flimsy, brightly colored paper printed in Cyrillic. "Look, I have tickets for the ballet tomorrow night. It's the last performance of the summer." She stroked Mel's face tenderly. "It's my favorite. *Giselle*. Come with me."

Nadia's grasp on her hands was almost painful, but Mel resisted pulling away.

"You know the story of *Giselle*?" Nadia asked. "It's wonderful. Very romantic, very tragic. The heroine has a bad heart. When she discovers that her lover, Albrecht, has been untrue to her, Giselle dies of a broken heart." She leaned in for dramatic emphasis. *"She dances herself to death."*

She exhaled a ragged, almost hysterical laugh, tears pooling at the corner of one eye. "That's what I'm doing, you see?"

Mel freed one hand, placing it over one of Nadia's. "I can't go. Tomorrow night I have something with my team. I'm really sorry."

Nadia pulled both of her hands away, smoothing them through her hair. She turned her face away, her expression bitter. She took the tickets and threw them in the air. They fluttered briefly and then fell limply to the ground.

The look of misery on Nadia's face twisted like a knife in Mel's chest. But she thought of her colleagues, and her mission, and what she had to do.

Mel leaned down and picked up the tickets, placing them on the seat next to Nadia. "I'm so sorry. Believe me, if things were different, I'd love to go with you. But I still have a job to do here."

Nadia's head whipped around, the wounded look giving way to something desperate. "You told me that if I had any suspicions of who the *Svisloch Dushitel* was I should come to you."

Mel felt a shudder of anticipation. "You have an idea?"

Nadia's gaze wandered over Mel's shoulder, and she startled as though catching sight of something alarming.

Mel turned around, seeing nothing out of the ordinary. But the panic in Nadia's eyes put her on alert.

"I think I've done something bad," Nadia whispered.

"What's wrong? Is there something I can do to help?"

Tears welled in both Nadia's eyes, and she moved closer to Mel, resting her head on Mel's shoulder. The gesture seemed almost childlike, spontaneous and poignant.

"I understand," Nadia whispered. "You will leave, I will stay." After a pause, when Mel was almost certain she'd nodded off, Nadia sat up abruptly and grabbed on to the bench to steady herself. "In the ballet, Giselle dies while the unfaithful lover lives." She smiled crookedly. "Just like in life."

"I have a friend. Someone in the *militsiya*. Maybe you could talk to him about your suspicions—"

Nadia placed a hand over Mel's mouth. "No. There are no friends in the *militsiya*. Please, if you want to help me, you don't talk to nobody. Promise me."

Mel nodded reluctantly. "Okay." Then, remembering the turquoise scarf, she stood. "Wait here. I have something to give you."

She rushed into the hotel and up to her room. Retrieving the scarf took less than ten minutes, but by the time she'd returned to the gazebo, Nadia had gone, leaving the two Bolshoi tickets on the bench.

20

SATURDAY, AUGUST 11, 1990

Unlike on the previous Saturday, William debriefed Dan, Ben, and Julie immediately and all at once. Mel waited alone in the living room for almost half an hour. She examined the two bookshelves at the far end and found that they were filled mostly with books on the hard sciences. She discovered that several of them had been authored by William, one of them titled *Heat and Mass Transfer in Nuclear Reactor Accidents*. She pulled the book from the shelf and opened it. Inside the front cover was a scrap of paper and on it was a handwritten note: *Happiness is beyond the mountains, but grief is just over the shoulder, so says author Svetlana Alexievich—she is not wrong*. William's book was dedicated to Alexievich, and she made a mental note to ask him about her.

She returned the book to its place and continued her exploration of the bookshelves. There were two award plaques from the American Society of Mechanical Engineers, and photos of William with a few well-known scientists, as well as one with noted author Isaac Asimov.

There were no family photographs, though. No pictures of children or of a woman who could be anything other than a colleague. Nothing to show that William had any roots. There was only one faded image, an old-fashioned studio portrait, of a blond boy about twelve years of age standing before an unsmiling couple. They looked stout and weather-beaten, as though they'd spent their life working on a farm.

It was almost six thirty by the time William reappeared. He crooked a finger at her to follow him back into the kitchen. Her colleagues were huddled around the sink, the water still gushing through the pipes. Dan's face was flushed and pinched, and Ben looked expectantly at Mel as though peering at an oracle who hadn't yet made her pronouncements. Julie caught Mel's eye once and gave her an enigmatic smile.

"Melvina," William said, "Dan has something to tell you."

Dan cleared his throat and pushed a lock of hair off his forehead. He stooped down and put his mouth close to her ear. "I just read a note that was delivered to William from the deputy director of clandestine operations, dictated by Director of Central Intelligence Webb himself. It said, and I quote, 'Agent Donleavy's mission supersedes all others while in Byelorussia.' It went on to say that we are to give all possible aid to you, and to not in any way impede, inhibit, or obstruct your assigned task. And lastly, we are not to ask you what that mission is."

He stared down at his hands for a moment, and when he raised his head again, he was grimacing the way a person will when they've decided to be a good sport about an uncomfortable joke played on them. "I need to apologize. I hadn't a clue." He paused. "William told us about the spy room. That was a bold move, Mel. But it provided some important information for the team."

Mel could feel everyone's eyes on her, waiting. What she wanted to say was that she *had* told him to back off. He just didn't want to hear it from her.

"Apology accepted," she said, warming up her smile. "We are working together toward the same end, are we not?" He nodded unconvincingly, and she sensed that, at heart, he was still agitated. "Is there something else you want to say?"

His eyes narrowed. "That was a hell of a risk you took, getting past the *dejournaya*—"

The front door buzzer sounded.

William looked at his watch, clearly relieved by the interruption. "Ah, that will be Sveta. Punctual as ever." He turned to Mel. "We didn't get to have our debrief. I'll pick you up tomorrow morning at nine?"

Without waiting for an answer, he grabbed the paper bag out of the garbage can and carried it to the hallway.

The four of them filed out of the kitchen and into the living room. Out of the corner of her eye, Mel studied the new outfit that Julie was wearing: a formfitting sleeveless silk dress with a matching bolero jacket. It was the kind of dress that looked spectacular on a full-figured woman like Julie. Mel thought, wistfully, that on her slender figure the dress would make her look disappointingly formless—like a fence post with hair.

Julie followed closely behind Mel, her high heels striking the floor provocatively. Grinning gleefully, she tapped Mel on the arm to hold her back. "Good job, partner. Not only did Dan get a spanking by the principal," she whispered, "but by the whole fucking board of education. I don't know about you, but I, for one, really enjoyed it. In fact, I could go for a cigarette right about now."

Mel swallowed a laugh, feeling vindicated. But she was also aware that it wouldn't ingratiate her with Dan if she made an outward show of it.

Soon after Sveta arrived, other guests began filing noisily through the front door, which William left propped open. The Alpha officer who had searched the apartment last week did not appear, which reassured everyone that Martin Kavalchuk would not be attending. It meant that the guests could fully relax. And even though Mel was relieved, she wasn't surprised;

his promise to see her again surely implied something more than a social encounter.

Oleg Shevchenko and Sergei Ivanov arrived together. Oleg made it a point to greet the Americans in his stunted English, while Ivanov merely gave an awkward little bow and retreated to the far side of the room.

"William was right," Ben said to Mel after Oleg had made his way briskly to the drinks table. "Looks like Oleg's warmed up to us."

"Or to our money," Julie added, returning with her own drink.

Soon the apartment was full of people, most of them now familiar, eating and drinking. Mel worked her way over to the piano and stood listening to William as he played a medley of Broadway show tunes. A bright flash of scarlet caught her eye, and when she looked up, Alexi Yurov was walking toward her. He was in full uniform, carrying a small suitcase.

Watching him move—his vitality, his natural grace, the sharp angles of his face—she felt dizzy, cut off from common sense. For all the times she'd pushed thoughts of him away, her mind a drill sergeant keeping unruly physical responses at bay, in that moment she felt powerless. She struggled to keep the muscles in her face under control.

"Alexi Ilich!" William cried, and stood up to embrace the young officer, kissing him on both cheeks. Alexi hugged William tightly as he might have done with a member of his own family.

"Melvina," William said, turning to her. "Alexi is a regular at my parties, and soon you'll know why. Will you make sure he gets plenty of food and drink? We want to make sure he's well energized for his *prisyadka* dancing."

"I didn't know you danced," Mel said, struggling to keep her voice casual.

Alexi laughed. "It's a tradition in the *militsiya,* as well as the Soviet army. It's a way to entertain ourselves."

"And show off," William said, grinning. "Go get some food and we'll clear the floor."

Alexi followed Mel into the dining room, which had emptied out as most of the guests had already filled their plates several times. He set his military hat on a sideboard and loosened his collar. Mel's own fingers tugged restlessly at her plain cotton shirt. Julie and the rest of the women were dressed in their party clothes, and she wondered how drab she must appear in her wrinkled slacks and flat shoes.

She handed him a plate. "I didn't know you'd be here."

"Are you disappointed?" he asked casually, his expression neutral. He started moving around the table, deftly spooning food onto his plate.

When she didn't answer right away, he looked up expectantly.

"Of course not," she said. "I'm…happy to see you."

The corners of his lips twitched as though she'd said something amusing. "And I'm happy to see you." He studied the breadbasket and carefully placed a seeded roll on top of his growing pyramid of food. "Have you been well?" he asked, returning to where she stood, her back to the table, both palms planted at her sides.

"Yes. And you?"

"Oh, I'm very well, thank you." He stood facing her, close enough for her to feel his breath on her face. She forced herself to meet his gaze. He slowly extended one arm and she thought for a moment that he was going to embrace her. But instead, he reached around her, picking up a bottle of vodka. He stared at her, unblinking. "Shall we talk about the weather now? This is what Americans call polite conversation, am I correct?"

"What would you rather talk about?"

"*Stakan dlya vodki,*" he said, laughing. When she looked at him, confused, he translated, "A glass for vodka."

In that moment, Sveta stuck her head in and called for Alexi in Russian. He nodded to Mel and walked back into the living room.

Mel stood for several minutes, leaning against the table, her pulse thundering in her ears. All her best intentions to stay clear-headed fell like burning bits of paper onto the rug beneath her feet. She closed her eyes and counted to a hundred before she rejoined the others.

When she walked into the living room, all the male guests had removed their jackets and were busily pushing furniture against the walls and rolling up all the rugs. Alexi had removed his policeman's coat and had changed into a traditional Russian-style peasant shirt, belted at the waist. He'd also put on a pair of soft leather Cossack boots. When he took the center of the floor, the guests moved away, forming a circle around him. William began to play a quick-tempo Russian folk song on the piano. Urged on by Alexi, the guests began to clap, and he held his arms out to them, palms up, as he circled the space. He waggled his fingers teasingly, inviting some of the women to move in closer.

Julie had removed her little jacket, and more than one man in the crowd looked at her with hungry eyes. She caught Mel's gaze and winked, fully aware of her effect on the men.

Mel had watched Russian dancing in newsreels and films, but she hadn't yet seen it live. The performances, typically by a group of classically trained male dancers, had seemed refined and well practiced. But here, the energy was raw, almost primal. The crowd began to shout out encouragement, the women's shrill catcalling in counterpoint to the men's bass voices. Both Dan and Ben had moved to the front of the crowd and were laughing and clapping along with everyone else.

Alexi started with simple moves, heel and toe, sidestepping in repeated patterns to the music. Oleg Shevchenko placed two fingers in his mouth and whistled sharply in tempo, making everyone laugh. His face had turned red and was slicked with sweat, and his clapping gained an unsettling fervor.

Some of the women sang along with the melody, and the pace of Alexi's dancing increased. He dropped to the floor, executing the recognizable Russian *prisyadka*—knees bent in a squat, torso upright and rigid, arms crossed over his chest, legs extended alternately out in front in rapid kicking motions. He leapt up, thrusting both legs out into a Russian split, hands touching his feet, and then down again into a squat. His face was rapturous. There was no sign that his movements were anything other than effortless.

Alexi began to spin in a kind of pirouette, one leg extended, arms flung outward, and the crowd began to count in Russian the number of turns. At fifty, Alexi came to an abrupt standstill, hands on his hips, his chest pumping deeply in labored breaths. The show had ended. His crowd rushed forward, the first to embrace him in a theatrical bear hug Oleg Shevchenko. He was then enveloped by inebriated men and women, cheering and laughing. Someone pushed a glass of vodka into Alexi's hand, and everyone toasted him.

Mel hung back, watching the crowd breaking off into smaller groups to continue drinking and talking. Julie and Dan sat together, looking relaxed and comfortable, while Ben talked to the female scientist from the institute. William resumed his glad-handing and refilling glasses to overflowing with vodka. Being an observer was familiar territory. But tonight, watching Alexi mixing joyfully with the guests—the men still clapping him on the back and the women flirting outrageously—Mel felt her aloneness more keenly than ever.

She worked her way around the edges of the room, catching bits of conversation, some in English, some in Russian, until she lost sight of Alexi. Finally, she was close enough to William to ask him if he had any novels she could borrow. She had to almost yell into his ear, the noise in the room was so loud. He nodded and pointed toward the back hallway.

"In my bedroom," he shouted. "Take whatever you want."

As she walked away, she saw Minister Ivanov crossing the room as well. Behind his black-framed glasses, his eyes were locked onto her. His complexion looked waxy, and, like most of the other men, he was unsteady on his feet from too much vodka. There was a frightening eagerness to his expression, as though he were a starving man and she a full banquet.

Mel moved quickly, hoping to duck into the bedroom and close the door behind her. Whatever he wanted, she didn't feel up for the game right now. The back hallway was dark, with no overhead lights, but she could see that at the end there was an open doorway. As she got closer, she glimpsed the wooden footboard of a bed. She ducked into the room just as Ivanov appeared at the end of the hall. She closed the door, feeling for a lock, and listened as his footfalls stopped and, after a moment, retreated toward the party again.

She rested her ear against the door, letting her heart rate settle, until there was a noise behind her. Mel wheeled around, only to see Alexi perched on a chair watching her.

"Oh my God," she said. "You scared me. I didn't know anyone was back here."

He stood up and faced her. He was shirtless, his trousers unbuttoned and draped low over his hips. The light from the one low-wattage lamp reflected sharply off the sweat on his chest. "I came here to change."

She gestured weakly toward the door. "I was trying to avoid someone—"

He sauntered to where she was standing, eased open the

door, and peeked outside. He closed it again. Resting both hands on the door, her body caught between his two arms, he lowered his face close to hers. "There is no one there."

His lips were a mere six inches away. She had only to lean in to feel his mouth on hers. It seemed all the air had been sucked from the room, and Mel realized she'd been holding her breath. Alexi waited for a few slow beats and then, when she didn't move, he took one of her hands, slowly passing her palm across his chest. His muscles were firm and warm; her fingertips dampened with his sweat. It was the most erotically charged thing she'd ever experienced. She had an impulse to run her tongue along the base of his neck, or to raise the tips of her fingers into her own mouth. But before she could respond, he stepped back and reached for the doorknob, waiting for her to step aside so he could open the door for her.

"Good night, Melvina Donleavy."

The sudden disconnect was as jarring as an arctic blast. Without another word, she stumbled out in the hallway, and then hurried to lock herself in the nearest bathroom. The noise of the party had reached a fevered pitch and she used the thrumming chaos to give herself over to a wanting so crippling that she sat on the floor until she could master her breathing again. The sweat on her palm had evaporated, leaving only the faint scent of cut grass and sea brine.

21

SATURDAY, AUGUST 11, 1990

For Russians, it has been said, pain is an art form.

The pain of death. And the sound of women crying. The two crowning pillars of Russian *kul'tura* during war.

Russians had for a millennium written about death, sung their way through it, and danced their way around it—fearing death, advancing toward death, retreating from death, wishing for death. And always, always the soundtrack to this dance the deafening sound of women wailing.

For the man, waiting in his blue Lada, the sound of a woman sobbing could bring back memories of the carnage like nothing else, even forty years after the Great Patriotic War. It was a visceral thing, his response to crying. Crying resurrected his fear of the abyss, the nothingness of the grave, and when he heard it, he had to take whatever measures necessary to stop it. Even if he understood that a crying woman was only fulfilling her God-given nature. A woman was born for pain.

The only thing that unsettled him more was the sound of a woman's laughter. Not the tepid, chaste giggling of schoolgirls, which was to be expected, but the full-throated, taunting laughter of a woman who had abandoned her nature. That is to say, a woman without fear.

That sound brought him to a towering rage. One that

burned like a penetrating acid—like the increasing roiling in his stomach—strong enough to pierce through metal.

His first noncombatant kill had been during the war. He'd been, in essence, still a boy. After losing his siblings, he had joined a small group of partisans, the oldest only twenty, and had hidden in the Byelorussian forests for months. Starving, cold, lost, and afraid. The cold was so bad that some took to sawing off their own blackened toes to save their feet. But throughout that long, frigid winter of 1945, he managed to fell a dozen Germans with his prized Mosin-Nagant carbine, a gun he had liberated from a dead comrade. It was his proudest accomplishment.

He had known, of course, that the great Soviet army had encouraged women to fight. With his own eyes he'd witnessed peasant women wielding knives, setting upon a lone German with a fury, and a savagery, that defied imagination. When they were done, there was not enough left of the German for a sausage.

He had seen women working as field medics and cooks and couriers too. But as the war dragged on, women were enlisted to do less and less natural things—driving tanks, flying planes, firing rifles. There weren't even proper names for these operators, as the nouns were all masculine. New words had to be invented for these creatures, which he refused to learn.

The day he saw the tank driver—April snow still on the ground, the smell of diesel choking the air—he and his comrades were in the last echo of the war. General Zhukov's troops were advancing toward Berlin, so intent on overrunning the Germans in his path that his furious artillery barrage annihilated hundreds, perhaps thousands, of his own soldiers too. The attacks had gone on for two days. On the third, there was at last a break in the fighting.

A KV battle tank, one of the largest made by Soviet hands, and rarer than the ever-present but smaller T-34s, roared to a thunderous stop close to where the man and his comrades were sheltering in a ditch. He'd never seen a KV before, but he'd heard that the behemoth was all but impervious to German armor-piercing shells.

The hatch opened and out of the turret peered a fierce-eyed woman, her face smudged with soot. She spat and then cursed like a man. She looked about, and when she saw him cowering close to the heavy treads, she laughed shrilly and cried, *"Ey, paren'! Ya dumayu chto pod vsey etoy gryaz'yu yest' kozha."* Hey, boy! I think there's some skin under all that dirt.

The men around him laughed. And from trench to trench the cry was repeated—*Hey, dirty boy, Hey, dirty boy, Hey, dirty boy*—followed by catcalls and rough, unforgiving laughter.

There was no fighting that night, and, relieved, the Soviet tank troops mingled with the infantry around small fires, trading stories and vodka. There were as many women drivers as there were men, and they strode about the camp, bold and unencumbered, as if they'd grown a cock between their legs.

In the dark he followed the woman around, waiting for her to drop into her blanket to sleep. He supposed she would bed down close to her troop, but he got lucky. She stumbled off into a small stand of trees to relieve herself, unbuttoning her trousers as she went. He followed her, soon realizing that he could have approached her riding an elephant and she wouldn't have noticed, so drunk was she.

He had taken a length of rope, knotted in the middle, and as he walked he wrapped the ends around his fists. He waited for her to squat and then, from behind, he dropped the rope over her neck and jerked it taut. To gain better traction, he fell backward, pulling her down onto him, his legs wrapped tightly around her struggling arms. Her legs thrashed, and as her body began to spasm, the friction across his groin gave him an immediate erotic pleasure. He arched his pelvis against her back and ejaculated the moment she stopped breathing.

He lay panting for a moment, the weight of her body still pressing heavily against him. He'd made sure that she'd never laugh at a man again. When he'd caught his breath, he rolled her away and covered her with leaves and branches.

It was an unnecessary precaution, as the next morning at sunrise the offensive reconvened and the men, and the tanks, in frenzied disorder, surged forward. Left behind were the dead, and the dying, and a lone KV tank gunner who searched in vain for his driver.

As the man sat in his car—engine off, windows down to allow in the dry evening air—he remembered that kill, and the many more that followed. He had hoped that Nadia would be successful in bringing Melvina Donleavy to him, away from his place of work, and away from her comrades so that he could savor her. But Nadia had failed. Of course the American had cut off contact. Why would she want to associate with a known prostitute?

And then, when he'd angrily told the skinny whore that the Swiss businessman had been a fabrication, the drunken shrill had laughed at him, saying, "I don't know who is more pathetic. Me for believing you, or you for thinking that I would deliver the *amerikanskaya zhenshchina* into your filthy paws."

He couldn't stop himself; he'd lunged for the greedy little *shlyukha* and begun to strangle her with his bare hands. But somehow, she'd managed to reach into her bag and pull out a knife, and before he could stop her, she'd viciously slashed at him. Cutting through his jacket and slicing through the meaty part of his forearm. The sight of his own blood only strengthened his fury. Her neck was so slender that her spine had snapped even before he'd felt the hyoid bone in her throat splinter under his thumbs. Now she lay in his backseat, waiting. She'd be no good to plant in the ground. This one he would leave on a main thoroughfare, in the garbage where she belonged.

He took a few steadying breaths. This was only a small setback. He'd been so close to Melvina at William's party that he could have touched her, stroked her skin, enveloped her with his body. He took another deep breath and squared his shoulders. If he'd learned nothing else, he'd learned patience. Patience and watchfulness.

As his grandmother used to say, "The wolves are full and the sheep intact." At least for now.

22

SUNDAY, AUGUST 12, 1990

Mel spent a restless night, sleeping fitfully, finally waking at five a.m. exhausted and not looking forward to the debriefing with William. But important wheels had been set in motion. One of two things would probably happen now that she'd made an initial sighting. The Agency would send more experienced agents for an intervention, or an "extraction." Or the State Department would bring pressure to bear on Byelorussia by threatening to withhold American dollars. Perhaps both would happen.

As she got dressed, she stared at herself in the bathroom mirror. Her eyes were red-rimmed and swollen, her skin especially pale. After only a little over a week, the amount of energy and cunning it took to avoid being watched and listened to every moment of the day was more draining than she could have imagined, no matter how many times she'd been schooled on the reality of Soviet life. She felt increasingly anxious, afraid to trust anyone around her, including members of her own team. Even Anton, their burly driver, seemed everywhere at all times.

And this apart from the frightening reality that the Middle East might soon obtain nuclear material.

She knew there was still more she could do. Dan had been

told to back off, but she sensed he was still bitter about not being briefed on her separate mission. Despite his apology, on the drive back to the hotel he'd been distant, and watchful.

It was no wonder she was so receptive to Alexi Yurov's attentions. Her uncertainty must be cascading off her in waves. It wouldn't take a genius to see she was vulnerable to seduction.

"You're an idiot," she said to her reflection.

She finished dressing and hurried down to the lobby to meet William.

"We're driving to Khatyn," William announced after she'd gotten into the car. "Dan knows you're with me. It's far enough out of the city for us to speak privately. And public enough for us to be safe."

Safe from what? Mel wondered uncomfortably. She knew that Khatyn was a national monument, a tribute to a village decimated by the Germans during World War II. Almost 150 people, at least half of them children, had been burned alive in a barn. Retaliation for a German officer killed near the village.

"There were over six hundred villages burned in Byelorussia by the Germans," William explained. "Thousands of men, women, and children slaughtered. Byelorussia lost more people than any other country during the war."

Mel tried to imagine what kind of lasting psychic damage would occur following that kind of epic brutality. She believed that the effects of violence could be generational, that the experienced carnage could be metabolized, absorbed at a cellular level, to be passed down from parent to child. How could a country *not* be left with a populace that was suspicious, slow to smile, pessimistic?

"Alexi's from Dubrova, by the way, which is not far from Khatyn." William rolled his window down and inhaled noisily.

"What a treat to smell pine trees again instead of motor exhaust. Sveta's dacha is not far from Dubrova. It's a lovely place. I've gone there often. If I can, I'd love to have you all out for dinner before you leave."

When Mel didn't respond, he looked at her over his glasses. "You look tired, Melvina. I know no one can ever be fully prepared for the Soviet Union. You have to experience it. That's why I recommend to the few Western friends who come here that they drink more vodka, sing more extravagantly, and throw themselves into an ill-advised love affair." When she looked at him, he smiled and said, "I'm speaking of Sveta, of course."

"How did you meet Alexi?" she asked.

The smile broadened under William's mustache. "I think you want to ask how Alexi became my go-between." He shrugged. "He, like a lot of young people in the Soviet Union, wants to defect. So, until I can help make that happen, he does what he can for me in return."

This was interesting. Not only might Alexi be a source of information for US intelligence, but might his interest in her be authentic? Perhaps he saw her as another ally in his defection, rather than as a target for Soviet intelligence.

"So, you trust him?"

"He's given me no reason not to. But trust should never be blind. A seasoned paratrooper would never take a jump without checking his parachute three times."

William had been glancing in his rearview mirror more and more frequently. "I'm not certain, but it looks like we've got a tail."

Mel craned her neck around and saw sunlight reflecting off a dark car about fifty yards behind them. "*Militsiya*?" she asked.

William pursed his lips. "More likely one of Martin's."

At the name, Mel felt a rush of nervous energy. William had

assured her they'd be safe at Khatyn. "Are they still buying the mistress story?"

"We'll soon find out."

He slowed the car until they were advancing at a crawl. Instead of passing them, the dark car did the same.

William snorted as he sped up once more. "If I really wanted to irk them, I'd pull over and take a nap."

William took the turnoff into the memorial park, the entrance fronted by a large concrete block with khatyn written in large Cyrillic letters.

"A man named Leonid Levin built this park," William said. "He subsequently won the Lenin Award, which was extremely rare for a Jew."

They parked in the already crowded lot, and as they walked toward the monument, Mel spotted the dark car parking some distance from William's.

The pathway ended at an enormous bronze sculpture of a tortured-looking older man holding in his arms the limp body of a young boy. Mel thought it one of the most poignant commemorative statues she'd ever seen. Anguish beyond endurance, made manifest in bronze.

"It's called *The Unconquered Man,*" William said. "Twenty feet tall. The man was one of the only survivors of the massacre. His name was Joseph Kaminsky and he's holding his dead son in his arms, burned to death by the Nazis."

As they walked through the complex, steering clear of the other visitors, William explained the meaning of the different sculptures.

"The three birch trees and the eternal flame pay tribute to the one in every four Byelorussians killed during the war."

It meant that every single family would have lost someone: mother, father, sister, brother. Mel was stunned by the genius of the memorial. It was visual, it was tactile, it had weight as well as emotional gravitas. It got into her pores, and she wanted to sit and weep.

She became aware of the frequent ringing of low tonal bells throughout the complex. The sounds vibrated in the hollow of her chest like the final notes of a funeral mass. "What do the bells signify?"

"They ring every thirty seconds to commemorate the rate at which these lives were lost."

Every thirty seconds, a man, woman, or child had died. Hundreds, thousands, millions dying in agony, side by side, by gunshot or disease or starvation. Most of the faces Mel retained were of the living. What would it be like to scan a battlefield with so many dead? Could she take in all of their distorted, terrified, bloated visages, until she too ceased to exist? Instinctively, she took William's arm for comfort.

He led her to the Cemetery of Villages, where 185 "tombs" held earth taken from vanquished villages. Each tomb was a squat concrete sculpture, painted black and red, with the name of its village spelled out in blocky letters. Mel could almost smell the acrid tang of burnt wood and flesh; the heavy atmosphere ached with pervasive, unavoidable tragedy.

"So much destruction," Mel said, struggling to keep her voice steady. She thought of the framed image on William's bookcase: the young blond boy. "The photograph of the boy and the older couple in your apartment. Are they your parents?"

William took off his glasses and cleaned them slowly on the edge of his jacket. "They are the Polish Catholic couple who took in this Jewish boy after his parents had been sent to the camps. I have no pictures left of my actual family, fourteen of whom perished in the gas chambers."

Mel was speechless. William Cutler, born Wilhelm Kolwitz in Poland, a fair-haired youth in short pants, had lost more than a dozen of his family members in the Holocaust. And yet, despite all odds he had survived. He'd maintained his dignity, his sanity, and, more astonishingly, his empathy.

It took Mel a few moments to trust her voice. "I saw a book in your apartment by a woman named Svetlana Alexievich. Is she your friend Sveta?"

"No," he answered, smiling sadly. "Svetlana's a brilliant author and journalist. A chronicler of women's experiences during the war. Sadly, what's usually written about are the exploits of men, the very same who started the conflict. She once wrote, 'What must be reclaimed is the small, the personal, and the specific.'" He waved a hand across the concrete tombs. "Most men only look. Women are better at *seeing*."

But what Mel saw now were two men, dressed in sports coats and patterned shirts, strolling casually in their direction. Even if she hadn't maintained a heightened awareness of her surroundings, Mel would have known they weren't merely sightseers. They wore dark glasses and spoke to each other tersely, their lips barely moving.

William took Mel's arm and they walked slowly around the Cemetery of Villages, the gravel crunching softly under their feet. She studied his face, deeply lined, slightly jowly, lips curled in a Buddha-like smile, and had a burning desire to know how this orphan became a well-respected scientist.

"Dan said you got your doctorate in the States."

"That's right," William said. "After the war, I was the... how shall I say it...guest of the liberating Russians for a year. And then I was sponsored to go to America by a kind, and very rich, Jewish lady. I attended college and later got my PhD from Columbia. I worked for a while at Caltech, which is where I met Richard Feynman. Then I taught briefly at Oxford and then the Weizmann Institute of Science in Israel."

Mel was relieved to see that the two men were keeping their distance. "What made you come to Byelorussia?" she asked.

"I was invited by Oleg. Our paths had crossed a few times in Frankfurt and Berlin at conferences. We got to be friends as well as colleagues. As you've seen, he can be quite charming when he's not puffing himself up. I'm an American, but I'm also Byelorussian in spirit. And so Oleg and Martin, and others, amuse themselves by trying to turn me. Make me into a double spy." He said the last in a dramatic whisper.

Like a splinter in the ear, Mel remembered Julie's mistrust. Her suspicion that William was playing both sides. As William had said, there was what was looked at, and there was what was seen. She believed that Svetlana Alexievich was right, that women were often more perceptive. But in a world where deception was key to surviving, did you trust people because you perceived them to be trustworthy? Or did you do so because to do otherwise would be to eventually go insane?

William had led Mel to another sculpture—two giant slabs of granite, leaning together to form a massive roof.

"This is the site where the barn was razed to the ground."

William turned to face the two men, watching them with narrowed eyes as they hovered in the distance. Every trace of humor and goodwill had drained from his expression. "Here's the dirty little secret that the Soviets don't commemorate. It was not just the Nazis who burned and killed and tortured. It was the Byelorussian police, the *militsiya,* who collaborated to extinguish the Jews and the resistance movement. Their fellow Byelorussians."

He turned his back to the men and stared at the granite sculpture. "I was saved because I didn't look Jewish. And, because I spoke Russian, German, and Polish, I was made a translator to an SS officer. I was twelve at the time. Terrified that I would be discovered and sent to the camps. You see, by that point we knew what was happening."

He reached out, laying one palm on the stone edifice. "The officers used to play a game. They'd gather up any male civilians they suspected of being Jewish, sometimes ten at a time, and make them pull down their pants. Anyone who was circumcised was arrested and shipped out on the next transport."

He turned to Mel, who stood frozen, staring at him. All the granite and bronze at Khatyn had been formed to overwhelm the senses, to transport the visitor to a place of unimaginable suffering. And yet the most powerful and inspiring embodiment of survival and remembrance was standing right next to her.

William gently took her arm and began walking again. "That's when I learned to be conspicuously invisible. To stand out in a crowd when I needed to be noticed, like making sure my language skills were acknowledged by the Germans. I made myself seamlessly useful to the very entity who could be my destruction. But I also learned to blend into the scenery, to step back when necessary. I fed a lot of information to the partisans this way."

"Like a magician's sleight of hand," Mel said. "Artistry and distraction."

He gave her a playful smile, tapping his forehead with one finger. "Exactly. That along with shrewdness and cunning." He took a few gliding steps. "And, of course, being light on one's feet. It's no small task to make this bulk slip between the shadows."

As soon as they had disappeared on the far side of the granite slabs, blocking them momentarily from view, William said, "It's going to be almost impossible to get you close to the thermophysics lab. But I've found out where the visiting scientists are being housed. It's a Soviet-owned facility for VIPs—a compound, really, with a large dacha and several sleeping cabins—not far from here."

"How do you know about this place?" Mel asked.

"I've stayed there in the past with Sveta."

Mel blinked in surprise. "Sveta Ulanova?"

William nodded. "The very same. Widows who were married to very important politburo members can be *extremely* useful." He put his mouth close to Mel's ear. "Listen, a contact close to Shevchenko told me that the institute is in talks with rogue agents in Almaty. With uranium from Kazakhstan, and the nuclear expertise from Belarus, hostile countries like Iran or Pakistan could have the bomb within a few years. Things are 'hotting up,' as my English friends say."

The two KGB agents had closed the distance and were walking rapidly in their direction, the sun flaring off their glasses.

"I don't have an exact plan yet," William said quietly, taking Mel's arm and moving away from the granite slabs, "and the institute has restricted Sveta's access to the dacha right now, but I'll figure something out."

One of the men called out sharply in Russian for them to stop. William turned in their direction, a pleasant, guileless smile on his face. They exchanged a few more words and William stopped smiling.

The vague anxiety Mel had felt turned to dread. She understood enough Russian to know that they were talking about her. "What's wrong?"

"We're to follow them back to Minsk," he said. "Martin Kavalchuk would like another word with you."

23

SUNDAY, AUGUST 12, 1990

At KGB headquarters, Mel was taken to the same room as before. The same young Alpha officer led her in and left her seated alone, the lone chair once again positioned close to the drain. She had no doubt that it was intentional, as were the lack of windows and the harsh, artificial lighting. The entire space gave her the claustrophobic feeling of being buried somewhere deep below a mountain. The walls sloped inward, the diameter slightly narrower at the ceiling than at the floor, giving the sensation of the space literally closing in. Mel struggled to keep her thoughts calm, her muscles relaxed.

William had again protested Mel's being taken in without his presence. But, as before, he was not allowed to leave the waiting room. He assured her that he would inform Dan and that he wouldn't leave until she was returned safely.

Now it seemed as if she'd been waiting a long time. She shut her eyes and concentrated on her breathing, running through all William had said on their drive back to Minsk, as he'd recounted Kavalchuk's personal history.

Martin Kavalchuk had been a young army officer in the war, and an enthusiastic devotee of Joseph Stalin. His talent for extracting information caught the attention of Yuri Andropov, newly named Soviet ambassador to Hungary. Because of his Hungarian mother, Kavalchuk spoke the language fluently and so accompanied Andropov to Budapest in 1954. He'd then helped to crush the first serious threat to Soviet rule, the Hungarian uprising. It was hard for Mel to comprehend the intentional cruelty; two thousand Hungarians had been massacred, and over two hundred thousand citizens made refugees. How had he not seen his mother's countrymen as his people?

When Andropov was named chairman of the KGB in Moscow in 1967, Kavalchuk was firmly his right-hand man, overseeing a tidal wave of crackdowns on dissidents. Mass arrests, involuntary psychiatric commitments, and executions were made by the tens of thousands. In 1986, two years after Andropov's death, Kavalchuk was named head of the KGB of the Byelorussian Soviet Socialist Republic.

At the sound of quiet footsteps, she opened her eyes. He'd arrived. Kavalchuk was walking toward her, carrying a file folder under one arm. She hadn't heard the door open and realized that the soundlessness of the mechanism was also intentional.

He sat at the desk once again, placing his hands over the folder. "Good afternoon, Miss Donleavy."

She nodded tersely in greeting and waited. He looked at her, unblinking, for a count of ten and then said, "When we last spoke, you mentioned the *Svisloch Dushitel*. The Svisloch Strangler. Where did you hear these words?"

She remembered first hearing the phrase in the Planeta Mir, from Larysa. The woman who'd lost her husband, and probably would lose her son. The woman did not also need a midnight visit from the KGB.

Mel shrugged. "I don't recall."

He sighed and opened the file. "Your father is a sheriff in Wisconsin, is this true?"

Again, he'd taken a direction that she'd not anticipated. "Yes, he is."

"How long has he been in law enforcement?" He cocked his head to the side, as though immensely interested in what she had to say.

"Over thirty years."

"So, he's a very experienced policeman. And he's been witness to a lot of crime, some of it violent."

"Yes."

"A pernicious ailment afflicting the United States."

She wondered if she would be getting the "Decadent West" sermon as a preamble to whatever point Kavalchuk wanted to hammer home.

"I think violent crime is a universal affliction," she said.

"Richard Ramirez, John Wayne Gacy, Ted Bundy. Do these names mean anything to you?"

The familiar names sounded foreign, almost exotic, spoken with such a heavy Russian accent. "Yes, they're all what law enforcement now calls serial killers."

Kavalchuk stood and began slowly pacing behind the desk. "Please define for me what 'serial killer' means."

His tone seemed offhand, relaxed. He could have been any professor in any university calling on a pupil.

"Well," she said, choosing her words carefully, "most commonly it means someone, usually a man, who has killed multiple people at different locations, often at different times."

He stopped and looked at her. "Yes. I believe that is the current technical definition given by your FBI. But perhaps it is also used by local law enforcement, such as your father?"

She'd given the general definition that was now common currency within federal law enforcement. As she regarded Kavalchuk's trim figure, his hands clasped behind his back, a benign expression on his face, she remembered her father's warning: the most dangerous interrogator would appear the least threatening. *Remember always who you're talking to,* her trainers had warned.

"Unfortunately," she said, "America has seen far too many serial killers lately, and our media can't get enough. Any schoolgirl could give you that same definition."

He nodded distractedly. "And what is this curious ritual of giving these killers romantic names such as the Night Stalker and the Golden State Killer?"

"I suppose it sells newspapers."

He smiled sadly and sat down once more. He leaned forward as though to draw her into a confidence. "Common wisdom within Soviet law enforcement is that we, as a society, do not have serial killers. It is taught that this aberration is a result of moral decay in the West. We have violent crimes, but they are *singular* events. This is what is taught in the academy, and this is official Soviet policy."

She knew this from her Agency training, but it was jarring to hear it from the lips of a faithful advocate. If, in fact, that was what he was. If it was doctrine that there were no serial killers in the Soviet Union, why would Martin Kavalchuk even entertain this discussion?

"Do you believe it?" he asked. "That we are somehow inoculated against men who kill and kill again?"

She looked at him incredulously. Joseph Stalin, the man who ran the Soviet empire for thirty years, was, at some estimates, responsible for the death of twenty million people.

"No, I don't," she answered honestly.

He exhaled with a satisfied hum. "Are you familiar with the killer Ed Gein?"

The name brought back a flood of memories. Her father had been the first officer to enter the killer's house, and what he saw there haunted him still. Gein's most recent victim, a woman named Bernice Worden, had been decapitated, strung up and gutted like a deer. Many more trophies were found throughout his property. Years later, Mel's mother would tell her it was this pernicious haunting that drove her to divorce her husband. The experience had changed Walter Donleavy from a personable, loving partner to a paranoid, untrusting man.

Mel realized that Kavalchuk was studying her intently.

"Was the killer not from Wisconsin?" he asked.

"Ed Gein was arrested in the same county where my father was a young deputy. I remember him telling me about it."

"I followed this case closely over the years. In Russia, Gein was referred to as *Sborshchik Kozhi,* the Skin Collector. Do you think all serial killers collect trophies?"

Surprised that he would have followed the case so closely, she answered, "I wouldn't know."

"Would you not?" He opened the folder, studied it for a moment, and then closed it again. "Let us say, for the sake of friendly conversation, and as a purely hypothetical case, I were to ask you what the criteria are for a serial killer?"

"The criteria?"

"Yes. Imagine your father tracking a serial killer. What would he look for? What do you think, Miss Donleavy, that the FBI would look for?" He gazed at her pointedly. "Let's assume, for argument's sake, that you have some knowledge, however rudimentary, of what the FBI would look for."

Her scalp tightened and her heart rate increased. She took a deep breath before answering, forcing herself to maintain his gaze. "My father hasn't tracked a serial killer since Gein. And I would have no personal knowledge of how this is done, other than what I've learned from watching TV."

He looked at her for a long moment and then slipped something out of the folder. Standing, he walked around the desk and placed himself directly in front of her. He held up a photograph.

Mel blinked several times, the spit in her mouth drying,

her eyes filling with tears. It was a black-and-white image of a woman, lying on the ground, lifeless. She was fully clothed, her long dancer's legs twisted by the awkward angles of death. There was a large, mottled bruise around her neck, and both of her eyes had been blackened, her nose broken. Some strands of long blond hair had fallen across her forehead, and she looked through them lifelessly, like a deep-sea diver peering through a bank of seaweed.

"You know who this woman is?" Kavalchuk asked.

"I know her from the Planeta Mir," Mel whispered hoarsely. She cleared her throat. "Her name is Nadia."

"She was discovered early this morning. A street cleaner found her, dumped like a sack of garbage onto the street."

Mel closed her eyes against the image. Nadia had told her that day in the gazebo that she had a suspicion about the killer's identity. Mel should have pressed harder, made more of an effort to protect her. "Was it the Strangler?"

Kavalchuk shrugged. "The morgue examiner thinks it was manual strangulation. There were definite thumb marks and the bones in her throat were crushed."

He returned to his desk and sat, replacing the photograph in the folder. "She was a prostitute, and violent death often accompanies such a profession."

Mel thought of the colorful Bolshoi tickets fluttering in the air and remembered the weight of Nadia's head resting on her shoulder.

"In three years, eleven women, including Katya, have been killed or declared missing in Minsk, prior to Nadia. Some of them prostitutes, but not all. Some of the bodies have been recovered, but not all. It's these differences that have convinced my colleagues that they are all separate incidents."

"But you…you're not so sure."

"Miss Donleavy, it is ideological heresy to form personal opinions about criminal methodology. There can be no 'gut instinct' in modern Soviet detection techniques. But, as a matter of curiosity, how do you think American law enforcement, such as your father, with decades of knowledge, would approach such a case? Would your father rely on 'gut instinct'?"

She resisted gripping the sides of her chair, knowing he'd notice the white of her knuckles. The first of the Moscow Rules was *Never go against your gut.*

He was waiting patiently for her to answer his question. A question that was heretical to Soviet law enforcement practices.

She licked her lips and said, "Maybe what we call gut instinct is intuition combined with experience."

He nodded heavily and stared down at the folder. "I have heard that there are...signposts, a blueprint, if you will, that guide American law enforcement to a serial killer. For instance, the killers often take souvenirs from their victims."

Beginning in the early 1970s, the FBI had developed a system of criminal profiling, and this discipline had been blended into Mel's academy training. She'd mastered it all already, of course, during the years of her own furtive research: the method and manner of a killing, an organized or disorganized killer, the differing routes to body disposal, and notable antecedents or postoffense behaviors.

When Kavalchuk met her gaze again, she got the uncanny impression that instead of testing her, he was asking her for some insight. Did he believe there was a serial killer at work in Minsk? She thought of Nadia's broken body and her face flushed hot, turning her sadness to anger—closer to rage.

A curious change came over Kavalchuk's expression as he studied her face. His chin lifted, his posture shifted subtly, his eyes narrowed. His body had tensed as though surprised by something unexpected. Some shift in her demeanor, however brief, had betrayed her carefully presented façade of naïveté. His face tightened into a near smile. She'd revealed an underlying intensity that he found revelatory. And satisfying.

"My father once said that criminals get better with practice," she said, struggling to return to a state of calm. "They refine their methods. But sometimes, because of the situation, their methods necessarily change."

"Go on."

"In the case of a serial killer, perhaps they've been interrupted, or they're angered into acting impulsively. I've heard my dad talk about a killer's 'signature.' The weapon they favor, or the location at which they'll dump or bury their bodies. But the methods can change." She was on sure footing now, gaining momentum, talking about something she'd studied for years. "Take, for example, the Green River Killer. He strangles his victims, all women, sometimes with a rope, and sometimes with his hands. But we're certain both sets of victims are his."

"But what causes a man to do murder time and again?"

"One aspect may be childhood trauma, which can account for certain abnormal behavior."

"'Childhood trauma,'" Kavalchuk echoed darkly. "You were just at Khatyn, were you not?" He got up and turned his back to her. "Over one million Byelorussians died during the war. More than half children. Most of them starved to death. The Soviet Union lost three-quarters of its men. Seventy-five percent. Bullets, bombs, starvation, dysentery, gangrene…It is a wonder we're not all mad." He turned to face her, his eyes narrowed, his lips pinched.

"And yet the United States of America, a land of plenty, whose cities were never bombed, never invaded, has had dozens of serial killers. There must be something more."

For the first time Mel caught a glimpse of something beyond the construct of the professorial interlocutor. A singular, unrelenting purpose, someone made of iron and razor wire. Reflexively, she looked down at the drain at her feet. Of course he was right. She'd never had to experience the desperate privation of a war-torn land. Her answer about childhood trauma seemed glib, naïve, unthinking.

"I don't have a good answer for that," she said.

He picked up the folder and Mel knew it was over. "There is something in your English…'The evil that men do.'"

"It's Shakespeare," she said. "'The evil that men do lives after them; the good is oft interred with their bones.' It's from the play *Julius Caesar.*"

"Yes," he said. "The emperor stabbed by his own men. We have the same problem in Russia."

24

SUNDAY, AUGUST 12, 1990

When Mel was led back into the waiting room, Dan was with William, both looking strained with worry. Without saying a word, the men stood and escorted her back through the garage to William's car like two bodyguards.

Throughout her life Mel had been grilled, trained, and interrogated, but she'd never spent half an hour with a single man—even such an erudite, soft-spoken one—that made her feel so menaced. And yet dangerously engaged.

"The banality of evil," Hannah Arendt had written. In the interrogation room, where time became irrelevant, the torturer spoke in hushed tones and took notes, opening his hands in modest supplication. All while his implements of torture hung glinting on the wall behind him.

Before William got into the driver's seat, he bent over and picked up a small piece of paper that had fallen to the ground. He showed it to Dan and Mel, gesturing that he'd left it inside the closed door. Someone had gained access to the car during Mel's interview.

When they were all seated inside, William motioned for them to stay quiet. Running his fingers lightly over and under the dashboard and along the steering column, he examined every surface, including the undercarriage of the radio. He then examined both visors, and as he gazed up at the upholstered roof, something caught his eye. There was a minuscule break in the seams of the fabric. William gently pinched the tear between his thumb and forefinger and nodded.

He craned his neck around to look at Mel and put his finger over his lips. The car had been bugged.

William drove them to Victory Park and the three walked until they stood at the bank of the river. Mel spent those moments gathering her thoughts.

"Kavalchuk showed me a postmortem photo of Nadia, the blonde from the Planeta," she announced finally, pausing to quell the rising sadness. "She'd been beaten and then strangled with someone's bare hands." Standing at the river, she fought off, as well, an image of Katya on its banks. "She makes the twelfth woman killed or missing in Minsk in the past three years."

"He believes there is a serial killer at work in Minsk?" Dan asked.

"He's going to have to tread very carefully if that's the case," William said. "Although I've heard through my Moscow contacts that women and children have been butchered in Russia and Ukraine *for decades*. There are whispers of one man, a 'Butcher of Rostov,' but Major Fetisov, head of the police task force in Rostov Oblast, has come under intense criticism for insisting this so publicly. Maybe *glasnost* is thawing the hard line on these investigations?"

"Kavalchuk knows that my father is in law enforcement. He also insinuated that I might have knowledge of FBI tactics," Mel said. "And that I could somehow provide him with what he called a 'blueprint' to identify the Svisloch Strangler."

"He's just fishing," Dan said. "There's no way he could know you've been to the academy. All of that's been scrubbed from your personal history."

"Nevertheless, he knew my parents' names."

"What else?" William asked.

"He made light of the idea that American law enforcement works off gut instinct. But my gut says he's not finished with me."

Dan turned to Mel. "I know I've been giving you a hard time. Tell me what our team can do to help you? What can *I* do to help?"

He appeared so earnest, the same lock of hair falling artfully over his forehead.

Mel sensed, yet again, a patronizing air to his words: the knight in shining armor coming to rescue the helpless damsel. In the end it didn't matter what he thought of her. It only mattered that she complete her mission.

She looked over the river, calm in the afternoon light, and envied the people strolling along in their ignorance. She had to give something to Dan if the team was going to be of assistance. But she'd have to tread carefully.

"There is a restricted area at the Heat and Mass Transfer Institute," she said. "Something is going on in the thermophysics lab, and I need to be able to see who's working there. But William has explained to me that it will be nearly impossible to gain access."

"This 'something going on' is a security threat?" Dan asked.

"Potentially." William stepped in. "As I explained to Mel earlier today, I may have a workaround. The person, or persons, that Mel needs to see will be housed in a dacha outside Minsk. I'm not sure I can get Mel into the dacha, but I may be able to get myself invited and take some clandestine photographs."

That would work, Mel thought. "Do you think you'll be granted access, though?"

William gave her a reassuring pat on the arm. "All important foreign scientists stay at the dacha. As academician of the institute, Oleg Shevchenko is the one coordinating the schedules of all visiting members, including their accommodations. I'm sure my very good friend Oleg will be persuaded to invite me if only because I can provide the best American scotch."

"One other thing," Mel said. "Nadia told me that there are rumors that the Strangler is someone 'high up.' But she didn't get the chance to give me specifics."

William met her eye briefly. "Melvina, I would steer as far away from that topic as possible."

"Even if Kavalchuk won't let it go?"

"I'm all too aware of some of my colleagues' less tasteful habits with women. But a serial killer? I'll tell you one thing, if I hear, or see, anything that raises a red flag, I'll let you know. Until then, please promise me you won't try poking the serpent to life."

"I agree with William," Dan said. "In this country it seems that everyone is guilty until proven innocent. I'd hate for that to become you."

Mel was in her room early that evening when Julie knocked on her door. She held a book in one hand and a bottle of wine in the other. In the crook of her arm, she cradled a small tape player. Change out the wine for a bouquet of flowers and Julie, with her worried expression, could have been visiting her in the hospital.

"I brought you the novel I just finished," Julie said, "because I know you weren't really enjoying the one you brought. Mine isn't very good, but it's escapist and the wine will probably make it better."

Mel examined the label on the wine bottle and made an approving sound. "It's French!"

Julie laughed. "I traded three chocolate bars and a bottle of Wite-Out with the barman at the Planeta Mir."

"Wite-Out?"

"Evidently, he has a girlfriend who's a secretary, and he said it would make her queen of the typing pool."

Mel knew that office items made in the West, like Post-its and sturdy paper clips, were novel in the Soviet Union, but it was a revelation what they all took for granted. "Imagine improving international relations with liquid corrector."

Julie set the tape player on top on the dresser in front of the two-way mirror and plugged it in. She turned up the volume on a Janet Jackson tune and perched on the edge of the bed. Mel poured two glasses of wine and pulled the lone chair closer so that they could sit knee to knee. They toasted each other and drank.

"Dan told me about your morning session with the Wolf," Julie said. "You okay?"

Mel leaned in and whispered, her lips barely moving, "He intimated there's a serial killer operating in Minsk. Eleven women killed or missing in three years. Larysa from the Planeta Mir had told me he's been named the Svisloch Strangler. Now she's his latest victim. His twelfth."

Julie's eyes widened, and the two women huddled closer together. "The gorgeous blonde? Jesus. Why didn't you warn me before now?"

"Because we're protected Westerners with an official group, constantly tracked and followed by the KGB. I didn't think we were in danger."

Julie smirked. "Oh well, then. I feel so much safer now."

"I think there'll be more interviews with Kavalchuk. He's interested in how my father, an American sheriff, would handle it."

"Your father would call in the Feds."

Mel held up her glass in silent agreement.

Something occurred to Julie. "Wait…does that explain Katya's death? She was strangled, right?"

"Yes."

"The KGB have any suspects?"

"Up until now, they've all been handled as isolated incidents. But the killings keep happening."

Julie shivered theatrically. "I can think of a few suspects. Maksim, for one. He tried entering my room the other night. I threw a book at him. Clocked him in the head pretty good."

Mel sat up straighter. "Why didn't you tell me?"

Julie made a wry face. "You kidding me? After our last conversation about the bad behavior of men? A fumble in the dark was hardly worth mentioning."

Mel wondered how many missions she'd have to complete before she became that toughened. "He did the same thing with me, the night of the blackout."

"Son of a bitch. You tell Dan?"

"I told Ben." Mel chewed thoughtfully at her bottom lip. "There's just been a lot going on." Nadia had said the Strangler might be someone "high up." Maksim was a creep, but he didn't fit the description.

Patting Mel on the knee, Julie pulled a pack of playing cards out of her pocket. "Well, then, before you're hauled in front of the Black Wolf again, you need some mindless distraction."

They began to play gin rummy, concentrating on the cards. While Julie dealt the first hand, Mel hummed along with the music, soothed by the gentle slapping of cards being dealt and discarded. She thought of William's advice to drink more. As well as to indulge in ill-advised love affairs.

After a few minutes, Julie said, "I told Dan a joke this morning. It goes like this. An Agency mission leader dies and goes to stand before the Almighty, who asks him, based on his deeds on earth, if he thinks he should inhabit heaven as an angel or hell as a devil. The mission leader looks at God and says, 'Neither. You're sitting in my seat.'"

Mel grinned. "Did he laugh?"

Julie picked up a card from the deck and discarded it. "No, he did not. And gin!"

"How did you do that so fast?"

Julie gleefully scooped up the cards and handed them to Mel for the next hand.

"It's how I made extra money in college," Julie said, filling their glasses again. She stretched out on her side, propped her head up with one hand, and studied Mel for a few beats. "Since your interrogation this morning, and subsequent meeting with William, Dan has gone from ranting against you to being your biggest cheerleader. He's going to try to rescue you, you know. It's his go-to seduction move."

She had just echoed what Mel had intuited. "Julie, you have nothing to fear from me—"

"Oh, relax," Julie said good-naturedly. She sat up again, collecting her cards. "It's over. I've broken it off. It never would have worked anyway." She took another swallow of wine. "He's not Jewish. Knowing that seeing him would have pissed off my parents made the sex that much better."

Julie drained her glass. "Anyone special stateside?"

Mel studied her cards for a few beats, forbidding her thoughts from summoning Alexi. "Nope."

A slow-creeping smile appeared briefly on Julie's face. "You're blushing. Look, can I play big sister here for a moment? I have no doubt that you're capable. You wouldn't be here if you weren't. But you are *literally* surrounded by killers. Both friend and foe. Don't let your guard down with any of us. And that includes me."

She discarded and laid down her cards triumphantly. "Gin. See what I mean?"

There was a quiet knock at the door and Julie bounded off the bed to answer it. She reappeared with Ben in tow.

He held out a bottle of vodka. "I hear this is where the party is."

Ben gave Mel's shoulder a reassuring squeeze, and she moved to sit next to Julie on the bed, letting him have the chair.

"Gin rummy," he said. "I haven't played this since college."

Julie dealt the cards, and they played a few rounds, the three of them switching to vodka once the wine was gone. Julie retold the joke she'd told to Dan.

Ben laughed long and hard, almost spilling his drink in the process. "Okay, okay, I've got one, but you two have to finish it. Let's see how quick you guys are. The CIA, the FBI, and the KGB are all trying to prove they're the best at getting the bad guys. The secretary-general of the UN decides to test them. He releases a rabbit into a forest, and each of them has to catch it. The Agency people go in. They place animal informants all through the forest. They question the plant and mineral witnesses. After three months of exhaustive investigations, they conclude that the rabbit does not exist."

Julie nodded sagely. "Good, that's good." She paused to study her cards and gather her thoughts. "Then the FBI goes in. After two weeks with no leads, they burn the forest, killing everything in it, including the rabbit, and make no apologies. The rabbit had it coming."

Mel snorted. She could feel the vodka relaxing her, making her feel silly, but she composed her face to finish it up. "Martin Kavalchuk goes in personally for the KGB. He comes out two hours later with a badly beaten bear. The bear is bloody and limping, one ear gone. The bear keeps yelling, 'Okay, okay! *I* am the rabbit, *I* am the rabbit!'"

She struggled to keep a straight face, looking at Ben's and Julie's troubled expressions. People had been arrested for less, and they hadn't spent their morning with Kavalchuk themselves. William had warned her not to poke the serpent, but the alcohol, and the company, had made her careless. When Mel finally cracked and grinned, Julie wagged a finger at her. "Melvina Donleavy, we'll make a killer of you yet."

There was another knock on the door and Ben got up to answer it. Dan walked in, carrying another bottle of vodka.

"I hear this is where the party is."

Ben looked at the two women and they all melted into laughter. He gave up the chair to Dan and began pouring a double shot of vodka into a glass for the newcomer. Mel realized it was the first time she'd felt completely relaxed with her team—and had no ex-Stasi officers, no minders, no clandestine KGB around. Dan smiled warmly and held his glass in a salute to Mel.

"Drink up," Ben told him, crowding onto the bed with Julie and Mel. "You've got some catching up to do."

Dan made a face when he heard they'd been playing gin rummy. "Oh, no. Real men only play poker. What'll we use for chips?"

Ben held up a hand, grinned, and pulled from his pocket a bag of almonds. "A Boy Scout is always prepared."

"Finally," Julie crowed, "a use for vegetarians!"

They played for a while, making outrageous bets on bad hands.

"Listen," Dan then said sharply, pointing to the tape player. "That's 'Rock You Like a Hurricane'!"

"The Scorpions." Ben named the German group.

Dan nodded as though he'd found the answer to a long-lost question. He leapt up and turned the volume louder. "Oh, man, that song was played constantly while the Berlin Wall was coming down."

Motioning the group into the bathroom, he said, "Bring your drinks." He crowded everyone together, closed the door, and turned on the shower.

"Hey," he said, addressing the group. "Where were you on November ninth, 1989?"

"Uh-oh," Julie said. "We've now entered the stage where

we get all nostalgic." She'd brought the bottle of vodka into the bathroom and poured another healthy round.

Ben smiled broadly. "I was on a brief furlough in New York City with some buddies, celebrating the election of David Dinkins, first Black mayor."

"And you?" Dan asked, looking at Julie.

"Paris, translating for a bunch of industrialists who were in reality running guns to the Middle East."

Dan looked at Mel. "I was still neck-deep in training at the Farm," she said. "But I watched it on TV. My dad called me to say he never thought he'd live to see the day. First time I ever heard him cry."

"I'll bet Dan was neck-deep in sand somewhere," Julie said.

Dan shook his head. "Nope. I was in the quaint Bavarian town of Hof, known for its hot pots and sausages. East Germans had been flooding in from Czechoslovakia and I was there to root out suspected spies. I was sitting in a little bar, drinking warm beer and watching it unfold on a crappy black-and-white television while oompah-pah music played in the background. I'm watching intoxicated Germans, from both sides, pulling down the concrete sections with hammers and picks and their bare hands. And in the back of my head, I'm thinking the world still holds sixty thousand thermonuclear weapons, the Agency is still toppling regimes across the globe, and human beings are still blithely, and enthusiastically, destroying our environment.

"And yet"—he paused, twirling the glass between his palms—"and yet, for a few moments I felt that something… profound was happening. That there was the glimmer of a possibility that we could stop marching into the abyss…"

Face flushed, wavering a bit on his feet, Dan trailed off.

"Oh, Christ," Julie said, not unkindly. "We've now gone from nostalgic to morbid." She opened the door to let the steam out and linked her arm through Dan's. "Come on, stud, back to poker."

Mel turned off the shower and joined the group back in her room. As they played, Dan told stories of his time in Afghanistan helping to train the insurgents on the newly acquired Stinger missiles, a hotly debated gift of the US government.

"The first battle came in September 1986 outside of Jalalabad," he said, popping several of the almonds from his pile into his mouth. "Half a dozen Soviet attack helicopters were returning to base when the first Stinger was hoisted onto the rebel commander's shoulders. He switched on the guidance system, locked it onto the heat signatures of the Mi-24s, and let her rip. But the motor failed to ignite, and the missile fell to the ground like a Pet Rock. Fortunately, two other gunners brought down two of the Soviet helicopters. The commander said a quick prayer to Allah, reloaded, and brought down a third."

"That was the beginning of the end for the Soviets," Ben said loudly in the direction of the two-way mirror, pouring more vodka into his glass. He reached for one of Julie's "chips," but she slapped his hand away. "Afghanistan is only ever a place you should be traveling through on the way to somewhere else."

"Yeah," Dan said. "Starting with Alexander the Great, any force that's ever tried to occupy it gets reamed in the end, if you'll pardon my expression. You'd have to flatten every mountain and fill every cave to win. Fuck, I hope we never get mired down in that mess." For a moment he stared morosely into his glass, but then he knocked back the last of the vodka, looked up, and grinned drunkenly. "Why is it so hard to do inventory in Afghanistan?"

The other three yelled drunkenly, *"Because of the tally-ban!"*

Through the general good-natured hooting and laughter,

they heard a pounding on the door. Dan got up, and when he opened it, the group heard the unmistakable sound of Maksim's outrage.

"You make too much noise," he said. "Other people complain."

He bustled his way into the room and Dan watched his quivering form with a bemused smile. At least until Ben scowled and looked at Mel. "Isn't this the guy who tried to get into your room the other night?"

Dan looked from Maksim to Mel and back again.

"He tried using his passkey to enter my room the evening of the power outage," Mel said.

Julie nodded. "This guy tried the same shit with me."

Maksim saw the look on Dan's face and began backing up. "I look after guests. These women are crazy."

Dan grabbed Maksim by his coat lapels and dragged him into the bathroom, closing the door. The words were indistinct, but there was no doubt from the heat in Dan's voice that threats were being made.

"I'm rather enjoying this," Julie said.

"Do I need to intervene?" Ben asked.

Julie shook her head and deftly shuffled the cards. "Not unless we hear the sound of tiles breaking."

A few minutes later Maksim burst free and fled. Dan sat back down in the chair next to the bed.

Ben leaned back, looking impressed. "What the hell did you say to him?"

Dan smiled unpleasantly. "I told him if he tried anything like that again, I'd personally tell Martin Kavalchuk that he tried to pass along Soviet secrets to a US State Department employee. The guy almost had a stroke." He reached out and squeezed Mel's arm. "I don't think he'll be bothering you anymore."

Julie sighed in exasperation, one eyebrow raised. She looked at Mel and muttered, "Told you."

25

WEDNESDAY, AUGUST 15, 1990

It was Wednesday evening, and the Americans were crowded around William's dining room table. He was sketching the layout of the dacha compound on a large piece of paper, indicating where Mel's target would be housed when he wasn't at the institute.

The volume on the radio had been turned up, the crashing sounds of Beethoven's Ninth Symphony filling up the apartment, but they still spoke in hushed undertones.

William squinted against the light from the chandelier and occasionally rubbed tenderly at his temples. He'd spent the prior evening with Oleg Shevchenko, plying him with vodka and caviar in exchange for access to the thermophysics lab, ostensibly to run his own experiments with computer microprocessors. William had promised he could help them improve their systems.

"The Soviets are having a terrible time with their own computers, with poor quality and worse reliability," he said. "I even ruffled his vanity by telling him that his biggest rival, Aleksandr Nadiradze of the Moscow Institute of Thermal Technology, just acquired a hundred state-of-the-art IBM systems. But he wouldn't budge."

But something was going on. For three days the Americans,

with William's cooperation, had tried every distraction and subterfuge they could to get Mel close to the lab, all unsuccessful. The guard had instead been doubled at the door and security teams appointed along the back side of the institute. Elena stuck to Mel like a Siamese twin, following her everywhere, including into the toilet. The few times she'd tried to engage Elena in conversation, the woman kept to the weather, national monuments, and food. The one time Mel brought up the murdered and missing women, Elena seemed to forget her mastery of English and lapsed into scandalized Russian. She'd shaken her head and pressed her fingers to her lips to signal the subject was off-limits.

The ambient measurement taken that morning on William's pen dosimeter had read 50 millisieverts.

"However," William added, propping his elbows on the table, "I did extract an invitation this Saturday to the dacha, where Oleg intimated there were some very important visiting scientists."

He turned to Mel, holding up a finger for emphasis. "Notice he said 'scientists,' in the plural."

Mel's pulse surged at the thought of identifying more targets.

"How did you get the invitation?" she asked.

"Ah," he said, "I'm pleased to say I had a burst of inspiration between my fourth and fifth vodkas." He walked to the living room and returned with a large book. On the cover was a star-studded sky with the title in Russian, *Meteory I Komety*.

"Meteors and Comets," William translated. He opened the book to a chapter titled "*Meteoritnyy Dozhd' Perseid.*"

"The Perseid Meteors," Julie said.

William nodded, a satisfied grin on his face. "Every August the earth is blessed with the return of the Perseids. *This* year the peak for Russia will be around August eighteenth, which just happens to be this coming Saturday. *And* a quick check of the lunar calendar shows that there'll be a waning crescent moon, which, along with almost no ambient light from the city, will make viewing of the meteor shower spectacular."

He removed a pill bottle from his coat pocket and dry-swallowed a few aspirin. "God, that man can drink."

Pulling a chair from the table, he sat. "Knowing that Oleg had a powerful telescope at the institute, I proposed to him that we impress his visiting scientists with a celestial show the likes of which they may never see again. He was very keen on the idea."

William pursed his lips, looking at Mel over his glasses. "I floated the idea of inviting you Americans too, which he forbade. No guests, *especially* no women. The regular female staff have been let go until the scientists leave. Also, no alcohol is permitted on the premises, which will put quite a crimp in Oleg's style."

"Religious restrictions?" Dan asked.

Dan was fishing for clues. He was smart and experienced, and Mel knew that he'd probably figure out what was going on without her spelling it out. He knew that "visiting scientists" who were on the US intelligence radar, and who didn't drink alcohol, meant they were most likely from Pakistan or Iran.

"I'll be searched, not allowed to bring in any recording equipment," William said. "I could probably get my hands on a Tropel pen camera, but it's not good at capturing moving images at low light. So we need to bring Mohammed to the mountain, so to speak, by putting Mel close to the dacha. The question is, how do we get her close enough to make an identification?"

Mel leaned over the table, studying the drawing. The central dacha was a building six thousand square feet in size, the front door oriented to the south. Two cabins flanked the main building to the east, and two more were situated to the west. The surrounding forest had been felled in all directions up to where a tall chain-link security fence circled the parameter. It would be patrolled at night by a guard with a dog.

Dan jabbed a finger at the forest behind the compound. "We need to get Mel positioned here. Are there any roads along the back side of the compound?"

"Not that I'm aware," William said.

"What time will you be setting up the telescope for the meteor viewing?" Mel asked.

"Midnight. Between twelve thirty and one thirty will be the best viewing time." William pointed to the back of the main building. "This grassy lawn area here will be an ideal position to set up."

"How far is it from the tree line to where you'll be standing?" Mel asked.

"Eighty, a hundred yards," William answered.

"It'll be dark," Mel said.

William agreed. "But I can make sure there'll be plenty of illumination beforehand. We can set up some tables with refreshments, string some lights. All Mel would need is a good pair of binoculars, which I happen to have."

"I'm not so worried about the security guard as long as he stays close to the fence," Dan said. "But what about the dog?"

Mel remembered hunting with her father and his special recipe for keeping other predators away from their camping sites: coyotes, foxes, and the occasional stray dog. "A dense mixture of citronella, ammonia, white vinegar, and hot peppers will do the trick. We just need to let it sit for a couple of days and soak the ground in a circle around our position. I guarantee you no dog will cross that boundary."

"Leave the ingredients to me," William said.

Dan swept his finger along the bottom part of the map. "Looks like we'll have to pull over on the main road and hike into the forest, circling around to the back of the compound. Not using flashlights will make it slow going for us."

Mel looked at him sharply. "Us?"

"You don't think I'm going to let you go into the forest by yourself, do you?"

She faced him, her arms crossed. "You realize that I grew up finding my way around the Wisconsin wilderness, often alone and at night."

"This ain't Wisconsin, Mel—"

"Melvina," William said, holding up a hand, forestalling further objections. "In this case, I think it's a good idea. If you get into trouble, you'll need backup. And, with his experience, I can't think of anyone more capable than Dan."

Mel looked at Julie, who said, "Points for chutzpah. But if it was me, I'd want Dan too."

After Mel nodded her assent, William said, "We only have two days to plan." He grinned and rubbed his hands together. "Time to practice a little old-school tradecraft. Work in the gap. Use disguises, if need be. Go black, if we can. It's going to be a matter of timing and patience."

He studied the serious faces around the table. "Relax, children. This is what we live for!"

26

THURSDAY, AUGUST 16, 1990

Mel spent the whole of Thursday with her three colleagues at the institute, gathering reports and asking questions, her nervous energy surging with many cups of tea and too much sugar. She was confident of her ability to recognize her target, or targets, come Saturday. But her ability to stay calm and focused would be tested; she'd have to trust that her training had given her the tools.

She'd once asked a commercial pilot how he stayed calm in a storm. He'd answered, "Practice and repetition. Rinse and repeat." She'd come to realize that it was the same for an agent operating clandestinely in the field. And on her first mission, practice was all she had.

The team gathered at William's apartment that evening to again discuss how they would outwit their surveillance on Saturday, getting Mel to the dacha without a tail. The radio was broadcasting Prokofiev, which William deemed too muted to shield their conversations. So he put on a Shostakovich album and turned the volume up.

"Symphony Number Four should do the trick," he yelled over the dynamic opening.

He sat at the dining table, and everyone leaned in to hear.

"All day today, I was followed by two not-so-subtle KGB

agents in a new-model GAZ Volga," he said. "It wasn't even black. It was *white,* if you can believe that. I mean, they're not even trying to be discreet. I'm sure they're going to be following me to the dacha on Saturday evening."

He spread out on the table a map of Minsk, which had been provided by US intelligence. American personnel had learned the hard way that the city maps provided by the Soviets were purposely misdrawn. For half an hour they discussed different routes—splitting up the group, hiding Mel in the trunk of William's car.

"The problem with all of this," Dan said, "is that we're usually together. If any of us is not with the group, it's going to cause suspicion. We can't even say Mel is spending the night in someone else's room, because they're all bugged."

"Since Mel seems to be the one under most scrutiny, what if Mel and I exchange identities?" Julie asked. "We go into a restaurant bathroom and change clothes. I leave as Mel, causing a distraction—"

"And then what?" Dan asked, interrupting her. "If only three of us leave, it's going to look suspicious. They'll still be looking for the fourth man."

Ben held up his hands. "Look, we're overcomplicating this. What if we come here to dinner on Saturday night? William, you leave after dinner for the dacha. The four of us stay behind to continue the party. Surveillance, which will most likely be Anton, will be situated at the main entrance. We disguise Mel and Dan and get someone to sneak them out of the building, say, from the basement. Or out the back. Julie and I will stay behind and continue making noise for our listeners."

"What happens next?" Mel asked.

"The person sneaking you out would have to drive you and Dan to the forest, where you could take up your positions behind the dacha."

"And when I've made the ID," Mel said, "this person would

have to drive us back and sneak us into the apartment again." She turned to William. "Do you have anyone that you trust to do this?"

William tapped his finger thoughtfully on the table, staring at Mel. Then his finger stilled. "Actually, I do." He nodded to Ben. "Kudos to our young accountant."

For an instant Mel's thoughts turned to Alexi. She felt the heat rise to her face and stopped herself from pressing William. She didn't trust the inflection in her voice to stay neutral.

"And what happens if our KGB friends get curious about the conversation in the apartment and come to investigate?" Julie asked.

Ben gripped Julie's arm. "We'll just have to dance our way through it."

Friday passed slowly and without incident, and despite the increased security at the institute, excitement built among the Americans. They were finally going to be doing the spycraft that every young agent longed for: misdirection in order to go black. And, for once, the Americans would be turning the tables on their Soviet minders—they'd be doing surveillance of their own.

At times, Mel would catch the eye of one of her colleagues. They'd each responded to her air of nervous expectation by giving her a sly wink or a reassuring nod. Ben once squeezed her elbow and muttered, "Tally-ban," making her smile. Since the impromptu card game in her room, the four had finally gelled into a cohesive unit. Ben, Julie, and Dan had all shown their goodwill by seeking her out. For the rest of the mission, Mel felt confident that they would be her supporters and her allies. Nothing like a little danger to harden the cement.

That Friday Shevchenko seemed in good spirits as well,

sitting next to Mel at lunch, practicing his halting English on her. Even the Germans in the Planeta, where the Americans went for a drink after their dinner, seemed less insidious than usual. William had not yet revealed who his trusted agent was who would be taking Mel out of Minsk. But her last thoughts before she fell into a deep sleep that night were of Alexi Yurov and his sweat on her skin.

At eight o'clock on Saturday night, Anton collected the group in front of the Planeta and drove them to William's apartment. Dan told him they might be very late, so if he wanted to go somewhere for dinner, he was free to do so.

Anton lifted a heavy grease-stained sack and grunted, "*Nyet. Ya zhdu zdes'*."

No. I wait here.

"Good," Dan muttered after the group had exited the van. "Now we can hope that Anton will be fast asleep in a few hours."

The desk clerk opened the front door and accompanied them to William's apartment. As they rode up in the elevator, the clerk stared at Mel as though measuring her by a yardstick that only he could see. When she met his gaze, his eyes lingered on hers for a few seconds before he looked away.

Once settled inside the apartment, they ate cold cuts and dark bread and drank bottles of stout German beer. When they'd finished eating, William turned up the radio and brought out a few board games and cards for the group to pass the time.

Julie picked up the Monopoly box. "Uh-oh, a capitalist tool. The authorities know you have this?"

William chuckled. "I admit it's a bit unorthodox. I once teased Martin by threatening to teach him the game."

"What did he say?" Dan asked.

William arched one brow. "He quoted Stalin. 'When we hang the capitalists, they will sell us the rope we use on them.'"

He then motioned for Dan and Mel to follow him down the hallway, leaving Julie and Ben behind, setting up the game board. Before he got to his bedroom he stopped and whispered, "I'll be leaving at nine to drive to the dacha. At ten o'clock your guide will come to take you out the back and drive you to your destination. Once you've made your identification, he'll bring you back into the city. The clothing you'll be wearing is in my room. I'm afraid everything's quite worn, but you need to look authentically Soviet and that includes the good honest sweat of hardworking comrades."

While William pulled the costumes together in the bedroom, Dan stood with Mel in the hallway, close enough to keep his voice low.

"You nervous?" he asked.

"A little," she answered, certain he was going to give her a pep talk.

But all he said was "Good. A little nervousness keeps you sharp."

William called them in and showed them their disguises. For Dan there were a pair of canvas trousers, a threadbare coat, and a worker's cap with a brim, which would come down low over his forehead.

William handed Dan a pair of well-worn work boots. "They're probably two sizes too big, but it was the best I could do."

Mel would wear a shapeless housedress, a sweater, and a scarf. He also handed her a pair of badly made but sturdy shoes—the kind of footwear found on every Soviet woman over sixty.

"You'll be two aging citizens, so watch your posture,"

William warned. "Slouch some, and don't walk too fast. In other words, don't walk like the healthy, confident Americans that you are."

"Who is our guide?" Mel asked.

"It's someone you already know," William said, and paused for dramatic effect. "It's Joseph."

Mel blinked a few times, trying not to be disappointed. "Who's Joseph?"

"He opens the front door for you every time you visit."

Dan made a face. "You're kidding. That old man?"

"That old man?" William drew himself taller. "The irony is not lost on me that you, who are about to don an old man's clothes, do not appreciate that appearances can be deceiving." William turned and walked back into the hallway. "After all, I've had to aver to more than one of my Soviet colleagues that you, Dan, are not just a vain government functionary who likes the sound of his own voice."

Dan's face colored for an instant, but by the time they'd returned to the living room, he was turning to Mel with a grin. "As a matter of fact, I do like the sound of my own voice."

The group played poker for forty-five minutes after William left, talking and laughing loudly for the benefit of the hidden microphones.

"You know what one of the institute guys said to me yesterday?" Ben asked, studying his cards. "He said that, in terms of foreign policy, the Soviets conduct strategy as though playing chess. We look at the long game, he said. It's elegant, thoughtful, and ideological. Then he told me that the US plays the game like this, like poker. That we're reckless, aggressive, and sloppy."

"I've heard that trope too," Dan said. "Of course, he meant it as an insult. American cowboys playing the lesser game. But just like in real life, there are many players at the table. Not just two. The US and the Soviets may be holding the most chips, but even a small-time bettor can win a hand. Just look at Afghanistan."

Dan called and laid down his cards. He had two pairs.

"Or Vietnam," Ben said, laying down three of a kind.

"Yippee-ki-yay, fellas!" Julie cried, laying down a straight.

Mel had a garbage hand. She shoved away, before it could take root, a dark, hairy little thought that it presaged some bad turn of events.

"A bad set of cards doesn't mean anything," Julie said, reaching out and squeezing Mel's hand reassuringly. "But just in case it does, I'll lend you my good luck for the night."

Mel smiled weakly, thanking her. Julie picked up her dinner plate and jabbed at the remnants of the mushroom casserole William had prepared. "Did you know that more than eighty percent of the earth under your feet is mycelium? The mushroom is just the tip of the iceberg. The largest organism on the planet is the honey fungus, which can stretch for miles underground."

"How do you know?" Mel asked.

"Encyclopedia, baby. I did my research on Byelorussia's favorite pastime. Russians spend more time picking mushrooms than the French. It's their therapy. It's in their blood."

Julie took a bite of the casserole and made a face.

"What is it?" Mel asked.

"There's something off about this batch. Some underlying taste…" Her voice trailed away, and she handed the plate to Mel. "See what you think."

"I've never really liked mushrooms," Mel said. "I'm always a little nervous that someone picked the wrong fungus." She took a small forkful and tasted it.

"Human beings are genetically closer to fungi than to

plants," Julie said. "Mushrooms breathe oxygen and expel carbon dioxide, just like people."

Mel shuddered and spat the mushrooms into a napkin. "You're right," she said. "It tastes like bad meat. Thanks, now I'll be having nightmares about mushroom people."

Julie grinned. "But I took your mind off the mission for a moment, though, didn't I?"

At the designated time, Mel and Dan took turns quickly changing into their borrowed clothes. When Mel passed the dress over her head, she caught a strong musky odor embedded in the fabric. She remembered someone telling her that even washing too often in the Workers' Paradise was suspect. It meant you were a slave to Western bourgeois hygiene practices. She'd been raised with the American ideal, covertly if not overtly, that cleanliness was next to godliness. That clean hands meant a clean conscience. But in a country where something as simple as soap was often in short supply, it was a type of arrogance for her to equate stale human sweat with moral turpitude. Whoever had worn this dress had probably experienced hardships she'd never had to face. She thought back to her earlier hot bath with soap she'd brought from the US, luxuriating in the aftermath of her recognition processing. Something she'd almost always taken for granted.

There was a knock at the door and Ben walked into the bedroom. "I just wanted to wish you luck for tonight," he said softly.

"Thanks, Ben."

"I know Dan can be an asshole—"

"But at least he's our asshole," Mel said, finishing the sentence.

"Seriously, though," he said, and paused. "Let Dan do any heavy lifting. When in doubt, run like hell. Dan's a big boy and can take care of himself."

"You think there'll be trouble?"

"Always," he said, smiling. "And, just so you know, you've made this trip bearable. See you on the flip side."

He held out a hand for her to shake. His palm was warm and dry and immensely comforting. "Whatever it is that you're really doing here, I wish you luck. Look sharp. For all of us."

Promptly at ten, the door to the apartment was opened with a passkey and Joseph beckoned for Mel and Dan to join him. Ben gave them a silent thumbs-up and whispered, "We'll be here when you get back."

He then closed the door after them.

The two Americans followed Joseph to the far end of the hall, where he took out a key and unlocked an exit door. They eased into a darkened stairwell and moved swiftly down to the first floor, their footsteps echoing softly on the marble steps. They cautiously entered another long hallway—alcoves on both sides housing buckets, mops, and chemical cleaning supplies—heading toward a door at the far end. There was only one low-wattage lightbulb screwed into the wall.

"When we get outside," Joseph whispered, "turn to the right and walk to the end of the block. No talking."

As they moved toward the rear exit, Mel heard a rattling noise, like a key in a lock. She froze, only dimly aware of Joseph slipping into an alcove to her left. The door was flung open to reveal a large man silhouetted by the faint illumination from the street. He startled when he spotted the two shadowy people in the hallway and called to them in Russian. Mel's nervous energy morphed into a paralyzing fear. She hadn't prepared to be accosted before they'd even left the building.

"Say nothing," Joseph hissed, pulling something from the long sleeve of his jacket.

The man began walking toward them.

"*Kto eto?*" Who's that?

Mel felt Dan stiffen beside her, his breathing rapid, fueled by adrenaline. The man was large and striding rapidly. At the same moment Dan gripped her arm, Joseph brushed past her shoulder with a surprising burst of speed. In his right hand was something long and slender, with a dull metallic glow. Without hesitation, he raised the object like a baseball bat and cracked it viciously across the man's neck. The man fell heavily onto his back, holding his throat with both hands. Joseph stood over him and calmly delivered a hard blow to his solar plexus. When the man jerked his hands from his throat to cover his stomach, Joseph delivered two more crushing blows to his neck.

For a full minute, the man made harsh, gurgling noises while his body spasmed, his heels raking the floor. Finally he stopped moving, and Joseph rested the iron bar against the wall.

"Take his feet," Joseph said to Dan.

Both Mel and Dan took a leg and the three of them dragged the man into the alcove, pushing him into a fetal position so his legs wouldn't stick out. Mel felt at his neck for a pulse, but there was nothing. She stood too abruptly, almost passing out, and grabbed at the wall to keep herself from falling. The killing had been effective and brutal, a universe away from the simulated defense classes she'd taken at Camp Peary. Thrust, punch, block, now you "play dead." She felt every nerve prickling below her skin like a colony of fire ants.

Instinctively she looked at the floor for trails of blood, but the man had been killed without leaving any trace except for the marks from the back of his shoes.

"He KGB?" Dan asked.

"What do you think?" Joseph asked, turning, and walking briskly toward the door again. "We need to leave."

Joseph opened the door and peered briefly outside before gesturing for them to follow him up the street. Behind them was the hulking KGB complex, but there was no movement on the sidewalk, and they saw no one until they got into Joseph's car.

"Get into the backseat," he ordered.

Joseph started the car and they sat without speaking until the car passed beyond the city limits.

"What are you going to do with the body?" Dan asked. His voice was shredded with tension.

Mel didn't trust herself to say anything. Her heart was beating so forcefully that she felt it thrumming through the soles of her feet.

"Don't worry about it," Joseph said.

Dan leaned forward, draping his arm over the front seat, his chin jutting angrily. "You better believe I'm going to worry about it. Who the fuck was that guy?"

Mel could see Joseph's eyes in the rearview mirror. His gaze shifted from hers to Dan's and back again. She realized that his demeanor during the whole incident had been calm and efficient. His breathing was never labored, his hands were steady, his expression neutral. There was no anger in his gaze, only cold calculation. The stooped and seemingly fragile man had disappeared.

"The building has a large incinerator," Joseph said. "He'll be gone before daybreak. As to who he was, I've never seen him before. But my guess is he's State Security. You've been attracting counterintelligence like a tall tree attracts lightning."

"They are sure as shit going to miss one of their own, and soon."

Joseph muttered something unintelligible. "You know what that is? It's Hebrew. From the Talmud. Translated, it means 'Rise, and kill first.' Next time, if you like, I'll let them shoot you instead."

Dan sat back as though something had just occurred to him. "You're Mossad."

Joseph shifted in his seat and sighed impatiently. "I suggest you stop talking now. Save your energy for your job."

Mel knew that Israeli intelligence had been operating clandestinely in the Soviet Union since the Six-Day War. It was also general knowledge that she'd have a better chance of seeing ball lightning than crossing paths with a Mossad agent. At least knowingly. The precariousness of her mission had, within the space of an hour, floated into the red zone. Joseph was now either a protective asset or a crushing liability.

They drove for another thirty minutes, Joseph checking the mirror frequently for any signs that they were being followed. At a seemingly random spot in the road, he pulled over and shut off the engine and the headlights. He turned and faced his passengers.

"The dacha is a mile up the road. We'll have to walk from here."

"You're coming with us?" Mel asked.

"Unless you want to spend a few hours losing your way in the forest." He handed Mel a pair of binoculars. "The chemical repellant you asked for is in the back."

The three got out and Joseph opened the trunk. Handing Dan a sealed bucket, he said, "I'll let you do the honors."

He slipped a canteen over his shoulder and grabbed a lightweight rain poncho. "We'll walk along the road, which runs almost due east, until we're closer. Then we move north into the forest."

Joseph set off at a brisk pace and Dan and Mel followed, single file. It was dark, but soon Mel's eyes adjusted to the ambient light from the sky, which was clear and filled with countless stars. She'd never seen the swirling brilliance of the Milky Way so clearly, except in the northernmost part of India. There the sky had seemed magnificent but benign. Here the celestial light was somehow cold and pitiless.

The forest was absent any animal noises, and she was

uncomfortably conscious of their footsteps crunching over the pine needles littering the shoulder of the road. Her shoes were tight, but she felt sorrier for Dan and his loose-fitting boots. He'd soon be rubbing blisters into both feet.

Joseph signaled for them to turn north, and the two Americans followed him into the deeper blackness of the forest. Unlike some of the thick woods back home, the pine and birch trees grew several feet apart, and there was very little coarse undergrowth. Some grasses and low ferns grabbed at their ankles, but their guide had slowed his pace and Mel was able to feel her way without tripping. It was cool among the trees, and she was glad she had a sweater.

After they'd been walking for ten minutes, Joseph stopped and knelt. He pulled the poncho over his upper body like a tent and, using a penlight, checked a small compass to get his bearings. He switched off the light and pulled off the poncho. He made a course correction and continued walking. He'd been muttering something to himself, and Mel realized he'd been counting steps.

Joseph held up a hand and whispered, "We've passed beyond the back perimeter fence. We'll walk east now. You will soon be able to see the lights from the dacha."

Within ten minutes Mel could detect the faint glow of fairy lights filtering through the trees. They moved slowly and cautiously, edging farther to the north to keep more distance. The sound of an animal panting made them freeze and hunker down. It was the perimeter guard and his sizeable German shepherd making a leisurely sweep outside the fence line. The dog stopped once directly opposite where they lay, sniffing at the air. He gave a high-pitched whine, but the guard tugged at his lead, and they moved on.

Once the guard was lost from sight, the three took their positions directly behind a fallen trunk, well within the tree line. Dan opened the bucket, releasing a powerful stench of ammonia, and he poured it in a large circle, creating a barrier between the three of them and any approaching animal. Mel's hands were shaking, and she steadied the binoculars against the tree. After a few minutes, she checked the faintly glowing dial of her watch. It was eleven thirty, close to the time when the visitors should be gathering on the lawn. Bright lights spilled from the windows of the dacha, and the shadowy forms of people moved inside, but she couldn't yet hear any conversation.

Fifteen minutes later, two men, waiters in white coats, began bringing platters of food and drink out to a large table. Off to the side, and pointing toward the heavens, was a large brass telescope.

Dan shifted restlessly beside her, the tension making him agitated. Out of the corner of her eye Mel could see him studying her. He finally leaned over and whispered, "William's pen dosimeter. It shows elevated levels of radiation."

She caught and held his gaze.

"I lifted it from his coat pocket tonight," he said. "Is the radiation coming from the institute?"

Mel made a minor adjustment on the binoculars, sharpening her vision. "I can't answer that," she murmured.

"Can't or won't?"

She took a slow, steady breath. His challenging tone set her teeth on edge, and she gave him a warning look. "Whatever makes you feel better, Agent Hatton."

"I've underestimated you, Agent Donleavy."

"That happens a lot," she said, looking through the binoculars again. "I'm used to it."

After a pause, Dan said, "You'll make a reliable case officer. You observe, you listen, you can keep a secret. And you're sharp, even though you don't always laugh at my jokes."

Keeping her focus on the lawn, she whispered, "I will when they're funny."

The back doors to the dacha were thrown open. Eight men, talking and laughing, walked onto the lawn, gathering around the table under the lights. Mel looked through the binoculars, easily locating William's stout form manning the telescope. Next to him was again the unmistakable face of Farhad Ahmadi, the Lion, tall, imperious, self-assured. After a few minutes William guided another, smaller man over. The man was pinched and studious-looking, with nervous gestures and thick glasses. He looked like a professor, which was what he had been at Tehran's famous university for sciences.

His name was Ibrahim Mahmoud and he'd been tapped by Persepolis two years ago. Another man joined him at the telescope. He was younger, with a robust, muscular build and a deep scowl. Abboud Saleh took to heart his prophet's edict that "there are no jokes in Islam, there is no humor in Islam, there is no fun in Islam." To help develop the bomb for *jihad,* he believed, was divinely ordained.

Mel lowered the binoculars and exhaled softly. She could feel Dan continuing to scrutinize her.

"Did you see what you needed to see?" he asked.

She nodded.

"From one to five, how important is it?"

Mel turned to him and looked at him solemnly. "Definitely a five."

"Does this complete your mission?"

"I believe so," she answered, filling her lungs with air. Even through the sharp tang of animal repellant she could smell the sap in the pine trees.

He smiled at her. "Glad I could help, then." He stared up at the sky and said softly, "Look."

Tiny streaks of light appeared across the blackness, some flashing faintly for only a second, others flaring more brightly. The Perseid meteor shower, named after the sons of Perseus, who slew Medusa—the namesake of Mel's mission. She felt her pulse quicken. What were the odds that the heavens would align at precisely this moment?

William clapped his hands, the sound carrying and breaking into her reverie. He was encouraging all the attendees to gather around the telescope. Mel peered through the binoculars again, easily identifying the remaining four men: Oleg Shevchenko, the Alpha KGB officer, and two other scientists from the institute.

Dan spotted the security guard again. He'd completed the circuit and was returning to the back side of the compound. He gently touched Mel's arm to alert her. The guard paused to watch the men on the lawn talking excitedly, waiting their turn at the telescope.

But the German shepherd began tugging at the lead again, his nose pointed at the woods. If Mel was at twelve o'clock, the dog's nose was directed toward ten. The breeze was blowing from the west, and Mel realized that it must have picked up their collective scent from where they'd hiked in. The guard ignored the dog until it gave a sharp bark. A few of the guests looked toward the sound. The guard turned on his flashlight and began moving toward the tree line.

Mel and her two companions dropped, hugging the ground on their bellies.

"Let's hope your animal deterrent works," Dan said quietly.

Mel could hear the dog, panting against his lead, and the guard stepping heavily through the trees. She followed the beam of the flashlight as it moved into the distance. But then the beam swiveled back. It was pointed directly at them, and the dog began barking excitedly.

When the German shepherd came to the chemical barrier, it stopped, rearing back on its haunches and rubbing its nose on its forelegs. The guard called out in Russian and withdrew his sidearm. The Alpha KGB officer had also walked to the perimeter fence, and he called out to the guard.

"He's asking what's going on," Dan whispered in her ear. "Telling the guard to quiet his dog."

In that moment the lights were extinguished so that the meteor shower would be more easily viewed, and the lawn was plunged into darkness. The guard's flashlight raked over the area a short distance from where they were hiding. Now there were two columns of light trained in their direction. The Alpha officer had turned on his own flashlight. There was a click of a metallic gate opening and the Alpha officer began walking quickly toward the guard. They continued their call-and-response in Russian. The dog was barking furiously.

"This is no good," Joseph rasped. "We need to leave. They're going to find us."

The security guard and the Alpha officer were getting dangerously close to their hiding place. Dan caught Mel's gaze and for the first time she thought she caught a true glimpse of the man ducking bullets in the Khyber Pass. Every expression of glib humor was gone and in its place was flinty determination.

"You're no good to anyone if you get shot," he said. He looked at Joseph. "Get her out of here."

Without another word he stood and began running, drawing attention away from Mel. The officer and the guard yelled for him to stop, but Dan continued crashing his way noisily through the underbrush. Joseph grabbed Mel's arm with surprising strength, and he yanked her roughly to her feet. They began running west. Behind them, Mel could hear the confused shouts from the party guests.

Joseph kept the lead, moving at a punishing pace. Mel would have matched it easily wearing the proper shoes. But her bad shoes pinched her feet, and her arches began to cramp. She stumbled and fell, skinning her knees. Two gunshots were fired off at a distance, and she stifled a moan. *Dan.*

Afraid she would lose sight of her guide, she scrambled up and ran face-first into a narrow pine. The impact knocked her to the ground again. Her hand went to her head and her fingers came away sticky with blood. She lay stunned, breathing heavily, until grasping fingers found both her wrists and she was pulled to her feet.

Joseph pressed her palm over the cut and said, "Keep the pressure on, but we have to keep moving."

He slowed the pace somewhat, checking to make sure that Mel was still following. The sound of another gunshot echoed through the trees.

"Jesus," Mel said. "They're going to kill him."

"Keep moving," Joseph said, and pulled at her arm.

Soon he turned left, toward the south, and they ran until they reached the road. Mel took the lead this time, the pair checking frequently over their shoulders for any sign of an approaching vehicle. The mile back to the car seemed much longer than when they'd embarked, and she was relieved when she spotted it.

Mel had barely gotten the passenger door closed before Joseph started the engine. He accelerated hard, fishtailing the car before gaining traction. He looked every few seconds into the rearview mirror and relaxed only after they'd driven five or six miles back toward Minsk. Mel, in shock, stared through the windshield at the black road ahead of them. Her head was throbbing, the cut over her brow stinging as sweat ran from her hairline to her chin.

It had only taken a few seconds for Dan to throw himself into action. He'd saved her from certain arrest and perhaps even death. This was more than field experience at work. The man she'd perceived as vain and arrogant had put himself in harm's way to save the mission. To save her.

Joseph looked over several times, his brow creased with worry. Or condemnation. He yanked his cap off his head, throwing it onto the backseat. He rubbed one hand over his head, his jaw clenching.

"If they haven't shot him," he said, "he'll be taken by the KGB."

The certainty that Dan was lying dead or wounded in the forest began to grow until Mel felt like throwing herself out of the car to return to the dacha. If he had been killed, it could have international implications. How had a seemingly simple task—watch, recognize, and report—become two deaths?

"I shouldn't have left him," she said.

"You have your mission, yes?" Joseph asked, and his eyes cut to her. "That comes first. Always." He pulled a handkerchief out of his pocket and handed it to her.

"If Dan's arrested," she said, dabbing the drying blood off her face, "they can only hold him for forty-eight hours, right?" When Joseph didn't respond immediately, she asked again. *"Right?"*

He clenched the steering wheel, hard. "Technically."

"What do you mean 'technically'?"

"It means this is the Soviet Union, and when it comes to espionage, they don't always play by the rules."

"And if I'm arrested?"

He looked at her through narrowed eyes. "Martin Kavalchuk already has a special interest in you. Why, I don't know. But according to your entry papers, you're clerical. Meaning that, in the wilderness of Soviet law, you don't matter much. People still disappear here all the time. It's best to be prepared for all eventualities."

He drove for a few minutes in silence. He could tell she was afraid, but she set her jaw and straightened her posture, as though readying for a blow. "We have to get you back to your friends as soon as possible," he said at last. "You'll be safer with the group."

They drove for another twenty minutes without passing another car, the road noise echoing like static between radio stations.

"I'm not Mossad," he said finally.

"You fight like you are."

"I was trained by Shin Bet. A month at the Black Sea a decade ago. Do you know what their motto is? 'The unseen shield.' That's me, a simple desk clerk. But for the past ten years I've been smuggling the refusenik Jews out of Byelorussia. The ones labeled dissidents or the ones who cannot afford to pay the emigration tax. Israel provides the forged paperwork, and in many cases the money. I'm the go-between, ferrying exit visas in and helping to get Jews out. Ten years ago, there were one hundred thirty-five thousand Jews here. Since then, over twenty thousand Byelorussian Jews have moved to Israel."

"Is William a part of this?"

He nodded. "A big part. He determines who will be moved. The Soviets have been cracking down on the exodus. All of the brightest minds are escaping to Israel. So now, the smart ones that Stalin managed not to kill are being held hostage by the State. They know once the Jews leave, all that will be left are the stupid and the cultist apparatchiks, which is the same thing."

He handed her the canteen, which she gratefully accepted. She drank deeply and handed it back. "William says you'll be going to Israel."

"I would have left already, but I stayed to help out our good friend, who is also an Israeli citizen. And by extension you and your colleagues."

Mel flashed on bumping into Joseph in the hallway, holding a paper bag of garbage. The garbage that a seemingly fastidious William made sure to take out before every party.

"Are you the one smuggling our reports out to the State Department?" she asked.

"Yes." He looked at her. "As well as to Israeli intelligence."

"Does the US know you're sharing the intel with Israel?"

He gave her a tight smile. "If you live, they will."

27

SUNDAY, AUGUST 19, 1990

Once they entered the city limits, Joseph reduced his speed, his eyes restlessly searching for anyone following them. It was after one in the morning; the streets were empty and quiet. But when they passed the KGB headquarters on Ulitsa Nezalezhnastsi, there seemed to be more lights than usual burning in the top-floor windows.

Joseph made a slow pass in front of William's building. Two large black Chaikas were double-parked on either side of the entrance. Anton's van was gone.

"This is not good," Joseph muttered.

"With the van gone," Mel said, "couldn't it mean that the others went back to the hotel?" She knew even before she'd finished the sentence that they wouldn't have left the apartment voluntarily. Not without her and Dan.

He circled the block and approached the building from the rear. Guards were posted outside the exit there too. Joseph told Mel to crouch down so her profile wouldn't be seen. Once they were out of sight of the guards, he pulled over and parked. He stared straight ahead, his brow furrowed in thought.

"KGB is all over the building," he said. "We have to assume that your colleagues have been arrested or soon will be." He exhaled a tortured breath. "And that may include William."

"What do we do now?"

"I need to find out what's going on." He studied Mel crouched on the floor in front of the passenger seat. She could only imagine what he must be seeing. A young, frightened woman with blood on her face and two skinned knees, wearing a faded, malodorous dress and a grandmother's scarf. How many terrified women had he witnessed in his life?

"I need to go into the building." He reached under the front seat and brought out a near-empty bottle of vodka. He drank some and dribbled the rest down his shirt. "Wait here. If I'm not back by morning you need to get to a safe house." He pulled a pen from his shirt pocket. "Give me your hand."

He wrote an address on her palm. "It's only a few miles away. Just follow the main street, Nezalezhnastsi, so that William's building is to your back. You'll pass the Lenin monument and the Church of Saints Simon and Helena. You will recognize it as the Red Church. Turn right on Ulitsa Sovietskaya and walk two more blocks, and there you'll find the address. I'll give you keys to the front door and to the apartment on the third floor. Repeat to me the directions."

After she had recited the directions, he handed her the two keys.

"Don't respond to anyone. Keep your head down. Pretend to be deaf. If I can, I'll come to you. If not, I'll send someone you can trust."

Everything was happening too fast. There were too many ways the plan could go wrong.

"Who?" she asked.

"You'll know him when you see him."

"Why can't you tell me?"

Joseph turned and reached for his cap in the backseat. "In case you're caught before you get there."

He handed her the water flask, opened the door, and stepped out. "Good luck," he said.

Staggering as though drunk and stooped as if he were simply a weak old man, he slowly approached the rear entrance to the building. Mel peeked over the seat and watched as he loudly greeted the guards. One of the guards held up his hands as if to block him from entering. Joseph pulled out a large ring of keys from his jacket pocket and gestured to the door. After another few moments of animated discussion, and Joseph showing his identification papers, the door was opened and one of the guards followed Joseph in.

Once Mel was certain there was no one on the street, she quickly crawled over the front seat and lay down on the floor in the back. The car was small, so she couldn't fully stretch out her legs. She made herself as comfortable as possible and checked her watch. It was one thirty; sunrise would be at five thirty, four hours away. Four hours in an airport or in a hospital visitors' room was not a very long time, if you had a book or could grab something to eat. But her bladder was full, she was cold, and the hard floor made her back ache. At least she had some water and shelter. It could be much, much worse. She could still be lost and wandering around a Byelorussian forest, hunted by the KGB.

But now, besides not knowing the fate of her colleagues, she was alone, with no money and no true Russian-language skills. Her only map was an address scribbled on her palm. She kept her fingers extended so her nervous sweat would not wash away the ink.

Closing her eyes, Mel directed her thoughts away from her bodily discomfort. As she'd been instructed, she searched for an image that would soothe and calm her nerves. Her mind grasped at the memory of Prashar Lake in India, the unplumbed body of water with the floating island. The lake where she'd lain on a raft, staring up at the sky white with stars, the countless pinpricks of light reflected back into the water like phosphorescent algae.

There'd been no wind and no sound, and, for an instant, she'd experienced a dizzying vertigo, not knowing which direction was up. As though she'd been cast into the deep vacuum of space. It was in that moment that she understood that the loneliness she'd felt as a child was little compared to the awesome, potentially crippling reality of infinity, of nothingness. The reality that her presence on the rock she called Earth was less than insignificant.

And yet, she'd also understood—feeling the steady pounding of her heart, the unfailing pumping of her lungs, the furnace of her blood—that she would fight ferociously to continue living.

A little physical discomfort could be endured, overcome, ignored. It would pass. *It's just the drugs, Alice,* she repeated over and over.

At last, she drifted off to sleep. When she later opened her eyes, the sky was a pale gray. Morning had come and Joseph had not returned. She unfolded her stiffened limbs and climbed carefully out of the car.

28

SUNDAY, AUGUST 19, 1990

Millions of the cheaply killed, have trod the path in darkness…

The line, repeated quietly under his breath, over and over, mirrored the cadence of his fevered thoughts. It was written by the Russian poet Mandelstam, he recalled, although the man in the blue Lada couldn't remember the rest of it. It put him in mind of the American poet Robert Frost.

But I have promises to keep, and miles to go before I sleep…

Both were about impending death. Mandelstam once famously said, "Only in Russia is poetry truly respected—it gets people killed." But to those burdened with a sentimental bent, Frost's poem was also a nostalgic ode to a traveler reveling in the rustic beauty of nature.

The woods are lovely, dark and deep…

Certainly *his* woods were lovely, dark and deep, enough to hide many secrets. It would be only a few weeks before the mushrooms would erupt through the rich soil behind his dacha.

The woman he was following had quickened her stride. He'd seen her face for only an instant as he passed, but he'd known. The woman-child with the wide-set eyes and elfin chin. With skin as pale as moonlight. As pale as the meat of a Veshenka mushroom, and just as delicious.

He could scarcely believe his luck. He'd been headed for an emergency meeting at the State Security headquarters. There'd been quite a lot of excitement the previous night, but as the dust began to settle, no one knew where the youngest American was.

Then, as though he'd conjured her, he'd spotted her walking past the Church of Saints Simon and Helena, right on the main thoroughfare. *Alone!* She was dressed in a formless housedress, one befitting a much older woman, but there could be no mistaking her luminous eyes.

By his usual criteria, Melvina Donleavy would be too slender for planting. But the idea of keeping this beautiful creature close to him forever gave him immense pleasure. She wouldn't yield a robust crop, but he could imagine slender rows of *Chesnochnik*—what the English call fairy ring mushrooms—blooming slowly like shy virgins until late in the fall. The proper Latin name was *Mycetinis scorodonius,* and the mushrooms mimicked the delicate garlic plant in smell and taste.

He remembered the old peasant saying that when fields of mushrooms abound, you'll find the dead of war around. The Russian countryside always yielded its best crops during deadly conflicts.

Five months after the taking of Berlin, he, along with ten thousand other veterans of the Great Patriotic War, had been sent back east. They traveled through Poland by foot, pushing, pulling, and carrying military matériel along the way. There was little food, and the nights were turning cold. The man couldn't recall ever not being hungry. But it was then that he'd learned from his comrade Misha how to pick mushrooms. He'd learned which ones were safe to eat, and which would bring a slow, painful death.

Misha was a fanciful fellow. Whenever they'd find a bright

surge of mushrooms growing over a hastily dug grave, he'd stop and say, "Here lies so-and-so," and make up their story, all the while plucking the edible fungi from the spongy ground.

"Here lies Alexander Gregorivich. He had a lovely voice in life, made the best sausages east of Potsdam, but had a very small pecker, which gave his wife no end of sorrow. He was felled by a cannonball, separating his head from his body, which is why he was buried in two graves..."

There were no females in the ranks, so, of course, any village that hadn't hidden their surviving women—women who had somehow miraculously escaped rape and death at the hands of the advancing, or retreating, Germans—had been made sorry for it. And after women were killed by the Soviet army to stifle their wailing, it wasn't uncommon for late-arriving, desperate men to avail themselves of their sometimes cold and rigid bodies. They could do no more harm to the lifeless, after all.

The man, remembering his excitement over the tank driver's warm, writhing body, was not, at first, tempted by these frigid remnants. What good was expending all that energy on leftovers?

One day, outside Grodno, though, the man came across the naked corpse of a girl. She'd been dragged into a small stand of birch trees and left with her poor peasant's clothing scattered about her like leaves, her dark hair spread out like a halo. She was recently dead, her skin waxy and smooth, the areolae still pink, the thatch of hair between her legs like a small sparrow's nest. There'd been no noticeable animals or insect disturbance, yet, but on her arms and legs grew the beginnings of a fine spray of oyster mushrooms, sprouting like gills on a mermaid.

Aroused and ravenous in equal measures, the man had plucked and consumed the mushrooms—the most delicious he'd ever eaten—at the same time releasing himself onto her body in mighty spasms. When he'd recovered enough to stand, he looked at her for a long moment, burning her perfect image into his memory.

She was the ideal woman, providing pleasure and sustenance alongside a dignified, unquestioning silence. Such a female would never, ever laugh at him. He hated to leave her behind, but he had no way to transport her back home before the inevitable decay began.

Until he spotted Melvina, he thought he'd never see her like again. The same graceful form, the silvery skin, the beautiful dark hair.

And now she was just steps ahead of him.

It was still early morning, and the street was empty. As she passed the looming shadow of the church, impulsively, knowing he might not have this chance again, he parked his car and began following her on foot. He closed the distance easily and, giddy, overcome, enveloped her in his arms, dragging her into the church's lush garden.

It wasn't until his hands had closed over her mouth and he had wrenched her around that he discovered his mistake.

29

SUNDAY, AUGUST 19, 1990

The entryway to the apartment building was dark, and, thankfully, there was no one around to challenge her as she climbed the worn, uneven stairs. Behind the closed doors she passed, Mel could hear muffled conversations, radios, hungry children looking to be fed, even a lone woman crying. Another Sunday in Minsk.

She had found the building easily, following Joseph's orders, keeping her head down and her scarf pulled low over her forehead. To keep herself from panicking on the long walk, she'd recalled Agency protocol: first, run an SDR—surveillance detection route—looking for possible escape options or anything that would allow outpacing, or outwitting, an enemy. But given her situation, her inability to have prepared only made her more nervous, and so instead she'd slipped into a mental state where she simply focused on moving her feet: left, right, left, right. There was no worrisome past, no threatening future, only the movement toward her destination.

Fortunately, very few people were out this early and no one had looked twice at her hunched form. She'd only had one close call. A man, very drunk, waving an unlit cigarette, demanding a light. She'd deftly skirted him, even as he made a grab for her sweater. He swore at her but continued weaving his way down the street.

The apartment key fit into the lock easily and she slipped through the door, closing and securing it behind her. She stood for a moment listening for any sounds in the apartment, but the air was thick with dust and silent. She pressed herself against the door, momentarily immobilized, as if all the adrenaline in her body had vanished at once.

Finally, she drew herself up and moved through the space, desperately searching for the bathroom. Happily she found a modern toilet, and, with shaking legs, she lowered herself onto it. She nearly wept with relief at the release. Looking at herself in the bathroom mirror, she saw a purple bruise at her hairline, a streak of blood down one cheek, her eyes glinting with fatigue and prolonged fear. She washed her face and hands with cool water, drying herself with a bath towel that she hoped was clean.

Mel searched the rest of the apartment in stockinged feet. There were only one bedroom, a small sitting room, and a dining area within the kitchen. It didn't appear to have housed anyone in a long time. She checked the tiny refrigerator, but it was empty. Turning on the faucet over the sink, she drank deeply, hoping the water was potable.

She removed her scarf and sweater and sat on the narrow couch in the sitting room. Her stomach had been growling, and even though the water had tempered her cravings, she felt dizzy with hunger. She resigned herself to waiting in the apartment until she had formulated a plan. Joseph hadn't returned, which probably meant he'd been arrested as well. She couldn't imagine that he would have willingly abandoned her. Her options were limited: waiting for the unknown contact; turning herself in to the KGB to be held for forty-eight hours and then, best-case scenario, sent back to the States; or attempting to board a train to Moscow and somehow make her way to the US Embassy.

The third option seemed impossible, and the second, based on Joseph's warning, made the spit in her mouth dry up. Imagining Martin Kavalchuk's cold, relentless gaze through two days of interrogations, and without her nightly processing, she wasn't sure how she'd hold up. She'd last been able to complete the ritual early on Saturday night. Twenty-four hours from now she'd begin to feel the negative effects. What if she became unglued alone with the head of the KGB? She could be shot, beaten, or committed to a psychiatric hospital, "for her own good."

The best option was the first. She'd continue waiting in the apartment until hunger drove her to seek help. The walls and ceilings were thin. She could hear somebody walking with heavy steps above her. A man coughed uncontrollably in the hallway as he passed her door. Somewhere in the building someone practiced their scales on an out-of-tune piano. She closed her eyes, telling herself that she had the strength and the fortitude to wait a bit longer.

There was a gentle knock at the door, followed by three more. Alarmed, she stood abruptly, the muscles in her legs tense. The knocking pattern was repeated. She tiptoed to the door and held her ear against the wood.

"Melvina," a voice whispered.

She opened the door to Alexi. He was wearing his *militsiya* uniform and carrying a backpack. Mel couldn't remember a time when she'd felt such relief seeing a friendly face. In a few steps he'd entered the apartment and secured the lock once more. He listened for any sounds in the hallway and then, taking Mel's arm, led her back into the sitting room. He sat on the couch facing her.

"Joseph told me where you were," he said, looking tired. He

gently pressed his fingers next to the bruise on her forehead. "You're hurt."

Seeing him, feeling his reassuring presence, his warm hand on her skin, threatened to unravel the thin veneer of calm she'd managed to maintain. "I'm okay. Just some cuts and bruises."

There was blood at the hem of her dress. He pulled the fabric away from her bare knees and gently examined the scrapes. On her abraded skin, his fingers were almost unbearably pleasurable. He unzipped the backpack and pulled out two thermoses and a paper sack. "I brought you some tea and soup. In the bag are sandwiches. First you eat and then we take care of your injuries. I brought some bandages and disinfectant."

The tea was strong, hot, and sweet, and Mel felt the caffeine hit her system like a pure shot of adrenaline. She drank the soup straight from the thermos and tore into one of the sandwiches. In five minutes, she felt her strength returning.

"What happened to Dan?" she asked at last, bracing herself for bad news. "Do you know?"

Alexi gripped her arm as though to steady her. "He was arrested, along with William and your other two colleagues."

She exhaled and slumped back against the couch. "So he's alive. Thank God for that. What's going to happen to them?"

"They will be held at KGB headquarters for questioning. Then they will be put on a plane and sent home. But Melvina, they are still looking for you. The longer you are in hiding, the more pressure there will be to find you. And the more evidence of guilt under Soviet law."

She wondered how much he guessed about her true purpose in Minsk. Surely by now he knew she wasn't merely a secretary. "Should I turn myself in?"

He regarded her steadily. "Joseph didn't say."

"Where is Joseph?"

"They suspect he's been helping you. He's gone into hiding and will leave Byelorussia as soon as he is able," he answered, not looking at her. "You will probably not see him again. Because he is a Soviet citizen, he will be shot for espionage if he's captured."

Oh, God. She hoped that within a few days he would be safe in Israel.

"What happens now?" she asked.

He sighed restlessly. "I have some contacts. They can try to smuggle you out of the country. For the time being you need to stay here and rest."

"I need to shower," she said, pulling at the dress, embarrassed. "I don't usually—"

Alexi held up a hand and smiled. "I'll wait here."

She padded into the bathroom and ran the water in the shower until it was warm. There was no soap or shampoo, so she stood under the shower head for a long time, scrubbing at her body with the palms of her hands. When she was done, she wrapped herself in the towel and stared at the clothes on the floor. She couldn't bear to put them back on. Not yet.

In the mirror, her face at last had better color. She touched her forehead where Alexi had brushed his fingers across her skin.

She opened the door and walked back to the sitting room, tugging the towel more tightly around herself. Alexi sat on the couch, holding the bottle of disinfectant. He averted his eyes for a moment before beckoning for her to sit next to him. He dabbed a few cotton balls with the liquid and gently patted it across the cut at her hairline.

When she winced, he said, "It stings. I'm sorry."

He knelt in front of her, carefully and methodically wiping disinfectant across both knees. She inhaled sharply and he blew on her skin to lessen the burn. His breath was warm and exquisitely intimate. He eased one hand tentatively around her bare calf, meeting her gaze with a questioning look. But she'd reached the limits of her endurance—her injuries and her fear draining any remaining strength from her body.

Instead, she slumped back onto the cushions, cradling her head in both hands. "Please stop," she whispered. Everything was coming unraveled and any decision she made in that moment would be unplanned, irrational, and probably unwise. "I just need to rest for a bit."

"Of course," he said softly, helping her to stand.

He guided her into the bedroom, his arm around her naked shoulders, and pulled down the blankets on the bed. When he turned to her again, she made the mistake of looking up. His face loomed above her, thoughtful, concerned, strikingly handsome in the morning light streaming through the window. When he lowered his lips to hers, as he'd done at William's apartment, she allowed herself to be kissed. He was gentle at first, exploratory, but as the kiss deepened she felt him slip the towel from her body, letting it drop to the floor. Without his arms tightly around her, she felt she too would have fallen to the floor. His touch was like fire; everything in her—the stress, the fear, the weeks of uncertainty—had melted away. He lowered her onto the bed. He stood over her, staring at her as he undressed too, letting his uniform drop to a heap on the floor, one item at a time. Mel remembered the drawing of the Vitruvian Man, the masculine ideal, perfectly proportioned, lithe, and muscular. So too was Alexi. He crawled to her from the foot of the bed and entered her as easily as a swimmer slipping into a thermal spring.

Later, when they could lie quiet again, he drew her to him so that she could tuck her face tight against his neck.

"Why are you helping me?" she asked at last. "It has to be dangerous for you."

He took a breath. "I did it first for William. And then—" He tightened his hold on her.

"Why were you helping William?"

"William was going to help me defect. He has many contacts in West Germany and America."

"And now that the wall has come down?"

He repositioned himself so that he could see her face. "I love my country. It may be that I can stay. William thinks that Byelorussia will declare full independence soon. I want to be a part of that."

She kissed his chest, running her fingers along his collarbone, amazed that his skin, his scent, his mouth on hers felt just as she'd imagined. "But right now, today, Martin Kavalchuk still has the weight of the entire Soviet collective behind him."

"Yes, we have to be careful." He was quiet for a moment, his fingers softly combing through her hair. "Joseph thinks you're very important to your colleagues."

"We're a close team."

"But…is there a special reason why you are here?"

Caution made her chest tighten. She looked up at him, searching for something disingenuous, any sign that he was probing beyond his concern for her well-being. He met her gaze. "Perhaps if I knew more, I could help more."

"Alexi," she said, willing him to believe her, "I'm just a secretary."

He leaned in and kissed her hard, almost bruising her lips. "I will do everything I can to help you. My uncle has a dacha. Maybe I can take you there?"

He pulled her on top of him, where she could control the pace of their lovemaking. It started tenderly, but soon it was urgent, almost violent, their hips moving in concert. After they'd both climaxed again, Mel at last fell into a deep sleep.

She woke to Alexi dressing, buttoning his uniform coat, pulling on his policeman's boots. Checking her watch, she saw that it was now nine thirty and bright light was filtering through the flimsy curtains. It seemed a full day had passed, not just a few hours. Alexi sat on the edge of the bed, his hand resting on the curve of her hip.

"I must report for duty," he said. "There is still more food. I'll leave it in the refrigerator. I'll return later and bring better clothes."

She panicked, for a moment, at his leaving. She had so many questions left unanswered. She wanted him to promise her that he'd be back with some definite plan of action; she was placing her safety entirely in his hands. The more time that passed, the more dangerous her options.

He leaned down and, cupping his hand behind her head, kissed her. He looked in her eyes resolutely, squeezed her hand, and then left. She heard the door close and knew she should lock it. But before she could summon the will to get up, she'd drifted back to sleep.

When Mel woke, the light had changed. Through the bedroom window the sky was dim and murky, somber with dense rain clouds. She'd been dreaming and still felt the disorienting effects of climbing out of a deep sleep. She'd been with her father again, feeding the livestock in the barn, breathing in the familiar, warm smells of the dairy cows. He'd been talking to her, giving her advice, but the only thing she could remember, now that she was awake, was his admonition to be especially wary of those who would befriend her. "Don't get killed with kindness," he had warned.

And now she'd slept with a man who could with a word either help her or betray her. She wrapped her arms tightly across her chest and noticed a new bruise on one bicep. It must have happened during their lovemaking. He'd held on to her fiercely when she was on top of him, but she'd never felt a moment's pain, only the most intense, overwhelming pleasure of her life. She allowed herself the briefest thought that if he defected to the West, they could be together. But then she reminded herself that hours had passed and he hadn't yet returned.

She got up, wrapping the top sheet around her like a toga, and went to the bathroom. Remembering the sandwiches and soup, she walked into the kitchen, only to pull up short and grasp the doorframe in fright. Seated at the kitchen table was a man. Behind him stood a stocky woman she'd never seen before. But the man, she'd recognized immediately. Minder #3.

He held up a hand, as if she were a frightened animal, and stood. "Miss Donleavy. You are to get dressed and come with us."

"Where are you taking me?" Mel asked, instinctively backing away, taking quick stock. She was wearing only a sheet, her bare feet cramping on the cold floor. Frantically, she looked around for any avenue of escape, any implement in the kitchen that could be used as a weapon.

Minder #3 gestured to the woman, who marched forward to firmly take hold of Mel's arm, dragged her stumbling back to the bedroom. The woman fetched the clothes from the bathroom and examined them carefully before she let Mel put them on, monitoring her with a hard, probing gaze. Mel dressed as slowly as she could, trying to buy time. But as though reading her mind, the woman snapped at her in English to dress faster or she'd be taken out in her bare skin.

When Mel was finally dressed, the woman and Minder #3 walked with her down the creaking stairs. A car waited at the curb with the engine running. She looked around desperately, hoping to see Alexi, but she was quickly maneuvered into the middle of the backseat, her two captors sitting on either side.

Anton was in the driver's seat. He met her gaze in the rearview mirror for only an instant.

"Where are we going?" she asked again, even though she was increasingly certain.

"Somewhere that will be familiar to you," Minder #3 said. "By the way, we're long overdue. My name is Dimitri. Next to you is Oksana. And I believe you already know Anton, your excellent driver."

But it became evident within fifteen minutes that they were not driving to KGB headquarters. Instead, they drove east, out of Minsk. Mel had a wild surge of hope when it became apparent that they were headed for the airport. Perhaps they would just bundle her onto an airplane and ship her out of the country?

Once at the airport, Oksana and Dimitri guided her rapidly past the ticketing area and into an elevator, which swept them up to a higher floor. She was led down a long hallway and into a room, past two KGB officers flanking the door. The room was not large and one entire wall was glass. Standing with his back to her, looking outside, was Martin Kavalchuk. Oksana and Dimitri left, along with the two guards.

Mel stood, alone, with the head of the Byelorussian KGB.

He gestured for her to stand next to him, and, when she was close enough, she could see that the departure lounge for foreign visitors was below. Huddled together were Dan, Julie, and Ben. All three looked haggard, and very tired. But they were all alive. Mel had a bright surge of hope that she'd soon be with them on a flight out of Byelorussia. She pounded on the glass and her team members at last looked up, relief flooding their faces. Mel felt as if she could weep.

"I wanted you to see that your colleagues were all well," Kavalchuk said, not unkindly.

She locked eyes again with Dan, who shook his head, holding up his hands in a helpless gesture. He had a black eye, and his nose appeared swollen. Julie looked scared, but Ben's expression turned only to anger when he saw Kavalchuk at her side.

He mouthed, *I'm sorry.*

"Am I going with them?" Mel asked hopefully.

"Not yet," Kavalchuk said, turning to her. "You and I must chat before we decide how and when you'll be leaving the Soviet Union."

Mel tried to absorb this calmly, but its implications were too vast. Potentially calamitous. Instead, she focused on the last missing piece. "Where's William?" she asked.

"Detained," he said, turning away again, as if the word meant nothing. "And his release may depend upon you."

30

SUNDAY, AUGUST 19, 1990

Oksana stayed with Mel in the holding cell at KGB headquarters as she changed into the faded blue shift. Every item of clothing she'd been wearing, including underwear and socks, was replaced by another utilitarian, and mostly oversized, article. Even her shoes were taken, and she was supplied with a pair of felt slides, completely useless for anything other than a shuffling gait. Oksana placed all Mel's discarded items in a large paper sack and handed it to the guard.

Soon another guard delivered a tray of food, which he set on the narrow bunk next to Mel. Oksana perched on the only seat in the cramped space—a small cane-backed chair that looked inadequate to the woman's weight. On a plate were a meat cutlet, several small boiled potatoes, and cooked carrots, everything covered in a gray, gelatinous gravy. Next to the plate was a large mug of tea. Mel stared at the food and her stomach lurched.

"You should eat," Oksana urged. "It is many hours until next meal."

For the briefest moment, Mel considered offering her minder the plate, but a voice inside her head whispered that she would need her strength. She took a small, tentative bite of the meat, washing it down with a large swallow of tepid tea.

She wondered if the food had been drugged, but she knew if they wanted to drug her, they'd find a way even if she didn't eat. Bite by bite, she managed to empty the plate, tamping it down with the remainder of the tea, which at least had been generously laced with sugar.

The tray was removed and Mel, overcome with exhaustion, leaned her head against the wall and closed her eyes. Her fellow agents had all been deported; William had been arrested; Joseph was in hiding. She was alone.

And Alexi? Had he been arrested as well, or had he been manipulating her all along? She replayed every conversation she could remember, recalling every word they'd exchanged that morning and, reluctantly, his every touch, every kiss. He'd seemed genuine in his passion, and in his declaration that he'd do everything he could to help her. But he'd also prodded, however gently, for more information about her. Despite her lingering doubts, she couldn't summon anger toward him, only frustration that she'd allowed herself to be seduced. She pushed thoughts of him out of her mind. To dwell on him would only weaken her resolve.

Martin Kavalchuk would soon be prodding her for information too. And not so gently.

She had no idea how vigorously her fellow Americans had been interrogated, although she believed—*had* to believe—that they would've done what they'd been trained to do. Safeguard not only their own secrets, but hers as well.

Of course, Dan had been arrested near the dacha where the three Iranians were staying. It wouldn't take a rocket scientist to determine that they were the US team's targets. But the US government would make noise commensurate with her importance to national security, which she had to believe was high. Even now, she expected that pressure was being applied through the official channels to Moscow to have her released.

Here was the conundrum, though. The louder the ask from

the States, the greater the perception by the Soviets that she was an important asset. Prior to the Berlin Wall coming down, and the newly declared sovereign status of the republics of the Soviet Union, a captured American spy could expect to spend between five and twenty-five years (or more) in a detention camp—and this only if they weren't "disappeared." In 1990 there was a newly negotiated, informal agreement that suspected intelligence agents be released within forty-eight hours—referred to as a processing period—and returned unharmed to the States.

But in reality, if she met with an "unfortunate accident," what could be done? A charred corpse can hide an abundance of secrets.

As her thoughts began to fragment, Mel lay down on her side, her arms pulled into her chest, her legs drawn up to her belly, like a child. She heard Oksana shift in her chair, but the woman said nothing. Her biggest weakness, Mel knew, could prove to be her own mind. If she couldn't do her processing every twenty-four hours or so, she'd start to fall apart. She had to hope she'd be out of here within the next day.

Finally, she fell into a deep sleep, one with no dreams and no awareness of anything outside her cell.

Mel woke to a metallic rattling and jerked upright just as the door to her cell was opened. Oksana was gone, replaced by the young Alpha officer, who was standing in the doorway. Mel shook her head, trying to clear the remnants of sleep, rubbing her palms across both eyes. They had taken her watch and, as there were no windows in her cell, she had no idea what time it was. She felt slightly dizzy and wondered if perhaps she had been drugged.

He motioned for her to stand, saying, "Please come."

She walked out of the cell and struggled to keep pace as

he led her to a cramped elevator and down several flights to a subfloor. He then led her through a pair of swinging double doors into a brightly lit, white-tiled room, which was so chilled it brought all the hairs on Mel's body to attention. She hugged herself for warmth, breathing in the unmistakable scent of chemicals and some underlying smell. Something organic, and in the process of decay.

Martin Kavalchuk pushed through an opposite pair of doors and came to stand in front of Mel. The overhead fluorescent lights carved deep shadows under his eyes and in the hollows of his cheeks, making his skin appear even more pallid. He motioned for her to follow him past a third set of double doors, where the smell almost brought her to her knees.

There was a bank of six steel tables and on one of them lay a figure, fully draped by a green sheet. She began to tremble involuntarily, both from the cold and from the realization that she was in a morgue. A tall, angular man wearing surgical scrubs and a thermal shirt stood on one side of the occupied table, and Kavalchuk took up his place on the other.

And so it begins, Mel thought. The terror of the unknown. Implied threats, physical discomfort, disorientation. A horrifying thought crowded into her head. Was it Alexi under that sheet? William? She locked her knees to keep them from trembling, but she couldn't stop the rest of her body from shivering.

Martin peeled back one corner of the sheet, revealing the still, bloodless face of a young female.

"Do you recognize her?" he asked, scrutinizing Mel's expression.

For a moment she thought she'd pass out from relief. Tentatively, she moved to the foot of the steel table and gazed at the woman's face.

"No," she said, shaking her head. The muscles in her

neck responded jerkily, as though the nerves had been short-circuited.

"Are you sure?" he asked, beckoning for her to move closer. It was a gentle gesture, as though he only wanted to show her something he found interesting.

"I'm sure. I've never seen this woman before."

The coroner, with a raised brow, traded a look with Kavalchuk. Mel had a brief but unsettling thought that he was testing her recognition abilities.

"Does she remind you of anyone, then?" he asked.

The woman had dark hair, a narrow chin, and defined bone structure. She was pretty, but it was the first time Mel had ever laid eyes on her.

"No," she said, her teeth chattering. Was this also an implied threat, showing her the corpse of a young woman? "I don't understand. Why are you asking?"

"Because she looks like you," he said somberly. "She could be your twin. Doppelgänger, I believe is the term." He waited a few more seconds for Mel to study the face. "She was found this morning behind the Red Church. Close to the apartment where you were found. She'd been strangled, manually. Like your friend Nadia. But there was some rope left at the scene. Rope of the kind used to kill the woman from the Ministry of External Affairs."

"Katya," Mel said.

"Yes, Katya." He gestured to the woman on the table. "Do you see it now?"

"No," Mel said emphatically. "Her ears are different. Her lobule is detached. The helix is curled in more. The pinna sticks out several centimeters more from the skull. Also, the perimeter of her lip is different, more angular. The zygomatic arch is higher, more pronounced..."

It was reflexive, this acknowledgment of distinctive facial

features. But the coroner was watching her as he might an exotic animal.

Kavalchuk was also studying her, his eyes narrowed, his chin lowered, his forehead furrowed in thought.

Mel cut herself off, trying to stay composed. At last Kavalchuk nodded to the coroner and motioned for the dead girl's face to be covered again. Turning to Mel, he said, "Let us begin our conversation, shall we?"

Mel sat in her customary chair next to the now-familiar drain. She'd been given another mug of tea, but, though she was burning with thirst, she was reluctant to drink.

"There's nothing in it but tea and sugar," Kavalchuk said, taking a seat at his desk.

Not fully trusting him, she pulled the mug to her mouth and took a small sip.

"What is your true mission here?" he asked, getting situated. His tone was easy, conversational.

She inhaled, preparing herself. "I'm a secretary."

"So you keep saying. That was an interesting response to seeing the woman in the morgue. Very...precise."

Mel shrugged. "I guess I'm just observant."

"Yes...," he said, drawing out the word. "A precision I've never heard after a glance before. Do you know why your colleague Dan Hatton was arrested?"

She met his gaze. "I have no idea."

"He was trespassing on restricted property." He studied her for a moment. "And we are certain there were others there as well. Hiding in the forest."

She stared into the murky tea, mindful that a dull, throbbing headache had started behind her eyes. There were no clocks in the room, and she had no idea how many hours had passed.

"What time is it?" she asked abruptly.

"What were you doing at the apartment at Ulitsa Sovietskaya?" he asked, ignoring her question. "Who told you to go there?"

Mel had an answer ready. "Nadia told me about it."

Kavalchuk blinked and sat back in his chair. "Nadia?"

"I told her I wanted some privacy, some free time unobserved. I'm not used to being watched twenty-four seven." She was going to say "spied upon" but decided not to tug the tiger's tail. "She told me it belonged to a friend and that I could go there to be alone for a few hours."

If Alexi had been collaborating with the KGB all along, Kavalchuk would know she was lying. The same held true if Alexi had been arrested for helping her. Either way, she wouldn't point the finger at Joseph.

"What friend is that?" Kavalchuk asked.

"I don't know. I didn't ask." She sipped at the tea, now cold, hoping the caffeine would help dull her growing headache.

As though sensing her discomfort, Kavalchuk asked, "How did you get that cut on your forehead?"

"I tripped on the stairs."

"Would you like a doctor to examine it?"

"It's fine. It's nothing."

Kavalchuk stood from the desk and began pacing, both hands clasped behind his back. "Occam's razor, you know this term?"

"Yes."

"The simplest explanation is usually the best one." He studied her for a moment. "And the simplest explanation for your presence here is that you work for American intelligence. No, don't object. Miss Donleavy, I am a practical man by nature. I like uncomplicated solutions to straightforward dilemmas."

He paused for a moment and stared at the concrete walls. Thick, impenetrable, soundproof. She recalled an illustration she'd once seen in a children's book: Alexander the Great slicing through the Gordian knot with his sword. Uncomplicated, straightforward, and deadly.

He turned to face her again. "But I'm also Byelorussian, which means that, alongside centuries of dirt under my nails, I have a thousand years of superstitions running through my veins. The Soviet dialectic never could overcome that internal conflict." He held up one hand and looked at it musingly. "No matter how many they've lost trying."

Returning to his desk, he sat, his head cocked, studying her. As though looking for the fault in a piece of granite. He held apart his two forefingers.

"I woke up this morning with two separate problems. Expelling American spies and finding a killer. The two seemingly unrelated. But now—" He broke off, bringing his two fingers to touch.

"*Smert' otvechayet prezhde, chem yeye sprosyat.* Death answers before it is asked," he translated. "Now there are thirteen women dead or missing, as well as one of my own agents, found in the basement of William Cutler's apartment. I suppose you know nothing of that?"

"No," she answered. But the memory of the metal bar slapping against the man's bare neck made her flinch.

She caught a faint flash of anger in Kavalchuk's eyes. "What are the chances, do you think, that of all the women in Minsk our latest victim looks like you?"

Again, he'd taken a tack that left her feeling off-balance. "It must be a coincidence..." She stopped, her heart beginning to race. Kavalchuk's expression was almost one of pity. The stress of the past few hours had distracted her from the obvious. "Are you saying that I was targeted?"

"Your father has been a policeman for many years. He deals in hard facts, evidence, yes? What would he say about coincidences?"

"I don't know. What were the other women like? I mean, I don't look anything like Nadia or Katya. Does this killer even have a type?"

"You've hit at the heart of it. He is an opportunistic killer, grabbing women off the streets. Usually at night, but not always. The victims are usually young, but not all. Some are prostitutes, some are not. And then there are the missing. I believe that many of these women were taken without a struggle. At least at first."

"So the killer was known to the victims."

"I don't think it is possible for all."

"Then maybe he's a person in authority. A policeman, or someone that the women trust—"

"Or are compelled to obey."

Mel paused to catch her breath, order her chaotic thoughts. Kavalchuk's practiced restraint had morphed into something else. Something bordering on feral enthusiasm. It brought to mind her father's old, docile hunting dog. Calm, until the scent of prey brought out the snarling jaw and snapping teeth.

Abruptly, Kavalchuk held up a finger, as though a thought had just occurred to him. "If I may, for my own clarification, what time did you get to the apartment this morning?"

"Early. About six o'clock..." Mel stopped, instantly realizing her mistake.

"And yet, when Mr. Franklin and Miss Reznik were arrested at William Cutler's apartment, you and Mr. Hatton were not there. We know where Mr. Hatton was. Where did you spend the night?"

Mel stared at the floor. Kavalchuk stood once more, slowly circling her chair until he stood directly behind her.

"I think you were with your colleague Mr. Hatton. You were certainly wearing what a Belorussian would wear for an outing in the woods. The question is, why? What is your true purpose in Minsk? And who brought you back to the city? These and many other questions have me perplexed."

Even though she couldn't see him, she could feel him, like the low hum of a powerful engine. Her headache intensified, making her eyes water.

"In one of our earlier chats," he said, "I showed you a piece of paper retrieved from Katya's handbag. It was a note addressed to you, saying that she wanted to meet. You had befriended her, and soon after, she was killed. Then you befriended Nadia, and she was killed as well. And now we have another dead woman, one who happens to look like you."

Mel could feel his breath on her nape. Could he be right? Could she be the link?

"I believe that you were with Mr. Hatton last night in the woods and close to a dacha where a gathering was taking place. A gathering including William Cutler…and others, important guests of the Heat and Mass Transfer Institute."

He returned to the desk and scribbled something on a pad of paper. When he finished, he looked at her. "You are not a simple secretary. You are something else. The question remains: Why do all roads lead to Melvina Donleavy?"

He pressed a button and an officer appeared.

"She can go back to her cell for the evening," Kavalchuk instructed.

Mel stood, her legs rubbery, and followed the officer.

At the door, Kavalchuk spoke a last time. "You haven't yet asked about your friend Alexi Yurov." His voice was matter-of-fact, as though talking about the weather.

She paused, afraid to turn and face him; afraid that what she'd see in his eyes might make her legs give out. She wouldn't give him any more ammunition to use against her.

The guard took her arm and guided her out.

31

SUNDAY, AUGUST 19, 1990

Soon after being returned to her cell, Mel was given another meal on a tray, this time thin soup with dark bread. And, again, a mug of tea. The soup was cold, but she ate most of it anyway, along with the bread. When the guard took the tray away, she lay on her back and stared up at the ceiling.

Her vision pulsed along with the throbbing in her head. She closed her eyes, counting back from a hundred, trying to relax enough to initiate her processing. But the lights in the cell were too bright, even when she squeezed her eyelids tightly together. She would have to wait until they turned them off to try again.

She tried to reassure herself that, as her colleagues had left for Moscow on the late-afternoon plane, they would have arrived around six thirty. The last flight into Berlin, where the US had kept a chancellery in the former Soviet section and in the Clay building in West Berlin, would have them landing around midnight. Of course, the US State Department was working to unify the two embassies, and potentially to move their presence out of Berlin into Bonn. Mel had to hope that wouldn't in any way delay the American response, or her colleagues.

Surely, she only had to endure another day before she'd be

put on a plane back to the States. Just another twenty-four hours.

She tried counting breaths, focusing on relaxing each part of her body. Occasionally, she'd hear the footsteps of a guard, the closing of a heavy metal door, the hissing of air or water through the pipes in the walls. But she heard no talking. She'd been told by her trainers that Soviet guards were instructed not to speak unless giving orders. It helped to increase the prisoners' sense of isolation.

After an unknown span of time, she drifted off. She found herself back in the apartment with Alexi, his body just out of reach. She stretched her hand out to touch him but found, instead, a void, her fingers grasping only air. Waking in a panic, she realized that she was close to falling off the narrow bunk onto the concrete floor. The lights were still on. Disoriented and nauseous, she didn't know if she'd slept through the entire night, or if they were never turned off. Perhaps she'd only slept for a few hours.

Recalling the dream, she lay in an agony of uncertainty about Alexi's fate. If he'd truly been helping her, he would be shot if captured. Soviet justice was straightforward and swift.

Officially, the KGB had stopped interrogating prisoners in 1953 after the death of Stalin. But she knew that the reality of Soviet prisons for its citizens was harsh, and sometimes fatal.

Her own father had always said, "That which does not kill us makes us stronger." She hoped that, if she survived her ordeal, it too would strengthen her. But in the past few hours, her headache had worsened. It was now like a steel band around her head. She tried to guess how many hours she'd spent in the cell, but it could be two in the morning, or it could be eight o'clock. She felt sick and frail. And it was only going to get worse.

The next time the door to her cell opened, a guard brought in a tray with a hard roll and tea.

"Can you please tell me what time it is?" she asked.

The guard ignored her and left. When he returned a short while later to retrieve the tray, she asked him if there was somewhere she could get cleaned up, a shower or a bath. He left without any indication he'd understood.

Standing up made her feel unsteady, and she traced her hand along the wall for support. She used the small toilet and washed her hands and face in the corner sink, the water trickling from the faucet in a slow, rusty stream.

The Alpha officer appeared at the door. With some relief, Mel knew that this must mean it was the beginning of another day. He led her back to the interrogation room, where Martin Kavalchuk was again waiting. She sat, cradling her head in her hands, rubbing at her temples and trying to ignore the flashing silvery lights at the periphery of her vision.

When Kavalchuk took his seat at the desk, he stared at her for a long moment. His eyes were red-rimmed, the lids puffy, as though he too hadn't slept in days.

"Melvina Donleavy," he said, "your ordinary detainment has caused an extraordinary reaction from your government. Do you know who is the chairman of the *Komitet Gosudarstvennoy Bezopasnosti* in Moscow?"

Mel did know who the head of the Soviet KGB was. He was Vladimir Kryuchkov, an acolyte of the terrifying Yuri Andropov. Kryuchkov had become a master at spreading disinformation globally and acquiring technical intelligence from the West. But, more recently, his absolute hold over the KGB had begun to weaken. Several of his high-ranking members had defected to the US. He also held a great hatred for Gorbachev, current president of the Soviet Union and champion of reform.

Feigning ignorance, she said, "I'm sorry. I'm not sure—"

Kavalchuk inhaled deeply, as though steadying himself. "Since you are merely a *secretary,* I will tell you that, even though we are an independent agency, we are still part of the Russian Soviet Directorate. Do you know how many times I have received a direct order from the chairman of the KGB since his appointment in 1988?"

She shook her head.

"Twice. Only twice. And this morning is one of those times." He held up two pieces of paper. "In one hand I have a letter signed by the chairman ordering me to hold you, indefinitely. In the other a letter from the Byelorussian minister of external affairs, Sergei Ivanov, whom you have met, instructing me to release you immediately into his care based on the firm request of the US State Department."

He set the letters on the desk, covering them with both hands. "At any other time, my duty would be, without question, to the directorate. The KGB was built on discipline. Our motto, 'Loyalty to the party. Loyalty to the motherland.' Party first and always."

He stood and faced her. "But the mortar is beginning to crack. You are here because Byelorussia has declared its sovereignty. Our current Soviet chairman, Kobets, wants stronger ties to the West. And his mistress, a famous gymnast, happens to be among the women who have gone missing in Minsk. He called me last night to give me a deadline in arresting someone, anyone. He is not a happy man. So you see, Melvina, the old structures are resting on quicksand. *I* am resting on quicksand."

He moved closer to where she sat until he could have reached out and touched her. "And there still remains the question of what to do with you."

The dull, insistent ringing in Mel's ears grew louder as he approached. She remembered Ivanov's unsettling stares at both the ministry and William's apartment. The thought of being turned over to either Ivanov or Kryuchkov made her stomach churn. Clenching both fists, she willed herself to find some way to change the course of the interrogation. Moscow Rule number nine was *Pick the time and place for action.* Kavalchuk wasn't the only one who could pivot.

Mel stared up at him and said, "Tell me about the missing gymnast."

Her demand caught him by surprise and his scrutiny intensified.

She forced herself to keep her gaze steady, even though her eyes felt like two brittle marbles. "When did she go missing?"

"A few days before you arrived."

It was hard to keep her thoughts together. She pressed her nails into her palms to stay alert. "What did she look like?"

Kavalchuk crossed both arms, bringing one hand up to cradle his chin. "She was blond, like Nadia. And athletic."

"Was there any other commonality to the other women missing or killed?"

"No. As I said before, the women were from all walks of life. The only commonality is that they are all female."

"Have the local police, the *militsiya,* formed any theories, or found any leads?"

He scowled but also retreated, perching at the edge of the desk. "The police are no longer involved. All of these cases have been turned over entirely to the jurisdiction of the *Komitet.*"

"Linkage blindness," she muttered.

"What did you say?" he said sharply.

She sat up straighter, resisting the urge to rub at her temples again. "Linkage blindness. It means that different law enforcement agencies do not, or will not, share information about a crime. Important clues stay isolated, like individual puzzle pieces. Without connecting each, a whole picture of the event, and the perpetrator, may not become visible."

"We of the KGB have the best criminal investigators in Byelorussia," Kavalchuk said.

The words sounded rehearsed. She'd hit a nerve. Almost as

though he'd had the same thought before. Kavalchuk abruptly returned to his chair and reached for something under the desk. He must have pressed a signal button, because the young Alpha officer appeared immediately. The officer bent down and Kavalchuk whispered something into his ear. The officer then left, and after a few moments, Kavalchuk said, "Let us assume, for a moment, that there is one killer who is also our abductor. How would the FBI go about forming the picture of this man?"

She opened her mouth to deflect, but he raised a hand to silence her. "The recording device has been turned off," he said quietly. "Whatever is said in this room from now on is between you and me."

She raised her eyebrows in surprise. If he had stopped the recording, he really was encouraging her to speak freely. But she also wondered how many times an interrupted recording hid evidence of brutality. The pressure band around her head squeezed tighter.

"How many women are missing and how many women were killed?" she asked.

"Nine women have been found dead. Seven strangled by rope, and two, Nadia and the woman we found this morning, by hand."

"So that means four women are missing." He nodded and she remembered the complicated ropes that twisted Katya's stiffening body as she was pulled out of the river. "Were the others strangled by rope tied in the same way as Katya?"

He nodded again. There was something familiar about the odd constraint—hands tied behind the back and a noose that would tighten as the legs were lowered—but she couldn't remember where she'd seen it before.

Kavalchuk had been watching her closely, and he leaned forward, his gaze intent. "What were you thinking just now?"

"I was thinking that it was an odd way to kill someone.

The killer obviously had the strength to manually strangle a woman. So why go through all the trouble of the complicated rope system? There's something familiar about it—"

Her voice trailed away as her headache pounded. She realized that she had started to pant, taking in shallow breaths through her mouth. Her nausea was getting worse.

"Are you ill?" he asked.

"I'm…I couldn't sleep. Too much light in the cell." Through watering eyes she watched him watching her. Not in sympathy, but in cold, hard calculation. The predator sniffing around the fence, looking for a way into the henhouse.

The fact that he was still engaging her in conversation, though, made her think she was still useful to his hunt for the Strangler. And that might be useful to her, in obtaining a quicker release.

"You asked for a blueprint," she said. "For your killer. I can help you with that. But I need something from you first."

One heavy brow lifted. "Oh? And what is that?"

"I need a hot bath. In a dark room. To get rid of this headache."

"Anything else?" he asked, considering.

"What's happened to Alexi Yurov? Is William Cutler still in custody?"

His lips tightened into an implacable thin line. "We'll continue our interview after you've rested for a few hours." He signaled for the Alpha officer. As she was led out of the room, she saw Kavalchuk spreading both hands over the two letters again, as if trying to eradicate the conflicting orders.

After an endless hour back in her cell, another guard led Mel to a new elevator. They went up to what looked like a private living suite. Its expensive, heavy furnishings were in stark contrast to the building's ominous function, and she wondered if this was Kavalchuk's personal apartment. She shuddered to imagine living over the internment cells and interrogation rooms of the KGB. There was no warmth in the rooms, no photos or even books. Everything was practical and soulless. Passing a large, imposing desk, she saw a black coat draped over the back of the office chair and three Bakelite phones lined up in a row, like soldiers waiting for duty.

Oksana was waiting for Mel just outside the bathroom, where a full bath had already been drawn. Mel turned off the lights, removed her clothing, and stepped into the warm water. At Oksana's insistence, the door was left open.

Her worries about her ultimate fate, and the fates of Alexi and William, were overpowered by the absolute necessity of clearing her head.

"It's just the drugs, Alice," she murmured, feeling her muscles relaxing in the comfort of the bath. Intoning her mother's name brought an unexpected pang of nostalgia as she recalled the last time they'd spoken. Her mother had been chattering on in her usual slightly manic way about her latest college production of *The Crucible*. Mel had known then that she would be going to the Soviet Union, and had thought of that irony as her mother retold the familiar story of Arthur Miller's reimagining of the Salem witch hysteria.

"You know they tortured some of those poor people," Alice had said breathlessly. "I researched it! It was brutal but *legal* in the Colonial courts."

Mel sat up abruptly, the water sluicing off her body in waves. *The killer's ropes.* Odd, yes. Singular, yes. But American as apple pie.

Oksana must have heard the slapping of water against the tub. Suddenly she was standing in the doorway. "You must get out now," she ordered.

Panic gripped Mel. She hadn't yet processed the faces of the people she'd scanned in the last few days. She vigorously shook her head, closing her eyes in the hopes that Oksana would relent. But she felt the woman's hand firmly clamping onto her bare shoulder.

"You must get out, or guards will come."

Mel's eyes jerked open, and she saw a look of open hostility on Oksana's face. The woman was as solid as a Soviet tank and could probably lift her out of the tub like a child. Reluctantly, Mel stood up. Oksana handed her a towel and refused to leave while Mel got dressed again.

Before she had even left the apartment, the waves of nausea returned, the pressure building steadily inside her skull.

32

MONDAY, AUGUST 20, 1990

The man standing outside the KGB headquarters took furtive sips of vodka from his pocket flask. The discomfort he had been feeling the past few months had recently sharpened into stabbing pains in his abdomen, driving him finally to his doctor for something, anything to coat his stomach.

He'd gone that morning for a follow-up to the tests the medical expert had insisted upon. But instead of the doctor providing a soothing balm, he had given his patient the fatal news. It was cancer of the stomach, very aggressive, and very far advanced. It had been growing and spreading in his gut like the mycelium he had so carefully, and dedicatedly, been cultivating. He had, at most, a few months to live.

The past hours had been an agony of a different kind for him. An agony of disappointment and thwarted desires. How many chances did he have left? The woman he thought he'd recognized yesterday had not, in fact, been Melvina Donleavy. Upon discovering his mistake, he'd been overwhelmed with a rage so powerful that he'd throttled the life out of the imposter before he could have counted to twenty. It surpassed even the anger he'd felt with Nadia. It had happened so swiftly, and so deftly, that it surprised even him. He'd still felt shaken the next day, sitting in his doctor's office.

The dead woman had been found quickly—which was to be expected, as he'd left her body in full view. He had no great worries that he would be connected to the body. The pressure he was feeling now was of a completely different nature.

He sipped his vodka again, the viscous liquid finally beginning to dampen the intense burning in his gut. Melvina Donleavy had been arrested by the KGB, and the demands from the American State Department to release her would only increase. He'd heard through the rumor mill that the chairman of the KGB in Moscow had taken a personal interest. There was good reason to believe that she had been with her male colleague, hiding in the forest. To believe too that they'd seen the Iranian scientists who had pledged millions to Byelorussia in order to advance their nuclear program. It seemed everyone had heard about Persepolis. The finance ministry, the foreign ministry, the KGB, the Americans, and probably even the *babushka* who swept the streets in front of the Heat and Mass Transfer Institute.

Gossip needs no carriage, the old ladies say. The entire country knew to spy on their neighbors. It was how the KGB and *militsiya* were able to keep tabs on millions of people. Asking them to keep quiet? Might as well try to tell rainwater not to run downhill.

It did not take a genius to understand that the Americans were gathering proof that the nation of Iran, the sworn enemy of the United States, was using Soviet technology to aggressively develop a nuclear bomb.

There would be fallout when the Americans openly protested. They would withdraw their proposed funding. He himself had stood to gain monetarily from the development of the program. But his position, at least, was safe either way. As long as he was alive, he would be insulated by his standing with the party. *Altinnovo vora veshayut, a poltinnovo chestvuyut.* Petty thieves are hanged, but great ones are praised.

Of course, he would soon be beyond such concerns.

He stared up at the massive pillars fronting the KGB headquarters, the pride of Minsk, the building he'd just left after an emergency meeting to discuss what to do with the American female. That angel of a woman who would, if he didn't act quickly, be taken from him forever. Either back to the States, or into the all-consuming bowels of the Lubyanka prison in Moscow.

He had to come up with a plan, a strategy to get her out of her prison cell, and into his hands. Perhaps some kind of barter, or bribe?

The man had discovered that, of his many talents, his most successful one was reading people's weaknesses. Every person had a vulnerability that could be exploited. He'd honed his skill in the years after the war, when needs had been simple. Bread, vodka, and cigarettes were powerful currencies in the wasteland that was Minsk following the relentless bombing campaigns of the Germans.

He remembered as a young man, standing in the ravaged streets before his university classes, the shadows of the predawn hour barely flown, waiting for the tender schoolgirls to emerge from their ruined basement burrows like young Persephones. He would stand as quiet and motionless as a trapper, waiting for the little doves to walk into his snare.

The university students, out of national pride for Stalin, were given a surplus of food, and he'd started hoarding it to use as lures. Some of the girls had maintained a semblance of cleanliness. Their faces were scrubbed, they wore bits of ribbon in their hair. He'd imagined a mother, or grandmother perhaps, tenderly washing off the coal dust with a bit of rag and water left over from the morning tea. Then sending their child off into the world like the blessings of a martyr, a useless shield against a dangerous and uncertain future.

Other girls had looked more animal than human. Feral,

wearing rags and butcher's paper for shoes. Girls who would growl at the man when he approached but became tame as house cats when presented with food.

How many had he strangled? A dozen at least. In the fractured aftermath of the war, the dead were still more familiar than the living. If a body was found, the local police were more likely to strip her to sell anything of worth than to try to solve a crime. After all, they had their own daughters to feed.

As the years passed and order was restored, he had become more cautious in his selection and more refined in his methods. There'd been travel to other cities, where he'd practiced. He'd spent some years in East Berlin, a place rich in opportunities among the many frantic women looking to escape to the West.

He'd honed his methods of bribing and bartering as well. He'd never met a man or woman who, with the right kind of leverage, could not be moved to act to his benefit.

But it was only later, after he'd settled back into life in Minsk as *vazhnyy chelovek,* an important man, that he'd developed his glorious field of mushrooms. His beautiful garden that would never be complete unless he could place his perfect woman in a place of honor. And after he had covered her over with the black, rich soil, he would lie down beside her and put a bullet in his brain.

Then they would be together, at peace, for all time.

He shook himself out of his reverie and put his mind once more to a plan. The KGB had Melvina Donleavy, and Martin Kavalchuk held the keys to her cage. But the head of the Byelorussian *Komitet* was being squeezed between two powerful and oppositional forces, and the man with the blue Lada had sources inside the headquarters too. Even KGB officers could be bribed now, something that would have been unthinkable before Byelorussian sovereignty. As well, he had darker, more secretive contacts who daily roamed the streets, and daily gained more power and influence.

He had, luckily, plenty of money set aside. A vast sum that even his wife didn't know about. But he would have to hurry. Time was running out.

He drained the last of the vodka into his mouth and got behind the wheel of his car. The man had miles to go before he could sleep.

33

MONDAY, AUGUST 20, 1990

Mel stared at the food on her lunch tray, eventually only able to drink the lukewarm tea. She could barely rouse herself when a guard arrived again, insistent she follow him once more to the interrogation room.

Kavalchuk was already waiting for her, seated at the small desk. In front of him, resting like unexploded grenades, were the same two letters.

As well as the throbbing pain at her temples, Mel felt a growing fear. Every hour brought closer the possibility of prolonged arrest, or of being "disappeared." And every hour held the dread of not knowing what had happened to Alexi. The longer she was a prisoner, the greater the possibility that she would not complete her mission at all. She hadn't had a chance to pass along her report. She was still the only person who could verify the identity of the three Iranian nuclear scientists. But in front of Kavalchuk, Mel forced herself to unclench her hands and resisted the urge to cross her arms protectively over her belly.

"You will be able to speak freely," he said pleasantly, motioning for her to begin. "As before, there is no recording."

Instinctively, she knew not to start the conversation with her worries, but with her certainties. "The killer."

Kavalchuk stirred in his seat, his head tilting in her direction.

She licked her lips, keeping her voice steady. "I've been trying to tie together the similarities. To form a blueprint, as you say. But I need to ask you some questions."

He gestured for her to go on.

"Did any of the murdered women have evidence of sexual assault?"

"No."

"No semen or other bodily fluids?"

"No."

"Did you rule out other suspects? Their husbands or boyfriends?"

Kavalchuk sighed. "There were arrests made to satisfy the procurator, and the citizens. But in every case but one there was no history of domestic violence. And, in most, there were adequate alibis. Regardless, some of these suspects are still in custody."

"And are you certain the ropes were all the same?"

"Yes." Kavalchuk stood and began pacing. "Same kind of rope and same type of slip noose."

She cleared her throat. She felt like she was executing roadside maneuvers; like a drunk person trying to walk a straight line. "The FBI have theorized that classifying certain types of crimes can identify certain types of offenders."

On Kavalchuk's desk were a glass and a pitcher of water. Pouring some water into the glass, he handed it to her and waited for her to drink all of it.

"Your hand is shaking." He said it casually, but she thought for the first time she detected a glimmer of concern. "You are ill, I think."

"No. I'm just tired."

He took the glass from her and returned it to the desk. "So, to your point, certain offenders can be disqualified from this exercise. Say, molesters of children."

"Exactly."

"Then we must determine why the offender chooses adult females."

"The 'why' is not important right now. The why may not be apparent until the suspect is detained and questioned. Sometimes the offender doesn't fully understand, themselves. They're just compelled to do it."

Kavalchuk pursed his mouth thoughtfully. "Go on."

"If we can start to form a list of commonalities, we can consider who fits. We can assume the killer is a man, because of the strength needed to overcome his victims. We can assume he's not a typical rapist, as there's no semen or other evidence of frenzied assault. Death by slow strangulation takes time, so the killer may gain satisfaction from watching his victim die. Most of the time, at least for the victims who have been found, he uses the same kind of rope. Perhaps he needs to set a certain scene? We can also assume, then, that the two women manually strangled were killed out of a sudden rage, or because he didn't have time to draw it out."

Crossing his arms, Kavalchuk stopped his pacing. "Yes, the last woman was killed in a very public place. The chance of detection was greatly magnified." He studied the ceiling. "Most of the murder victims discovered were killed at night, which could possibly mean that he works during the day."

"Possibly," Mel said, nodding. "Or, conversely, that he works as a night guard and is killing while on duty. One of the biggest questions is the matter of the women not found. You said that there was no commonality between the women found and the women missing. But perhaps those comparisons are clouding the equation? If we exclude the women who have been found, is there a similarity to those still missing?"

Kavalchuk quickly turned to her. "They were mostly substantial women. Fleshy, we would say." He paused. "Although the gymnast had been quite slender."

"'Had been,'" Mel repeated. Competing gymnasts reached their prime before their twenties. "How old was she when abducted?"

Kavalchuk shrugged. "Forty, forty-five?"

"A woman's body can change a lot over twenty years."

"Yes, yes it can," he said, looking at her as though seeing her for the first time.

Mel could almost read his thoughts: *Here is forward momentum*. Pieces of the puzzle were falling into place, presenting a cohesive picture.

"He's being selective, then," Kavalchuk said, resuming his pacing. "He has some purpose for them. Perhaps he's attracted in a sexual way to large women. He's taking them somewhere to rape them in private."

"There is often a deviant sexual component to torture and sadistic murder," Mel agreed, fighting the urge to grind her teeth. "And some serial killers, I've read, experienced sexual release only after they revisited the crime in their fantasies. So the lack of bodily fluids on the dead women might not mean anything. But we also don't have proof it's sexual in nature at all."

"What else could it be?"

"With all due respect, you're thinking in conventional terms." When his expression darkened, Mel hurried to add, "You're equating rape with sex and not violence. Every woman knows it's about power."

"Then what else could he be doing with the women he takes?"

She hesitated for a moment before going on. "There have been instances of cannibalism in sadistic murders. You mentioned Ed Gein. He kept trophies of his victims. Skin and body parts. Perhaps he has use for them after death?"

"To do what?"

The overhead lights were pulsing in erratic waves and she lowered her head to shield her eyes. "I don't know."

Kavalchuk sat once more at his desk. "Tell me what you think you do know."

Mel took a deep breath. "Your killer is a strong man, highly organized, and supremely confident. His methods are sophisticated. He's been practicing killing for a long time, which might make him an older man. Someone who's professional, intelligent, and highly exacting in his routines. He commands respect, or fear, as he's often able to lure, or compel, women to go to private places. That he killed the most recent woman in broad daylight behind a church means not only that he's bold, but that he would blend in with other common, respectable men on the street. He would need a car to execute his crimes and transport the women, alive or dead.

"And lastly, the murder weapon. Something was tugging at my memory. And I realized: his ropes. The way he ties them. It's a little-known torture technique from Colonial America, used during the so-called witch trials of the seventeenth century. It's called the Bow. Only someone who had studied early American history would know about it."

Kavalchuk stood rigidly motionless, his gaze eager, almost feverish. "This could be another vital clue. One we'd not considered."

"Unfortunately, the West has had its share of violence toward women."

Kavalchuk shook his head, running a hand over the dense bristle of his gray hair. "The West is not unique in this regard." Rising to pace once more, he continued. "The description you have given of the killer could apply to half of the men in Byelorussia and most of the men in the politburo. It could even be me."

"Are you married?"

"No, I am widowed," he answered curtly. "Heart attack. Dead two years now."

It seemed oddly personal, and chillingly unemotional, this

confession. If the apartment where she'd been taken was in fact Kavalchuk's residence, there was no evidence that he'd ever had a private life. Even a widower would normally keep evidence of a family, at least for a while. But then again, what would be normal for the head of the KGB? Especially a man who'd been responsible for countless arrests, and deaths, during his tenure. What kind of woman would be wife to the Black Wolf of Byelorussia?

She took a breath to order her thoughts. At Quantico she'd once been able to obtain an official psychological profile of a killer nicknamed Pogo the Clown, who'd buried dozens of young men under his house. The FBI had documented how he was superficially charming, successful at his job, and married. But there was no way she could mention the FBI now.

"What I say next is based on things I read in my college psychology class about the serial killer John Wayne Gacy. But I think it applies to similar killers as they've been profiled by US law enforcement. I'd guess the Strangler is probably married, possibly with children. It gives him cover. As in Colonial America, a man unmarried for a long period of time will fall under suspicion. He also has a place, maybe a dacha or second apartment, to take his victims to."

"You've told me what your mind informs you about the *Svisloch Dushitel*. What does your gut tell you?"

"He's going to kill again. And he'll keep killing until you stop him."

"And the murdered woman who looks like you?"

To Mel, the dead woman's face had been that of a stranger. *Every* face was distinct, with a million different variations, but in ways that most people couldn't detect—at least not instantaneously. But she had to now admit the possibility that she had been the Strangler's target. Here was a new fear to add to her growing list.

"I think...that means the killer is someone who's been in

my company. Who has perhaps formed either an attachment, or a dislike—"

"Perhaps even an *obsession* with you?" he asked. He looked at her with a raised brow, his tone gently mocking.

She had the uncanny feeling that he was somehow teasing her. His menacing air, his very posture, had, at some point in their conversation, softened. It both reassured her and put her on high alert.

The young Alpha officer entered the room following a quick knock and whispered into Kavalchuk's ear. Kavalchuk looked at him sharply and then dismissed him. He handed Mel a piece of paper and a pencil.

"I want you to write down every man with whom you've come in close contact who you feel is capable of being our killer. At the ministry, the institute, the hotel, and even here, in this building. If you don't know his name, put down his location and a physical description. Underline the name of any man who's been inappropriate with you, or who's made you uncomfortable."

She caught and held his eye for a moment. Incredibly, there was not the slightest hint of irony in his last uttered sentence. Nadia had said that every woman in Minsk had a boyfriend, or a husband, or a boss, who could be a suspect. Sadly, someone Nadia had encountered had proven her right. The terrifying question now was, did Mel know that same someone?

As she made her list, Kavalchuk once more paced the floor methodically, slowly circling her chair until he stood behind her, out of her range of sight. She felt the intensity of his focus directed like an arrow at her back.

After fifteen minutes, she'd written down the names or descriptions of the dozen or so men she'd been in daily contact with. It was only a small fraction of the remembered faces she'd scanned during her time in Minsk. When she'd finished, she handed the paper over her shoulder to Kavalchuk. He took it from her hand and was silent for a moment.

"I must tell you that you cannot be correct with some of these names," he said with conviction. "I asked you to write the names of the men you feel *capable* of being the killer."

"Yes, that's what I did."

He shook his head vigorously. "You are accusing highly ranked members of the Communist Party."

She turned in her seat to face him. Whatever had caused him to relax his stance with her earlier had hardened again. "They are powerful men with resources, and they fit the criteria—"

"Enough!" Kavalchuk said forcefully. "It is simply not possible. Some of these men are war heroes."

He returned to his desk, his expression strained. He took a few moments to compose himself.

Her body ached from sitting in the hard chair, and from the tension of being questioned for hours. She was physically and emotionally drained and wanted nothing more than to sleep, but she made one more attempt to get him to think past his own prejudices, and perhaps his own arrogance. "My father used to say that no matter how strong the boat, if it's got holes in it it's going to sink. You can recite official policy from now until doomsday, but it doesn't change human nature."

Kavalchuk stared at her, unblinking, entrenched in a lifetime of Soviet doctrine. Believing that something was true because the party said it was so. She leaned forward, willing him to hear her.

"You're going to have more murdered women if you don't broaden your search. My guess is, you've already arrested the usual suspects and yet the killings have continued. Can you at least consider all the men I've listed?" When he didn't respond, she said, "Beyond what I've told you, I can't help you."

His eyelids lowered to half-mast, and he clasped his hands over the desk. The shadows in the hollows of his cheeks and at his temples had deepened, as though his body were caving in on itself. "I've just been informed that the First Directorate of the KGB is sending an envoy from Moscow tomorrow morning. I'm ordered to turn you over to him for transport to Lubyanka prison for further questioning. You've been named as an agent of *Glavniy Vrag*."

The Main Enemy. Stalin's name for his greatest foe, the United States. A label like this could easily mean a death sentence. Her eyes darted frantically along the walls to the far door, sure to be locked and guarded.

"I'm an American citizen," she whispered.

"But you are suspected to be a spy. It cannot be a coincidence that you are here, now, when Byelorussia is fortifying ties with a foreign entity hostile to America."

She peered through bloodshot eyes at Kavalchuk, searching for some compassion. "I was sent here as a secretary."

His mouth twisted unpleasantly. "Years ago," he said, "I was assigned as head of security to Leonid Brezhnev at a forest retreat in Brest, close to the Polish border. It was toward the end of his life. He had cancer, lung ailments, gout. The man could hardly walk, but he would still drink vodka and smoke ten cigarettes in an hour. He wanted to hunt deer and so I was tasked with finding deer, drugging them, and tying them to a tree. His personal aide would help him hoist the rifle. And still the man couldn't hit his mark.

"Yuri Andropov was with us. He said to me, 'Martin Gregorivich, Brezhnev is perceived as a great hunter. If you have to wear antlers yourself and let him shoot you, he will get his kill. He's first secretary of the Soviet Union and will not be embarrassed.'"

Mel remembered seeing newsreels of Brezhnev, a stern, robust man with eyebrows as thick and black as boot brushes, and a deep belief in Soviet doctrine. She could imagine that he would never forgive a perceived slight or humiliation.

"I hid with a rifle in the trees behind Brezhnev," Kavalchuk said, "and timed my shots with his, bringing down the deer. If his remaining security detail had seen me, pointing a rifle in Brezhnev's direction, I would have been shot."

He said it matter-of-factly, crossing his arms. "But I was willing to take the risk because I am a true believer and it meant something to my country."

He took up his pad of paper and wrote something. When he was finished, he tore the sheet off the pad and folded it.

"There is only one person, I believe, who can countermand the order from the First Directorate," he said, holding the note aloft. "I have written here that you may be the key to helping solve the mystery of what happened to the famous gymnast, mistress to the chairman, Vyacheslav Kobets. Chairman Kobets believes that Byelorussia may become independent. There is disagreement about this in our parliament, but it may be useful for the chairman to flex some of his political muscles in thwarting Moscow right now."

She looked at the man seated across from her. A man who could, with a word, and within the hour, arrange to have her corpse placed alongside her doppelgänger. "Why would you do this?"

He stared at her through hooded eyes. "I could tell you that it's because I think you are a true believer as well. That you are someone willing to risk their life for the good of their country. There are very few of us left in these days of cynical compromise." He pressed a button on his desk and the young Alpha officer appeared to take her back to her cell.

"But the truth is," he continued, "I have a killer to catch, and very little time to do it. I will revisit your list of important men, Melvina Donleavy, and if you are right, you can congratulate yourself that a mere *secretary* will have shaken the government to its core."

34

TUESDAY, AUGUST 21, 1990

For what felt like the hundredth time, Mel rolled in her bunk from one side to the other, trying to find a position that would relieve the tension in her neck and the roaring in her head. Light continued to flood the cell. She'd managed to drift off into sleep a few times, but always some noise or bodily discomfort would yank her back to consciousness.

Despite the pain, she still had control of her motor functions. But she didn't know how many more hours of rational thought she had left. If her experience during training held, there would be no warnings before her switch was triggered. Other than the pain, it would be like slipping under anesthesia—awake one minute, unconscious the next. Except that her body would be left on autopilot, defensively and blindly striking out.

Luckily, it seemed she'd only been in the cell for a few more hours when a guard opened the door and Oksana walked in holding a change of clothes.

"You must get up," she ordered, and stood by silently as Mel took off the prison dress and put on a plain, summer-weight skirt and blouse with a bright yellow cardigan.

"What's going on? What's happening?" Mel asked, slipping her feet into a pair of flats.

Stony-faced, Oksana only gestured Mel out of the cell and

into the elevator. With a sinking heart, Mel realized she was being led back to the interrogation room. But this time, when the guard opened the door, she saw Kavalchuk standing next to a man in a white doctor's coat. Next to the man was a cart with a stethoscope and what looked like several hypodermic syringes. The young Alpha officer was standing on the other side of the doctor.

She started to back up, but the guard pulled her into the room and forcibly lowered her into the chair. Her elevated heart rate set the cadence for the throbbing in her head, and she felt bile at the back of her throat. For a moment she thought she'd start retching.

"You're not well," Kavalchuk said. "The doctor will check your heart to make sure you're fit to travel."

Her panicked gaze searched the enclosed room. "Travel? What do you mean?"

The guard tightened his grip on Mel's shoulder as the doctor approached. He held up a hand to show her the stethoscope and said, in heavily accented English, "I will check only to see if your heart is strong."

He stooped down and moved the stethoscope diaphragm over her chest, listening. When he was finished, he straightened and turned to Kavalchuk, saying something in Russian. She understood the words *ochen' bystro*—very fast—and guessed that he was talking about her accelerated heart rate. They exchanged a few more phrases before the doctor shrugged and picked up one of the syringes from the cart. It was filled with a milky-looking liquid.

"What are you doing?" Mel had meant to sound firmly outraged, but her voice cracked with fear.

"Ergotamine," the doctor said. "For your headache."

"It's not that kind of headache—" The guard pulled Mel's wrists together behind her back. Oksana wrapped one arm around her neck in a wrestler's hold and squeezed.

The doctor tapped one finger against the glass cylinder and expressed a little of the liquid through the end of the needle. With surprising speed, he approached Mel, jabbing her in her shoulder, delivering the drug. When the doctor returned to the cart for the second hypodermic, Mel renewed her struggles. She tried biting Oksana's arm and kicking out with her feet.

Kavalchuk approached and said quietly, "I will have you restrained if you do not cooperate."

"What's in the second shot?" she demanded.

"Something to help relax you."

"Please," she begged. "Tell me what's going on."

Kavalchuk paused, clasping his hands behind his back. "You are being driven this morning to Minsk-2 airport. There will be a plane waiting to take you to Moscow."

Everything was happening too quickly. Being taken to Moscow could only mean that the central KGB committee was determined to prove that she was a spy.

There had always been the slim possibility that she could be killed on this mission. Her trainers at Camp Peary had told her so. But she'd never fully entertained the idea. How arrogant she'd been to take for granted that, because she was young, and American, and unique, she would be valued. Soldiers younger than she had gone to war and not come back. She shook off Oksana's hand from her shoulder.

"What about the Soviet chairman?" she asked, relieved that at least her voice sounded strong. "Did you petition him?"

Kavalchuk turned his back to her. "He refused my request. He will not challenge the First Directorate."

He began to walk toward the exit door. There was nothing she could do. Escape was impossible—even if she tried, she doubted she'd even make it past the tank calling herself Oksana. But the part of Mel that had walked six miles in a Wisconsin snowstorm carrying a heavy bottle of bleach wouldn't give up.

"Wait, Martin Gregorivich!" Everyone in the room stiffened at her tone. Even Oksana moved away, as though to distance herself from the blast zone. The doctor looked nervously at Kavalchuk as he turned to face Mel. She'd spoken his patronymic, used only in informal settings and by his peers. She had dared to call out to the Black Wolf as though they were intimates.

Mel stood unsteadily. "Did you even care about the women? Or was finding the Strangler just another potential medal for you?"

Recovering herself, Oksana tried to wrestle Mel back down into the chair, but Kavalchuk motioned to the woman to stop.

His expression went through several rapid changes. First angered, then puzzled, and finally something that looked like regret. "I'm sorry that we didn't have more time to solve our mystery, because I surely would have gotten another medal. As it stands now..." His voice trailed away, and he shrugged.

"You didn't answer my question," she said.

He resumed his exit, but before he'd left the room she yelled, as forcefully as she could, "Linkage blindness!"

The door closed behind him. As soon as it had, the doctor approached her with the second syringe. It was only a few moments before she felt a crippling warmth spreading through her body, making her limbs impossibly heavy, her head too weighted to stay upright. She could barely keep her eyelids open. She felt herself being lifted and strapped into another chair, which had been wheeled into the interrogation room.

In the long dark hallway she saw, for the briefest moment, two men standing together at the far end, observing her. One was Martin Kavalchuk and the other was Alexi Yurov, in uniform and wearing his high-crowned military hat.

Losing consciousness, she woke briefly in the elevator, but, despite her best efforts, everything went black as she was lifted into the backseat of a car, a blanket tucked around her. When the engine started and she felt forward motion, she managed to open her eyes for only a second. Anton was driving and another KGB officer was in the passenger seat.

"Anton, help me," she rasped. Both men swiveled their heads to look at her.

Anton shifted uncomfortably in his seat and then stared at the road once more. After a heavy pause, he said, "I'm very sorry, but I must drive you to the airport."

She closed her eyes and gave herself over to a growing hopelessness. She had failed her mission. *Ahmadi, Mahmoud, Saleh,* she mouthed silently, a new—and maybe last—mantra.

As they drove, her eyes opened and closed at unknown intervals, like a camera's shutter set to its slowest speed, capturing only fleeting images of blue sky through dense trees, a blur of green and brown. She was conscious enough to register that the car was traveling at a high speed, which meant that they would be at the airport all too soon. Occasionally, she could hear the two men in the front seat speaking in Russian, but they spoke too softly for her to make out the words.

At some point the roar of highway noise decreased, the pulsating vibration of the car began to slow, and she opened her eyes just as the car came to a complete stop. Thinking they had arrived, she fought a rising tide of panic.

She heard Anton bark at the KGB officer sitting next to him. He sounded irritated and then impatiently honked the horn. Rolling down the window, he called loudly to someone, *"Uydi s dorogi, idiot!"* Out of the road, idiot!

Footsteps approached the window, and then another man was speaking rapidly, his tone apologetic. From her vantage point in the backseat, Mel could only see his torso. Then a hand holding something dark was thrust through the window. There was a surprised yelp from Anton and the deafening roar of a gun being fired. The force of the bullet rocketed Anton's bulk sideways. Another shot was fired, and the KGB officer slumped forward. The gun was fired rapidly several more times and Mel recoiled into a protective fetal position, her face and arms flicked with wet, sticky patches.

She waited to feel her own bullet. For an instant, when the impact didn't come, she had the wild hope that maybe someone was rescuing her—Joseph perhaps, or one of his contacts. But then the back passenger door was yanked open and a pair of hands grabbed her roughly, and painfully, around the ankles. Whatever this was, it was not a rescue. Defensively, she began kicking. A man swore in Russian. Another pair of hands slipped under her armpits, and she felt herself being carried. Blinking against the bright day, she saw a white van with a farm trailer attached to its back parked crossways in the middle of the road. With narrowing vision, she looked at the man holding on to her legs and recognized the kitchen worker from the Planeta. Anton would not be rescuing her this time.

"Privet, krasavitsa," he said, winking at her.

Hello, pretty girl.

She was carried like a sackful of enraged cats past the trailer to a vehicle parked on the side of the road. This one was blue. As blue as the limitless sky above.

Before she could see who was driving, she lost consciousness again.

35

TUESDAY, AUGUST 21, 1990

In a certain kingdom, in a certain land…"

The old *babushka* would start all her fairy tales in this way. "The Thieving Peasant," "The Nightmare," "The Slandered Maiden"—she knew hundreds of stories, and Oleg loved every one of them. But his favorites were of Baba Yaga, the terrifying witch of the forest. His first memories of these retellings came from a time when he was so small, he couldn't see over the top of the table where his mother and her mother would sit for hours, drinking tea and shelling broad beans and gossiping.

He must have been very young, as his sister was still in the cradle and his brother hadn't yet been born. The only light in the small room he shared with his sister came from a narrow candle that wept wax under the flame the way a saint shed tears. When his grandmother would come to tuck him in, the shadows they cast were like long dark fingers reaching toward his bed to swallow him whole.

"Baba Yaga," she would begin, her tongue moving around what few teeth she had left, "lived in the forest, catching and eating whatever little children came her way. Grinding them to paste with her sharp teeth."

As she talked, the old woman would ease her hand under

the covers, pinching him hard whenever she uttered the witch's name, on his arms and legs and belly, and sometimes even his pale little penis. She often left bruises on Oleg's flesh, which would last for days. The physical pain added to the almost unbearable suspense of the story and brought home his *babushka*'s favorite lesson: that he could never, never eat the only other food that Baba Yaga consumed, the thick-bodied, red-hatted fly agaric mushroom.

It was only after the Great War, when he studied science at the university, that he would learn the exact reasons why the fly agaric was so dangerous. Its mix of chemicals—muscarine, muscimol, and ibotenic acids—generated a toxic buffet of nasty, potentially fatal, side effects. But when he was a child, his grandmother had only warned him that death would come to call if he so much as put a tongue to its red cap. And so, as an inquisitive child, Oleg had needed to verify her warning, and had stealthily dropped several pieces of the fly agaric into his grandmother's stew. She didn't die, but for days the old woman had hallucinations, severe muscle contractions, and seizures. After his *babushka* recovered, she never again told Oleg her fairy tales. Instead she would sit in a corner and stare at him fearfully through her tiny button eyes. Eyes that now recognized him for what he truly was.

Intrigued, he'd later read of Siberian shamans, the Evenki, who, through carefully controlled rituals, took minuscule amounts of the fly agaric and became convinced they were invisible, able to fly through the frigid air wrapped in reindeer hides to visit some vengeful act on their enemies. He'd even experimented with isolating the psychotropic chemicals himself, consuming small quantities to varying effect, some of it quite pleasant. Often, after drinking a tea with the extracted alkaloids, he'd experienced a heightened sense of joy, at times bordering on the ecstatic. Once, he'd felt compelled to lie on his belly in a nearby field, his ear pressed into the dirt until he could hear the roots of the grasses and flowering plants growing into the ground. He'd been led home by his wife, who thought he'd merely drunk too much vodka.

Now, Oleg decided, for this last act of planting, he would finally consume a larger amount of the mushroom's extract. He'd give some to Melvina too. Together they would exit the world in a happy fog.

Oleg checked his rearview mirror and saw that she was still unconscious, lying motionless across the backseat of his blue Lada. Her face looked serene, as though she'd already begun entering the Eternal Sleep. Of course, he would have to wake her when they arrived at the dacha. He wanted to share with her his lovely garden, so she'd know that she was soon to become a part of it, its final crowning jewel.

He briefly considered going south into the Exclusion Zone, to another colleague's dacha, where the fallout from Chernobyl had encouraged glorious mushrooms to flourish in the irradiated soil. He'd visited it many times already. But it was too far now. Time was of the essence. He would be discovered missing soon. And besides, he wanted Melvina to see his own beautiful fields.

Nothing else mattered except this final act of passion. This final act of dedication. And, yes, he could even say, as he hummed a Byelorussian folk song, a lasting expression of his love.

36

TUESDAY, AUGUST 21, 1990

Mel was only vaguely aware of the movement of the car, a continual gentle vibration. She felt trapped in a twilight state: poised between the world of knowing, and of not. Slowly, and then ever faster, faces began to flow across the inside of her closed eyelids—the guards, Oksana, the new members of the Brotherhood Mel had never seen before—and she felt the pressure in her head releasing. The muscles in her body relaxed slowly, and the fear of her mind fracturing abated. Tears of relief leaked from her closed eyes, and finally, she fell into a deep sleep.

Coming back into consciousness, Mel realized she had been staring at the lifeless eyes, seven pairs of them, for what felt like hours. But the hand on the wooden wall clock had advanced only a few minutes. She felt disconnected from her body, as though a camera had been placed above her and she was watching the video from another room. With a shock, she realized that the unblinking eyes staring back at her were painted onto the shellacked surfaces of *matryoshki,* the iconic Russian nesting dolls, seven of them placed side by side on a shelf next to the clock.

She blinked slowly, her eyelids like sandpaper across her irises. Her hands and feet felt numb, and she carefully flexed her fingers and toes, willing them to obey her thoughts. Elated, she realized that the drug had worked in place of her nightly ritual. There were lingering physical symptoms, but her mind was free.

She sensed that someone was there with her in the…what? House? Apartment?

It was a man humming, moving around in another room.

Breathing deeply, flooding her brain with oxygen, she carefully turned her head. She was on a narrow bed, pushed up against a wall. The wall was paneled in smooth pine and partially covered with an intricately patterned carpet in faded colors. Next to the rug was a weathered piece of wood, bent into an arc. Mel recognized it as a harness for a brace of oxen.

Turning her head, she took in the rest of the cluttered room. Old Soviet-era furniture—a dining table, a ratty, misshapen sofa, and a large dresser—was all pushed against the far wall. There was only one window, but it was covered by a thick blanket. A ceramic lamp stood in one corner, the light haloing brightly through the paper-thin shade. There were a few black-and-white photographs in cheap frames on the end tables and she scanned them quickly. On every flat surface were placed more *matryoshki*. Dozens of them. In a corner, a small birchwood basket was also filled with the dolls, their eyes wide and unblinking.

With shaking arms, she levered herself into a sitting position. A wave of dizziness threatened to throw her backward onto the mattress, but she closed her eyes until the droning in her head stopped. She heard the footsteps of someone walking into the room.

She opened her eyes and then blinked a few times in disbelief.

It was Oleg Shevchenko, head of the Heat and Mass Transfer Institute. He also startled, clearly surprised that she was sitting up. She recalled, in a fragmented series of images, the trip to the airport, the horror of Anton and the other officer being shot, the members of the *Bratva* pulling her from the car. How she'd then been placed in another car. Was Shevchenko the one who'd rescued her from the KGB?

"Thank you," she said groggily. "For saving me."

He made a vague gesture with one hand, looking at her as though suddenly confounded by her presence. Instead of his usual suit and tie, he was dressed in an old work shirt, the sleeves rolled up past his elbows.

"Vody," she tried again. Water.

He stared at her for a moment before turning and leaving the room, returning with a glass. Silently, he passed it to her and watched as she swallowed all the water in one go. It tasted slightly metallic, but it was cold, and she almost fainted with relief.

Holding the glass out to Oleg, she said, *"Spacibo."*

He took the glass and stood; his brow furrowed.

"Eto tvoy dom?" she asked. Is this your home?

His frown deepened, and, turning on his heel, he abruptly left the room.

Mel sat wondering if she should try to stand, but she wasn't sure her legs would hold her upright. Wherever she was, it was someplace quiet. There were no street noises, no sounds of water running through building pipes. She heard a faint birdcall, identified the far-off, strident cawing of a crow. From the rustic furnishings and antique farm implement, she guessed she'd been taken to someone's country dacha.

There was a slight rustling sound from the next room, and she called out, *"Izvinite…Akademik Shevchenko?"*

There was no answer, but an earthy, pungent smell had started filling the air. She'd just begun to climb to her feet when Oleg walked back in and sat again, hunched in a chair facing her, resting his arms along his thighs. For the first time she noticed an angry red cut, recently scabbed over, on one of his tightly muscled forearms. And then she noticed that from his two hands dangled a rope with a noose tied at one end.

His head was turned away slightly, as though he couldn't meet her gaze head-on.

She looked from the rope to his face, immobilized like an insect swallowed in the sap of a tree. This was no rescue…

"You sleep," he commanded in heavily accented English. The gruff timbre of his voice was like a slap to her face, momentarily clearing her head and sharpening her thoughts. Everything coalesced into a meaningful pattern: a kidnapping, an isolated dwelling, a man holding a rope—a strong, authoritative man with a car and a second home.

In the largest photo on the end table, she'd scanned Oleg, one arm draped around a young man in police uniform. She felt a dawning recognition. The young man in the photo was unmistakably Alexi Yurov.

Alexi had told her, soon after making love to her, that his uncle owned a dacha. She should have put this together, asked more questions. Oleg Shevchenko was Alexi's uncle. Her eyes dropped again to the rope in his hand.

Svisloch Dushitel, she mouthed, and her breath stuck in her throat.

Oleg stood, fidgeting the rope between his palms. He took a few steps toward her, his face flushed with a fine sheen of sweat, and then veered off into the other room again.

She felt the explosion of adrenaline in her chest. Snapping her head around the room, she looked for any potential weapons. But her vision faltered, and she grew light-headed again, the sedative churning like molasses inside her skull.

She could hear Oleg in the other room. His breathing was ragged and labored, and he was pacing erratically. It sounded like he was winding himself up, steeling himself to take some action that was either agitating or exciting him.

She had to find something to defend herself with. There was

a small desk across the room with some scraps of papers in disarray, but no sharp objects like scissors or a letter opener. But propped up against a stack of books was her missing driver's license. Mel groaned. The last time she'd seen her license was in her coat pocket, which she'd worn to the spa with Nadia. Nadia, who'd been murdered by the Strangler.

She could pull the ox harness off the wall, but she didn't think she had the strength, or the necessary speed, to swing it hard enough to make an impact. Oleg returned to the room suddenly, holding a mug of steaming liquid. He sat in the chair again, the rope now draped across his lap.

He cradled the mug in his two large hands and began speaking to her in Russian. A long string of passionate words she could only partially understand. He had the wide face and rounded cheekbones of an Eastern Baltic Russian, with unremarkable gray eyes. She tried and failed to see, to *recognize*, the gaze of a killer. There was nothing yet in his expression but sentimental brooding—no rage, no obvious disgust. And it was this lack of murderous intent that she found most frightening.

She caught a few words, *night* and *garden* and *love*. It sounded almost scripted. Had this been the last thing each woman heard before she was killed? Was it a well-rehearsed play justifying his actions, or a verbal jump start, fueling what was to come? His eyes now brimmed with tears, which he wiped away with the back of his hand. Mel didn't know which was more monstrous, the thought that he was crying for her or for himself. He closed his eyes. And began singing.

It was a mournful song, pitched in a minor key. She tensed, and then prepared to bolt while his eyes were closed. As though sensing her intent, he abruptly stopped and pinned her with his fixed gaze.

He held out the mug to her and demanded, *"Ty p'yesh'."* You drink.

She took the mug, bringing it to her nose, but the smell was sharp and overpowering, like dirt boiled in dishwater. The liquid was dark and viscous, with little specks of organic material floating along its surface. Oleg pulled a small pistol out of his pants pocket and again ordered her to drink.

Taking a few small sips, she started to gag, but Oleg stood, gun in hand, and gestured for her to finish it. There was no way of knowing what was in the mug, but the taste was noxious, unwholesome. He used the barrel of the gun to tilt the mug toward her mouth. She drank more and fought to keep the liquid down.

When she'd gotten through half, he took the mug from her and swallowed the remaining drink. If it was poison, it seemed they'd both be going down together. He ordered her in Russian to stand and gestured with his gun for her to go into the adjoining room. She stumbled into a sparse country kitchen with faded curling wallpaper, dark with water stains and mold. There was a pan of foul-smelling liquid still simmering on the antiquated stove.

Oleg moved past her to open a door, flooding the room with bright sunlight. He signaled, again with his gun, for her to go outside.

She had to purge her system of the drink, and soon, but she was afraid that if she vomited, he'd just make her drink more. She stepped out slowly and he prodded between her shoulder blades with the barrel of the gun, prompting her to begin walking away from the house. Slender pines grew closely together within a few yards of the door, the ground underneath dense with fragrant, browning pine needles. The light was slanting and golden, and Mel guessed it must now be late afternoon. There were no other houses or buildings within sight, the only sound the soft breeze rustling the trees. Even the birds had gone silent.

She approached an area that had been cleared of most of

the fallen pine needles. The ground was lumpy and raised into hillocks, and each of the mounds—there seemed to be dozens of them—was topped with rich, dark soil. And erupting through the soil, as dense as barnacles under a rotting pier, were mushrooms of all shapes and colors and sizes. A field of monstrously large mushrooms, not growing singly as they might in nature, but in vast, dense swaths, intertwining, their stems and gills and caps all crowded together.

Mel could barely keep herself from being sick. The mushrooms looked like pale alien limbs crawling their way up through the moist dirt. And closest to where she'd stopped was a freshly dug shallow pit, black and gaping.

She fell to her knees, the trees canting at an angle, bile rising to the back of her throat. Oleg was saying something, his tone remorseful, pleading. Whoever had strangled Nadia and the woman in the morgue had done so savagely, violently. And yet, Oleg's tone was almost apologetic.

"*Akademik Shevchenko,*" she said, trying to make her voice sound reasonable, conversational. But when she tried to stand, he pushed her back to the ground.

She looked around for anything that could inflict an injury, but there was nothing, not even a stone. His voice had increased in tension, his speech becoming rushed, as though he was coming to an end. Mel knew she had to act soon, or she'd be dead.

She placed her head in her hands, sobbing audibly, her shoulders shaking, her body now morphed into that of a frail and frightened little girl. The sound of her crying seemed to move Shevchenko and he began making soothing noises.

"*Oish, oish, oish,*" he cooed, as though quieting a squalling baby.

He bent closer to where she crouched. Out of the corner of one eye she could see the rope dangling from his hand. If she didn't act now, he'd slip the noose over her neck. Clenching two handfuls of loose soil, she twisted and, with every ounce of strength she had left, hurled them into Oleg's face. He stumbled back and yelled in outrage, furiously rubbing at his eyes. Scrambling to her feet, Mel charged, the top of her head connecting solidly with his solar plexus.

Oleg howled in pain, falling onto his back, folding both arms protectively around his middle. She made a grab for his gun, savagely biting his hand and drawing blood, but he yanked it away, firing wildly into the air.

Panicked, she ran for the woods, gasping for air, mindless of the direction she was headed. Her only thought was to put as much distance as possible between herself and the house. Oleg bellowed like a wounded bull and fired twice more into the trees, one bullet shredding bark a few feet from her churning legs, shooting a long splinter of wood into her thigh. The pain brought her to her knees, but, pushing herself to stand again, Mel sprinted on.

This, she realized, was a game she knew well. One she had practiced with her father in the wilds of Wisconsin. Quickly assessing the terrain—what could be used for cover, trees, bushes, boulders, ravines, rotten logs. And using it to her advantage. It was still a few hours until sunset, but the shadows in the forest had begun blanketing the ground and would aid in making her invisible.

She was weak from lack of food, and from the drugs, but the adrenaline of fear worked like rocket fuel, propelling her onward. She knew she had to find a hiding place before dark.

As she zigzagged through the forest, anxiously looking back over her shoulder for Oleg, it was another five minutes before the hallucinations began.

37

TUESDAY, AUGUST 21, 1990

Alexi Ilich Yurov sat on the chair where Melvina had sat only a few hours earlier, facing Martin Kavalchuk. Kavalchuk knew what he saw: one of the new generations of *militsiya,* spoiled by Western goods, eager to see the wider world, dangerously hopeful of a new order at home. Despite all this, Kavalchuk—chairman of the KGB of the BSSR, recipient of the Hero of the Soviet Union medal, along with the Order of Lenin, the Medal for Valor, Order of the Patriotic War, and Order of the Red Star—knew that the entire weight of Soviet law and order still lay within his power to execute. The look in Alexi Yurov's eyes told him that the young man knew this was still true.

The medals he wore only during official state ceremonies. In the interrogation room he wore only black.

Kavalchuk leaned over his desk, reading the latest reports. Two of his officers had been assassinated that afternoon, and more alarmingly, Melvina Donleavy had disappeared. But the only outward sign of his displeasure would be the veins that throbbed at his temples. He was a man whose officers had never heard raise his voice. In fact, it was said, if you angered the Black Wolf, you'd only hear his footsteps when he was carrying your coffin.

The envoy from Moscow's First Directorate was on his way from the Minsk-2 airport to KGB headquarters. He would want a full accounting of why the American was allowed to escape.

There were three possible perpetrators: the Americans, the Israelis, or the *Bratva*. Tire marks had been found perpendicular to traffic on the road where they'd discovered their dead men. A team was working on identifying the treads, although Kavalchuk already knew what had happened. A car had blocked the road. Anton had stopped, only to be shot at close range, and Melvina had been taken.

His Alpha officer walked into the room, laying another update on the desk. Shell casings had been found at the scene. The ballistics report noted they were 9-millimeter Parabellum ammunition. Israeli assassins favored the Beretta 71, also referred to as David's Sling, and the CIA often issued a Glock or SIG Sauer to their agents. So the gun was most likely a Russian-made TT-33. A Tulsky Tokarev. Supplies were still plentiful decades after the war, and prices so cheap that often the *Bratva* hit men left their guns at the scene, as they could be so easily replaced by clean weapons.

This narrowed the field considerably. Kavalchuk scribbled a quick note on the report and, after walking over to let Alexi read it, handed it back to the Alpha officer. It called for a citywide sweep of known *Bratva* members, totaling twenty in number. The actual number they arrested, however, was irrelevant. They simply needed to make a statement that the Black Wolf was past winking and nodding at their misdeeds. Almost as an afterthought, he scribbled a postscript: *Shoot three in front of the others to encourage a productive dialogue.*

Kavalchuk looked at Alexi from under weighted lids. Misery, on the younger man's face, was like the Greek mask of Tragedy. His mouth was downturned, his eyes blank holes of despair.

"Well?" Kavalchuk asked finally.

Alexi stirred. "Some of those men will be heroes of the Afghanistan conflict."

Kavalchuk shrugged. "We'll give a bonus to the widows." He pressed the button on the desk once more, telling his officer, "Send in the clerk."

A woman carrying a stenographer's pad entered the room. The Alpha officer set a chair next to Kavalchuk, and she took a seat.

"I have, at most, twenty minutes before the envoy from Moscow arrives. The clerk will take down our words and you will then sign the typed confession. Swiftly. Agreed?"

Alexi looked down at his hands clasped together in his lap and nodded.

Kavalchuk asked for his full name, place and date of birth. "What is your current position in the *militsiya*?"

"Corporal, entered into the academy in 1982."

"When and how did you first meet William Cutler?"

"A year ago. Because of my English proficiency, I was directed by the Ministry of Internal Affairs to be his personal aide and to report his activities to KGB headquarters weekly."

"When did your relationship to Dr. Cutler become more... personal?"

Alexi blinked as though looking into a bright light. "Within a few months. He urged me to consider defecting to the West."

"And you considered because this had been in your mind for some time." It was not a question.

"Yes. But this was before the Berlin Wall was dismantled. And before reforms were begun."

Kavalchuk waved his hand, dismissing the last sentence. "To be clear, Dr. Cutler had begun plans to help you defect a year ago. Almost as soon as he had arrived in Minsk. Without the arrival of the Americans, you would have enacted that plan in September of this year. It is not enough to nod; you must answer in the affirmative."

"Yes."

"When you were found out, I gave you an opportunity to avoid arrest by reporting on Melvina Donleavy. But you formed a personal attachment to her as well."

"Yes," Alexi whispered.

Kavalchuk got up from the desk and stood looking down at Alexi. He signaled to the clerk to stop writing. "Did you imagine that once you were in the West, you could resume your affair? How does the saying go? 'Love is like the wind. You can't see it, but you can feel it.' My dear Alexi Ilich, you live in a veritable typhoon of emotions. How very Slavic of you. But now, you see, we have a problem. Or rather, you have a problem. My assurance of William's safe passage out of Byelorussia was dependent upon your extracting information from Miss Donleavy. And now…?"

He ran his hand over his head and began to pace. "Why did the *Bratva* take Melvina Donleavy?"

"The usual reason is for ransom," the younger man quickly volunteered.

Kavalchuk grunted. "How did they know she was being taken to the airport?"

Alexi counted off on his fingers. "Select workers in the Soviet chairman's office or in Ivanov's department would have known. Also, there was an emergency session held here with the Academy of Sciences yesterday."

Kavalchuk lowered his chin. "Are you suggesting that members of the academy are working with the *Bratva*?"

Alexi let out a cynical laugh. "Are you suggesting that members of the academy are above paying the Brotherhood to get what they want?"

The older man wagged his finger. "You are still on thin ice,

Comrade. You didn't push her hard enough when you had the chance. Now we may have lost her for good."

"I did my best," Alexi said, staring back down at his hands.

Kavalchuk made a face. "Your best was not enough to keep your good friend Dr. Cutler from being arrested." Frowning, he stood lost in thought for a moment. "If she was kidnapped for ransom, we would have been contacted by now."

"Why else would she have been taken?"

"Because perhaps the *Bratva* have already been paid." Kavalchuk studied the wall, as though he could decode the cracks in the cement. "But by whom? And for what purpose?"

"Western women, especially Americans, just don't go missing—"

Kavalchuk turned on his heel, facing Alexi. "What did you say?"

"I said, Western women just don't go missing."

Kavalchuk turned to the clerk. "You can go now. We'll complete the interview at a later time."

He sat at the desk again, gesturing to the Alpha officer. Kavalchuk told him, "After you've taken Corporal Yurov back to his cell, I need the names of all the workers in Ivanov's department, and all of the attendees from the Heat and Mass Transfer Institute who were in the meeting here yesterday. I want to know their movements in the last twenty-four hours. And that includes Ivanov and Shevchenko. But most importantly, I want to know if anyone is missing today. *Do it now!*"

"What about the envoy?" the Alpha officer asked. "He'll be here any moment."

"Ply him with vodka and a hot meal—" He stopped, startled by a novel thought. It was the first time the Alpha officer had ever seen Chairman Kavalchuk smile. "And tell the medical examiner to have the body of the woman found murdered behind the Red Church bagged and ready for transport."

38

TUESDAY, AUGUST 21, 1990

The slender pines surrounding Mel had begun to shimmer and glow, light breaking through the cracks in their bark like the gold filaments that join broken pieces of pottery together. *Kintsugi.* The Japanese word came to her easily. She hadn't even known that she knew it. She realized the murky tea she'd been given must have been a strong hallucinogen, something she'd never indulged in before. She'd always been too afraid it would somehow affect her recall. The only drug she'd ever done was marijuana, smoked a few times in college. But never again after entering Quantico.

She could feel the world around her vibrating, as if preparing to shatter.

In the distance she heard an animal lowing, crashing through the ferns and ivy that covered the forest floor in seductive mounds, like green pillows. She wanted to lie down and sleep. Maybe if she just pulled the vegetation over her like a blanket, she'd become invisible?

The sounds were becoming louder. It wasn't an animal. It was Oleg Shevchenko, with a gun in one hand and his ropes in the other, looking for her. There was still too much daylight for her to disappear into the ivy. She needed to keep moving, to keep ahead of him, until she found a fallen tree or an animal burrow large enough to creep into and hide. She focused on her scurrying feet—they were solid, real. She had to focus on what was real.

There was a small rise ahead. It was a risk. He might easily see her at the elevated position—but she might be able to change course and head in an unexpected direction at the bottom if there was a depression below it where she could crouch and stay hidden from view. It was one of her father's simple deceptive strategies.

Mel turned and ran diagonally up the slope. To her relief, she saw an old streambed below. But as soon as she crested the rise, she heard the crack of the pistol and felt a bullet zing past her head. She dropped and rolled into the depression, half-buried stones bruising her arms and legs on the way down. Finding her feet again and pivoting left, she began running. She'd made it fifty yards when she heard labored wheezing as Shevchenko ran up the rise behind her. The splinter of wood in her thigh stabbed painfully every time she flexed her muscles.

Ahead, a large, vine-covered boulder in the middle of the streambed provided shelter. Hunkering down, she peeked around it and saw that, as she'd hoped, Shevchenko was in the streambed running the opposite way. She felt something delicate brush against her cheek, like a spiderweb. One of the vines close to her face moved. It now appeared as a long, thin snake, with iridescent green scales and hard, glittering eyes. Rearing back its head to strike, it flicked its tongue in the air as though tasting her sweat.

She screamed and threw herself back, away from the boulder. Instantly, the snake became a vine again. And Shevchenko had corrected his course and was running toward her. Dragging herself upright, she scrambled up to the top of the opposite bank and looked frantically for cover.

The last of the sun's rays were almost horizontal to the ground, the beams of light running like rivers of liquid fire.

Shevchenko crested the rise after her, his face furiously intent. But as the radiance coursed over him, it distracted him, and he turned to face the setting sun. The light enveloped him, showering him with a halo of gold, expanding around him until he looked like a man on a burning pyre. He spread his arms out wide and made an ecstatic sound. He began to tear his shirt off, rubbing his hands over his chest, as though kneading the lucid particles into his skin.

Mel wanted to stand with him, hypnotized. But a sliver of rational thought intervened: the drugged tea was affecting him as well.

She turned her back to the sun and ran. With every passing moment the light diminished, turning first to pinkish gray, then to ash. The forest floor became more difficult to negotiate—stones and branches and vines made her slow her pace. She was weakening. She had to find a place to hide and rest.

Looking up, she saw the first evening star appear between the branches of the trees. As she watched, it swelled in size, grew a face, and winked at her. She barked her shins on a fallen log and, at the same time, heard Shevchenko bellowing in the distance like a wounded bull. The log was not hollow, but it was covered with ferns, lush enough to hide in. Crawling over it, she eased into the leaves and tried to quiet her breathing. For a full minute she grasped at the end of the splinter in her leg and tried pulling it out. But it was too large and too rough to come out easily and she left it buried in her flesh.

There were tiny denizens in the greenery, insects blindly moving about, their numerous legs thrashing noisily against the stems and leaves. The worry was overwhelming: they were being too loud, they'd give her position away. She shushed them. They quieted for only a moment and then began gnashing their mandibles together until the air was filled with the deafening sounds of chewing.

She clapped both hands over her ears. *It's just the drugs,*

Alice, she told herself. Her mother's voice reassuring in her head. *It's just the drugs and it will pass...*

The gnashing ceased abruptly, and she was anchored again in the real. Listening for Shevchenko, she heard only a gentle wind shaking the pine branches high above her head. The temperature had dropped, and she began to shiver. But all the winter months she'd spent camping in the snow with Walter had toughened her. She could do this. If she could just rest for a few hours, she'd be able to find her way to another dacha, or a road. And then what? She was unarmed, unsure of her location, with no water or food. At Quantico, the Bullet had given her two pieces of advice, should she ever need to escape pursuers. *Don't be a rabbit.* Keep moving and don't pop your head up more than once in any location. *And plan like it's the last plan you'll ever make.* He'd given no advice for planning while under the influence of a hallucinogen.

Mel closed her eyes and drifted into a vivid dreamscape. Russian domed cathedrals grew around her like enormous mushrooms, filled with dancing *matryoshki.*

She woke to someone calling her name. It was a plaintive male voice, a lovesick yodeling into the darkness, seeking her out. Calling to her tenderly. To her ears the sound was terrifying. Shevchenko was nearby. She could hear his tortured breathing. Soon he stopped saying her name and began singing in Russian. Her brain filled with an explosion of volcanic colors, and she had the irresistible urge to stand up, to confront him and end this game of chase. But she clamped down on the impulse and froze in place. Surely, he'd wander off in a different direction if only she stayed quiet.

Another strategy from her training: a sharp, self-inflected pain can focus the mind away from dangerous impulses, especially when one is exhausted and edging on hopelessness. Grinding fingernails into the palm, biting the soft inner lip, raking a heel along the inside of the tibia. At the time, it'd been hard to imagine feeling so close to betraying oneself. Now, gritting her teeth, Mel jabbed the splinter of wood farther into her thigh.

He was getting closer, his shadowy bulk stepping, halting, then wheeling around, sniffing the air as though he could find her by her scent alone. He was naked from the waist up, the expanse of his pale skin reflecting the anemic starlight. His body looked bloated, larval. Her hand closed on a rock, and as soon as he'd turned his back to her, she stood and threw it fifty feet into the brush. Shevchenko turned and, staggering, followed the sound. Once he'd disappeared into the forest, Mel crouched down again in the damp ferns. He'd tire eventually. Maybe he'd have a stroke or a heart attack. Collapse into the underbrush, his body discovered only after a long winter and the spring thaw.

But no. That wasn't a plan. She'd rested long enough. As quietly as she could, Mel stepped gingerly away from where Shevchenko had appeared, weaving cautiously through the darker patches, where the pine branches grew closer to the ground. In a small clearing she came upon several large boulders nestled together, forming a natural cleft between them. Climbing into the cleft, she piled up handfuls of ferns until she had a natural barrier, one that she could see through.

Soon she heard a chuffing, rustling sound. Tensing, she peered through the ferns. Into the clearing lumbered a gigantic, woolly form with a distinctive shuffling gate. Its giant paws showered sparks, as though its nails were flint striking stone. A great brown bear, sniffing at the air. Slowly, it approached the boulders, then sat back on its haunches, the pads of its rear paws comfortably touching, its two forepaws settling in its lap. The middle of its chest bloomed into swirling particles of light, orbiting a central nucleus. The particles moved so rapidly that they left elliptical pathways, glowing an iridescent green.

Mel closed her eyes. It had to be a hallucination. But when she opened her eyes again, the animal seemed to be looking at her, expectantly, patiently. She had a flash of a memory—crouching in a deer blind that she and her father had built together, waiting for hours for the deer to come. A black bear had approached the blind once, deftly climbing up the ladder. Walter had sat on the trapdoor, keeping it from entering.

He'd told her, "The best thing to do if a bear charges is play dead, be boring. He may take a bite out of you, but he just might leave your head on your shoulders."

But this brown bear was easily three times the size of the Wisconsin black bear. Mel stayed very still.

"Dobryy Vecher," the bear said finally. *"Kak dela?"*

The bear spoke in Nadia's voice.

Mel's throat tightened with unbearable sorrow. "I'm fine," she managed to say at last, "and you?" She couldn't tell if she had said the words out loud or only in her head.

"Not so good." The bear shook her woolly head. "I've been to the Exclusion Zone. Now all my cubs have died."

The bear pointed to her chest. The particles glowed with a painful brightness. Mel felt a warmth in her own chest, and she rubbed her fingers along her sternum. Hiroshima, Chernobyl, the near catastrophe of Three Mile Island. She was so small in contrast to the will of nations, the enduring arrogance of humanity that had brought death to so many. Before she came to Minsk, it had all been so abstract, nuclear destruction only an old newsreel or photo. Numbers on a chart. She felt wetness on her face and realized she'd begun to cry in earnest. Larysa's son, born with his heart outside his body, her parents and husband dead. The great bear looked at her with infinite sadness. All her children were dead too.

"Is it inside me now as well?" she asked.

The bear nodded. "It will soon be inside everything and

everyone. Go to sleep now. There's nothing left tonight that can be done."

She closed her eyes. Behind her lids a replay began of every face she'd ever seen, beginning with the shining, happy faces peering over her crib, to her first fumbling days at school...to sports...camping...dance classes...theater practice...shopping malls...traveling to vast and faraway places...training...the academy...and finally to Byelorussia, with all its beleaguered citizens, sad-eyed, suspicious, persistent, poetic. Millions of faces, all unique, all memorable, all seemingly infinite. And yet, in truth, each one finite, fragile, fungible. Hurled like galaxies through the limitless black of her internal universe.

When Mel opened her eyes again, it was morning and the bear had gone. She was left with an aching optimism that conflicted with the desolation of her dreams. As though revisiting those numberless faces had shown her the truth of human existence: *I strive even as I'm dying*.

Her thoughts were still fragmented from the drug, and she felt not quite solid, as though she were in a vaporous state—hydrogen, helium, nitrogen swirling together—the molecules of her skin and organs not quite solidified...

Hydrogen!

She remembered once reading that hydrogen is a light, odorless gas that, given enough time, becomes people. But with that hopeful thought, she also knew that, under the right circumstances, hydrogen can also become a thermonuclear weapon. Galvanized, she was brought back to the here and now, and to her real purpose: fulfilling her mission. Reporting back that Iran was in Byelorussia to develop nuclear weapons.

She crawled out of her hiding place, hungry and very thirsty. She felt hollowed out, light as gossamer, her limbs trembly and weak. The sound of rushing water made her quicken her pace. She came to a small stream and, kneeling, she cupped handfuls of it into her mouth. It was cold and pure and invigorating.

When the ripples subsided, she saw, reflected cleanly, the surrounding pines, the sky, and Oleg Shevchenko standing behind her. Then she felt his pistol press against the base of her skull.

For an hour Mel walked in front of Shevchenko, the constant pressure of the gun at her head. He'd tied her hands behind her back, and she stepped carefully so she wouldn't trip and fall. Several times she tried talking to him, softly, soothingly. But each time he'd jammed the barrel so viciously against her back that she'd stumbled, almost losing her footing.

He was still shirtless, his torso covered in scratches, some of them oozing blood. He kept up a constant stream of Russian curses through his cracked and swollen lips. Mel had stopped hallucinating, but she could still feel her perception of reality balanced on a knife's edge. Colors were still too bright. Sounds too sharp.

She didn't feel the lightning strike of fear, though, until she saw Shevchenko's dacha, dappled in the shade of the trees. The mounds of dirt through which the mushrooms grew were even more terrifying in the cheerful light of day. When they got nearer to the freshly dug pit, he pushed her down onto her knees again, slipping the noose around her neck. The rope felt unbearably rough against her skin, and she felt a tidal wave of blind panic building. He dragged her to a slender pine and tightened the noose until she started to gag and spots like a swarm of silverfish darted around her vision.

He tied the length of rope around the tree to secure her and walked into the dacha. Desperate for escape, her mind summoned frantic thoughts of her evasion training, what to do if captured. But there was nothing in her memory banks to aid in freeing her from being tied like an animal ready for slaughter, even as she continued to strain, muscle and bone, to break through the ropes.

Within a few agonizing minutes, depleted of all energy, her

body sagged in acceptance, and her mind searched for a place of peace—the first snow of winter, her mother playing the piano. She finally settled on an image of her father. Walter was reading a book, next to the fire, his feet up, all worry about the wider world erased from his face.

He was saying, "Mel, I think we need more wood for the fire."

Shevchenko was returning. His hair was wet and slicked back and he'd put on another shirt. He stood over her, barely controlling his rage, fists clenching, open and closed, open and closed. All traces of the maudlin romantic had vanished.

He said something harsh in Russian. Mel didn't know the words, but she could guess the meaning. Time to die. More than afraid, she was furious. Not just that she was to be unfairly killed, but that no one would ever know where her body was buried.

Her last act of defiance was a bold-faced, unblinking stare, fierce enough to give him pause for a final moment.

"Idi na hui!" she screamed.

Frenzied with anger, he furrowed his brow and stepped forward.

An echoing crack broke the silence, and Shevchenko was thrown to the ground with such force that he raised a plume of dust and pine needles. Mel blinked reflexively. Somehow, the back of his head had become a bloody crater. She looked up, trying to make sense of it. Martin Kavalchuk was striding toward her, a hunting rifle cradled in both arms. Alexi Yurov stood behind him.

Mel heard the two men speaking quietly in Russian before she saw them. She was on Shevchenko's bed, resting, again watched over by the *matryoshki* on the shelf. Shevchenko had given her one a few weeks ago. Could there be a doll for every woman the Strangler had killed? If so, there would be dozens of graves behind the dacha.

Alexi came and sat on the edge of the bed. Both he and Kavalchuk had helped her into the house.

"We only have a little while," he said. He spoke in a soft murmur, and Mel struggled to grasp the meaning of the words.

"Oleg Shevchenko is my uncle...I didn't know." He took a deep breath. "As I told you, William was going to help me defect...Kavalchuk found out...He will let you and William leave if I stay behind and identify other defectors. If I don't..."

He stared miserably at his hands clenched tightly between his knees. "He says I will be promoted for this."

Alexi looked exceptionally handsome in his uniform, illuminated by the morning light. His blond hair, his expressive hands, the grace with which he carried himself. But Mel felt no more relentless pull to be held by him. To be kissed. Those feelings had been snuffed out the moment she'd seen him at KGB headquarters.

"Did you ever care for me?" she asked at last.

"Yes, yes. Of course!" He took her hand gently in his.

She believed him, but only partly. He had hesitated a fraction of a second too long. She closed her eyes and turned away, her face to the wall.

Kavalchuk later guided her to his car, and they drove in silence back to Minsk. Alexi was not with them, and she supposed he'd been left behind to sort things out, to smooth over the rough edges for the official report. Like a theatrical set designer arranging props to tell a story. One that the audience expected. One that would delight or terrify, depending upon the script. And with the Black Wolf both the playwright and the director, she was sure it would be a convincing one.

39

FRIDAY, AUGUST 24, 1990

There were only four folders marked sovershenno sekretno, emblazoned with the red Soviet hammer and sickle. They had been placed in front of the four attending members of the Byelorussian Committee of State Security. The report inside was so secret that, once it had been reviewed, all four copies would be locked away in the protected archives of KGB headquarters.

Four of the five attending members were Head of the Supreme Soviet BSSR Vyacheslav Kobets, Minister of External Affairs Sergei Ivanov, Minister of Internal Affairs Gregori Lavrov, and First Deputy Minister of Defense Viktor Zakharenko. All of them sat in heightened states of agitation. Both Kobets and Ivanov looked especially shaken. Although none yet had all the details, there'd already been dark murmurs: assassinated KGB agents, dead bodies, a special envoy back to Moscow, and a female CIA spy held for days, invoking the ire of the US State Department.

The fifth member of the committee was Martin Gregorivich Kavalchuk, chairman of the BSSR KGB. He had no report before him, as he was its author and he knew it by heart. Kavalchuk had also chosen to stand rather than take his seat, as it forced the other members to look up at him, like students at a university lecture.

He directed the four to open their folders and waited as they read the cover page. Zakharenko first labored impatiently to remove his lighter from his uniform pocket, which was stiffened by the number of medals across his chest and stretched tightly around his massive gut. He then lit a cigarette and roughly opened the folder. He was the least familiar with the events of the past few weeks, and, after scanning the page, he looked up at Kavalchuk, uttering a spectacularly vulgar oath. As the others also finished up, Kavalchuk began to speak.

"On the second of August a group of four Americans, posing as accountants for the US State Department, arrived at Minsk-2 airport. They were here ostensibly to offer substantial financial aid to Byelorussia on the condition that there were no active nuclear programs currently being conducted within the republic. The first envoy of this kind. And although the minister of external affairs was not initially suspicious, I kept a careful eye."

He paused and looked pointedly at Ivanov, who removed his thick-framed glasses with shaking hands, cleaning them slowly and methodically with his tie.

"As I suspected all along, these four Americans, along with Dr. William Cutler, were working for, or with, the CIA and, in the latter case, Israeli intelligence. You can read their timeline of activities before our meeting adjourns. On the evening of August eighteenth, scientists and foreign guests from the Heat and Mass Transfer Institute gathered at the official state dacha east of Minsk. Two of the Americans, Dan Hatton and Melvina Donleavy, spied on the gathering, along with, we suspect, an Israeli intelligence officer. We have reason to believe this Israeli officer has already passed over the border into Poland. Melvina Donleavy was subsequently detained by me after her three colleagues were expelled. She was held at headquarters by order of the First Directorate in Moscow. William Cutler was also detained."

"Under strong protest from the US State Department," Ivanov added.

"Yes," Kavalchuk said, "which proved to be a difficult quandary for the chairman."

Kobets looked red-faced and angry, and Kavalchuk thought, *The chairman is close to having a stroke.*

"And now the woman is dead," Kobets roared, banging his fist on the table. "Her body removed by special envoy to Moscow. This will cause a major international incident. An American intelligence officer has been murdered. You have much to answer for—"

Kavalchuk held up one warning hand, his eyes fixed on Kobets's face, his expression unyielding. Instinctively, Kobets stopped speaking. Without the support of the KGB, and Kavalchuk in particular, his elevated status meant nothing.

"I'll remind you, Chairman, that you were given the choice to return her home, and yet you turned a blind eye to benefit the First Directorate. Now read the second page of the report."

Kobets turned to the second page and began reading, his balding scalp reflecting the harsh overhead lights like a mirror. His head jerked up in surprise. "Is this true?" he asked.

"Yes. Fortuitously for us, Miss Donleavy looked remarkably like another woman murdered by the Svisloch Strangler. It was this woman's body that accompanied the special envoy back to Moscow, not Miss Donleavy, although I explained to the envoy that the Donleavy woman had been, unfortunately, kidnapped and killed by the *Bratva*. I further informed him that, following our rescue of her body, more than a dozen of the Brotherhood had been taken into custody, three of them already executed on my order."

The defense minister, Zakharenko, made a dismissive sound. "Knowing Comrade Kavalchuk's methods, luck had nothing to do with this. How did the envoy not realize it wasn't the Donleavy woman?"

"Because I assured the envoy that it was. And there is no one to say it's not. Am I not right?" Kavalchuk looked at his comrades for any dissent. "Moscow will keep it quiet to prevent protest from the United States. And the United States will not protest, because the real Melvina Donleavy has already been flown to Berlin on my orders, accompanied by Dr. Cutler."

There was a collective expression of surprised outrage.

Kavalchuk continued speaking, his voice calm and steady. "Moscow will assume that the silence from American intelligence is an affirmation of her spy status. They would otherwise make a lot of noise over a missing US citizen. She will just be another CIA officer missing in the line of duty. Another star on the Memorial Wall at Langley. I strongly urged the real Donleavy woman to never again put a foot on Soviet ground, ensuring that our little secret stays safe. I now direct you to the third page of the report."

After a few moments, Lavrov from internal affairs, whose narrow frame and pallid complexion had earned him the nickname the Undertaker, started stabbing at the file with one sharp finger. He said, "Two KGB agents shot. Melvina Donleavy abducted by the *Bratva*. How did you track her down?"

Kavalchuk turned to Lavrov. "The *Bratva* only kidnapped her. Soon after, she was delivered to the man we now know was the Svisloch Strangler. This was verified by certain members of the Brotherhood following rigorous interrogation. As you know, Minister Lavrov, I have been working diligently to find the Strangler." He glanced at Kobets. "The chairman had a special interest in one of these cases."

Kobets's face turned scarlet. It was not a state secret that he had a mistress, but he didn't want to discuss his private life here.

"There is no such serial killer," Kobets thundered.

The skin under Kavalchuk's right eye had begun to twitch. "At the dacha where Melvina Donleavy was rescued, my men discovered twenty-six buried bodies in various stages of decay. Including the badly decomposed body of a once-famous Byelorussian gymnast. Some of these women were from Minsk, others were most likely taken from different towns and villages."

Kavalchuk waited for the shaken chairman to collect himself.

"One Corporal Yurov of the *militsiya* here in Minsk put forward a suspect, based on his intimate knowledge of the man, as well as clues uncovered from the previous killings. I have recommended Yurov for a promotion."

Zakharenko stubbed out his cigarette. "What do you mean, 'intimate knowledge'?"

"What I mean," Kavalchuk said, "is that the Svisloch Strangler, the 'serial killer' as it were, was Director Oleg Shevchenko of the Heat and Mass Transfer Institute, Colonel Yurov's uncle."

Ivanov started to stand, but his legs gave way and he collapsed back into his chair. "It's not possible."

"And where is Shevchenko now?" Zakharenko demanded.

"He was shot and killed."

"By whom?"

"By me."

All the crimson in Kobets's face drained away, leaving him with the pallor of the deathly ill. "One of the most important men in Byelorussia, with ties to the scientific community worldwide. This will bring disaster to our move toward sovereignty. A scandal of epic proportions."

"No, it will not. And I'm going to tell you why." Kavalchuk paused, carefully taking his one cigarette of the day out of his coat pocket. He used the defense minister's heavy gold lighter to ignite it. He took his time—reminding the flock that it's not the wondering *if* the teeth will be shown but the dreading of *when* they'll snap shut.

Enjoying the tension in the room, he inhaled deeply and turned to Lavrov. "As head of internal affairs, you will make a public announcement that the *Svisloch Dushitel* was a member of the *Bratva* and that he was tracked down and shot by officers of the KGB. Let the public know that the remains of the murdered women will be processed by our medical examiner for identification for the families. The body of the Strangler, I will provide. Fortunately, we have three from which to choose.

"Secondly," he said, turning to Ivanov, "it was discovered by the medical examiner that Shevchenko was dying of stomach cancer. As his closest comrade, you will address the members of the institute, telling them that he was greatly depressed and committed suicide. A single gunshot to the head. And, as your closest comrade, Shevchenko will have sent you a letter telling you of his intent to save himself from a terrible, lingering death. I will, of course, provide the suicide note, and you can hand-deliver it to his widow. He will be buried with all the honors due to a high-ranking Communist Party member in good standing. Thereby keeping his reputation, and ours, intact."

He moved to stand in front of Zakharenko, who had loosened the buttons on his uniform to ease his labored breathing. "I'm sure I can rely on you to supply men and equipment in our continued efforts to eradicate the *Bratva* from our midst. Nothing attracts foreign investors like safe streets. The revelation that the Strangler was one of the Byelorussian Mafia is the opening we've needed to counter this 'war hero' rhetoric. Our citizens won't care how many Afghani *mujahideen* a soldier has killed if he's coming home to murder our sisters, wives, and daughters."

He shifted his gaze to the chairman. "Comrade Kobets, I

know about the Persepolis project. And by now the CIA will too. A statement to the US State Department of your shock and dismay over the discovery of this clandestine project, as well as assurances that the Iranian scientists will never again be given entrée into Byelorussia, will go far to strengthen our ties to the West."

Kobets curled his hands into fists. "Persepolis was bringing millions to Byelorussia."

"No," Kavalchuk said, his carefully modulated voice rising. "Iran was bringing millions to a few in this room. It's not an exaggeration to say that Stalin killed the best and the brightest of his countrymen, fearing a coup by men smarter than himself and leaving an intellectual vacuum that we've still not rectified. With idiots such as Shevchenko heading up our nuclear program, we would have another Chernobyl on our hands. Or worse, a nuclear war initiated by men who are still living in the Dark Ages."

Kavalchuk placed both palms down on the table in front of Kobets, causing the chairman to sit back in his chair. "Do you realize that our fellow comrades have begun to identify not as Russians or Byelorussians or Ukrainians, but as Chernobylites? A new nation, without pride, without honor, without purpose. A faulty facility run by imbeciles did this.

"No," he said, emphatically, straightening and picking up the chairman's file. He tucked it tightly under his arm. "I am first and always a Byelorussian. And there is not a person in this room who can doubt that I will use whatever methods I have to defend her against ignoble opportunists. Especially if those efforts threaten to kill multitudes of our countrymen indiscriminately." He looked at each man in turn. "Any man who challenges this is welcome to come to KGB headquarters and read his personal file, written in blue ink and in triplicate. I will gladly give the tour personally."

He stood for a moment, comfortable in the silence, knowing

that each member had been reminded of where the true power lay. As long as the central KGB committee in Moscow existed, he, Martin Kavalchuk, would be the true seat of power in Minsk.

"But I am also a practical man," he said, appearing to soften, "and what I've offered is a practical solution. I'm sure that there will be plenty of other tempting opportunities to try to skim the cream. The Americans are notoriously lax in accounting for their foreign spending."

As Kavalchuk picked up the other three reports, Zakharenko asked quietly, "Why was the First Directorate so keen to obtain Melvina Donleavy?"

Kavalchuk paused as though considering how much to reveal, taking his time crushing the stub of his cigarette into the ashtray. "A Russian source inside the CIA messaged to Moscow that the Americans had a kind of...savant at Camp Perry. He reported that she could be shown a photo of a target for thirty seconds, only to pick out the individual in a crowd of thousands."

"Ridiculous," Kobets muttered.

Kavalchuk shrugged. "Moscow wanted her for their psyops program. I found out about this only after speaking to the envoy from KGB Central."

"And now they have only a body," Lavrov said. "At least Moscow will now leave us in peace. You will get a medal for these actions."

The KGB chairman placed the four reports inside his briefcase and locked it. When he turned to face Lavrov once more, the man blanched and pretended to study his hands. "All of us in this room cut our teeth on the winter tale told by every *babushka* of the hungry wolves chasing the sleigh. It's a cruel and perplexing tale, and perfectly Russian. In the sleigh are a lone woman and her two children. As the wolves are about to attack the horses, the cunning woman throws one of her children out into the snow, hoping to save herself. The child only whets the wolves' appetite, and they renew their pursuit. The woman then throws her second child out of the sleigh, with the same result. Despite her monstrous efforts, the wolves down the horses and devour the woman.

"Comrades, Moscow will open the supposed Donleavy skull and dig and dig, looking for something singular, something unique. But they will find only the gray matter of a simple Byelorussian peasant. And when they don't find what they're looking for, they'll be back. The wolves will always return, no matter how many children we throw into their jaws.

"But," he said, exhaling with the satisfaction of a job well done, "as I am counted one of the pack, it will be others who will be eaten, for now. Perhaps some of you in this room."

As he headed for the exit, he remembered Stalin saying, *It's not how many people vote that counts, but who counts the votes.*

"I vote this meeting adjourned."

40

SATURDAY, AUGUST 25, 1990

Every city had its own smell, Mel remembered. As soon as she deplaned onto the tarmac at Schönefeld Airport, she caught the particular odor of Berlin, even though the city proper was miles away.

The flight from Minsk on Lufthansa Airlines had been uneventful, the attendant chatting cheerfully about flying the sick children of Chernobyl who'd vacationed in Berlin back to Minsk the past summer.

"Interflug Airlines brought three hundred of them into Berlin," she whispered conspiratorially, "and all of their 'minders' worked for the KGB."

"The *K* in this case standing for *Kinder*?" William had asked teasingly, holding up his glass for more champagne.

Mel had slept through the beginning of the flight, her head on William's shoulder, his comfortable bulk obligingly quiet so as not to disturb her rest. She'd still felt the course of the hallucinogens throughout her body, a remaining glimmer that tempered the edges of surrounding objects, as though at any moment they'd run and melt like butter on a hot griddle. Or swell into a ball of light and break apart like supernovas.

When, midflight, she'd awoken, somewhat refreshed, she'd finally asked him about his experience in the KGB prison.

He'd said, "Compared to my first detention with the Russians after the war, I was quite comfortable. Even so, the food was awful. I was sleep-deprived. But you had the worst of it, I think."

The shade on the window had been pulled down, and she'd pushed it back up, letting in bright sunlight. The warmth had felt good on her face, giving her the energy to recount her last few days in Minsk. She'd told him about the interrogations by the Black Wolf, about being kidnapped by the Strangler and her night in the woods, lost and hallucinating, although she still could find no words to share what she had experienced with the great Russian bear.

Identifying Shevchenko distressed William greatly. He took off his glasses, covering his eyes with a napkin.

"I can't believe it," he said, choking with emotion. "I've known the man for so many years. I never suspected…"

She took his hand. "You couldn't have known, William. He'd spent decades hiding in plain sight. He fooled everybody."

"How were you rescued?"

"Martin Kavalchuk put the pieces together. It was Alexi who gave him the clues. Did you know he was Shevchenko's nephew?"

William started to nod, and then with a dawning realization his face crumpled in agony. "Oh my God, you and Alexi! I encouraged your friendship. I put you in harm's way."

She didn't want to reveal to him yet that his own release from prison was dependent on Alexi's staying behind, informing on others who'd sought to defect. Maybe at some point in the future when they were both not so emotionally raw she could tell him the truth. "Both Martin and Alexi came to the dacha to rescue me. Martin shot and killed Shevchenko. If he hadn't come when he did, I'd be another one of the Strangler's victims."

"What did Martin Gregorivich say to you at the airport?"

Kavalchuk had accompanied Mel and William all the way to their plane.

"He said...he told me he admired my fortitude."

William shook his head in amazement and called for more champagne. After downing a few more glasses, he fell into a deep sleep. When a meal was placed in front of Mel, she looked down, dismayed, and immediately covered it with a napkin. It was mushroom soup.

Mel gazed out of the window at the cloudless sky, revisiting the few days following her rescue. She'd been taken to a hospital and treated by the same doctor who'd given her the injections at the KGB headquarters. He was still stiff and unfriendly, but he assured her she would be released, and free to return to the West, within forty-eight hours. She didn't fully believe him, especially as there was a KGB officer always stationed outside her room, but she was determined to get back to Berlin even if she had to walk there in bare feet. Her ordeal at Shevchenko's dacha had only strengthened her resolve: she was an American intelligence officer, and she would complete her mission, no matter the cost.

She'd been given a single room in a wing that seemed to house no other patients. They'd drawn blood, examined her for assault, treated her wounds. She was allowed to take a bath for the two nights she was there, enabling her to do her usual recognition processing. And as her body recovered, she began to experience moments of intense, delirious, triumphant elation. Even staring at the concrete walls of her room couldn't dampen this powerful, mystifying optimism. Did everyone who narrowly escaped death feel this way? Her occasional outbursts of manic laughter, as she thought again and again of all that had happened, and how close she had come to dying, caused her stoic nurses to look at her with growing suspicion that perhaps she'd suffered a nervous breakdown.

When they finally released her from the hospital, she was given new clothes and shoes and picked up in a long black car, a sleek GAZ model, favored by the KGB leadership.

William was in the backseat, Martin Kavalchuk situated next to the driver. Mel, relieved beyond words to see William again, alive and well, impulsively hugged him, letting go only when he gently untangled her arms from around his neck. He squeezed her hand and signaled for her not to talk. Kavalchuk neither spoke to them nor looked at them until they reached the Minsk-2 airport, where the two men escorted them to their gate. As William went ahead, Kavalchuk had taken Mel's elbow and pulled her aside.

"Are you well?" he'd asked. "Do you need anything before the flight?"

"Yes...I'm..." Her eyes filled with tears. There could be nothing more disturbing or disarming than a proven killer being solicitous. Her body felt unmoored, as though gravity had lessened its hold, her arms so weightless she worried they'd float up above her shoulders. She willed herself to absorb her tears; she would not cry in front of him. "You saved my life."

He gave her a formal nod but didn't respond. She was acutely aware of the stares from the other passengers, who instinctively moved farther away until the two of them stood in an island of quiet. Even the bray of the intercom had ceased. She watched all the other passengers to Berlin boarding the plane, including one little girl holding a stuffed toy bear wearing a Russian hat. For a moment Mel had felt the bright burning in her chest that she'd experienced while hiding in the woods.

A flight attendant stood patiently at the departure gate waiting for her and William, who lingered just ahead under the watchful eye of their driver.

"You are never to return to the Soviet Union," Kavalchuk

said at last. “Or to Byelorussia, even if the unlikely happens and we declare independence.”

She nodded.

“When you land in Berlin and you are debriefed by your State Department and your Central Intelligence Agency, you will hear reports that the body of a woman named Melvina Donleavy, killed by members of the *Bratva,* was transported to Moscow by the First Directorate. You must tell your handlers not to dispute this. If you are dead to the KGB in Moscow, they will not come looking for you. Do you understand?”

She nodded again, remembering the woman on the autopsy table. Her doppelgänger.

“I would imagine that you will want to stay in the United States for a while to recover fully,” he said.

“Perhaps.” She searched for a glimpse of William, still standing next to the driver. She’d not seen Kavalchuk even glance in his direction. The Black Wolf had played chess with William every week for almost a year but was treating him as though he were a stranger. She wondered if they’d exchanged their final words at the prison.

William met her gaze and raised his eyebrows in concern. She signaled that she was all right.

“I want to show you something,” Kavalchuk said, reaching into the pocket of his black coat. He pulled out what looked to be a grainy security photo of two men in close conversation. “Look at this. Memorize these faces. I am right, am I not, that you will forever after recognize these men?”

“Who are they?” she asked, unnerved that he knew. When had he learned about her ability?

“The man on the left is Zana Ghorbani, although he goes by many aliases. He is an Iranian national. He was here in Minsk, briefly. Now he is in the newly declared sovereign republic of Kazakhstan, looking to secure an Iranian embassy in Almaty.”

"And?"

"Kazakhstan supplies nearly fifteen percent of the world's uranium."

"Why are you telling me this?"

"Because this man is yet unknown to your intelligence services." He put the photo back into his pocket. "He's a ghost who will haunt every mine in Kazakhstan until he has enough uranium to make a bomb. I want you to seek him out. Keep both eyes on him."

"Can you give me the photo?"

"The man on the right is the current president of Kazakhstan. The photo was taken inside a safe room. It would not be good for relations if he knew that we were spying on him."

He took her elbow and began slowly guiding her toward William and the departure gate. "You ask yourself, why would such a man as myself be concerned about this? A man with such a reputation for violence." His fingers tightened slightly on her arm. "It is because a cannon fired leaves a hole a few feet wide. Then the dust will clear, the resulting dead will be manageable, perhaps even predictable. And the damage is done. But a nuclear explosion poisons everything, everywhere.

"It's not only out of compassion that I tell you about Ghorbani, but out of common sense. It's madness to assume other countries will be responsible when it comes to using the ultimate weapon."

Mel had a moment of intense vertigo, a startling déjà vu, as though the floor had been shaken in an earthquake. The bear in the forest had told her there was nothing that could be done. And yet the Black Wolf had just given her a way to continue her work.

Kavalchuk halted and turned to face her. "I believe that you can help stop this man." If Mel hadn't been looking at his face, she would have missed the ghost of his smile. "And lest you think I've grown sentimental because I admire your fortitude,

I tell you all this because you may be useful to me as an ally in this cause. Although it's not likely you and I will ever see each other again." He turned his head to the large windows revealing the runways and planes and the dense expanse of birch trees beyond. "To answer your question, I did care about the women. They were, after all, Byelorussians. Like me."

He signaled to his driver that it was time to leave. "You were right, you know. The poem I quoted to you for dictation was Pushkin's. It was my wife's favorite."

Once the plane had landed in Germany, William and Mel emerged into bright sunlight. They linked arms and descended the ramp slowly onto the tarmac, led by a Lufthansa official who accompanied them into the terminal. William took exuberant breaths of what he called the *Berliner Luft*—the Berlin Air. It was heavy and organic, with errant traces of wet sewage. He told her it was because the old sewers were built too close to the city's surface. Also, he said, Berlin was built on a swamp, that the city name came from the Slavic word for swamp, *berl*.

Two consular officers from the Clay building, the US Mission Berlin, located in what had been West Germany, met them at the internal arrival gate. Mel would be taken to the embassy; William would stay to catch his flight to Tel Aviv.

William grinned wickedly. "The Germans converted their VIP lounge, their 'special room' for the Stasi, into Terminal C to accommodate security-sensitive flights to Israel. Evidently, there's still some scandalous, anti-Semitic graffiti scratched into the walls. Now I'll know."

He turned to her, giving her an enveloping, paternal hug. "Take care, Melvina. Come visit me when you need a break from chasing villains."

Mel felt as brittle and thin as an eggshell. There was so much she wanted to say to him, but the words were thwarted by the conflicting emotions roiling within her, threatening to crack through her skin. Instead, she watched William until he was lost in the crowd of restless travelers, the numberless strangers who were swept up into her memory banks and stored forever. Strangers who were not as they appeared to be.

She'd realized from an early age that most people spent a good portion of their waking hours masking their true selves behind ever-changing wardrobe and hairstyles. Glasses, jewelry, makeup—all of it working to separate the inner self from the outer self. Masking the secret internal places where the monsters hid from the glaring light of day.

Mel turned to let the two embassy officers lead her to their car, noticing for the first time that one of the men was carrying her suitcase. Kavalchuk must have had her things from the hotel packed and put on the plane. Her first thought was to burn everything inside. It would all smell of fermenting cabbage and disinfectant. But then she smiled, trying to remember Julie's translation of that very description upon their initial arrival.

The two officers were young, probably close to her own age, although she felt a hundred years old now. They kept trading looks when they thought she wasn't paying attention. They had not, of course, been told the whole story of her mission. She was hesitant to ask after her colleagues Ben, Julie, and Dan, in case they'd already been reassigned. She desperately hoped that they would still be in Berlin to welcome her.

While driving from the airport, one of the officers informed her that there was a doctor waiting at the mission. So they knew she'd had a bad time of it, at least. The bruises on her arms and legs were still vivid. Her neck was still visibly scratched red by the rope. She imagined the look on the doctor's face if, in response to his asking how she was doing, she said, "Actually, I'm dead."

Mel felt a rising bubble of hysterical laughter and made a

small hiccupping sound. The officer in the passenger seat gave her a concerned look.

The constant feeling of dread was dropping away, and in its place was the expansive sensation of being safe and alive. She was out of the crumbling chaos of the Soviet Union. She was out of Byelorussia, soon to be back in US territory. She'd survived it all: the Svisloch Strangler, an ill-timed love affair, and the Black Wolf of the BSSR, who'd called her a potential ally. Although she too hoped that their paths would never cross again.

But Kazakhstan...what did she know of Kazakhstan? A Central Asian country, part of the Soviet Union, bordered by China and Russia, homeland of the descendants of Genghis Khan and the ancient Silk Road. Rich in uranium deposits. For now, that was it.

She remembered what Special Agent Thomas Hunter, the agent who had initially recruited her for the CIA, had told her. "In your training, you'll be learning about the four potential blast rings following a nuclear detonation.

"But Donleavy, there are really only two you have to worry about. The 'You felt it' ring, and the 'You saw it' ring. If you felt it, you're dead, sooner or later. But if you've only *seen* it, you can survive. If you're smart and if you take the right precautions."

Mel had been near the innermost ring, not of a nuclear detonation, but of a serial killer. And of the decaying, noxious core of the Soviet Union itself. Her mission had changed her in a way that no desk job or domestic field assignment could have. As her father would say, that which does not kill us makes us stronger. She wondered how long a flight to Almaty would be, but then she pushed the thought away. Time enough for that in her debriefing.

"Thank you for being my taxi service," she said to the officers.

"Our pleasure, ma'am," the driver said. "Berlin's finest."

She thought of one of Dan's jokes and finally understood that, for him, they were a coping mechanism. Gallows humor. Whistling past the cemetery at night. A way to balance out the world's dangerous absurdities. She hoped she'd get to hear another soon.

Mel smiled and asked, "Why do Stasi officers make such good taxi drivers?"

A pause. The officer in the passenger seat turned, earnest and eager. A young, optimistic American.

"You get in their car," she said, "and they already know your name and where you live."

Acknowledgments

Although this is a work of fiction, it is based partly on true events. I've changed the names of some of the Soviet leaders in Byelorussia (now Belarus) who were in power in the 1990s, but many of the towns and cities, monuments, street names, and landmarks are real. The prolific serial killer known as the Butcher of Rostov, Andrei Chikatilo, was all too real and was the model for the Svisloch Strangler.

This book is dedicated to Lowell A. Mintz, entrepreneur and visionary, former chairman of the Board of Governors of the Commodity Exchange, Inc., in New York and chairman of Byelocorp Scientific, Inc. (contracted by the US Department of Defense), which introduced previously unknown Soviet technologies to the US, as well as my boss for twenty years.

Dr. William Cutler is based on Dr. William Begell, a brilliant chemical-nuclear engineer, talented linguist, partner in Byelocorp Scientific, and survivor of the Holocaust. A frequent travel companion of mine to the former Soviet Union, he was a colleague and friend. He is greatly missed.

This is my seventh novel with the Little, Brown/Mulholland Books family, and I feel incredibly fortunate and grateful to have been supported and encouraged by the following dedicated and talented magic makers: Josh Kendall, Helen O'Hare, Ben Allen, Pat Jalbert-Levine, Massey Barner, Alyssa Persons, Liv Ryan, Bruce Nichols, Lauren Hesse, and Gabrielle Leporati.

Many thanks also to Barbara Perris, whose copyediting skills kept the manuscript sharp and consistent, and to my agent, Danny Baror, who helps steer the ship. Happily, once more, Pamela Marshall has, with a keen eye, corrected many of the things I got wrong.

Gratitude to my friends and family and, as always, to my husband, Jim.